Finn
Fairlane

The FAIRLANE Series

Finn Fairlane

THE COMPLETE PACKAGE

NICK SAVAGE

4 Horsemen
Publications, Inc.

4 Horsemen Publications, Inc.
1497 Main St. Suite 169
Dunedin, FL 34698
4horsemenpublications.com
info@4horsemenpublications.com

Cover and Typesetting by Autumn Skye
Edited 4 Horsemen Publications, Inc.

Library of Congress Control Number: 2023930368

Paperback ISBN-13: 978-1-64450-872-5
Hardcover ISBN-13: 978-1-64450-830-5
Ebook ISBN-13: 978-1-64450-831-2

Table of Contents

THE
Fairlane
INCIDENTS

DEDICATION

For Kris, my love and my inspiration.

Table of Contents

CHAPTER 1

Wonder What's Next

I stand outside a greasy hamburger stand, shaking my head of purposefully unkempt hair in both awe and amused disappointment of the greater City Beautiful that surrounds me. Yet, there is an enchanting magic in this warm Orlando summer night as the mix of tourists and locals, all dressed in a variety of T-shirts, cargo shorts, and flip-flops or sandals, wander about. I look past them toward the giant buildings with facades designed like a drunk developer binged on the Mouse and his movies too much the night before, finished the night off with *Vegas Vacation*, and then made his distorted, haunting dreams into one long, wonderfully tacky street known as West Irlo Bronson Memorial Drive. I stand, shaking my head because I know it is here I am meant to be. Here is where I will find my inspiration.

I notice a man staring at me through a crowd of mismatched tourists. An ordinary enough looking man in his mid to late twenties. He's a bit bewildered. I look at him and nod. He thinks he knows me. Recognizes me from somewhere but can't place where. I've seen this look before... many times. It's fun watching the wheels turn in their heads as they try figuring out if I'm a friend, foe, ex-lover, or something else. I don't want to stare too long; you never do. It gets weird for them long before it gets weird for me. His face lights up. He tries to keep it subtle, but I see. He's figured out why I look familiar. His first encounter with a star—fading or otherwise. He realizes I'm Finn Fairlane, producer and songwriter extraordinaire, muse to the stars. He nods, smiles, and says he loves my work. I am far enough away that I didn't actually hear him say those words (not that it matters to him) but I've learned to read lips a bit over the years. If only a few phrases.

He walks off as I wait for my food outside this borderline edible, walk-up hamburger joint, taking in all of Kissimmee/Orlando's once glorious tourist trap Old Town, as the conversations of others continue to drone in the background like multiracial noise. The screams from teen girls as the Vomatron whips them around and around at seventy-five miles an hour dot the verbal cacophony like an overdriven crash cymbal in a Nine Inch Nails song. Ah!... Ah!... Ah!... But my attention slowly shifts, and the noise builds and swells like "Pinion," overtaking my visual attention. Just when it all amplifies, layering sound upon sound upon sound, so much my ears cannot stand the noise anymore, it falls away like the end of "Hurt."

It all stops.

For all I know, I could have gone deaf. The world around me could have caught fire. Hell, I could have been on fire. But none of that would have registered on my radar this second. Gleaming under the glow of the streetlamps and neon stars is beautiful, porcelain (just sweaty enough on this hot, summer night to be sexy) cleavage. I can't notice anything else. I am stuck in this moment, my eyes are feasting, and mouth-watering fantasies start to form. I am a man, after all; of course my eyes are drawn to her (what I'm guessing is a full C) cleavage. Also, to the elaborate ink on her left arm peeking out from her rolled-up sleeve: the beautiful color palette of black, blues, reds, greens, gold, and more making what, at first glance, seems to be a collage of superheroes. A woman after every man's heart.

As I was saying, there's something magical in these warm, summer, Orlando nights. A magic that makes the already large droves of people grow even more massive as the sun goes down. The gentle breeze that cools off the warmth of the day. The skyline of countless billboards, resort hotels, discount gift shops, restaurants, and churches to the gods of gaudiness and gluttony from the day that plunges into the vast, stark night. A deep purple night sky, polka-dotted with neon constellations of Vomatrons, Slingshots, sky coasters, and anything else advertisers can backlight to bleed tourists' pockets dry. Despite all that, this is where I belong. This city quietly calls to my fast-approaching, middle-aged self, making similar, sweet promises whispered by Hollywood to young starlets. To inspire. To be my muse. I know it. I feel it in my bones—a fast, agitating force that overcomes my senses, my muscles, my body. A feeling of being inspired that only comes along once in a great while. I feel it here.

What different musings I may find here compared to my time in New York or Chicago, I do not know. I left behind what life I had made for myself in the Big Apple: the chart-topping clients I produced in the music industry; my three-bedroom, three-bath brownstone; the few people I would call friends. I followed an internal calling, or an external beckoning if you will, to travel south. I'm not sure if it's an idiosyncrasy solely reserved for artists, the small, nagging child called wanderlust nudging me along, or maybe my deep-seated need to uproot my life once I start to find a comfort zone. I heard it calling me over and over again. It had been calling to me for a while, and Finn Fairlane listens to the call. Yes, I do. I apparently also refer to myself in the third person sometimes. But moving on.

The taxi top ads, radio, and television commercials all advertising Florida vacations. The dead-inside feeling that comes with working for big-name labels. Writing songs that had no passion left in them, only the ability to make dollar signs. I wanted something more. The internalized, unstoppable, ongoing struggle to better this thing I have come to call myself. Always moving, pushing forward. And it whispered over and over to me, "Orlando." To this, I listened. I am here.

It is my first night living in the endless summer that is Orlando, the city next door to that magical kingdom. That beautiful machine of childhood joy and adult misanthropy and cynicism. Dreamt up to make you forget the prejudice, arrogance, and misogyny with which it was built. Designed so each step farther inside makes you believe in your childhood more and more, washing away the jaded eyes of adulthood.

But that is Orlando.

Look past the epidemic of crystal meth, coke, and heroin so evident on these Florida streets in the leather-skinned, emaciated man with long, wispy hair as he twitches uncontrollably in his dirty, torn rags, or in the missing teeth of the haggard woman as she begs for change. Not just in Old Town, or Kissimmee, or even Orlando, but the whole of Florida. Look past it all because there you will find a place where the original concept 4,022 miles west could be so abominated by corporate culture to create something so wonderfully tacky, invitingly dominating, monstrously huge, and still pale in comparison to the egos of the people who run the place. Maybe, it's just what I see.

Welcome to Orlando.

And the city welcomes me with her. This fair-skinned beauty. Inked in all the right places and a look in her eye of deviant desires. She notices me leering. Since I'm standing not too far from where she waits in line and leering is meant to be obvious, I shouldn't be surprised she saw me, but I am. Not so much that she caught me, but that she didn't look away. Is this how fans feel when they recognize me? The roles have reversed because I am a fan of hers. I try to hold my surprise inside. I try not to react, but something gives it away. Perhaps an involuntary upturn of the corner lip. Or an unknowing eyebrow raise. Something gave my surprise away because she smiles, just a little. Just enough to let me know she knows, and that she's okay with it.

Her hazel eyes, outlined in the blackest of black liner that extends just past her corners, stay connected with mine. Ready to devour. A fleck in her left eye, accented by an eyebrow ring, adds to the allure. What some would deem an imperfection only makes this stare sexier. There's something about her stare. Hauntingly familiar, like a scene from my memory playing out in front of my eyes. We keep each other's gaze. A slow waltz of our eyes in our minds. A waltz that gently takes her closer to me, dancing around the unspoken subject of the moment. Who speaks first? I'm dancing with this stranger. Neither of us whispers a word. Just dancing and waiting. Observing her as she watches me.

This dance is pleasant. Like the joy of the earlier drive down I-4 to my new abode. Waltzing through clear traffic. I was taking in my new surroundings at 80 plus miles an hour. Screaming along in my 80-grit voice to post-Black Flag, Rollins Band's song (though some could argue I was blaring Mother Superior) "I Want So Much More," popping my speakers while passing palm tree after palm tree. Broken and abandoned cars scattered along the median and shoulders, momentary scabs on the city's beauty. As my pepper hair that has become dashed with salt blows in the wind of the open windows, I looked at the intertwining highways that make up the circulatory system of this city; I couldn't help wondering how my life would get intertwined into this city's lifeblood. I have yet to find where I fit into this metropolis among the more than two million people that run around this semi-tropical paradise every day. I will discover my place, though.

I do take note of the irony of the green dominating the floral pattern on her low-cut, button-down blouse. The green flora lines her bosom like the palms line the highway. Her shirt says to me, "Come, drive here." Take that for what you will. For a split moment, though, I ask myself why I know it's a low-cut, button-down blouse. Then I see the gentle bite she gives her bottom lip that gently pushes out her snake bite studs, and my manhood returns to me. That simple gesture says it all. Green she is anything but, and I want to know how far from green she is. I have to play it cool. React too strongly and come off as the upturned collar, golfer cap, polyester-wearing, wild and crazy guy. Play it too cool, and she'll think we both play for the same team. So, I do the only thing my muscles will allow me to do, as my mind unhooks her bra to reveal breasts that could bring a nation to its knees. With every ounce of my being, I summon the primordial gods of love and lust to give me power. They look down and bestow upon me the almighty ability to smile and give a slight nod.

I fucking smile and give a slight nod.

I've flirted before, hundreds of times, thousands even. This evening is no different from any of my previous one-night stands, three-night stands, or the plethora of quasi-relationships I've had. They all begin the same way: a subtle look, a dog-eat-dog-sly smile, a wink. God forbid a word, like hello. Something small. Though tonight, all my wiles abandon me in my moment of need. So, I smile and nod. Play it cool though. Wait for her to come to me.

Or am I wrong? Is this just a chick oiling her engine for a steamy night with her man? Damn. Am I the pregame mental porn she's using to rev her freshly oiled engine? Some real-life, soft-core PornHamster clip playing out in her mind to fantasize about later? (Which is a fantasy in and of itself for me.) Am I being used in her mental game?

Perchance this could be my first intertwining with the city. Perchance to sin. With her.

Perchance.

Then again, it was for this "perchance" that I left my life in New York behind me. Finished up album productions, cover concepts, and whatever other current affairs I had with clients and said, "Adios." Bid my fond adieus to the giant, light-polluting, prostitute-ridden, yet ever endearing and always loved area known as Times Square. Said goodbye to my favorite bartender at Sunswick 35/35 in Astoria. Stood there for one last moment, my hazel eyes taking it all in. The cool, crisp air slightly stung my weather-worn face on a chilly night, adding to my growing crow's feet as I squinted through the cold. Not sure when, or if, I'd ever breathe in New York air again. A part of me wanted to stay. A part of me wanted never to leave that moment because that moment was the accumulation of everything I've done in my life.

It was hard to believe it could ever be better than it ever was. But it was calling me—the stranger in the night that was Orlando. I was unsure if Orlando would be what I expected, except that I had no expectations. A part of me knew that it would be okay. That it would be the right place to be. But I stood there, engraving that moment in my mind: the green and brown leaves on the trees, the cars that lined the street, brick building after brick building housing countless people I'd never know, the sounds of people laughing a block away, the sirens in the distance, and the wind blowing against me. The love I feel for that great city, all of it. I took a mental snapshot of that moment in time before I got into my car. I drove off into the sunset (well, sunset on my right since I was heading south). The poetry fits better, however, if I had driven into it.

Not every client was happy to see me go, and that's understandable. That's a good thing for me. It means I've done my job, but I can't help my clients if I have nothing that inspires me. I can't muse my people, produce records, write songs, and do what I do if I have no muse myself to inspire those things, to make me want to create something bigger than myself. New York is a city that has endless inspiration for some. CBGB launched the careers of many musicians and inspired countless more. New York is the city of Gershwin. Cole Porter. The city of Philip Roth and Woody Allen. Every turn hides something new. From a mouse scavenging for food to the beauty in the blue-gray eyes of a homeless man that still clings to hope, to the stories you hear from the old woman sitting in the corner seat at your local bar. The late-night coke deals at gas stations with NYPD's finest filling up a pump away, to the bartender betraying the location of all the security cams so you can smoke inside when it's ten below and windy outside. Screaming Andrew W.K.'s "I Love New York City" at the top of your lungs when you're three sheets to the wind. Every day something new. Something wonderful.

But for me, I had somehow managed to overstay my welcome in a city of over eight million. When everywhere you turn you see memories of a better time, you don't feel inspired. You don't feel much like writing lyrics. Don't feel much like turning up the snare or adjusting the EQ of the floor tom. You don't feel much like doing anything. I found myself wallowing in my studio, quickly becoming the brooding musician the nineties were so rife with. Even my hair is in that in-between stage of long and short, either in dire need of a haircut or a better way to style it. I hated those brooding musicians and hated myself for becoming something I hated. So, I left. I left before I got stuck in a routine that spiraled downward, unable to ever get up. I needed to see what the next place held for me. And it was Orlando that called.

The eye contact we held breaks, returning me from my thoughts about New York as the hamburger stand worker hands her an already melting vanilla cone she promptly lifts to her deep red lips. Red lipstick that deep in color makes a statement that she takes control. She gets what she wants. I hope she wants me. A drop of melted ice cream disappears into her radiant, porcelain cleavage. Somehow that falling bit of ice cream makes me notice her long, curly, jet-black hair, unnoticed before perhaps because her hair disappears into the now black of the night sky above. Illuminated only by the surrounding neon stars. Maybe because her cleavage and eyes consume me in an all-encompassing fire that can only be doused by her. But now I notice. Curly hair is sexy. Almost dangerous. Curly haired ladies are the kind that breaks hearts. The kind of girl you don't bring home to your mother. Yes. Curly haired girls are super freaks.

It won't get to the point of heartbreaking. She will take control of nothing tonight, at least not with me. Or perhaps she already has and I just don't know it yet. Our moment seems to be over now that her creamy treat on a cone is delivered. She walks away from the pick-up window and past me as I stand, still waiting on my food to be made. She smiles as she passes and whispers something.

"Fate?"

"Feint?"

"Eighth?"

Hell. Did she say, "freight?" Did she want me to ship something? Is she looking for weed? A little Mary Jane for tonight? I couldn't hear clearly. The screaming man on the Slingshot and the laughter of his female companion drowns out the clarity of her word. She could have said, "Take me right here and now," and I would have been none the wiser. My mind is frantically going over every word, every phrase she could have said, and each time my mind thinks of something new that is more obtuse than the thought before. This deluge of thoughts makes my mind think more and get caught in a pattern that only makes things worse. A game of telephone I play with myself, ever distorting the original phrase spoken. All this because she enthralls me, and I'm unable to say something cool in hopes of releasing tension later on. But at least I won't be the only one not getting any tail tonight. I'm sure whatever man card the guy on the Slingshot held was stripped away the moment he started screaming like a preteen girl at a J. Bieb concert.

Did I get her name? Was it a message? The name of a place, perhaps? Maybe the heartbreaking does start tonight. For that one fleeting moment, it hurts. A hurt I haven't felt since I lost a $10,000 hand of blackjack at Circus Circus in Reno. I may have been up that $10,000 and playing with the house's money, but for a few moments, my table was surrounded by people with all eyes on me and that moment was mine. Those ten-thousand dollars in one hand. Only a few seconds for the card to flip and the dealer to win. For those few moments, though. For those few moments, that money was mine.

And for a few, she was mine. For a fleeting moment, we were cosmically entangled. A planet-sized meteorite on a crash course for earth, ready to make extinct all previous carnal knowledge I possessed. But no, Bruce Willis and his ragtag team of oil rig drillers had to blow her up. Had to destroy what could have awakened in me some previously undiscovered Chakra. It's cool though, Bruce. You killed Hans Gruber.

I whip my head around to see if she is still looking at me. I could have been more discreet, but after the leering and the ever-so-smooth smile and nod, I figure, "Fuck it." So a whip of my head it is. But no. A man whose dated, gigantic, arm-wrapped tribal tattoos and overly sculpted muscles make him look as though he's preparing for gladiatorial, hand-to-hand combat in a real-life version of a Bethesda© Softworks game has his arm around her shoulder. His shoulder blades bulge out of his bleached white tank top. The style of tank top that is often associated with either domestic violence or under-educated people of Mediterranean descent. His carefully frayed, bootcut jeans sag off legs that have been bullied out of every day in the gym by his over-sized torso. He leans down, his lips entwining with hers.

How I wish those were my lips pressing against hers. They look so soft, like a moist red velvet cake. So ready to taste something new. My arm wrapped around her shoulder. Or waist.

I watch them, casually. Or at least what I think looks casual. Nonchalant. I want to know how she feels about him. To understand why she flirted with me. I want to know why the hell I'm so entranced with her. No conversation. No physical contact. Just one muddled and misunderstood word she whispered.

They continue walking after an all-too-short public display of dwindling affection. Dying love could mean good news for me. I think. If I'm right. If I ever see her again. She turns her head back to me and winks her flecked eye. Damn that eye, both eyes. Haunting. They disappear into his metallic blue '98 Camaro, flames painted on the hood and sides to give the illusion of going really fast. I always thought that's what the pedal on the right was for. Hell, I'd bet ten to one he only drives with two pedals.

So here I am, left standing, abandoned by my wiles and by fate. But I smile. Soaking in both my surroundings and the events of the evening: the modern-day, casino-free Reno, the not-so-redneck Pigeon Forge, the little Vegas strip. This street numbered 192. At this moment in my life, I know this is where I need to be, where the winds of fate and fortune want to steer me. So, I stand outside the neon lilac and turquoise gate of Old Town, staring across the street at a shop I shorten to "Chine Gun 'Murica" with giant gift shops next to other giant gift shops. All of which brings "trying too hard" to whole new levels, with exterior murals painted top to bottom and oversized, eye-catching relief art. Not great art, mind you. Just eye-catching enough to put their vanilla overtones off.

Then you see the ad. "Gifts here. Towels at $3.99." But inside, they are all filled with the same gifts: generic clothes and countless items all stamped with that symbolic, mouse-eared "D" or ORLANDO sprawled across it. Items that end up collecting a half inch of dust on a shelf in a cabinet not long after purchase. But in these stores, they scream to be purchased. Puppies in a kennel crying out for a new home if you will. It's all so you can buy stuff as your reminder of time spent here, which I am all for. But if you are going to surround yourself with stuff, just make sure it's the right stuff.

Damn. Damn it all. I can only laugh at the events of the night.

What the hell did she say to me? And what did it mean? If I don't know what she said, I guess the meaning is pretty much a cow's opinion. Moo. Pointless. Yes, it's moot, I know, but I heard that somewhere once, probably on some hotel room tv while watching some sitcom rerun about a bunch of friends or something, and it stuck. So, moo it is. On the other hand, if I can figure out what she said, then I can ponder the meaning more.

Moo.

I am here surrounded by people, drifting in the loneliness of the passing moment. I wonder what's next. Tonight, the fates gave me a teaser of an intro to this city in the form of my mystery woman instead of a hands-on preview. Fine. I'm okay with that because as I'm standing here, inspiration swirls around me: from the clothes worn by the line of people waiting to eat a burger, to the cars that drive in and out of Old Town, past the Ferris wheel, to the distant early 2000's pop rock playing that barely carries this far. I find inspiration in everything around me.

In this moment, I take what I can—everything that it is this night. And a fantastic night it is. The sounds of young lust and fading innocence that gets so quickly pushed away. The never-been-kissed girl in braided pigtails flirting with the leather-clad rebel boy who is finally showing interest. He makes some joke I can't hear, but she laughs and playfully hits him. She makes her move and kisses him. A moment of unsure shock and joy on his face, but then he grabs her and pulls her in. They make a connection. The collision of two souls, intersecting on this path we call life, coming together in a moment of glorious happenstance. If only for a moment. She will never be the same. I can see her quiver with anticipation. His hands slowly slide down her back, stopping at her hips. She puts her hands on his as if to stop him, interlacing her fingers with his.

The girl hesitates, squeezing his hands for a moment. She lets that linger, enjoying the moment as their lips explore each other. She untangles her fingers and moves her hands, running her unsure fingers through his hair. He pulls her in closer, trying to have both bodies occupy the same space at the same time. Defy the laws of physics, good sir! If there's ever a time to defy them, it's now. It is this moment that begins the loss of her, or both of their, innocence. She'll spend as much time trying to lose it as she will regretting who she lost it to. But tonight, beneath the neon stars of the night sky, none of that matters. Just this moment is all that's important. The right here and right now. A fleeting moment we all try to hold on to as long as we can. Each time it happens, every time it happens.

Damn her eyes. I return to my forest green Grand Am. Two Door. Nice stock rims. Nothing that screams "I have a tiny penis!" but not understated. I blink as I open the door and her eyes haunt me. I can't remember the last time I saw eyes that were both so serene yet so filled with raw energy. Such potential energy waiting to explode in a nails-deep-in-my-flesh, sweat-dripping, soul-connecting, tangled-tongues-and-lips sex session that can only lead to both of us in the midnight hour crying, "More! More! More! More!" All I do is blink.

While this first night is not quite the start to my time here like I hoped, it sticks with me. Not just because it is my first night, but because of the events of the evening. The haunting familiarity of her gaze sticks in my mind, an icy reminder of what should have, or more properly stated, could have transpired tonight. It haunts me over the next eight weeks as I unenthusiastically gather clients to try and inspire, produce, and make great. I say unenthusiastically not because I'm not happy to be getting new clients, but because I know as of right now, I can't properly do what I do.

Damn those eyes.

CHAPTER 2

She's Gone

I settle into my soundproof studio, reading the news on my phone of the approaching tropical storm and its growing momentum. The schoolyard bully that is my computer's screensaver teases me as it scrolls across the monitor. It yells, calling me on my procrastination, "Get Back To Work." As if I don't know that behind the black wall of words is a program waiting to record my lyrical genius. Waiting for me to create, to bring to life a new Finn Fairlane musical masterpiece for the world to embrace as its new anthem. The spontaneous birthing of new and exciting ideas is why I came here. To be inspired. To write. To create.

My deep purple, sometimes black depending on the way the light hits it, six-string Washburn sits strapped around my shoulder. Condenser microphone hides behind the pop screen in its stand, tempting me to say something. Anything. Some simple phrase sung into its steel mesh that brings it bursting to life. Pen and notebook on a silver music stand next to me. Lyrics lying in wait to scribble themselves onto paper, but I sit empty-headed on my stool. Nothing. My mind feels constipated. Too much mental cheese stops up the tubes. When I try to play, it gives forth no sound. Its wires do not vibrate nor give music. I sit a music-less musician. Geddy Lee would be so disappointed in me right now.

I've had writer's block before: times when nothing good comes to mind, when the words I write are more representative of a junior high girl scribbling love notes about the cute boy across the room than lyrics written by an Emmy-winning professional, when the words read more like "Without You" than "Kickstart My Heart." Blocked times when music I write sounds more reminiscent of a bad video game soundtrack from the days of first-gen Game Boy and not so much the rock 'n roll it's supposed to be, stuff I should have tried selling to I Fight Dragons. Those gents could have made the riffs worthy, but I can't recall a time when nothing comes to mind, a time when all my creativity abandoned me—the unwanted dog left on the side of a central California county road.

Don't get me wrong; I've never done such an inhumane thing as leaving a dog. One afternoon, however, I was driving through (what some would call) a town east of Merced, California. The brown landscape of dead and dying plant life, underfed cows, sheep, and livestock surrounded me as far as the eye could see. The only savior to this was the occasional tree that had managed to somehow thrive in this Easy-Bake Oven the cartographers call the Central Valley. That and the rolling hills and mountains on the distant horizon to break the monotony. But there I was, driving through the isolation when a rundown, rust-coated, white-and-brown suburban a little way ahead of me coasted to a stop. The kind of stop that somehow seemed more like a skeezy leisure suit skulking his way to an unsuspecting female than a van coming to a stop.

As they did stop, they let out a dog. The suburban sped away. Nothing too fast, just accelerated as if the situation was typical. I kept driving, thinking nothing of it. Until later that night when I returned down the same road and the dog was still there, unmoved from where it first sat down all those hours ago. The good soldier he was, seated at attention, awaiting orders from his sergeant, little did he know his commanding officer was never to return. So, I called out to him. He remained unmoved.

I took some caution in my approach, knowing the worst that this thirsty mutt would try is a meager attempt at a defensive bite. But he sat resolutely. No collar. No name. Just a sad, short-haired mutt: white, brown, and covered in fleas. I'm sure the state of the dog reflected the conditions inside the vehicle. I petted him—soft and gentle. Tried to turn my 80-grit voice into something a little less rough. More 800-grit but the best I think I was able to muster was 120. He started to perk up. Tail wagging, tongue hanging out from dryness. I coaxed him my way and into my car. It didn't take me long to name him: Lieutenant Dan. It somehow seemed to suit.

Much like Lieutenant Dan when I found him, I sit abandoned. I refuse to be the one that's deserted. I leave my guitar and microphone. I am the white-and-brown truck, not the dog. For the moment, I leave them behind. Guitar and mic stand at attention—waiting for me, the obedient dogs they are. I'll be back. Just not right now.

I need to get my writing mojo back. I haven't had any since before moving down here, and it's not coming back. To paraphrase the immortal words of Maynard James Keenan, I need it, even though I don't want it. To breathe, feel, and know I am very much living. Without it, I feel useless, lifeless. A shell of a man attempting to live in a world in which he has already died. The ability to tap into an emotion that isn't readily there and write from it is what makes me Finn. To put myself in another's shoes and feel what they feel is something that comes to me—usually at the ready—but doesn't come at all for others. There is this innate ability to become someone else for a few moments: enough to write, to make music, to have an authentic feel as if I've lived those moments over and over again. I can't do any of those because my mojo is gone. New York pulled it all out of me. The few clients I've taken on in the two months I've been down here are more than grateful, but in all honesty, they are getting the short end of the Finn

Fairlane stick. I don't give the short end in any situation. I give a huge, long, rock-hard stick. And it all comes from mojo. I'm still a stranger in a strange land. So, I do what anyone in need to see something inspiring would do: grab my car keys off the ledge by the door and drive.

It would seem the gods of rock 'n roll are not on my side today. Two miles onto I-4 and the traffic slows to a crawl. Who knows why it slowed down—stalled car, horrific wreck with blood all over the road, a slow-moving truck that's trying to change lanes, out-of-state driver. Could be anything. Though it gets me thinking about this machine that is Orlando. Built West Coast by one man. One wildly misogynistic man and a dream. And he did it. He built it all. His corporate team of money-hungry, bloodsucking, anything-for-a-dollar white collars continue to build on his dream. Perhaps bigger than he could have imagined. Maybe this larger-than-life monstrosity is how he precisely imagined it. Maybe that's the problem. I don't dream big enough anymore. Instead of just building a park, he built a park and a town. Bought land and built more. And more. And more. And more. And people came. I came. I've written songs. Sold songs to the best of them. But the well ran dry. It's why I'm here. No offense, Fred, but if Limp Bizkit can arise from this, I sure as shit can rise again.

I turn on the radio to rambling tropical storm updates. Tropical storm Castle Heat, Cataratan, or whatever it's named, has been officially upgraded to a category one hurricane, which sounds extremely dangerous, but this far inland, it's more wind and rain than actual destruction, if it ends up even making landfall. And with that long-winded yet otherwise seemingly mundane announcement, a ton of bricks from the late nineties blares out of the speakers, hitting me straight across the face. As a ton of bricks racking your face should do, it reminds you of something. Mostly something you forgot. This song so eloquently refreshes my memory that it was all done for the nookie. If ever more juvenile, yet truer words were spoken. Only in Limp Bizkit's hometown of Orlando—well, Jacksonville, but to the geographically challenged and purposes of my locale, all Florida is just Orlando—can you still hear this song twenty years past its relevance without it being a call-in request. Ah, the good ole' days of pay for play. But true the words were. I don't know any prepubescent teens who pick up a guitar thinking, *It's all about the art, man.* No. They pick it up thinking sex, drugs, and rock 'n roll. It's what it's about.

Rock 'n roll is the embodiment of it all. Hot females dripping with baby oil, ready for action. Guys ready to give and receive. It's the musician's setting that encourages such great, uninhibited hedonism. Coke-fueled orgies that end in chain-smoking cigarettes and Mary Jane for an hour or two. And somehow this piece of shit song is reminding me of exactly what I need.

Nookie.

Damn you, Durst.

But damn him as I may, he was right. So, I do what every red-blooded American does while idling in bumper-to-bumper traffic. I swipe right on my blood red-and-black cased cellphone and make a call. The statistics show that driving on your cellphone is the same as driving drunk, but I, much like every other driver on the road, don't think that statistic applies to me, them. You know. Self-entitlement is the backbone of today's society. Especially in an area that outcries for the death of every alligator because of the unfortunate death of one small child. Unfortunate it was, but to place the life of one child above countless alligators in the lake to calm the masses is what makes Dismal Land the pretty-hate machine that it is. Quelling innumerable lives behind the scenes, keeping it out of the public eye, just to keep the look of their park clean and the grand illusion maintained. It's moments like this I hope, deep in my soul, karma has something big in store for the damned rodent.

At least my client answers his phone.

"D.B. What's up, my man?!" I say, knowing damn well he's sitting in his studio either surfing *Imgur Gone Wild* for boob shots of exes or dickin' around on his eight-string guitar. The eight-string guitar. I have such mixed feelings about that thing. If you want to play an instrument that gives off such low tones, play bass. On the other hand, the damned thing does give them a sound that a six-string could not. So, I keep my opinions to myself. Mostly.

"Working on some new stuff. Down for a few?" he replies, already knowing my answer.

D.B., short for Danny Boyle, is a good guy. In my short months here, he and his bandmates are one of the few clients I like beyond the work and enjoy doing anything with. Possibly the only. D.B. has bright, fire-engine red hair that hasn't changed since his infancy. The only reason I know that is his mother stopped by the studio my first session with them to drop off some homemade beef-and-cabbage soup. What an underrated dish that is. The smell of it might be enough to put some people flat on their asses, but the smell aside, it's one of my top five favorite dishes after that day.

Eileen Boyle can cook. Also, one good-looking lady too. Long red hair. Waves that almost turn it curly. Pale-blue eyes. Light freckles dotting her thin frame, concentrations around her high cheekbones. Eyes inset just deep enough to give her an almost perpetually sorrowful look. But her smile lights up the room.

After the first time I met her, there were these fantasies that started to creep into my mind. I didn't want them to creep in; they just would. Like a yearning for a cigarette each time you try to quit. I just thought of her in that flowing, blue & cream bohemian-chic dress she wore the day of the soup. They were choice fantasies too. Her hand slides up the inside of my shorts to tease me a bit. My hand works its way up her shirt to gently pull on her nipple. Some start in full session. Her legs wrap around me as I fill her up inside, embracing in hours-long passionate kisses. They were fantasies like that. Half-chubbed before getting anywhere juicy with them. I wouldn't let myself get anywhere juicy with them. I had to cut my mental movies short because every time I wanted to run with them, I knew two things. One, each time I started fantasizing about her, all I could think of is that scene from *The Goonies* where they find that large rock and Martha Plimpton says, "Brand, God put that rock there for a reason..." He moves it anyway, and bats fly out. Which brings me to two: Some things are best left unexplored.

It all started because I noticed her in a certain light. Literally. The light hit her in a way that made her look more aged, and she still looked beautiful. Perhaps, in a way, more than she is. She's always going to look graceful. She noticed me too. Not in the same way, of course. Maybe in the same way. Hell, I don't know. Even though our ages are closer than that of mine and D.B.'s, I refuse to find out in which way she sees me. It's a respect of boundaries, I think. At least that's what I'll go with.

She still looks at D.B., or as she calls him always by his full name Danny Boyle with her fading brogue, forever as a small boy playing in the fields behind a home back in Ireland where he never lived. Her courtesy toward the rest of the band surpasses motherhood into a friendliness of sorts. She well knows that the image they project is just that, an image. And after our introduction, she knew I was there to help them with that. The appearance. The words. The sound. The publicity. It's what I do, and more if needed.

I think the other reason nothing could ever happen is D.B. Respect for my client aside, the guy is enormous. Not fat, not orca fat, or that. I mean meat and potatoes, benches 425, bar room brawl champion big. The guy that never needed an ID to get into a bar. Here is a guy that got arrested one time, no stereotypes, for public drunkenness, and it took six cops and two tasers to take him down. While there may have been added strength because of the liquid courage, it wasn't much. I'm not afraid to fight, start a conflict if I need to. It's part of my job. Sometimes. Spurs creativity. But pick your battles. D.B. is a guy you want on your side, not a guy you go toe to toe with. Even if he was a guy to go toe to toe with, I'm more of a lover—less fighter, given a choice.

But bright, fire red hair since infancy—Eileen showed pictures like a proud mom. She carries a few in her purse like a small photo album. Sentimental reasons I assume. For D.B., the picture show was almost embarrassing, but it gave me a moment to be close to such beauty. And being close to raw beauty is where creativity is born.

I think Eileen is the sort of woman I could picture myself with, had life turned out differently. If I chose other roads, other options. Made different decisions. I would have loved to grow old with someone like her. But looking back on wouldas, couldas, shouldas doesn't help anyone, especially not the person doing the pondering. So, I appreciate her and her beauty at face value.

Back to our conversation though, yeah, I was down for a few. Maybe more. It's why I called D.B. He's not only a good client but one hell of a wingman. If nookie is what I need, this guy will help me land it with minimal effort. Not that I can't bring it in on my own. I can. I don't know many people who can't. But when the mojo is gone, it's gone, and getting all the help I can is much appreciated.

Grabbing drinks with D.B. is always an event. Sure, I get recognized sometimes. I have my moments when a lady, man, or person walks up to me and pays their respects. But I've faded from the spotlight. My time in it is over. I'm okay with that. I've had my fun with it. I've enjoyed the daily conversations with strangers about myself. The kisses from random women who wanted to be close to a star. I also grew to loathe it, getting to a point where going out was dreadful because I wanted to be left alone. Not that hordes of people were rushing me like screaming Usher fans, but there is always that one person who has to say something to you. It's never the guy who can just say, "I'm a big fan," and walk away. It's the guy who needs to dominate your time for a half hour while you are holding ice cream you just pulled from the freezer case while grocery shopping. Nowadays, I don't mind it so much. Most of the time when I get recognized, it's a silent nod of recognition, a quick autograph, or a handshake. So goes the life of a producer. Leave the spotlight to those wanting the lime hue overtones, for those wishing to be seen. Leaving the spotlight is good like that.

In the public's eye, out of sight, out of mind—unless I'm with D.B. Three albums, all gold, still looking for their platinum. Three. I want to help them get their platinum. So anywhere he goes, he plays the rock star. He still craves the attention, the uncertain and exciting feeling of an ever-changing entourage, the ladies he meets, especially the ladies, oohing and ahhing over every little thing he says, like musical scripture and infallible idioms are spewing forth from his mouth. In short, drinking with this guy is always an event.

It's dark by the time I finish my ten-mile drive into Kissimmee to get there, which means the daily thunder-storm has already passed. If you've never lived in Florida, it's strange to experience the first time. You'll be driving, walking, whatever. You'll see gray clouds overhead, but that's it. Then, out of nowhere, it starts. Light rain. You think to yourself, *This isn't so bad.* But no sooner do you finish that thought than the light rain turns into a torrential downpour that reduces vision to a few feet. Your thoughts turn to panic mode as you slow down your driving or find shelter from the rain if you were unlucky enough to be walking when it started. You think to yourself, *Did I miss the news? Is this how hurricanes start?* But as you finally grasp hold of the situation, it stops. A light, barely notice-able drizzle.

The first time it happens, you can't help but wonder what just transpired. As if some Cthulhuian portal just opened up and the gargantuan mass of glowing orbs and eyes known as Yog-Sothoth is making its way through to devour us all. But no, that's just a standard three o'clock shower in Florida. It gives the humidity time to settle by nightfall. Now there are enough people here for the pre-hurricane-party party. Yes, the hurricane parties have begun. And yes, in Florida hurricane parties are a thing.

As befitting a rock star, D.B. has commandeered the patio section of our usual day-of-the-week-fried-food-two-hundred-grams-of-fat-per-entree-overpriced-restaurant we meet up at. The late nineties music flows softly from the sad excuse of a sound system, whispering below the mixed noise of conversations. Two of D.B.'s bandmates, Vincent and Neil, brown acoustic guitars in hands, strum a modern-day rendition of Simon & Garfunkel's "A Most Peculiar Man" while the females swoon around them as if this is the first time they have ever witnessed such musicianship. I'm not saying Simon and Garfunkel aren't musical geniuses; they are. But these chicks are either feigning newfound awe and amazement to get close to the band, or they need to listen to better music. D.B., complete with his signature, frayed, dark gray golfer's cap, leather wristbands, torn jeans, and Spear Fist T-shirt, is in the center of a circle with everyone's attention on him—for he is the star of the show.

Sitting atop the back of an outdoor, woven plastic, black couch with red cushions, he makes a grand he-ho gesture and lets out a laugh, beer in hand, spilling a few drops as he does. The crowd follows suit, making me wonder how many understood the humor and how many laughed to avoid falling out of his good graces; as if he gave a crap about people who only care about him because of his money from music laughing at every joke. Half of these clowns could never see him again and he'd be no worse off. He has feelings of his own, but I doubt if anyone here cares much about those. He is human, after all, and (as The Smiths alluded to so many years ago) he needs to be loved, just like everyone else.

I enter the patio through the welded metal, waist-high swinging door. D.B.'s attention, and thus the attention of everyone surrounding him, turns to me. He sets down his beer as he stands and strides over. As much as he is into his nu-metal, rock 'n roll, bad-boy image, he'll always do the handshake into the one-armed hug with certain people. I'm glad in the short duration of our relationship I've made that list. It's always nice to see a friendly face in a strange town.

I've met some people in the few months I've been down here, people outside of clients, but they are all still strangers to me. People I've met through clients. Single-serving friends who want to hear every word I have to say but offer little to nothing in exchange. People sure are strange when you're a stranger. It's just a relief to see a friendly face.

"Finn!" His excitement turns to a quieter tone I know is meant only for my ears. "Thank the gods you're here, man. These people tonight! I tell ya."

I smile. Having been in his shoes before, I feel his pain of false friendships and passing acquaintances. "Nice to see you too, D.B. What's on the menu?"

As if in some Soviet-Era spy vs. spy game of espionage, his finger gestures to the crowd of Lt. Dans that moments ago were gathered around him and still eagerly await his, or the suburban's, return.

"A redhead I think you'll dig. Dyn-o-mite in the sack. Great head..." D.B. hesitates on something.

So, I chime in, "What's the but?"

He tries to hold in his words, "Strange amount of ... long nipple hair."

I think the twisted face I make (that, in my mind, is a frightening version of the famous Reese Witherspoon face from the car ride scene in *Cruel Intentions*) says it all for him. He laughs a quiet laugh of understanding and continues. He eyes a gal sitting two to her left. She is turned away from me at this moment. All I see is long, black curly hair. It brings me back to my first night outside that greasy spoon of a hamburger-and-fry stand. I can't see her arm, tattooed in all its superhero glory. I can't even see her face as she talks to some Harley Quinn wannabe who stands, staring at me. She is cute, but at this moment, those eyes pierce into my mind again. Haunting me of a distant memory from better times never had.

"The one staring at you is an actual fan of yours. When I told her you were coming tonight, she stuck around just to meet you. No tricks there. She just wants to say her graces."

D.B. says these words and I hear them, but they are distant. Faded into the background of the moment while I try to send mental messages to this raven-haired woman to turn around toward me so I can see if she is the same woman who has been haunting my dreams of late.

"But the girl sitting with her back to us," D.B. says this and the volume of his voice shoots to the foreground of my senses, as if nothing else around is of consequence.

"Yeah!!" I respond, reverting to a sixth-grade schoolboy version of myself about to see his first set of real-life boobs. My heart races so fast and beats so hard, I feel a Death Star-size explosion coming on.

"She's the catch of the day if you can reel her in. She's been chatting up that girl she's talking to all night."

"What's her name?" I ask, nodding at what could be either lady. The Harley-esque one I meant to nod at notices me and smiles. It worked.

"Her? Vivian." He corrects himself, "Viv."

"The other? The black curly hair?"

"Jeanine."

He says it softly, but she turns around to glance at us as though she heard him whisper her name. My racing heart comes to a dead stop. Not in the butterflies-in-the-stomach way you felt when you first fondled a pair of breasts back in grade school. No. This moment is a heart-stopping, loss-of-a-beloved-pet way. The way I felt when Lt. Dan was too old to move, too decrepit to enjoy any aspect of life, and had to put him to his final rest. That pain, or something close to it, is what I am feeling right now, at this moment. Her eyes have no fleck. They aren't hazel. They are brown. Her nose is not the same characteristic, Romanesque nose. The nose on her is small and cute, which is nice but lacks character. Freckles, yes. Not nearly as many or as nicely laid out. More crowded, larger freckles that make you think she had a rough childhood in school before the boys figured out the meaning of life. The sadness at this moment is harsh. I stare at a loss, even though there was never a win that could have occurred.

D.B. sees me staring past the night's options into the void of disappointment. He nudges me. "You okay?"

"Yeah. Just thought I knew her."

I look around and my attention is anything but focused. I again see the guitar players making sweet love to the dark wood Ibanez acoustics and their harem. The numerous other small conversations that go on around me. A fire lit in a fire pit, always a necessity at 75 degrees. I shake my head clear and turn back to my momentary savior.

"I need a drink."

"No worries, my friend. I already have one waiting. Shanghai Tea. As you always."

He knows me so well. I smile a half-cocked smile and nod an appreciative nod. We walk back to his circle and, like a trophy awaiting its champion, my beautiful, translucent green drink sits. As I pick it up, I watch the alcohols swirling about, mingling with the green liquor and rocks. A party in a glass. I take a sip and the party is now in my mouth. A sweet, pleasant, refreshing sip of alcoholic goodness that is a Shanghai Tea.

A quick note in case you've never heard of one: one part each gin, vodka, rum, and Triple Sec. Fill with sour mix, sweet & sour mix, whatever. Then top with a splash or two of Midori. It gives it the beautiful green color and a flavor like no other. That said, I am drinking my libation. The sip hits my tongue, and I am savoring the taste. I have to enjoy any small win I can to get my head in the game. Knowing that a woman named Viv wants to meet me helps with that.

After enjoying a moment to myself with my drink, I look at Viv. She is already trying to make eye contact. Not like a desperate barfly looking for love in all the wrong places, just casual. Her head is tilted down a tad. A slight, forced smile on her thin lips. Her long, blonde hair lends a view to the deep red-and-blue peekaboos underneath. She wears these black rim glasses that give her a look somewhere between a sexy librarian and a goth chick, both ready to tear your clothes off and rock your world while simultaneously having a most intellectually stimulating conversation with you. I figure tonight I'd be down for either, or both. Her blue-gray eyes stare into mine, waiting for me to make a move, to say something. But at this moment, I notice the Van Halen T-shirt she wears under an open plaid button-down. I smile at seeing her because her shirt makes me know that tonight, at least, she "Ain't Talkin' 'Bout Love." I nudge D.B. on the arm, a signal amongst men that a move is to be made. And it is. I make a casual move closer to her, nothing that will be mistaken for the up-turned collar, wild and crazy guy or anything else.

"D.B. says your name is Viv." I find my spot standing next to the patio couch they are squatting on.

In my impeccable timing, I say this as she takes a sip of some blue-red cocktail that matches her hiding hair. She hurries her sip, a little spilling out of her straw as she does. She wipes her lips; it is an adorable gesture that makes me chuckle.

"It is. Oh, God." Viv stands up as if some big bomb will need to be dodged. "What else did he say about me?" Her face scrunches, unsure if she should already be embarrassed.

"Just that you were a rabid fan who has been stalking me for a while. Pictures, shrine, incense: the whole nine yards."

She laughs. Her ability to discern dry sarcasm from true sincerity is a welcome sign. The sigh of relief in her laugh relaxes her as she takes another sip. This time without spilling.

"It's all true. Many, many posters and pictures." She laughs and smiles a real smile.

"I assume your face has been cut out of other pictures and taped next to mine," I retort.

"Yes, all of my pictures have us together," she adds.

Then, before things can get awkward, she downshifts the tone with the smoothness of a pro racecar driver. "But seriously, I do own all your work. My absolute favorite stuff."

How else can I respond to such a gracious comment but "Thank you. It means a lot."

From the couch, Jeanine looks up at me. She cocks her head just a sliver to the side, as if a thought has entered her mind and she's not sure if it should be there or not.

"I know you," Jeanine interrupts us. A quizzical look is painted on her face at me, "Knew you."

"I've been on the radio once or twice." I'm not exactly sure how to respond.

"No. Like, actually knew you. You knew my mom." A statement that made a subtle, borderline standard moment shift past awkward to just short of uncomfortable.

"I've known a lot of moms. Dads too. Sisters, brothers..." I respond, not exactly sure where she's going with this.

"Holy shit! Tricky Finn?!" She says this and the world around me closes in. I can feel the physical shift of my pupils contract. From all angles of my peripheral vision, a black wave closes in and shuts out everything except for her. All noise around seems to cease. It's still there, I know it is, but my ears have stopped functioning. All I can hear is the sound of the blood rushing through dilated vessels of my inner ear and the pounding of my heart beating in my chest. And a high-pitched buzz that sometimes lingers like a bad hangover.

I want to collapse. I want to crash to the ground and let the world fade away. For the first time in my 38 years of existence, my body is incapable of functioning. All systems are at a loss on how to operate. Ceased. Breathing has stopped. I mentally have to force myself to breathe. Much more difficult than you could imagine. Speech is turned off. All systems are no-go. The moment paralyzes me. Those haunting eyes enter my mind and stab me right through my cerebral cortex (or whatever part of the brain controls function), making me unable to move. Those haunting, beautiful eyes with a brilliant fleck, the Roman nose. The freckles. All thrown off because of black number 1 hair dye, a curling iron, makeup, and a tattoo sleeve.

I think I feel a tear rolling down my right eye. I'm not sure. I try to move my hand, but it won't budge. Stuck. Stuck in this moment and unable to move as my mind scrambles to comprehend what is going on at this moment in my life.

This woman that sits in front of me, a woman I thought I didn't know. A woman I don't know, at least not anymore, knows me. Well, knew me. And it's because this woman in front of me knows me, I now understand why those eyes have been haunting me. Now my ears hear what she said as the emasculated man on the Vomatron was screaming like a little girl: "Faith," as in "You gotta have faith."

Why didn't it register that night? Damn that screaming, girly man.

It was her name. It was also a message; a message that dated back two decades or so to my first year of college. The flood doors have opened and all these memories come flooding in, a torrent of memories out of chronology hitting my optic nerve. They all flash: so random, so fast, so overwhelming. I need to sit. But I still can't move.

Faith.

CHAPTER 3

Sidedish Friend

*S*he was the only one to call me Tricky Finn; it was a reference to a singular event. Almost meaningless. Except that the name stuck. For Faith. This woman in front of me was not Faith. Faith was the love with whom I spent four years. She was the love that drove me insane like no other, that pushed me to try harder than no other, that inspired me to write more than any other, that inspired me to create better than any other. Everything I did, I did better because of her. She was my muse—my reason for leaving Chicago behind after college and moving to New York.

The first thing I remember from our introductory night together was the candlelight, the stereo softly playing Dave Matthews' "Say Goodbye." Soft sheets. So extraordinarily comfortable that I almost made mention of it, almost. The way she looked as she raised her arms, and I took off her top. The look in her eyes as she took off mine. I held the back of her head with my left hand as we deeply kissed. Tongues tangled around one another. Lips silently speaking to each other. My other hand reached for her bra clasp. She hesitated for a moment. I stopped. The night was for her, not me. We continued to kiss, and she nodded her head. Yes! My middle and index finger snapped against my thumb, clasp between them. It sprung open. Her breasts joined us as willing participants in that night's rendition of The Drunken Match Game.

Now her breasts were there, opened and on display. I did what all men do. I stopped and took a moment to admire. They were beautiful. Not ordinary. Marvelous. Magnificent. Greek wars scribed by Homer would have been fought over these breasts. Arabian Nights legends could have been written about just the beauty of the areola and nipple. That night, she chose to share them with me. She decided to share herself with me. I don't think a hot, fat child in hell getting a gigantic bowl of cold ice-cream could have been happier. And she knew it. The shit-eating grin on my face said it all.

Now, if you want your life to change, do something different. Not extreme. No skydiving, bungee-jumping, or anything like that. I'm sure it's fun and all. But I'm talking subtly different from your everyday. The events that led to the candlelit Dave Matthews incident only took place because of a poetry class. Class registration began at some ungodly early hour, and I knew if I went to bed, I'd never wake up on time, so I stayed up all night. I had help staying up thanks to Anastasia in 304, but I stayed up. Registration was during the start of finals week at the end of the first trimester. All this seems pretty mundane but staying up without sleep let some bug I was harboring run rampant, making me god-awful ill. I lost forty pounds. I didn't mind that since I gained the freshman fifteen, so I was looking pretty good after my flu. Nothing big. Just a bad flu bug. But that's why I remember signing up for this class.

It was some poetry class about war's refugees. As a musician, I thought the topic was, as I put it back then, dope. I needed an elective, and I figured this class might give me some insight, some inspiration, some way of looking at things I'd previously missed or overlooked. I didn't know it then, but I was using the biggest hammer around to hit the nail smack on the head. I just thought I might get a couple of sweet lyrical sets out of it. Instead, I *found her. The nail the hammer was hitting had nothing to do with the class, of course.*

To know where the following is coming from, the time is important. The era. The feeling of the decade. Saddam was still at the height of his power. Corporations were frantically starting to prepare for what could be the downfall of society, Y2K. We all know what a joke that ended up being. It was the last of the feel-good times of the eighties that trickled into and lasted throughout—though being horribly twisted by—the '90s. The end of the millennium. Political turmoil was brewing, as it always does on some level. Social values were shifting, which of course the older crowd was pushing back against. But we were going to be heard, as every generation will be heard, even if we had no clue what we were saying!

The class itself was okay. The instructor was some renegade, a gray-haired priest who had multiple warrants out for his arrest from decades-old swords to plowshares protests (which he was all high and mighty about). All the students were soaking in every word he was saying like it was scripture. All I could think about was the pay he was getting at this Chicago, Catholic university. Where was his vow of poverty? Or did the renegade part allow him the luxury of money? Either way, something seemed off to me about him, but the rest of the students soaked up the rays of sunshine he seemed to illuminate. The skeptic in me couldn't help wondering if he had soaked up altar boys back in his day like these students are soaking him up now. Maybe it was the cynic in me.

For the first couple sessions, I was the Judd Nelson in the leather jacket. Daydreaming out the window, writing poetry while the teacher taught:

I sit watching the leaves fall from the trees
Listening to the crackling sound as they hit the building
While in the background is the ambient talking of
the teacher.

SIDEDISH FRIEND

I realize as we sit, 42 individuals, all being taught the
same thing
Becoming unconsciously institutionalized, that
Will was right
"They may take our lives... but they can never take
our freedom."

*That was a real crap bag right there, first one from the
class. The cynicism may have been dripping off my chin, but
all that was about to be challenged. He gave us an assignment. Write a poem. That was it. So, of course, he got the
barrage of zombified hands waving around, about to fall
off dare they stop moving. All were asking questions in the
same vein. "Write about what?" And like any good writer of
any genre knows: write what you know. But these weren't
good writers. Those students were only in that class for
elective purposes. The same reason I was there I guess, but
I was too holier-than-thou to see it back then. I thought I
was too good for these other students. Figured everything
I wrote was going to be gold.*

*I never liked writing songs directly about myself. I
enjoyed making them a bit more worldly. Political. Lovely.
Fantastical. Whatever the case. Not as introspective as
Father Renegade Lorenzo Lamas may have wanted. So,
the next class, I came in with my sarcastic, cynical look at
America. Some would have said it was unpatriotic. Some
said it was misogynistic and, therefore, I must have been.
I just wrote what I saw.*

The Dirt Will Climb

I love America and rightly so.
Only in this country can women be raped
And still men rule.
I love America and rightly so.
I see indifference grow,
Hate and love diminish

THE *Fairlane* INCIDENTS

Hateandlovediminish.
America is loved for what it stands for:
Freedom, Equality, Happiness
All for the upper class...
The upper ass...
Yeah, up your ass.
Women raped and children die.
This isn't freedom.
This is free dumb.
Just beneath the surface.
It's there you'll find
Dirt and slime, scum and grime.
The dirt will climb on cum and grime
But we should love our country...
God has blessed her...
We have blessed her...
We have caressed her...
I love America and rightly so...
Only in this country have I seen such change
To take segregation toward integration
And make it right...
Make it white...
We sing our song.
The right becomes wrong.
Follow along.
It's all so wrong,
But still, we love America.
I love America.
Burton loves America.

Now the last line was a direct reference to a Fear Factory song "Big God/Raped Souls," to which Burton C. Bell does lead vocals. The song starts with sad statistics on American violence, especially such acts perpetrated against women. And finishes with an ironic declaration of love for the country. I assume it's a lash out against those whose morals are in direct contradiction of their actions.

So, the whole poem was inspired by what I saw in life, in the news, and that opening to the song, which I had only heard once before while in a client's old red Trans Am getting double meat Chorizo burritos from this old Chicagoland joint called El Famous Burrito.

"The Dirt Will Climb" was my vocal introduction to the class. While it didn't have quite the introductory impact of a nursery rhyme and baseball bat upside the head as I would have liked, it was still enough. I figured it would piss off a few people, make others think, and stir up some thought, discussion, and controversy, which is precisely what the class needed. Get these dead brains thinking.

That's just what it did.

The next class session we, of course, had to write other poems. I chose stoic silence this time around. Wanted to give someone else the chance to stir the cauldron of our minds. And one did. This stick-straight, dishwater blonde with freckles on a makeup-free face and a fleck in her left eye, wearing an earth-tone flannel shirt and fitted, faded jeans, who had been quietly sitting in a window seat, decided to pipe up. She straightened herself up, as if she was ever that slouched to begin with, cleared her throat while getting her poem, neatly printed on computer paper, out from her blue folder, and stared at me. A look in her eye that said, "This poem is for you. You fucking douchebag of a man. Scum of the earth. Here's looking at you, shithead."

She then proceeded to read off this poem about being a woman. How hard it was to be female. Growing up middle America, some sect upper class, big city suburbs because once a month she bled for a few days. And oh, the pains of it all. How my eyes rolled. How everyone's eyes rolled. Yes, she saw my eyes point toward the ceiling, and it made her read her self-sacrificial poem all the more intensely, like someone-at a microphone-doing an open jam-slam poetry night-encircled by wreaths of smoke-while reciting what sounds like-every other-fucking-spoken-word-poem-where every-other word-is stressed-and thus-the meaning-of the poem-is lost-unlike Frost. Or Kerouac. Or Angelou. Or even Silverstein.

But she finished. And the class applauded its forced applause, and I applauded because she tried to write and however amateur, flat, or contrived the poem may have been, there was real emotion in her voice. Real feelings seeped out of her pores, and they were not encircling her like a wreath. Oh no. They shot at me, the poison-tipped arrows they were, trying to take me down with each shot. But I remained standing, well, seated. Alive. Her words could never hurt me. No one cared about the struggles of being a spoiled girl from a well-to-do house where nothing dreadful had ever happened. There were no real struggles.

I was a grade-A asshole back then. Sure, she may have called me out on it, but perhaps that's why I ended up doing what I did—Because she called me out. The beginning of the bettering of Finn Fairlane all started with this one incident. Perhaps.

The class let out thirty or so minutes later, and we all rose and hastily exited. I rushed out. One of the firsts. I didn't feel like being told off by someone who knew I thought lowly of their work. But I know I wasn't alone in how I felt because other classmates and I talked about it and her and whatever comments may have been told that I can't remember now, looking back. But I knew what I had to do.

For my next assignment, I wrote this poem called "I Will Build My Cross," and it was formatted to look like a cross. The poem itself was about individuals' exceptional ability to martyr themselves for any small cause just to garner attention while sweeping important issues under the rug of martyrdom. And yes, it was all aimed at her. While I read each line of what I thought was a poignant poem, her eyes stabbing deeper and deeper into my soul, trying to rip apart my heart, I knew she felt it. And the class ate it up. The round of applause I received was an unspoken thank-you from every other student for writing that poem for her. But no wars were going to start there. The applause *was it. We read more poetry for the rest of the class and mine was seemingly left wayside.*

The class ended for the day and I left. No war cries or rallies from the other side. No small group discussion was held dissecting line after line and how it fed on her poem. The round of applause was to be the end.

I opened the door to the outside world of wind screaming through the trees and whipping leaves. The crisp, late autumn breeze hit my face with a sharp sting. It also could have been the over-sized pebble that hit square against my cheek, sending a cool pain spreading throughout the right side of my face. As I said, her words could never hurt me... but sticks and stones on the other hand.

A voice called out. Screaming. Shaking. Mad. It called out to me, and I knew it. "Asshole!" When someone speaks that word to you, you know it. It doesn't matter if you've ever heard that voice or not. The letters scream your name. My name may be spelled F-I-N-N, but at that moment it was pronounced, "Asshole."

I rubbed the side of my face with my hand and smiled through the minor, but annoying, pain.

"Did you rush out here after class just to ambush me?" I was searching for a wittier repartee, but the pain was blocking intelligent thought.

"Yes. No." She paused for a split moment, unsure of her actions as if she didn't know why she assaulted me. "I did. But not to throw a rock at your face. You're an asshole. You know that? A real asshole."

"So, I've been told."

"Well, you are. I'm not a writer. I'm taking this class because I thought it would be fun. Different. A break from business courses. Then you have to go and ruin it for me." The anger in her voice was fierce. Fiery. The wind blew her dishwater hair across her face, rhythmically whipping it with the fury in her words in vicious prose.

"Tell me how you really feel." As those words escaped past my teeth, I felt a shit-eating grin take over my lips.

"You sit in the back of the class all quiet and brooding. Not talking, not making friends. People talk. You seem interesting. Somehow, in a university of 14,000, you have a reputation. But you make yourself unapproachable. You think what I wrote was somehow self-righteous martyrdom?! Take a look at yourself."

I couldn't tell if she was angry anymore or just yelling to yell, but the passersby were watching, and she was so beautiful at that moment that I was just happy she was talking—yelling—at me and not anyone else. The hair blew across her face as she continually tried to move it back, as if the wind would listen to her pleas and calm down. The furrowed brow that crinkled her nose as she said I, "seem interesting." She didn't want to be mad. She just was. I'm sure the shit-eating grin on my face did nothing to quell the anger and frustration inside her. But I couldn't help it. She was beautiful in her passion. And I loved that moment. I loved her at that moment.

"Can I buy you a coffee or a drink or something?" I asked, hoping she didn't honestly want to be mad.

"What?" The surprised look on her face, unsure how to respond.

"Coffee, a latte, a margarita. I'm thirsty." Now I was just trying to break the tension. The passersby had all stopped spectating, and the scene had returned to normal. Students walked up and down the sidewalks. Leaves blew on the ground from the wind. Cars drove up and down the street.

Something in her had also returned to normal. Her breathing had slowed, and her brow un-furrowed. She looked at me, unsure of my intentions.

I pulled out a pack of red-and-white boxed cigarettes and flicked my wrist, so one flew out into my lips. I extended it in her direction, and she accepted with a raised brow.

A sounding relief in her voice as she told me, "Margaritas sound great."

Glad to have gotten that all out. It was that moment. Third trimester of my freshman year for which I was waiting. For whatever reason, my college was done in trimesters for the year, not semesters. Stupid, I know. But that's private schools for you. Nothing before that day seemed important anymore. I didn't know where this might lead. A drink with a stranger that never crosses your path again, or something more. But the magic in that moment of all her yelling in the chilly winds had sappy romance songs playing in my head. I was living out my very own teen romance flick and didn't care how cliché it looked.

"I know a place that doesn't card. Come on."

We started walking down Fullerton Avenue along the row of (possibly Victorian) townhomes that decorated the southern side of the street, a nice contrast to the apartments on the opposite side. It was not as awkward a walk as one might think. Looking back on it, one might say it was almost pleasant.

"Fairlane. Finn Fairlane." I went for the understated Bond introduction.

"Yeah, got that from class," was her reply.

I smiled a bit. "I know, but we never had a formal introduction. So, I figured."

She retorted, "Oh, I caught the gesture. Just don't think you're getting off that easy."

"But I don't know your name," I replied. Honestly, I didn't. Never paid attention really to people outside my circle. I guess wanting to know her name was my attempt at expanding that circle.

"Siubhal. Faith Siubhal."

She was beautiful and mesmerizing, and I wanted her to be mine. There was a hypnotic tone in the way she spoke. Very sexy. I had to play it cool and make sure not to overplay my hand. We already got off to one bad start. They say you never get a second chance to make a first impression. Logically, that is true, but if there ever was a chance this was it.

The icy feel of frozen watermelon margaritas hitting her taste buds was just what she needed. She relaxed deeper as the watermelon's smooth, calming voice echoed in her mind while slowly counting back. Ten... Deeper. Nine... That's it.

Relax. Eight... Imagine steps. But her eyes were open. We were talking. She was from the suburbs but wanted to live on campus. Naperville area. I never much made it out that way before. Meeting her, wish I had.

She was telling me about her boyfriend halfway through our second pitcher. Maybe he was soon-to-be-ex, ex-something. Something about how he tried too hard to turn her into something she's not. She used to go to Scotland every summer with her family. Visit relatives. See the sights. But once she started dating whatever his name was, the trips stopped. He said establishing new roots was more important than the past. Some lame crap, but she bought into it. She had childhood dreams, as she called them, of traveling the world. She wanted to go back-packing through Europe. But no. She now thought living up to the social expectations of landing a corporate job was more important.

There was something in her voice, unsteadiness or unsure, that made me not completely believe her. Maybe it was the alcohol. Hell, the tequila made it a bit difficult to concentrate and the more she drank, the more she leaned forward. The more she leaned forward, the more her cleavage popped out of her top. While I tried to be a gentleman and not sneak a peek, they were handcrafted by an artisan very close to the creator, if not himself. And I was a tad bit inebriated. I continued to listen to her as she finished talking about the inevitable demise of her latest relationship, all while sneaking peeks at her lovely bosom. It looked such a place I wanted to fall into a deep sleep on, after doing such activities that afterward require a deep slumber.

"I honestly thought he was going to be the one I spent my life with," she reflected on her naivete, "but at fifteen, doesn't everyone think that?" She looked at me for confirmation.

I nodded, if only to comfort her. There was no way at fifteen I thought whatever girl I was with was the one I was going to spend my life with. At fifteen, all guys want to do is get their dong played with. Hell at nineteen, twenty, twenty-five that's all we wanted. Still, I nodded.

"I wrote that poem you so wonderfully attacked as a way to deal with him." The truth comes out. "He pissed me off. So many times. He always makes these promises but never follows through. Ya know? And he always has an excuse. For everything. It's like I'm only there for him when he needs. It wasn't always that way. He told me it would change come college, but I didn't listen. No! I am just his little..."

"Were," I figured now would be a perfect time to interject.

"What?" She was stunned I spoke.

"You were just his whatever. Now you are your own, to be yourself. Find yourself. And do whatever you want," I finished that sentence as the last of the once frozen watermelon margaritas slid down my throat.

"Yes. You are right. You're such a good listener." She smiled.

"One of my many talents." I spoke as if I were some embodiment of a walking, sexual inuendo in her wilting world.

"Let's get outta here." The sinful grin on her face said what her words did not.

Which leads us back to her breasts, candlelight, and Dave Matthews on the stereo. I grabbed her, pulled her close to me. I wanted to meld our bodies together. So did she. She reached into my pants and said hello to my other half. She played around for a moment, exploring the newly discovered territory. Who was I to say no? But then she left. As quickly as she found this new land, filled with toys to play with, she evacuated the premises.

She took my hand and slipped it down her pants. Slid it down? Whatever. It was my turn to explore exotic, new lands. The anticipation was palpable as she piloted its crawling descent down. The feel of her soft skin as my hand made its way to the unexplored. But there were no jungles, no shrubs of any sort. She was smooth. Well groomed. And when a man internally compares in his mind how turned-on a female is to how hard he is, she was unmistakably turned on. These were wetlands. Florida Everglades waiting to turn into the Niagara Falls, excuse the geographic jump. As I slid my middle finger in, she quickly inhaled a short breath. A quick draw in that let me know I hit the right spot. I continued my spelunking adventure for only a few moments when she stopped kissing me. She gently pulled away from my hand. My finger slid out of her and her pants. My heart dropped. I figured this was it. Perhaps my talents were lacking, and she wasn't going to be my teacher. The ride ends here. Please exit to your left and have a great day!

She looked into my eyes for a moment. The abyss of my soul reached for her; she searched for herself in there. I stared back. A half-cocked smile broke on her face, and she leaned over to her nightstand. She opened the drawer, tossing me the holy grail of any first date.

"Put it on." Those were her words. Short, sweet, to the point. They were not a request. A demand. She knew what she wanted and for that night, at least, she wanted me.

She took her jeans off to reveal black lace panties, and the beauty of those lasted three point five seconds until she took those off as well.

So, I took off my jeans and put on my raincoat.

"I just want you to know, this wasn't my end game tonight." I was just adding for clarification. I realized I just sounded like almost every other female I had been with. A guy's version of, "I'm not normally like this." There, that night, it was true. I wasn't lying.

"Shut up. When a girl's ready, don't shut yourself out."

Yes, ma'am.

CHAPTER 4

The Devil's Dance Floor

"**A**re you okay?" Viv sees my thousand-yard stare into the past. Her words jab me, snapping me back to the present. I blink, shaking my memories from my mind.

There, in front of me, still sat Jeanine, a version of Faith that always pales by comparison. The annoying off-brand when the real thing isn't available. The irritating little sister who never failed to make her presence known: a fly at the picnic, a mosquito by the campfire.

"Yeah, sorry, Viv." I am trying to get my head into the night. I don't like disappointing fans. "It just so happens we're old acquaintances."

Jeanine looks down to take a drink as she shakes her head, a mixture of disappointment and unchanging expectations.

Viv looks to Jeanine for confirmation. "Something like that, yeah." Jeanine's dry reply could be served as a martini.

"Me and her sister used to be a thing. It was a long time ago." I hope she drops it.

"Hmm. You'll have to give me some details later." She takes no time in dashing my hopes.

"Perhaps." I leave it short and to the point.

Viv and I take a seat where we stood. Plop down on two red cushions in the dead center of a patio love seat. I somehow get maneuvered between Viv and Jeanine. I take a giant slurp that finishes off my Shanghai Tea. This irony here stares at me from both sides. And even though D.B. had no knowledge of my past with Jeanine's sister, he finds humor in something. He approaches with a new green savior of a drink in hand, laughing about something while nodding in my direction.

"Please join us," I beg of him as he hands me my drink. I notice the winds picking up. The palm leaves dance around wildly, playing air piano of some Rachmaninoff piece. The tiny lizards scurry about for shelter, lest they might get blown away. Even the little sparrows that usually keep company here, scavenging for food scraps, have abandoned us this night. A few early signs of the approaching hurricane.

"I see you're all getting along." D.B. settles back in across from me. A gust of wind tries to steal his golfer's cap, but he stops the would-be thief.

"Like old friends." The sarcasm drips off Jeanine's chin.

D.B. tosses a glance my direction, looking for clarification. I subtly shake my head no. Nodding his head, he drops it like a good friend.

"So," D.B. begins, "what ideas do you have in store for Badaboom?"

All heads turn to D.B. The minstrels stop strumming their guitars, giving the swooning companions a chance to scoot in a little closer. Conversations surrounding us hush down, waiting to hear something about the man or his band. Even the wind quiets for a moment before picking back up.

Viv chimes in, "What's ... Badaboom?"

"Their fourth album," I say. "Actually, plans for the record release party are coming along. The date's been finalized, which means we need to finish the opener. And the date is not as far off as you'd like."

"Did we get the amphitheater?" D.B asks.

"She couldn't book it, but I'm working on something" is my best reply.

Viv chimes in, "Anything you can tell us about the album?"

"Yes. Come to the record release party. The date is on their website. Enjoy live music, great beer, and good food." I pause for a moment as the crowd looks on. "The album, though, it's gonna be big, Badaboom. Spear Fist's best."

Heads turn to their cellphones to look up dates and conversations return to normal. The guitars are silent as the magic fingers of Neil and Vincent are now playfully flirting with the female fans who were so entranced moments earlier.

Viv turns her attention—and positioning—back to me. I take note and turn to her. D.B. notices, smiles, and nods approvingly. Caught up in the introduction earlier and the awkward moment of running into Jeanine, I didn't notice the small, jeweled bull ring she wears in her nose. Not my go-to cup of tea but she pulls it off nicely. A gracious accent on a smooth complexion.

Some person I've only seen around here a few times and whose name I have forgotten, if I ever knew it, sees D.B. sitting unattended to and saunters up to him. Normally this is not a noteworthy moment, except that this person has unknowingly caused D.B. to leave me to my own devices. No safety net for things that may go awry.

Christian: that's his name. Whatever—it doesn't matter. I have a beautiful lady sitting next to me.

"What is it you do for them?" Her first inquiry. I know she's just trying to make conversation, unsure of what to ask. Not wanting to sound like every other female who has sat in her seat, metaphorically speaking. But all fans sing the same basic praise, no matter how hard they try to stand apart. It's the nature of the beast. And it's okay. I never hold it against them. At least not the ones that look like her. She is just a fan wanting to talk.

"Not really sure how to explain it. I'm a producer of sorts." I try to keep it simple. Producer, writer, publicist, prodder: anything that helps the band stay motivated, inspired, and playing. In other words, doing their jobs. But musicians don't like that sort of stuff admitted about them, so I just say I'm a producer.

"I know what a producer does," she says, half offended.

"It's not a normal producer-musician relationship. I'm a muse. Sort of."

"You sort of amuse?" Viv's confused, almost embarrassed response by her misunderstanding was not masked. That's when I notice what makes her so beautiful, a mesmerizing sadness in her eyes. A driving need to never be wrong and then be ashamed when she is. A wondrous melancholy that makes her so enchanting.

"No. I'm a muse. Like those figures from Greek mythology who inspire creativity." I hope to eschew obfuscation.

"Weren't Greek muses all women?" she inquires.

"Now you know what I'm talking about." I smile.

"Now that my misunderstood wordplay has been clarified, yes." She smiles back. She might be smarter than I think.

"Yes, I believe they were all women, but it's the closest analogy I could think of." I want to move this conversation along.

"How does that work? Do you just show up, sit there, and they stare at you until they come up with something? Or is there more to it, I assume?" she jokes.

"Yes." I laugh. "There is more to it. I have my ideas as they have theirs. I take good ideas and make them great. I take great ideas and make them genius."

"Where do you get your inspiration from?" she asks as she puts her hand on my thigh. Her eyes connect with mine, and she gazes into them, a longing, lingering gaze that attempts to ensnare my soul. I dive back deep into her eyes, searching her soul. Looking for the roots of her sadness so that at least tonight, if only for a moment, I can take it away. Remove all of it and make her smile again. Smile like she did when I first made her feel relaxed.

I am just a man. And from her hand slowly creeping up my thigh, she wants to verify that. I am no longer mildly irritated by Spear Fist's two members, who have resumed their playing and are now strumming "Mrs. Robinson" for their fans. I suddenly find their music a perfect setting for tonight, even if I'm Mrs. Robinson and she's Dustin Hoffman's Ben Braddock.

"Where do I get my inspiration from?" I pause. Keeping eye contact, I put my hand on her hand. I just rest it there, not stopping her. Just letting her know that she has permission to continue.

"Yes, where do you?" Her coy words need no direct reply. She turns her hand to grab mine. She puts my hand on her thigh, just above the knee but slightly toward the inner side. An open door, if you will, to come in for a drink.

Perhaps it's the liquid courage from the green drinks instilling in me the confidence that Bruce Banner has in his strength when he's in Hulk form. Maybe it's the simplicity in the mood of the night air as the hurricane approaches. Perhaps it's the feeling of false impending doom of the hurricane that everyone is using as an excuse for the behavior of the evening. Or it's the simple answer I give, proving that sometimes genius doesn't have to be complicated or wordy—just stated.

"From moments like this." I hope the words I speak will let me see her good graces, as D.B. put it.

And they do. Viv leans in to kiss me but stops. She is inches away. I can smell her faded, sweet perfume. The smell of mixed liquor on her breath whispers to me that a kiss is waiting. She stops and pulls back. Scared, perhaps. Hesitant because of who I once was. Who I still may be in her eyes. A man who's written some songs, but as it begins, "a man." I am just a man. A man who wants her at this moment, as she wants me. So, I grab her hand and pull her toward me. We inch closer and closer together. Our eyes slowly close as our lips begin to touch. Such gentle, soft lips. She frees her hand from mine and places it high on my thigh. I, not wanting to leave my hands with nothing to do, put one on the small of her back and the other behind her head. Our tongues waltz around, enjoying the moment in their temporary homes.

She stops for a moment, not to pull away, but to gently bite my bottom lip. She tugs on it with her teeth, and it feels great. I open my eyes to find her looking into mine. We search the abyss of our souls. She lets go and runs her tongue across my bottom lip, as if to put it back in place. Her eyes swim up from the depths of where they just were and close. She kisses me again, no tongue but a deep kiss still. Perhaps more passionate than before. More enthusiasm and eagerness in the performance.

She pulls back and opens her eyes again.

"Thank you," she says.

As if I did her a favor.

"No. Thank you." The only thing I can come up with. My mind has blanked; all wittiness is gone. I just look at Viv as any man would—with amazement—and with a longing for more. Maybe simplicity is the right word choice.

"Perhaps I'll see you again, Finn Fairlane." She stands up.

"That would be nice, Viv." An unsure response from a slightly confused man. I'm not used to a one-kiss wonder.

She turns and exits out the same swinging door I entered through, the loud clang of metal on metal as it hits against the frame. No one seems to notice. No one turns. At least not that I see, and if anyone did see, no one appears to give a crap. Down a sidewalk lined with parked cars facing her, she walks away with a confident sway in her hips. A happy swing with equal parts excitement. I watch as she disappears around the corner of the building. One last glance back to me and a not-so-subtle gesture with her finger that I should follow her.

I look around at all the people, too enthralled in what they are doing to have noticed her. The young gals too entranced by learning that heaven does hold a place for people who pray. Hey, hey. And I think I may be about to find out if heaven is a place somewhere on Earth—and know what it's worth. We could just do the deed right here. The others drink their martinis while waxing existential. At most, they would comment on the futility of the act. A few are merely comparing their just finished night at work. They might cheer us on but more for laughs than anything. I finish off my drink as I stand up, tapping D.B. on the shoulder. D.B. looks up, and I just give him a nod and a wink ... and my glass. He nods back, takes my empty drink, and raises his in a silent toast.

I step beyond the swing gate I entered through and turn the corner Viv ducked behind. I look around; she has seemingly disappeared. There's a bustle in the trees that line the back of the building. Not my hedgerow, so to speak, but I'm not alarmed. Tonight, I shall find my stairway.

I take a few suave steps to the trees, doing my best Ben Affleck a la *Good Will Hunting* bar scene, hoping she can see me. A little laugh lets me know she can. I make my way through the trees to her. Once I'm within arm's reach, she grabs my belt loops and pulls me toward her, not wasting any time.

"I wasn't sure you'd follow me." She wastes no time in unzipping my pants.

"If you walk away, I will follow." I paraphrase.

I look her in the eye while I say this. It was sincere, and I want it to come across that way. I want to see if I can remove some of that infinite sadness from behind her melancholy eyes, if only for a moment.

She smiles.

I move in, and our lips touch. Gently. Gliding over each other, waiting for the right moment to interlock. Something about this moment sent shivers down my spine. My hands reach around as Viv's back forms an involuntary arch at the touch of my fingertips. I slowly lift up her shirt to reach her bra clasp.

Her hands make their way up my shirt, knowing she has free range to explore my body. Perhaps a charade telling me what she wants me to do to her. I unclasp her bra. Her muscles quiver in anticipation of the coming moments. The realization of this delights me; for where else may my fingers excite?

Her breast fills my whole hand as it rests its glide over her chest. Soft-skinned and perfectly perky. Her nipples are hard and magnificent. I move my right hand to her jean button and start to undo it.

She pulls away, slightly. Even our lips stop caressing. The potential reasons are running through my head. *Are we done again? Bathroom break? Did she hear someone heading our way?* The list goes on and on and all in about 2.1 seconds.

I look her in the eye, waiting for her next move. She pierces me with not just her eyes, but her subtle smile too.

"I can't tonight." She frowns.

All my boyhood hopes go rushing out of my mind. Spewing forth at the wrong moment on a night of drinking, the drunkard's projectile vomit that is her words have hit me in the face, and I can taste the bitter saltiness of each of those three words. **I:** Bitter, a reminder of what Campari and all its crappiness taste like. The acidity of the single letter. **Can't:** Salt added to the mix of the moment. **Tonight:** The chunks of partially digested food covered in the previous. My only saving grace is that they are just words. No actual vomit to accompany them, but still, I want to scream to the skies above, "Why then! Why would she do this to me?! What have I done to her that she damns me so?!" But I remain calm.

"I understand" is the only calm reply I can utter, as my hands retreat from under her shirt.

"It happens," she responds with a scrunched look on her face that says it all.

"Usually about once a month," I retort, resting my hands on her waist.

She smiles and little laughs escapes her.

"Perhaps another time," I say, assuming this is the end.

She whispers coy words, "I never said we were done."

She grabs my belt loops again and lowers herself down. The fact that she grappled my belt loops twice tonight, each time with a single finger per loop, made me wonder if this was her move. Like John Cena waving his hand in front of his face, crowd chanting "You can't see me," before winning the match with his "Attitude Adjustment," she pulls on belt loops and does her thing.

As much as I'm a fan of Mr. Cena, the feel of Viv putting me in her mouth slingshots me back to this moment. No offense, John. The warmth. The wetness. The puppy-dog-look in her eyes that searches for approval as she peers up at me. I look down, smiling. I put my hand on the top of her head and let out a soft moan. She shuts her eyes and goes back to doing what she does. And man, does she do it well. The feeling of hitting the back of her throat as she takes me all in. The quiet moans she makes. A woman who truly enjoys her work.

The talent in this woman only takes a few minutes before both my hands are on her head. The sure sign that things are coming to a close. I am waiting for her to come up from the ground and tell me to finish elsewhere or to leave me blue-balled. But a true artisan of her work she is. She takes me all-in moaning just a bit louder, enough for me to feel the vibrations as I slide ever farther down her throat. With one hand, she cups the boys a final time. A gentle press of her fingers against them and that is it. She swallows every last bit of me, as the warm ecstasy of the moment washes over my body. Toes curl in my shoes. She looks up at me as she forces out the last drop. Licking the last of the batter off the tip of the beater, she stands up.

"I wore this shirt for a reason tonight. I'm glad you caught on." Her choice, whispered words to me as I zip up my pants.

"Happy to oblige." What else can I say? Blood flow has still not returned in full to my brain.

She steps out from behind the trees and I follow behind, the puppy dog I've become for the moment following my new master. She stops for a moment as my senses return. My world that was focused solely on her has widened, and

I hear footsteps close behind me. We start to walk back to the patio as I turn my head to see who's approaching.

In the shadows of the parking lot lights, I see the unmistakable tribal ink on the arms of a torso too big for the legs that supported him at Old Town and are still too big to support his frame. I stop. I have become a deer frozen in headlights. Faith, standing next to him, eyeballing Viv up and down, hasn't noticed me yet.

"A cup of male tears for the lady. Nice." He attempts some form of brute-sophistication, a Neanderthal's version of calling out that he knows what just transpired.

I may not be the most mature man on the planet, but I do think I have a bit of decorum about me. My eyes squint a bit, and my nose furrows a little. My head tilts to the side and as I stare at him, trying to find the place in him that spews forth such audacious and crude things, then I see them: his oversized muscles.

Viv turns, sees me stopped in my tracks, and takes the few steps back to me. Faith and Viv make eye contact. Viv just smiles, knowing Faith is judging with condemnation in her eyes. Viv's "fuck all" attitude makes her more attractive at this moment. For all Viv cares, Faith could vanish out of existence, and all would be well. She has no idea of the full depth of our relationship, our past. Faith's eyes break contact with Viv, and for a fraction of a fraction of a second, my body floods with relief of the ending moment. Faith will walk right by and not even look at the man who defiled this lovely, carefree woman.

But no.

Faith's eyes move to me, the deer about to be slaughtered in her headlights. My mind in all its wisdom and glory shoots back to my first night here and remembers how it failed me. How I needed my mind to give me power beyond anything I've used before. How in that moment when I needed my mind the most, it failed me and let me fucking nod. My thoughts swim fast, knowing it must make up for that first night. Understanding, at this moment, I need something so strong, so powerful that no one will be able to retort back. She'll smile. All will be right in the world. And nothing awkward will happen. The overgrown behemoth will continue making caveman remarks. Viv will go back to the patio and have a good conversation with me. Faith and her little sister will talk and not bring up the past. And my mind delivers its redemption for past failure.

"Just finding some faith in Orlando," exits my mouth as she stares, possibly hoping for some growth and maturation from years gone by.

She stares, the look in her eyes of familiar disappointment. The three seconds they've been standing here feel like forever to me because in some parallel universe it has been forever.

"Let's get a beer," he says.

It's nice to know three seconds is his attention span. I knew this Neanderthal would help me out somehow.

Faith's attention shifts back to her man and she smiles, shaking off the moment.

She adds, "And a shot. Something strong."

He nods, and they walk off.

Viv stands next to me once again.

"I think I got all the details I needed." Viv motions to Faith and her man.

I just look into her eyes, searching for something to say. Viv is such a nice woman, and this night has gone so well.

"Look. We just met. You're nice, and your past is your past. I have a feeling that some of it is going to get dug up here tonight and I like the impression I have of you so..." Viv pauses mid-sentence.

My mind is racing on what is about to happen. It sprints back and forth in an empty room, searching for possible scenarios about to play out. But nothing pops up. It can't think of anything, good or bad.

She reaches into the front pocket of her flannel and grabs a pen. Viv has a receipt on which she writes down her number.

"So take this. And you'd better call me cause I had fun and want to do it again," she finishes.

Not the ending I thought was coming, but considering I couldn't think of any to begin with, I can't think of any better way it could end.

She leans in and kisses me one last time. I kiss her back for a moment, then she pulls away.

"Till next time." Her parting words as she walks to her car.

I stand for a moment watching, in awe of the events that transpired and the fact I got out dodging all bullets, for now. Viv enters a silver BMW and pulls away.

Good graces all right and graceful. I pocket the receipt and head back to the patio.

As I enter, D.B. turns to me and applauds. I smile a forced, modest smile, knowing damn well I want to soak in the cheer. I wave him off, but it only makes him clap louder. A few others from the crowd join in. While I'm unsure if they know why they are applauding or not, it doesn't help my situation at the moment. Faith and her giant take a seat next to Jeanine. Jeanine is leaned over, whispering in Faith's ear. She follows me with her eyes as I cop-a-squat by D.B.

D.B. tells me about something, but his voice is faded to the background. All I can do at this moment is sit, sip my watered-down drink that D.B. replenished while I was behind the trees, and stare at her. At Faith.

How did I miss her that first night? Yes, her hair is drastically different. Different color, different cut. Her arm is now adorned in splendid ink. A masterwork started and completed in the years gone by since our final college rendezvous. She does her makeup differently too. Hell, she wears makeup now. While I can rationalize the many, many things that have changed in the seventeen or so years since I last saw her, I still can't grasp the fact that I didn't recognize her.

She shoots a glance my way. D.B.'s voice rises to the foreground, and I hear him.

"You know what I mean?"

Crap. What a sentence to come back in on.

"Yeah" is all I can muster.

"Bro, you are so out of it right now. Still thinking about Viv?" His attempt to help me through whatever this moment is.

Shit. I had forgotten so soon; I didn't mean to. Viv seems like a pretty rad chick. But here I am, 21 again: stupid and naïve and indecisive. Wasting moments that cost me days. Wasting days that can cost me months if I'm not careful. And months into, well, you get the point.

The thing is the time between when Faith and I last saw each other and now, filled with the moments movies are made of. All those stories, as fun as they are, are not filled with real emotion, real meaning. It's all faceless sexual partners, countless drugs, and time forgotten to the hang-over in between. Yes, it was fun. Yes, it made me who I am. A once glorious rockstar producer with a following enough to give me a big head for a few years, wreak havoc on my body, and ruin relationships. That time has passed. I've paid my dues and earned my respect in the industry. That's why I get my royalty checks and land the clients I land. But all those years—all those stories—they would never have happened if I had not been with Faith before. If I had not had a weight to carry on my back, a burden to bear, so to speak.

Here she is again. The universe is telling me something. I would say to myself to take this moment and shake it, come carpe diem baby, and go after her again. But the breathing metaphor of the roadblock between us is a bit much right now.

I look at D.B. I give a look that says it's time to take off the mask of rock star for a moment. His grin fades. "What's up?"

"You know your girl?" I'm not exactly sure how to tell him without telling him.

"Which one, Finn?" A slight cocky smile comes across his face.

"THE girl," I say.

"Yeah." The smile fades from his face once more.

He knows what I mean. Musicians, actors, entertainers: we all come to a choice at some point where we must choose, love or art. The great ones struggle against the love they left behind for the art that called to them, an obsession that holds them like a dangerous addiction. Then, of course, their art becomes a reflection of that love they left behind. The cocaine and alcohol-fueled pornucopias for which music is so well known. They are all just ways to drown the past. The struggle against the tide and undercurrent that perpetually tries to pull us under.

So yeah. He knows. He knows all too well, too.

A slight head nod toward Faith is all I motion, and he now knows. Now he knows the whole story though no details were needed. He sees the face of my pain. The one who shaped me. The one I left behind, not that I had a choice.

But now I do.

I sit close enough to Faith, her man, and Jeanine. Figure I can work myself into a conversation somehow. Keep it casual. Maybe Faith has forgotten me. Maybe that night, when she said her name, I read too deep into it. Maybe that's been her move all along. A play on her name to lure guys in. Perhaps not; the stares she and her sister give me say I was anything but forgotten. Much like Napoleon, I'll just wait and see how this plays out.

So I'm sitting near them. D.B. is enjoying himself but keeping an eye on me. Watching. He might be as hopeful as me. He and his bandmates are the only other ones here who understand, who know what I feel and what I've been through to get here. But his bandmates have moved on to play "A Hazy Shade of Winter."

I sit and wait.

The machine of a man that is Faith's boyfriend extends a hand.

"Name's Ronnie," he says to me as I shake his hand. "Nice job behind the trees. From what I've heard, her BJs are the bomb."

Faith shakes her head.

At least he's not shy. I'm figuring, with his quick intro, he has no idea about Faith and me, our past. I also imagine a guy his age describing the sensual act that was her blowjob as "the bomb" isn't an intellectual equal. But at least he's friendly.

"We had a nice time. Name's Finn. Nice to meet you, Ronnie."

He gives me the look, the "are you him" look.

And he starts, "Are you..."

"Yes. I am, but let's keep that between us."

"Love your stuff, man. I've gotten laid to your music so many times," he says, his inner schoolboy coming out.

His words put a smile on my face. My eyes shoot toward Faith, knowing she's had sex while listening to my music after we were an us. Makes me feel warm and cozy inside knowing she's held on to something we once had.

She sees me, and from the slap on the arm she gives Ronnie, heard us too.

She glances between both of us. "It seemed a suitable way to defile us," she chimes in.

That was a perfect jab to two men. Respect.

"Whatever helps." Not my wittiest but it'll do.

Ronnie turns to Faith.

"Do you know who this is?" he asks her, a gleam in his eye.

"Yes, honey, I do. We went to college together," she says, hiding what she wants from Ronnie.

"Good times, I say," I respond.

"Damn, that must've been awesome. Knowing him as he makes it big." Ronnie is oblivious to life.

"They were something all right." She smirks.

"Something, yeah. I think they were fantastical," I shoot back.

Shit's getting real. And I see the ever-so-slight wrinkles of her furrowed brow she gets when she wants people to stop talking about whatever it is they are talking about.

"Honey," she says to Ronnie, in a tone of voice usually reserved for small children. "Why don't you go get us a drink?"

Ronnie stands and takes a step, but stops.

"What do you want?" His words ring earnest.

"Surprise me." Borderline irritation seeps through in Faith's response.

He turns to me. "You want somethin'?"

I shake my head. "No thanks."

He waddles inside, making a perfectly timed exit for us to continue.

"What are you doing here?" Faith cuts to the chase. I can tell the answer she wants is vacation, or just leaving, but it's not.

"He's polite, asking if I wanted something."

"Don't avoid the question." A demand I shall have to meet.

"Me? I live here. Moved down from NYC. Needed a change of scenery." I pause for a moment, making sure I won't have to eat my next words. She waits. "You look drastically different from back in the day." I shift subjects, hoping it lightens the mood.

"Time will do that to a girl." She cracks a smile.

"Time's been good to you." I smile back.

She stares into my eyes for a moment, searching for something. Perhaps the "why" of why I'm here, on this patio, tonight. Or why after all these years fate brings us together again. It could be a simple stare, injecting me with thoughts of her wanting me to leave—or jump off a bridge. I think the preceding smile means it's the former of my thoughts.

I continue, "How have you been?"

"How do I sum up seventeen years? Good. I guess. Still doing my thing," she summarizes, trying to figure out my intentions.

"And what is your thing, as of late?" I inquire. An ineffable need to know on my part.

"Makeup and cosmetology. The business world wasn't doing it for me anymore. Just needed a change. A better place to practice my brand of it. Florida worked. Art scene and all."

"I see. It works for many people, including myself."

Jeanine interrupts, "As fun as rehashing the tragedy of your past will inevitably be, I'm going in to keep Ronnie company. I'll drink your drink."

Jeanine stands up and starts toward the door.

"I'm sorry, sis. We could talk about something else." Faith reaches for words.

"No worries. You kids have fun. Just not my scene." Jeanine pierces me with a look that screams "beware."

"Nice seeing you again, Jeanine. We'll have to catch up." I try to sound honest.

"Yeah, like behind the trees? You wish," she smarts off, walking into the restaurant, leaving my face a pale shade of embarrassed red.

I turn back to Faith. Memories surge into my mind, a deluge filling every corner till it bursts through the top. I can't help but to think about how we started, how we loved, how we hated, how it all came to a halt. But as quickly as those thoughts came, she pulls me back in the harshest way.

"So a quickie behind the trees in a restaurant parking lot? A little passè, don't you think?"

"We didn't have sex." My mind is searching for a way to end this conversation. Grasping for anything to finish this before it goes further.

"You took a girl behind the trees and didn't nail her? Poor boy. What happened to your skills?" She delights in my misery just a little too much.

My mind wants to say anything to end this. And of course, it doles out the first thing it conjures up.

"She gave me some head. We couldn't boink."

She laughs, lightening the mood for the moment. "'Boink?' Did you just say boink?" It's nice to see her relaxing a tiny bit.

"I did. It was the first thing that came to mind." I shrug.

"Some things never change." She shakes her head.

I wait for her to continue that thought. I don't want to be the one to say it. She stares at me, maybe she's waiting for me to say it. But I can't. I won't.

And she continues, "That's not always a bad thing."

I smile, hoping for something. For anything.

"I didn't come here tonight to get back with you. We ended years ago. You made a choice," she reminds me.

Not what I was hoping for, but since I didn't know what I was hoping for, I guess I can't complain.

"You left me. You gave me no choice. But let's not do this again." A weak rebuttal on my part.

She holds back what she wants to say, to scream in my face. She laughs the laugh of someone who thinks they've never been wrong. That conceited, pretentious laugh of superiority, but I let her have it.

I wait. I'm not saying anything that can fuel the fire. Nothing that will make what minute progress we've made tonight fall further back.

She eyes me with cautious intent, wanting to say something new. But she holds out and looks at my face, not my eyes, but my face. Searching for a tell, for a twitch or jerk in my muscles that says, "I'm not really here, in this moment." But I stay still, wanting to hear what words she has to say.

"Coffee." Her one-word response to the standoff. Not nearly as tantamount to the evening as I thought it would be. But with Faith, one can never be too sure.

"You want me to get you coffee?"

"Ha." She forces the worded laugh. "Silly boy. Tomorrow evening, after I get off work. Coffee. A chance to catch up without Ronnie, Jeanine, or anyone around."

"Sounds good. Where?" I ask.

She stands up, ready to head in to see her man. "Coffee Shop of Horrors. 6:30."

"Word."

She nods and smiles before turning to step inside.

D.B. is staring at me, jaw agape at the miracle of me not getting slapped, punched, or stabbed but instead asked for coffee. A miracle it may be, but only time will tell. D.B. swigs from his drink. He wipes his mouth with his forearm.

"Bro. She's what led you here in the first place." He casts his warning in a sage-like way. Nothing cryptic. Just a matter of fact with the knowledge and experience to back it up.

"I know." My head hangs, as if this isn't going to be a good idea. Of course, it's not going to be a good idea. It's never a good idea. They say the definition of insanity is doing the same thing over and over, expecting different results. I'm just hoping I can change one variable to shift it to my favor. But sometimes it's better to let sleeping dogs lie. My thoughts once again turn to our past.

CHAPTER 5

Life Loves A Tragedy

*T*he college years were kind to us, or so I thought at the time. Looking back, not even the rose-colored glasses of time past can hide the tragedy that was Faith and Finn. Hell, even Tommy and Gina had a prayer to live on, which worked for them because years, later Mr. Bon Jovi informed everyone that they never did back down. If only Faith and I had built a stronger foundation.

That first night was everything a musician, a budding man, anyone really could ask for. Wild, intense, passionate. Romantic in its own way. It was fueled by desire and feelings that were, perhaps, new to both of us. Faith thought she hated me. Then next thing you know, I'm balls deep, pulling her hair, and smacking her ass. Maybe it was a hate fuck. I think we've all been in a situation where we either have or have wanted to screw someone out of our hatred for them. Perhaps that's what this started as for her. Perchance it was to spite her ex-boyfriend or whatever he actually was. No matter what her reasons for riding me like Slim Pickens waving his hat as he plummets to his doom on a nuclear bomb in Dr. Strangelove were, the fact that we did what we did changed our futures.

Had she not thrown the rock at me, had she just kept her hatred of my writing to herself, had I not been a pompous ass and written that poem in response to her, had what's-his-face not treated her the way he did to make her want to write the verse, had business classes not been such a bore that she needed to break the monotony with a left field elective, had any of those things and a million more not happened, we wouldn't have been in bed that night, losing ourselves in one another and forgetting our problems for a few moments.

What a great night for either point of view. I remember sometime in the early part of the nineties, the phrase "wild, passionate sex" was used all the time. The stupid conversations I'd have with friends about the phrase. We'd be laughing, trying to understand how something like passion, which is supposed to be a slow, candlelit romance, could be wild. Which, by definition, is anything but candlelit, unless you want to knock it over, starting wildfires in the Hollywood Hills. But that night was it. Wild. Passionate. What a grand description of our relationship. Wild it was. Worldview-changing.

After that night, things slowly went downward. We started something akin to an affair. College is a time for exploration. We both knew it, yet we were drawn to each other. We tried to make this aberration of a relationship we created work. There were regular accusations that flew around the room. The Mondays she would throw fists, accusing me of sleeping around. Even though the Friday before, she would tell me she needed time away and a break from us. A lot of accusations flew. Not all the time, mind you. Though when they did, the room was covered in a veritable Jackson Pollock wallpaper of shit from the fan, flinging it everywhere. It was disgustingly glorious that two people could be so passionate and angry with each other on such a level that we let things get to the depths, heights, level, whatever, that they did.

Then there was the passion. Romeo and Juliet could be so lucky. I always felt ours was more akin to Clarence and

Alabama. If you don't get that reference, see True Romance, the most romantic love story ever told on film. Yes, I include Titanic in that. Titanic didn't have the to-the-ends-of-the-earth bond of love that True Romance had. Ours did. At least when it did, but don't we all hold onto the best parts of the past, the parts that don't hurt? The times that don't remind us of why we aren't still there, until we need to.

Yes. It started out rocky. Unsure of what really attracted Faith to me, of what drew me to her. Looks matter. Sure, they always do, and anyone who says otherwise is deluding themselves. No one is going to walk up to a person with open boils on their face, front teeth missing, and flies buzzing around their unwashed hair, snot dripping down their nose, thinking to themselves, Let me get on that 'cause they may have a glowing personality. So yes, looks matter. But there was something there more than looks. The ability for her to challenge me, for me to challenge her. To push each other to be better than we were. Always moving, redefining, pushing forward to better yourself, your being, and your art. Yes. It started out rocky, but it started out great. It started with a bang. No one wants a boring, uneventful relationship. And ours was not. Nights out on the town followed by great sex back at her place. Or mine. Sometimes we didn't even make it back there. Hell, once we were in an empty car on the "L" train late one night, coming back from somewhere downtown. We couldn't wait. Didn't want to wait. No, we didn't Risky Business it. But she went down. Like a goddess. And it was amazing.

But here's the thing: all those memories I have about great sex, great times with her, other things were going on, things that don't look so great.

Our first few months together was a casual thing. We weren't exclusive and didn't expect each other to be. I spent my time away from Faith working on music. Finding inspiration where I could, which meant a lot of different women. Don't get me wrong: she wasn't waiting around for me, twiddling her thumbs. She had her fun, too. Though I never inquired into what that may have entailed. It's not like I meant to sleep around. Things happen. It was college, and I was on a hot streak. I did meet a few chicks who inspired me to write a few songs. Some of which a few years later turned into Hot 100 Billboard songs: break-up songs, songs to have sex to, songs to drink on the beach to. But those gals, as inspiring as they were, were empty. They didn't hold any real meaning, but damn if it didn't help my art. And that's what mattered.

I remember this one chick who worked the front desk at my dorm. She was cute, innocent, smart, but still naïve enough to fall for the "I don't have game" game. Probably the only one I felt bad about hooking up with. Not that it wasn't consensual. It was, but there was this look in her eye when she told me she wasn't usually like this. In college, every female says that line. And every guy follows it up with either "I know" or "I can tell." Both of which were crocks of shit said to advance the porn playing out in the guy's mind that was manifesting in front of him. The same look when she asked me to call her that said she actually wanted me to. That said, she wasn't actually like this, that she was letting me into a world that not many hold sacred, that she didn't share with just anyone.

But here I was being let in. She didn't want me to disappoint her. The way her eyes lit up when I told her I would, and this wouldn't be just a one-night stand. It was the only time I felt bad after. That was the moment the realization solidified in my mind that I was the type of guy who became the reason people stopped holding their bodies sacred. Because guys like me would find a way to weasel ourselves in and defile their sacred dry lands by opening floodgates. And they wouldn't even feel bad about it till the next day—on their walk of shame back to their dorm rooms, not even breakfast money on the nightstand for them.

Nights like those happened. The people I met, we shared dreams, philosophies, ideas about life and death and love and war. What hopes have passed at such a young age and what dreams may come. What dreams the future may hold. Existential crap that then seemed so intense, so profound, when really we probably sounded like we were talking out our asses. I still have thoughts on existentialism and things more profound than the immediate. But back then, we were just figuring out life with the idea that we already knew it all ingrained in our heads. We were nineteen years old and just discovered the joy of our genitals only about six or seven years earlier.

But as the months went on and I added a few more notches on my belt, I came to a realization. I wanted more; more of what though, I didn't know. Just more. I felt like I was headed in the right direction. The only problem was I didn't know what direction I was heading in. I was lost at sea.

For about two months, I shut myself out for a bit. Just classes and music. I wrote. A lot. It was great. For me. Not a terribly long time in the big scheme of life. But to a college student during the school year, it was forever. To the woman I shut out, it may have been a little longer than that. I think in that time span, I was with Faith maybe four times. Maybe. I did make it a point to call her every day and talk. I wanted to stay close to her. I honestly did have feelings for her. She was not happy about the lack of time I had, though, but I was honing my art, perfecting my craft or some bullshit. But that's the mind of a creative soul. It never really changes.

Some time, I'd say in our third year of college, Faith noticed me starting to pull away. I didn't mean to. She was amazing. She was my best friend, my confidant and my partner in crime. She continued to push me to be better at my music, to be a better version of myself, as I did her, in her own ways. But pushing can be construed as poking and prodding. No one likes being poked and prodded, at least not outside the bedroom.

We got mean. The Friday/Monday accusations. Not every Friday, just the ones she let slip that she met a hot guy. So, I let her do her thing. But as I said, neither of us were waiting around the telephone for the other to call, all the while twiddling our thumbs. I was out with the ladies, as she was with other guys. We were young, and honestly, I didn't care. Not that I didn't care about her but that I realized the statistics of relationships that age lasting the long haul were slim. I can name one, but that's beside the point. Or maybe that is the point. But I didn't fuck every chick she accused me of. I did several of them, but not all. I never called her out on her strayings, indiscretions, or whatever you want to call it. Like I said, I was playing the statistical odds.

What started out as a hot and heavy relationship, based on wild romanticism, began turning stale. But we were, still are, stubborn. No one would admit things were declining between us or that things already had.

She wanted things to be steadier, not in an exclusive way. Yes, she wanted that, and to be honest, I did too. I think. Hell, I still don't know what I wanted. Maybe I just didn't want to lose her.

She wanted to know where things were going. She had plans for her future. She wanted me to fit into them. I wanted her to fit into my future. That became a point of contention. She didn't want to be a glorified groupie, her exact words. I didn't want a white picket fence in a suburb, working nine to five for a company that'd give me a gold watch after thirty years, causing me to recreate a Keanu/Bullock movie.

This was it, our inability, or unwillingness, to compromise—the cliched beginning of the end. Once this was out in the open, everything turned into a fight. From what movie to watch, to where to eat, to how often we were having sex. That last one though is a bit more legitimate of a point than the others. But nevertheless, everything was a fight.

We said we had both stopped seeing other people, which I did and she did too. I trusted her when she said that. But the damage was done. From the first part of our relationship being open, non-exclusive, free, polyamorous, whatever bullshit label of the moment you put to it, the feelings were there. And yes, the label was bullshit. No relationship stands the test of time when you're sticking your dick in other women and she's getting pounded by other guys. It doesn't work. Someone eventually wants more. Whether you call it intimacy, emotion, closeness, whatever. Someone, in some way, always wants more, and that doesn't come in a non-exclusive relationship. If I know anything, I've learned that in life, anyone who says differently about monogamy is, or will be, wrong. It didn't help any that we were both still friends with, and talking to, some of those people we previously bumped uglies with. And that led to suspicion and jealousy and mistrust: all three are not a basis for excellent relationships.

As I said, we were stubborn. The fights we had about who called, who we saw that night, why the other couldn't go with. As much as we both wanted time apart with just our friends, the ones that were not mutual between the two of us, we didn't see it that way. Not when it came from the other person. We saw red. We saw everything that was in our minds. We saw the other person doing things that we may have done in the past with them happening now. And it snowballed. All because our perceived futures weren't as smoothly blended as Neapolitan ice cream. So neatly packaged and yet separate in the packaging.

But it stayed like this till we graduated. Almost four years of ups and downs, four years of pushing and pulling: all because neither of us wanted to admit that after about the first year, it should have ended.

I think we were both holding onto something. Holding onto what could be. What we thought the other could be if only the other would change a little, not looking at who the other was. What the other really wanted. No. We held onto the idea of love and the notion of the changes the other could make so that our relationship would be a picture-perfect Norman Rockwell. But honestly, who wants to be with someone if so many little things need to change about them to make the relationship work? Who wants to be that person? The one who takes a happy, functional, moderately well-adjusted individual and tweaks so many things about them—gives them such a makeover—that the end product is so far off from where the person once was they are almost, if not wholly, unrecognizable.

As time went on, I think we held onto that. But my art was my work. I loved my art. I loved Faith. I didn't want to let go of her. I didn't want to admit that things went wrong so long ago. But things add up. They seem little at first, but they add up. And when you see the sum of what they've become, it ofttimes isn't pretty.

We were at some party. A graduation party, I believe. Not that the type of party matters but the devil's in the details, right? We were both there. We had arrived with each other but quickly went our separate ways once inside.

The party itself was lovely. Hors-d'oeuvres laid out. A large selection of mid to high-end wine and alcohol I probably should have abstained from. An enjoyable buffet of Chicago delicacies, like Vienna beef hot dogs, Italian beef, and Lou Malnati's pizza. I do remember those details. I had conversations with people about future plans: who had jobs lined up, where some people were moving to, what we thought the future held. But I got talking to some guy. Hell, if I remember his name, or even what he looked like. Jay, John, Jack, whatever. It's not important.

What is important is that we were talking about me. My plans. I was saying to him how I wanted to stay here but maybe head to New York. Chicago had a good music scene. But so did New York City, and Orlando, and Venice Beach. But here was home. Here was where my music was rooted. But on the other note, New York City had a good scene for rock, punk, and underground. What I didn't realize then was the sum of everything I was saying was about my goals. I hadn't put any thought into what Faith wanted. But that was our relationship, all about the individual. Her plans didn't put me into account. Not saying that what I did was deserved. Neither of us deserved it. But as I talked, I didn't realize that somewhere in our conversation, Faith had crept up behind me.

To this day I still don't know why she didn't make her presence known, but she didn't. Hell, maybe she did and I was so wrapped up in the conversation I didn't notice. She could have been all, "Finn. Finn! Finn!!" and I was just too damned caught up in the sound of my own voice, laying out my future plans that she could have been screaming bloody murder and I would have been oblivious. Which would make me a huge asshole, but I was used to being called that by this point. Maybe she didn't make herself known to me at that moment because she was searching for a reason. Wanting to find her excuse to blow it all up, but she heard me say something. Something about my upcoming album and going on tour via the record company's dime. That was when she chimed in.

"News to me." Her words were simple, pointed, sharp.

I did the quick introduction. "Blah blah, this is Faith. Faith, this is blah blah."

"I was waiting for a good time," I excused.

"Well, now's a good time," she attacked.

Blah blah saw that this was not going to be a polite conversation and snuck off somewhere after the introduction.

"So, I got signed." I kept my reply short.

"You've been playing enough and promoting enough," she said, as if my work was just play. A hobby.

People think that. They look at music, acting, art in general as just play. Something to do when bored. Something fun to do that doesn't take real time or energy. Like this shit just happens. Like we don't pour our hearts, souls, blood, sweat, and tears into every ounce of it, hoping, praying, screaming to the skies above that it one day might be almost possibly worth all the pain and torment we put ourselves through. "Playing enough and promoting enough." Fuck her. Getting signed is not as easy as a label exec being at a show, papers ready, and signing you because they like your sound. It is much more complicated than that.

"And they want me to tour. Not headline. Just opening or mid-act. But tour," I continued, hoping this would calm things.

We had our public fights and her side fist beating me in a desperate panic of name-calling, hoping to make some significant breakthrough in our relationship. But damn if I wanted to do this here.

"And where am I in all of this?" She questioned my upcoming tour as if it was centered around her.

The record company didn't exactly give a crap about what woman was involved in my life or whether or not I needed Mommy or Daddy to tag along. Hell, they wanted to make money off me, and I wanted to play and, hopefully, pad my pockets.

But that's where things escalated. What was a quaint, peaceful party with a few drunken shenanigans had turned into a shouting match between us. I don't remember all of the argument, but I do remember bits and pieces.

"You said you didn't want to be a glorified groupie." The sarcasm wasn't just dripping off my chin; it was spewing everywhere. Sarcastic was how most things were said between us. "So, I didn't tell you yet. It's not like you want to be a part of that anyway. Don't you have a job lined up in fucking Michigan or somewhere?"

"On Michigan Avenue, you dumbass! I have no plans on leaving this city!" The volume of her voice rose above all other conversations.

People were watching by this point. I remember because of how stupid I felt over the "dumbass" comment. I remember because of how it ended.

At this point, she was crying. She didn't care who saw. She didn't care about being vulnerable. She wanted out.

"Things could have been wonderful. Full of life and love. But you pushed. You always cared more about yourself and your dreams than mine. All you needed was just a little faith in me," she wept.

I was not a crier. I'm still not a crier. I stood there, watching her cry, not shedding a tear. Maybe I was an ass-hole. I know I looked like one. I guess I was. Asshole is as asshole does.

"Your dreams never compromised to mine. We never compromised, even in the beginning. We are two uncompromising people. That's what makes us ... us." I was oblivious to the beckoning end.

"Made," she whispered. One word. And the tense of that word represented everything she needed to say. One little word: Made. And the resonation of it was deafening. The points were sharp, and they shot through my heart.

I pleaded. "What are you talking about, 'made'? This'll pass just like all the others." I was desperate. I sounded desperate, and I knew it. I didn't care. I didn't want to lose her.

"No. No, it won't because no matter what we do, no matter how hard we try to pretend that things work or that they will work... they won't. They haven't. For a long time, if ever." Faith sounded beyond defeated.

"But they will. You have to believe me. You gotta have faith. In me." I turned the phrase on her. I was hoping it would make her realize we both played a part in this and that there was still hope. If only we had faith.

"Perhaps. One day. In the future, perhaps. But now, our time has passed," she cried.

"No, it hasn't," I continued to plead. "It's only passed if we give up."

"And I've given up. I'm done. We can't pretend to be something we're not, and it's time to move on," Faith finalized, turned, and walked away.

I stood, not knowing what to say. Nothing witty came to mind. Nothing charming popped into my head to convince her to stay. No quick phrase to cause her to turn her head and smile at me, all anger swept away by my smile. No thrown punches from her that say in all their rage that she still loves me. Nothing. I just stood and watched as she walked away. Thinking, shouting in my mind to the universe to get her to turn around. To look me in the eye one last time. To see that I still want to be the man she needs—the man I thought I should be. But she didn't. I felt the universe had abandoned me.

The universe had other plans—for both of us.

CHAPTER 6

Garden Of Eden

W hatever her reasons for choosing Coffee Shop of Horrors I don't know, but I'm excited, nervous, and uncertain. Not to mention I'm curious about this place. I'm not sure what her life had in store for her. I'm not sure about anything. But she said coffee, and I wasn't about to object.

My day has only just begun and I need to chillax, to do some deep breathing. Meditate on my current situation if you will. Clear my mind. Since I'm not good at yoga, I figure what better place to shake the anxiety away than the Orlando Garden of Eden. The big magical kingdom fully equipped with a castle at dead center. The mouse and his little Mouseketeers. The local news changed the landfall time of the approaching hurricane to later tonight, so I went. If it rained a little, I wouldn't melt.

After leaving our little get-together last night, I spent a good portion of the remaining evening writing a new body of lyrics. Not sure if the words are poetry alone or if they need music, but I wrote. Perhaps the essence of poetry crept back in because of my encounter with Faith last night. Maybe it was something that has been trying to claw its way out of me for some time. A chick pounding with its egg tooth, finally breaking through its shell. Perhaps it was all coincidence. Possibly I'm just full of shit, but I wrote. Not my best work admitted, but far from my worst. "Remnants" I call it.

Across the horizon ashes and debris.
The only remnants of what once was
When once we're we.

Ruins remain that once stood tall,
But the path always pushes forward
Making giants fall.

Massive machines move mountains aside
Tearing down what walls we have built
Behind which we hide.

A spark ignites, and forests burn
But still, we keep on forward
Life lesson learned.

Smoke still lingers from fires now doused.
Reminding me of happier days
Before smiles turned shouts.

Across the horizon ashes and debris
The only remnants of what once was
When once we were we.

Maybe a waltz? Something sad and melancholy. With a touch of The Animals to give it a timeless feeling. Or just pass it off to Nick Cave and have him give it the life, emotion, and style that only he can. After all, he wrote an entire album called *Murder Ballads*, and that was after his song, "Loverman."

As my forest green Grand Am comes to rest in the theme park's overpriced parking spot, I look over and see it on my passenger seat. Right next to a small, old coffee stain from a few years back, a receipt. Not just any receipt, mind you. A receipt with a phone number: Viv's number. I hold the torn edges of the crumpled paper in my hands, staring at it for a moment, thinking back to last night. The ecstasy and the agony of it. I pull out my phone and dial her number, deliberating if hitting send is the best idea I've had since moving here or the stupidest. Sometimes there is a spark of genius in stupidity, seldom but rarely. I was hoping this was one of those times.

Send.

My heart starts pounding in my chest with such force it hurts, causing physical discomfort from the number of butterflies I am feeling. More than butterflies. An intestinal churning that pulls and twists, making me want to taste my breakfast again. But I hold it in. Her voicemail saves me from having to deep clean my car later.

"Hey Viv, it's Finn. Wanted to say thank you for last night. Thought I'd see if you'd like to accompany me to the parks today or if you follow the two-day rule and I broke it. Perhaps another time though. 212-867-5309."

The pounding in my chest calms down, and I swallow what mix of food and bile has made its way into my throat.

I hit end on my phone and thoughts pour in. Why did I have such trouble calling this woman? Did I call her too soon? Does anyone still follow that two-day waiting rule? If there is a waiting rule, is it still only two days or has it increased, making me seriously break it? What is it about her that makes her different from the countless others? There was no difference in our meeting. No difference in the way we flirted or the conversation that led up to the wondrous activity that transpired behind the trees. Since I've learned the joys of my genitalia, I've done the song and dance countless times. Sometimes the song finished, while sometimes, like Billy Idol, I ended up dancing with myself. Throughout the years, the dance may have changed a bit, becoming slightly more sophisticated or complex, but it's still the same at the root of it all. So, what's different? Something I must ponder.

I walk through the magical kingdom, looking around at the facade. The buildings, the workers, the life that flows through each animatronic as they sing about tiki rooms and shit. I pull back the veil and notice what's beyond the facade. The mansion and all its ghosts, the exterior walls and how if anyone took more than two seconds to admire the craftsmanship, they could see that they were built with wall hangings you can buy at any pop-up Halloween shop. Yes, it gets the job done, and perhaps it's only here for temporary purposes, but I notice it nonetheless, and for a split second, I see the ever so slightly exposed underbelly of the beast. But damn it if this isn't one of my favorites. So I enter, wait through the intro, as most of his rides have, and sit upon the throne of a tilt-a-whirl car that glides me through these family-friendly ghosts.

Having not been on this ride since childhood, I remember it quite differently. Back then, it had an aura of mysticism and awe to it that made me buy what he was selling. Made me believe that these ghosts were real. Trapped in an eternal dance they must endure, never leaving their dancing partner, which made me hope for them back then that they were with the one they wanted, instead of having to settle on loving the one they're with.

Now, it's still just as good, but for a different reason. Now I see it for what it is—smoke and mirrors. Perfectly executed to make even the wizard behind the curtain believe in it all. It also houses a countless assortment of mixed quality haunted house props. Something I notice only because of my skepticism. It's both enchanting and somehow disheartening all at the same time. The memories of my childhood naïvete replaced with the jaded cynicism of adulthood.

Screw it. Speed metal for those lyrics. Or thrash metal. Something reminiscent of Slayer circa *Seasons in the Abyss*. Write the music fast and hard, so the juxtaposition of the words on top gives it an almost sarcastic, begrudging feel.

Maybe throw in a bunch of processor effects, overdrive on the vocals, give it a disco tempo, and turn it into something Rob Zombie would admire.

Now, he's a performer that doesn't get the full credit he deserves. Yes, he gets a ton of credit but also a ton of slack. Very phenomenal in concert. I never thought I'd see such an outwardly brutal, metal guy line dance to such heavy music, but essentially that's what he does. And somehow this guy makes it work. Makes everyone, as savage as they think they are, want to be him. A line dancing, unapologetic vegan of badassness who makes some of the best music around. Also, great to dance to and have sex to. A master ability to equalize us all and help us forget our problems for a short while.

After my thoughts settle down, I find myself ho ho ho and a bottle of rum halfway through the pirates. Another ride perfectly executed. It calms me down, brings me back to a happy spot, which is nice because in just over an hour, I'm going to have to sit down with Faith and face my past. Why would I agree to this? Why would she propose such an idea? I don't know. Childish excitement over things long past? Maybe. A naïve notion that sometimes fairy tales do come true? Perhaps. Possibly I can act grown up enough to have her not walk out on me again. Maybe she'll see I am a real boy. By the time all these thoughts stop marathoning circles and finally settle down in my head, the faux British lady who guides my GPS has safely navigated me to the coffee shop.

Nestled in the corner of an unremarkable road next to a gas station and across from railroad tracks, it doesn't look like much. A small mom-and-pop coffee shop. I am not sure what to expect once I open the door, but the logo of a man-eating plant on the door lends a clue. The outside belies what is in. A giant LED TV plays *Puppetmaster*. Classic. The owner sits working on her laptop while casually watching the flick. Lamps for sale sit on numerous shelves, each individually made and hand-painted with skull bases. Very cool stuff. A giant hand-painted canvas with an artist rendition of Deadpool. Small paintings of original and artistic interpretations of horror themes decorate the rest of the walls: all also for sale. Two couches and two small tables fill the seating area. Then there's the coffee selection. The wall of blends is enough to make a coffee lover cry for joy. The shelves of flavored coffee don't lack variety either. Flavors like JudgeMint Day and V is for Vanilla Cinnamon and unflavored roasts like Burial Grounds and Shrieking Toad make this place feel like it may become one of my regular haunts, an adult's place of fantasy and caffeinated fun. That is if this meeting, date, whatever it is with Faith, goes well.

After looking around some more, I grab a cup of coffee and take a seat at a table. The couches are open, but I don't want to sit too close to Faith. Things may get uncomfortable, more so than last night. I only get to see about two minutes of the horror movie masterpiece before she walks in. She wears the same breathtakingly sexy outfit she wore my first night in Orlando. I'm not sure if she thought maybe I wouldn't recognize her if she wore something else or if it's just coincidence, but she is wearing it.

She smiles at me as she grabs her coffee. After putting in an inordinate amount of cream and sugar into a perfectly roasted coffee, to which the shop owner shakes her head and disappears into the back, she plops down on the couch I so strategically avoided.

"Much more comfortable." She gestures toward the couch.

I look at her waiting, wondering if I should sit there too or if this is where we are going to stage our long-awaited, possibly overdue, rendezvous.

"Come here." She pats the couch. "It's not like we're going to lose control of ourselves and go at it all hog-wild right here."

We laugh. It is nice, relaxing in a way that is also nerve-racking. She has a man. I should know her by now. Or at least know who she used to be. And that comment should be taken for what it is. A joke. Nothing more. So, I decide a seat on the couch isn't a bad idea after all. But I sit propped against the arm, a place I can lean against comfortably and make myself as far from her as I can, while still accepting her invitation to sit here.

Perhaps I don't know her at all anymore. Hell, she could have the clap or HIV. I don't know. How does she know I don't have either of those? She doesn't. Seventeen years is a long time.

"I like your outfit. Very Stepford goth chic." I figure a compliment is a good way to start things.

"Figured you would since the last time you saw me in it, you didn't even recognize me." A backhanded way to say thank you. Typical Faith. Some things never change.

It feels nice. New but familiar. An oxymoronic sentence if there ever was one. Like a new sequel to your favorite film: you know all the characters; you know the premise. Just excited to see how it all unfolds.

Time seems to stand still. The old laughter comes back, and it feels nice. Faith fills me in on her post-collegiate life. Her time spent in the business world, effectively being a white-collar woman in a corner office an elevator ride up each day and hating every minute of it. The corporate environment wasn't who she was after all. How repressed she felt. Suffocated. The enclosed elevator a daily reminder of her rat status in the race. She wanted a simple eyebrow ring, but office policy dictated otherwise. No piercings allowed except ears, no visible tattoos. (Which doesn't work well for someone who loves sleeveless tops.) But more than that, she says it was "the stifling of any and all original thought." The corporate brainwashing, the manifestation of the faceless kids from *The Wall* all grown up, carrying out the whims of their masters. No fighting back, no talking back. No resistance.

"I just woke up one day and asked myself, 'How did I get here? This isn't who I am.' I'm not sure it ever was." A big smile breaks out on her face. A smile that's so big it looks like it could hurt. "And I want to thank you for that. I think after all the ups and downs, you helped me get out of my shell. Discover who I was deep inside."

I've never had such kind words sting so strongly. I remain gracious and say nothing for a second, as my mind searches for the right words. Nothing about how she couldn't have realized this back then; we wouldn't be who we are now if she did. The story of us would not have ended the way it did. So, I say the only proper thing to say.

"Thank you. That means a lot." A forced smile comes out, but part of me still wants to run, kicking and screaming, throwing anything and everything I see. Some part of me wants to destroy something beautiful as a fuck you to the gods for ruining what could have been. My rebellion against the universe, but I just smile. I figure I'll turn this into some lyric set and music disaster piece later.

Time has a very peculiar way of opening old wounds at the worst possible moment. Possibly those are the only moments they can open up, as if the universe prevents the scab from being ripped off at the wrong moment. Planning and plotting to make sure the scar that forms has enough tissue to prevent any further injury. If only it would ever heal.

They don't heal. And as old wounds get scratched at like a bad mosquito bite, she has unknowingly scratched at mine.

As soon as I think she finishes, she takes one more strike at me. This time gouging away all formed scar tissue, plus an area around it, making sure that she got everything as if she were a doctor excising cancer. She tells me about him: the one-man wrecking crew of a boyfriend—Ronnie.

It's been nearly two decades since I've seen her. I should think this wouldn't hurt so bad, but it does. And it's her eyes. Those haunting eyes that make it hurt. If only they had not haunted my mind. Had her eyes not been the *Dream Police* living inside of my head, invading my sleeping mind, maybe hearing all this wouldn't feel as bad as it does.

But it does.

What is important to the point is this, I can't exactly get up and leave. I can't tell Faith to stop. The patheticness of either would be colossal. So, I listen as she recounts about how she met him at a concert. I hear her tell me about her vacation in New York half a decade ago. She had already been living in Orlando for a year and wanted to see the Big Apple. So, she went, a lone vacation to see what all the buzz was about. The bar in Queens she stopped at had the flyer for a local concert she saw promoting some up-and-coming bands. She was a fan of one of the musical groups and went. And that's where she ran into a guy also there on vacation from Orlando, a muscle-bound man hunk nick-named Ronnie Frown.

The funny thing was, as she tells me about this show, the bands, the venue, something occurs to me. I helped set up this show. I helped get the bands lined up. I was helping promote some new punk trio that imploded on themselves in true punk fashion before they could explode onto the scene. But I helped put together the show that introduced my lost love to her current companion. I was the eagle shot with the arrow fashioned from my feathers. And the icing on the cake of this steaming pile of shit she is telling me is, "There was a part of me that was hoping to run into you while I was in New York."

Fuck me.

My mind shuts down; a protective measure to prevent permanent damage, I'm sure of it. Faith sits there talking and I hear the noise of her words, but I can't make them out. I see her lips moving, but I can't read lips that well. I am sure she knows I have faded from the conversation, but she keeps talking anyway because it would be rude of her to assume I'm doing something so bold.

Then she smiles, a smile I've never seen on her before. Or one she never had when she was with me. It looks happy.

"And that's why I asked you for coffee," she finishes.

Fuck me with a sideways dildo. *What did I miss? What did she say?* I can't ask. I can't admit that I spaced out because I am in grievous amounts of pain unintention-ally caused by her. I'm not going to be that assface I was in the past.

"I was just surprised you asked me in the first place." I figure a neutral response would be fitting. Nothing that says I pretended to listen and hope this is what you want to hear. And nothing that can be so far off center that she walks out.

"It just threw me to see you that first night. At first, I thought you recognized me and weren't sure how to approach. But once I realized you didn't realize who I was, I thought I'd drop a subtle reminder for you to pick up." Her words just as I would have said them.

"I'm sorry about that. You just look so different."

"I know. More like someone you would have wanted back then."

That hurts. Deep. My stomach drops. I feel my heart slow. Is this the moment I pay the piper? I never was a crier, but I feel tears welling up in my eyes. But I hold them in. She doesn't mean for that to penetrate like it does. She is making a sarcastic comment about the state of tail I chased back then and how she outwardly appears now. But it shoots through my heart and clear through the other side because she is right.

She continues telling me that her current look has nothing to do with a deep-seated need to get me back or piss off her father. It has more to do with herself. Being who she is at the core of her soul, an outward expression of her innermost self. No arguments there.

I think it is at this moment I understand myself more than I ever have. All I have ever done is try to express that. In every song I write, in every chord I play, but it is just that. The pain flowing through me right now is also very relieving. Very soothing. I let the pain overtake my senses and heighten them. I feel more alive now, sitting in this wonderfully quaint Coffee Shop of Horrors, in more emotional pain than I've ever felt, as well as some manifested physical pain, than I ever have in all the sexual encounters, drugged-out states, or drunken nights long forgotten. I feel so alive because of her words. Both the pain and the joy they bring. The agony and the ecstasy.

She sees a change in my expression. She knows I want to say something that will be sentimental, something that can quite possibly ruin this moment. She grabs my hand.

"Don't get all pussified on me now. Whatever you are about to say, don't. I regret nothing. I wouldn't be who I am today without it all. I am very happy with that so far. And your dreams would never have come true if you sacrificed back then. So, don't say it. Just do what comes to you so unnaturally and force it down. Force yourself to keep it in."

Damn, she has grown. Changed. And it's the person she has become that seems so wonderful that even more now, I want to say something stupid enough to ruin the moment.

I smile a smile that says I'm happy and holding back tears of joy. The out-pushed lips and wrinkled nose. All my facial muscles are trying to reabsorb the salt water that has collected on my bottom eyelids. I swallow.

"It really is nice to see you again," I say, searching for words better suited for this moment.

"I'm glad," she says, pointing outside.

How did I miss it? Was the sound of the outdoors blended in with the soundtrack of the movie? Was I that enthralled with her? How did I miss the start of the storm? The lightning flashes in the not-too-far distance. The roaring clap of the following thunder. Hurricane Spiffy Giggle Bunnies, whatever the fuck it is named. *How the hell did I not notice? More importantly, how the hell is anyone going to drive in this crap?* The raindrops are the size of gumballs. Not the ridiculously big gumballs that crack your jawbone if you bite down on a stale one but the small gumballs. The orange-flavored ones that come in the mesh sack to make them look like Florida oranges. The darkening sky overhead says this storm is going to be anything but a party. Already the winds have picked up and are threatening to topple over anything not anchored down. Those meteorologists sure as shit screwed the pooch when timing this one out.

The owner emerges from the back, and much to her surprise, we are still there. We all lock eyes for that awkward moment you know is coming in a situation like this.

"Didn't think you two would still be here," she admits.

"Lost track of time. Apologies," I offer. But still, she must deliver the inevitable.

"We're closing up early. I hate to do this to you with the conditions, but..." she trails off.

"No worries." I alleviate her guilt.

I look at Faith and she looks at me, half smiling. Still getting a feel for the full layout of the greater Orlando area, I don't have much usefulness to add at this moment. She just stares as if she is waiting for me to say something. So, I stare back deeper into her eyes, hoping to uncover what she wants from me. Her smile widens from a half-cocked smile to a full-blown, brilliant idea, lighting up her mind smile.

"What?" is all I say, not sure where her thoughts are leading her and because of that, I'm not sure what else to say.

I find it interesting that for someone who writes as many lyrics as I do, I'm at a loss for words an awful lot of the time.

She laughs a half-forced, quiet laugh, then jumps up off the couch, smacking my thigh as she does. "Come on."

"Where're we going?" I ask, thinking about the fact that in like three seconds, I'll be outside in a torrent of hurricane winds and rain, being possibly smacked across the face by Anoles caught up in the wind. I'd like to know what I'm stepping out into that for.

"Don't you trust me anymore?" she asks.

Nice retort, but do I trust Faith? I haven't seen her in almost twenty years. We have had a pleasant conversation so far, and even the parts of the past brought back up didn't seem to deter any forward motion. So, as she stands before me, hand outstretched and staring down at me, I ask myself, *Do I trust her? Now, after all this time, do I have a legitimate reason not to believe her?*

Sure. Why not? What could possibly go wrong?

CHAPTER 7

My Heart, Your Hands

I am not sure what to expect. I don't think Faith is going to lead me to a forest, tie me up, and kill me. Though, the falling rain aside, the freshly dampened woods, and being tied up might make for a fun time. I think that maybe she knows a place close by that will be open. Possibly a friend's house for a hurricane party. As I said, I am not sure what to expect.

I drive, following behind her through the hurricane, King and Foxtail palms swaying in the wind and rain. My mind is continually trying to focus on the barely visible road and not die, but at the same time, all I can think about is where she might be taking me. The possibilities are endless. Each raindrop that tries shattering my windshield is a momentary torment teasing me about the fragility of this life. They are also incomprehensibly shouting at me the innumerable places yet to see in The City Beautiful. We stop in the parking lot of an apartment complex. Each building identical to the next in color and height: tan with terracotta, Spanish tile roofing. I don't recognize this place. Though what little I can make out through the torrent of water gushing down from the skies above, I see no neon signs. No restaurants beckon for business. The rain still pounds down on our cars, but at least we are not moving. It strikes down in full force and gives my mind a new place she might take me. The drive was maddening, and we both somehow survived.

I sit in my car, engine running, trying to re-oxygenate my body after an hour of what was apparently me holding my breath. I quickly flip down the sun visor to check myself in the mirror. My pale face slowly regains color as the terrified expression that had taken control gradually relinquishes power. I'm alive. And here I sit, parked next to her in this lot.

I see her exit her car and wave me to follow. So, I do. I get out and, in about point two seconds, am drenched head to toe, again. I was halfway dry after the dash out of the coffee shop. But it's cool. I figure we are going to a hurricane party at Ronnie's or something.

Up a flight of covered stairs that should provide cover from the storm except that the wind is blowing the rain almost entirely horizontal, Faith stops at a door labeled 217. From outside the windows, there appear to be no lights on. At least not enough illumination to warrant a hurricane party. I can't hear much as the rain relentlessly assaults my ears to a deafening point. Faith pulls out an unremarkable gold key and opens the door.

Hung, framed pictures of her family and friends decorate the walls. A dirty ashtray beside a half-smoked pack of reds, topped with a green, plastic lighter, sits on her relic of a coffee table left over from the early nineties, complete with a black porcelain cat base that holds the glass tabletop. But the smell of the stale cigarette smoke takes my mind back to our happier times. The days of wine and roses, so to speak. Days when she would sit beside me as I wrote songs on the guitar, drinking whiskey, and smoking cigarette after cigarette.

She shakes out her long, pitch-black curls, whipping me back to the present tense where her hair is no longer straight and dirty blonde. She asks if I would like some bourbon, but the tone of her voice tries to mask the true intention of her words. My only thought is a throwback to the TV show *Friends*. "Does Joey want two pizzas?" I smile as I fruitlessly squeegee myself off in her doorway. As the water drips from my body, so does the weight holding back my words.

"Booker's, if you have some."

Faith grabs two cordial glasses from her cabinet and some ice from the fridge. For herself. Then as she holds my glass up to the ice dispenser, she tosses me a silent question.

"Neat, please."

She refrains from assaulting the glass with ice and fills it in bourbon. Beautiful, oaky bourbon.

She hands me the glass while looking me up and down. She sets her glass down on an end table littered with unopened mail, conveniently located both right next to the door and the couch.

"You're soaked. Let me put your clothes in the dryer." Faith starts undressing right in front of me.

"Um, what?" I say, completely caught off guard. All I can think is that this is not the same woman from Coffee Shop of Horrors, telling me, "It's not like we're gonna jump each other right here." Or whatever she actually said. This isn't even the gal from our first night of margaritas and definitely not the lady who walked away at the end. But then again, we weren't at the coffeehouse, and she was way past any other moment we shared.

By the time my thoughts die down, she is in her bra and panties. She's wearing next to nothing and still wears it as well as she did back then, if not better.

"Come on, cowboy. Not like it's nothing we haven't seen before," she says, solidifying her case.

"Okaaayyy," I say, a bit off guard.

But still, I undress down to my boxers and give her my wet clothes. She walks only a few feet down a short hall and opens a set of louvered bi-fold doors to her laundry machine. She tosses them in the dryer and grabs a couple of bath towels so we can finish wiping ourselves off.

As I pat myself down, I watch as the towel slides across her damp skin, soaking up the moisture in its path. The towel climbs her leg that I wish was begging for me to kiss it. The curls in her hair try to re-stake their claim from the water. Her hips used to call out to me to be kissed, to be held. Perchance tonight. The towel glides up and past her chest. A chest topped with two of the loveliest breasts a person could wish for, perfectly shaped and sized to match her figure. At this moment, my mind cries out to every inch of flesh that stands in front of me and shouts to the past to reenact every position that ever was. But alas, that is only in my mind.

She proceeds to turn on some Static-X. Wonderful, techno-thrash. The funny thing is, this album is such a far cry from their other works before it. But, at the same time, it could never have happened if it wasn't for the previous albums. It is the perfect blend of everything before and yet a unique monster unto itself.

We sit on her couch in nothing but towels, drinking wonderfully aged bourbon. I do wonder what warrants her accommodating my request for such an elegant spirit. At least my cellphone is next to me, karmically saving me if and when I need. Hopefully.

There's an awkward silence. We both sit, mostly naked, sipping our bourbon. Faith on one end of the couch and I on the other with the middle of the sofa the barrier between us. Her eyes look me over, examining twenty years of change. The left corner of my lip turns up. I feel myself smiling both awkwardly and happily. My eyes turn toward the ceiling. I know I'm making this more uncomfortable than it is. I don't want her to think I am here just for a wham-bam-thank-you-ma'am. Yes, I want to have fast, explosive sex so intense it induces an aneurysm. Anyone attracted to the female form would desire the same. Some have even been so bold as to say they ain't too proud to beg if need be. But it's not my intention. So, I look toward the ceiling in all its flat, off-white glory. I hear a small, dismissive laugh. I sit unsure of what to say or do next, as if time has looped and this is our first night together. Both ready to explore new lands, uncertain of the other's willingness and, at the same time, afraid of what the expedition might have in store.

My hesitant eyes turn back to her. A dubious answer to her chuckle. We both quietly stare into each other's eyes. Not searching for their soul. Not even looking for answers to the moment's unanswered questions. Just silently waiting for them to make a move. Whoever moves first loses the fight of the wills. So, I sit. I want so badly to say something to her: to tell her she still has the body of a goddess, to tell her that looking at her in her towel that has all but fallen off has me half-chubbed, to tell her that this night is so unclear in my mind as to what it means that I'm paralyzed, not with fear, but by the unknown. I start to say something, but it is really just noise. Something a toddler would gargle with uncoordinated vocal cords. So, I stop it quickly and finish the solid three shots of bourbon left in my glass.

She grabs my glass and heads back into the kitchenette. "Ronnie's a nice guy." She pours me another glass of bourbon. "And he loves me. But it's just ... sooo boring. There's no excitement. No surprises. The thrill is gone."

Choice words to shatter the silence.

I think the moments proceeding her words prove Depeche Mode wrong. There was nothing to enjoy in the silence.

"And I'm your excitement for the evening. A sort of take-home entertainment?" I say half- playful, half-seriously, inquiring if this is leading somewhere.

"I didn't think you'd mind." Honesty pours forth from her as she sits back down—this time a little closer to me.

"I don't ... but what about Ronnie?" I inch closer to her.

"Didn't I just cover that?" Always the quick wit. She leans in toward me. Not close enough to touch, but I can smell what perfume is left from the rain.

"I don't mean that. I mean the guy's literally twice my size. He could kill me without a struggle." I lean in closer to her.

She laughs, backing off a bit. "He's not going to find out."

"Unless he comes home."

"He's stuck at work till God knows when." She stands up and drops her towel. Her still drying bra reveals her gorgeous dark pink nipples. She turns and slowly struts her way to, I assume, her bedroom. Her panties tease me as she walks away.

I stand and take my first step toward re-entering a world I've long been estranged. My phone lights up. A number not yet programmed into my phone but recognizable all the same: Viv. The universe hates me, or it's trying to save me. I've done many, many, many, many things in my time that I am sure I need to pay for if I haven't already. But here I am. The one that made me who I am today, half-naked and ready to go on one hand. On the other hand, calling me is the new girl I can't get out of my mind, who is amazing in her own right. A devil on one shoulder and a seemingly less mischievous devil on the other. Whatever I may have still owed the universe, whatever karma there was left to pay back, this conundrum cleans my slate.

I pause. My head shifting between the phone and the woman down the hall, the phone cosmically beckoning me while Faith literally beckons me. This is the moment I've been waiting on for close to twenty years. I let the call go to voicemail and take a hopping step toward her room.

I turn into her doorway as she lights a candle. Three others already lit. It makes me wonder how long I was staring at the phone, but they are lit. She holds a joint between her lips as the smoke encircles her face. A moving frame. The universe whispering, "This is the choice you should have made tonight." I'm glad I did. She takes a hit and hands it my way. I inhale a short sample of the wares. I stop to get a feel for the product. I find it worthy. I inhale more. Deeply. Not only to take in the smoke but to inhale this event, take it in for all I can. The color of the deep red, softly scented cinnamon and sugar candles, the dark blue color of her matching set of bra and panties. Static-X's "Invincible" playing in the background, perfectly timed for this moment. I savor it for all the fleeting moments it provides, for this may never happen again. And even if it does, it will never happen like this again. Never like this. This is a unique, once-in-a-lifetime chance to change everything.

So, I will.

I exhale. My mind has captured all it can. And all it will. The THC starts doing its subtle job on my mind, relaxing me to a state I am far more comfortable with. Much more familiar with over the passing years. I try not to but accept the fact that a boyish grin has taken over my face. I let it happen as my smile raises my left eyebrow and lowers my right. Silently saying, "Yes! Yes, I can smell what The Rock is cookin'!" And it is glorious.

She points her finger at me with her upturned hand and motions me to her. As the Rock did when he entered the ring, I too will dominate. Or be dominated. Whichever. Tonight, I don't mind.

I drop my towel. My soldier is standing at attention. We both stop for a moment out of renewed admiration for what we see—out of the fact we just smoked some fantastic shit—and, well, because we're both comfortably numb.

She looks me up and down, biting her bottom lip as she unclasps her bra. As her lacey bra slips down past her nipples, Victoria reveals her best-kept secret. Oh, how I've missed those. They say you can never go home again. Damn those fuckers. Damn those fuckers to hell. Daddy's home. And I am happy to be here again.

I step to her as she moves onto the bed. She turns on her back, looking at me, smiling. I find I still fit so perfectly between her legs as they wrap around me. She pulls me in close, kissing me as we hover somewhere between sitting up and lying down. I return her kiss with gusto. A kiss I've thought about for years, lips whose touch I've missed. A woman whom most of my songs were about. A moment.

This moment. This singular moment that's been ingrained in song over and over, manifesting in my THC and alcohol-fueled mind. And it feels better than I have ever imagined. Every song that I wrote about this moment. Every chord ever strummed in an ode to this moment all pale by comparison. Those weren't the greatest. No. They were just a tribute. You gotta believe me.

She playfully bites down on my lower lip, pulling me down onto the bed. I put out my arms so as not to fall on top of her, but I misjudged my distance. Her teeth scrape my lower lips, drawing a drop of blood as she releases. I don't flinch. Don't say a word. Just lick the inside of my lip, taste the crimson, and smile. Lowering my head to wrap my lips around those nipples that have been so longing for my touch.

As the Static-X album comes to an end and our quiet moans of consent are all that fill the otherwise silent air, Tenacious D's "Fuck Her Gently" comes to mind. I am going to take this as a cosmic sign of what I should be doing. Because, to paraphrase the song, sometimes you must fuck gently. Then fuck hard. And as if the universe gave her the same message, without the pomp and circumstance that is the dance we call foreplay, she slides me inside her. Deep.

"Fuckin' metal!" The words slip out of my lips. Verbal diarrhea to kill the mood. A phrase I haven't uttered in a long time, a phrase I've never used to describe sex. She looks quizzically at me. A first in a long, many years. A smile breaks out on her face as she begins to laugh.

"Fuckin' A, it's metal!" a perfect reply.

This is going to be fun.

So, I follow the lead of Tenacious D. I lean in. I kiss her chin and make my way down her neck. She quivers a bit. I begin to slide my hand up her stomach as I kiss my way down. I feel every inch of me slowly slide in and out of her. Her breathing deep and intense. I slide my other hand behind her arching back. I feel the seventeen years of unspoken love, or some feeling perceived to be love, spilling out at this moment.

She leans in, nibbling on my ear. Then a commanding whisper. "Hard and fast, loverboy. Don't puss out on me now." A demand I did not expect, nor one that I will ignore. Sorry, Mr. Black; tonight, there will be no gentle fucking. Only hard, fast, dirty, and fun.

And at that moment, I hear the guitar riff. Unmistakable in its sound. Simple yet always drawing in the listener for more. The opening riff that embraced what the eighties were all about. "Talk Dirty to Me."

So, I begin to speed up, finding how hard and fast she wants it. My man is in no mood to finish anytime soon. We have as long as we need.

The headboard begs for mercy with each smack against the wall. The frame starts squeaking more and more with each pump of my piston into her well-oiled, overflowing engine. The deluge of juices flowing from her is something new to me. Not that I've never had a lady gush or squirt on me, just not her. Faith was not that woman before. This is a welcome change. I, like many of my brethren, can appreciate the puddle, the squirt, and all of its sprinkler, water park-like qualities.

We explore the changed landscape of our bodies. Seeing what is new and what we have missed over the years. Soaking in the pool of sweat and juices dripping off our bodies. Faith's painted claws scratch down my back, over and over, digging into me. Deeper and deeper. Leaving their marks, claiming me for her. The floorboards joining in the chorus of plaintiff cries for mercy the headboard first started. The speed increasing exponentially. First a fast-paced sports car. Now a jack rabbit after ten lines of coke and a bottle of NoDoz. All at her moaning behest. As she tenses her kegel muscles, only a few p.s.i. from separating the manhood from the man, she stops me. Pulls me down next to her and whispers into my ear the three little words, the holy grail, the most elusive phrase that every man secretly wants to hear but that after all these years, I never expected to pass my ears.

"Fuck my ass."

Generally not a first date activity, but then again this wasn't our first date. I pause for a brief moment out of shock. The audacity that someone who hasn't known me in years would assume that such a request would be met. But then again the look in her eye shakes me free. I am not one to deny this request from such a beauty of a woman. I flip her around and get a view of her heavenly, heart-shaped ass. If I weren't a participant at this moment, it would bring a tear to my eye that such a smooth, perfectly shaped ass exists. With tan lines in the perfect spot to exemplify the heart shaped-ness of it all.

I give it a nice, hard smack for good measure. Faith cries out in pleasure, "Yes! Daddy!" Also, a phrase we never explored back then. A most welcome addition.

I spank her again and grab her hair. A handlebar, if you will, to steady my way in. With all the wetness provided from tonight's activity, entering her presents no challenge. She has done much self-discovery in the years between. I'm enjoying the spoils of her explorations.

"Yes!"

"Yes!!"

"YES!!!"

I spank her again as I thrust harder, deeper, faster. The slapping of skin against skin has never sounded so good. This is the moment the midnight hour was made for.

"I want you to cum," she cries out.

"You'd better not cum in her, asshole!" Ronnie yells out.

We must've missed the sound of him coming in. The turn of the handle, the slam of the door, drowned out by the sounds of hurricanes and sex.

I pull out, fearing for my safety as the behemoth of a man charges toward me. But it's too late. Bodily functions quickened by the emotional yearning for the climax can only be put off so long. I may be out, exposed for all my glory, but my guy has something to say. Ronnie sees me spitting on his floor my batch of Wite-out and stops in his tracks. I juke passed him, out of the bedroom. I reach into the dryer for my clothes while sprinting down the hall with a full erection, but all I manage to grab is a sock. No pants, no wallet, no keys. Just one sock.

I can't make another pass at the dryer. The only exits out of the apartment are the door I entered through and the balcony with its two-floor descent, both of which are on this side of the hallway.

I run into the makeshift dining room and bunker behind the dinner table. Ronnie runs into the living room and stops upon seeing me. His chest heaves up and down. Veins on his arms bulge out, ready to explode in a torrent of pain all over my face. His mind calculates the countless ways he can tear each limb from my body in the most painful way possible.

"Calm down now, big guy!"

I say the first thing that comes to mind, but not what Ronnie wanted to hear. He circles around the table as I round the other direction. A newly started game of cat and mouse, but he stops where I just stood.

His silent intimidation breaks. "Calm down?! Calm down?! You just had your dick in my woman's ass! Then came all over my fucking bedroom and you want me to calm down!? I'll fucking kill you, you piece of shit!"

He jumps onto and over the dining room table, hurtling toward me.

Faith, still in her birthday suit, bolts into the living room and gets in his path.

"Ronnie! Stop!" she pleads.

He stops. Looking at her, his face turns a darker shade of red, as a vein in his forehead bulges out so much I may be saved by an aneurysm.

"I'm not even close to stopping." He shoves her out of the way.

A gesture that I do not take kindly to, I forget the size difference for a split second.

"Hey! That's not very gentlemanly of you, bro," I say, stepping toward him. Like I can actually do anything to intimidate this Goliath.

"Gentlemanly?"

He lets out a chuckle. Maybe I was wrong. Perhaps he possesses the ability to reason and things will turn around.

"Fuck you! Bro!" His fist connects with my head. The sound of which echoes through my ears. A thud rings through the apartment as the sudden stop of my head and torso against the floor pulls all the air out of my lungs.

Or reasoning is beyond him.

I'm stunned. I know I'm dazed but my brain, much like Ronnie at this moment, says, "Fuck you" to me. I can't move. I see him towering over me. All three hundred pounds of attack, but I can't move. I can't run. At least for this moment. I am stuck. He looks down, shaking his head at the patheticness that is me right now. He spits on me as he turns his head back to Faith.

Right in my face. I guess in some way I deserve this. I knew this night was too good to last, too perfect to end well. But at least my senses have returned to me. So, I stand and wipe the spit and pride off my face. And while I don't appreciate the spit on my face, I'm confident he's not going to cut out the pieces of carpet or sheets with my semen on it and have them framed. I'm doubly convinced he's not thrilled about my sperm on his girlfriend.

"So, are we even now?" I hope to calm the situation.

He turns back to me after he and Faith finish some inaudible exchange that I'm certain was not loving. He looks into my bruising face, swings again, and hits the other side.

Once again, I find myself kissing the carpet. But at least this time I can get back up.

"Get out." He sidesteps a direct answer.

"Can I least get my clothes?"

"Can I hit you again?" He opens the door.

While the thought of my clothes is a nice one, it is much outweighed by the pain induced by his massive sledgehammer of a fist. I stand naked for a second and look at Faith. She mouths to me words that usually end a date with no further contact. "I'll-Call-You."

Ronnie turns back to see what she's saying, a moment I seize to grab my phone and run.

The door shuts behind me, leaving me standing in the hallway of an apartment complex.

Naked.

Wet.

With one sock.

And a phone.

I take the sock and cover my cock. A cocksock if you will. It's better than nothing. Not that anyone is out in this storm this late at night. The floor above me provides little shelter from the raging storm. But enough to use my phone.

I dial D.B., but he does not answer. Voicemail, a savior, does not make. As the rain beats down on my naked body, I know I must do something fast before someone sees me, before the cops are called, before this escalates worse than it already has. Peering down at the clock reading 12:30 on my phone, I can think of only one person. One person who will answer my call, because she is waiting for me to return her call—hoping for me to call. There is this voice in the back of my mind telling me not to call. Not now. Not when nothing I can say to her about this will paint me in a good light. Another voice chimes in. It reminds me that I shouldn't care, that I owe her nothing. One good conversation and a blowjob is not the foundation for a monogamous relationship. For all I know, she could be in bed being railed by some guy right now. It's not my business. Though I do find that thought a little less appealing than I'd like.

The rain is a little cold. And it's not doing my guy any justice. It looks less like those old children's toys that slipped out of your hand the more you tried to hold onto it and more like a scared turtle hiding in his shell. Just the icing on the cake that is this hurricane.

So, I find a place to lay low. I duck behind these valet garbage bins that seemingly double as benches and find shelter for my body. No need to alarm any busybodies that inevitably peek out the windows, checking to make sure no burglar is taking advantage of the rain to commit robberies.

I dial.

Before my mind begins to doubt my latest action, I hear it ring. I can't hang up now. That will just look weird. It rings again. I can only hope that her voicemail picks up. It rings a third time. Voicemail may make a savior yet. Fourth ring. If she hasn't picked up by now, she won't.

"Hello?"

Damn. Here's hoping.

CHAPTER 8

Down In It

*T*he events of the day got me thinking about New York, why I loved it and why I needed to leave it. I wonder if my actions here are nothing more than a new way to repeat the same mistakes. I wait naked in the rain, thinking about my last fling in the Big Apple.

I remember looking around the stranger's room I was lying in. The abstract artwork reminiscent of, but not quite, a Rothko stood out like a sore thumb against the beige walls. The iPod dock in the background played some rock radio station. The thirty-five-inch LED screen waited to be clicked to life. It was nice but ordinary. A female voice on the radio started talking about Florida. Something in the smoky, yet nurturing tone of the lady's voice struck a memory I once held close but had been a little lost as of late. Something once said to me, "Never do anything you wouldn't tell your parents about."

I have about twenty years of memories I would never tell my parents about. Nights of love and lust, topped with the smooth creaminess of more desire and more moments lost to the demon known as alcohol, when all you wanted to do is hold onto the memory of what was happening right then. Days when a good bag of weed could take away all the worries of the next tour, the next song to be written, the album cover to design, but instead of a much needed bag of weed, you find yourself talking down three gunmen in a Truxican standoff all over some misunderstanding that probably wouldn't have happened if they weren't high in the first place. And while I guess what someone tells their mother or father depends on the type of relationship they have, the premise still stands. Nights like that are not what a parental figure wants to hear about. No mother or father wants to hear about the latest romper room activity of their adult child or the name of the one-night stand lying in bed next to them.

But I make no apologies about who I am. I'm not a horrible person. I'm not down with the needle or the torched spoon. I don't raise my fist to the ladies. I don't needlessly berate people for some sick enjoyment. I'm a person who is playing the hand life dealt, and while I may have played into that hand, I am doing the best that I can because life doesn't let you go back and change the past.

I stretched, arms above my head, elbows bent in a full body stretch I felt in my toes. As I rubbed the sex out of my eyes, a thought entered my mind. I didn't know her name, the one-night stand that was next to me. I didn't know her name. I smiled a smile on my face that became more weathered each year, a smile that she'd think is real. It was real, to a point. But only in so much as to let the inner Hustler magazine-reading teenager in me have his moment. The blue satin sheets on her bed strewn about, tangled, and intertwined in a way that only a sweaty, heart-pounding, roll in the sheets can do. I finished my stretch and turned to her to see her staring at me: Finn Fairlane, Producer-Extraordinaire.

Who the hell cares? That's right. Her. It's why she continued talking to me barside at Sunswick once she realized who I was. I needed some strange, and here she was: a beautiful stranger with hazel-brown eyes, a mile-wide smile, and cosmetically enhanced breasts that were on full display. This is how I get inspired. The sexcapades that help *me write, help me get direction to songs that have yet to be written. No, I'm not going to say they're getting old, or that they're losing their value for inspiration. They just haven't been doing it for me. There's been nothing in them to take away from. Like a Michael Bay flick, they are fun and full of adventure and excitement, but when the movie is over, there's not much to say about it except it was fun. All I could do at that moment was listen to the radio in the background finish the commercial about Florida vacations and how incredible they are. I thought maybe they are incredible. I didn't know. As an adult, I'd never been. But why the hell was I thinking about Florida when I had a naked woman lying next to me?*

"You doin' okay?" She asked as she smiled at me. She fell back on the pillow, her blonde hair in need of a root touch-up, either that or ombre hair, billowing out as if she was in a shampoo commercial.

That's a loaded question: I was not doing okay. If I were, I wouldn't have been thinking about the radio commercial. I'd have been thinking about the naked lady next to me. But that wasn't an answer she wanted to hear.

"Dandy." I turn to get out of bed.

She laughed a little, coy laugh. "Dandy. I like that."

I could have said "Super Duper" in my best Peter Boyle a la Young Frankenstein or even done a damn air guitar while saying "Excellent" and she would've responded the same. She was just hoping I'd listen to her Bandcamp or ReverbNation page and make her and her band the next big thing. I wouldn't have landed her otherwise.

There I went giving her the same line I've given a hundred times to others: "I thought you would."

"Last night wasn't about anything," she started.

I looked at her curiously as I pulled up my dark wash denim jeans. "What did you think I thought it was about?" I asked.

"Didn't want you to think I was only sleeping with you..." She trailed off for a moment. Her head tilted as I waited for her to finish her thought, jean button in my hand paused

for her. "Cat Claw. I didn't want you to think it was about my band or anything."

I finished buttoning up my jeans and reached down for my shirt. I knew she was waiting for some sort of affirmative response that fooled me into thinking that she was honest. But one, an upfront person wouldn't feel the need to make the statement. And two, if it really had nothing to do with her wanting me to help her band, then why not-so-subtly drop the name in there? And three. Cat Claw? Worst. Band name. Ever.

I took my time pulling my shirt over my head. "Of course not. Why would I?"

The look of both confusion and relief that mixed on her face was funny. It made her look both beautiful and ugly at the same time. "Oh. Okay. Just making sure."

"We're good. But I have to go meet a client."

"At this hour?" She slinked toward me a little in a meager attempt to get me to stay.

I huffed a small laugh. "It's early tomorrow morning. I need to actually get some sleep."

Her eyes widened with hope. "Can I call you?"

I felt my face start to grimace. I stopped it in the hope that I caught it early enough so she didn't notice.

"I don't give out my number. Too many unsavory individuals who present fine enough at first."

She nodded an almost imperceivable nod of understanding and disappointment that somehow a one-night stand didn't make the cut. I looked around and grabbed a torn-open envelope and a pen that was next to it.

I handed them to her, and she jotted down her number. I hugged her, giving the obligatory, "I'll call you." The funny thing though was as I hugged her, I thought that maybe I should listen to her band. Possibly I should call her again. I wasn't thinking that she was going to turn into something more than that: consensual sex between two consenting adults with no commitment to each other. But she did take the time out of her evening to give me some strange. But then, that was the same pattern of thoughts I had every time someone wanted me to do something for them and preempted the hopeful favor with sex.

As I walked down the hall to the cramped elevator in that Brooklyn building, a thought stirred in my mind: a sense of déjà vu. I got an eerie feeling about that hall. Maybe not that hallway in particular but that building. I didn't notice it on the way to her place, possibly because she had her legs wrapped around me while directing me as my eyes were staring at her chest. I wasn't really taking in my surroundings. But on my way out, free of distractions, free of blood being taken from my brain to fuel other body parts, I realized I had been there before.

The elevator buzzed and the door opened. A well-built man stood in front of me. Lean and muscular with a tight, maintained haircut. Chiseled jaw and tan skin. A Godsmack sun logo tattooed on his left arm. A gray tank-top and black workout pants. He looked at me with a slight head tilt. He grinned a slight gap-toothed grin. It hit me—why I recognized this hall—why that guy was maniacally smiling at me: Patrick.

I dashed toward the stairwell door, his words echoing in my head. "I thought I told you never to come back here, you piece of shit, Fairlane!"

I swung the metal door open and frantically started down the concrete stairs in dire need of a new paint job.

"I wasn't with her tonight!" I yelled back, hoping he would have stopped pursuit.

But I heard him enter the stairwell and a memory came to my mind clear as day. Another reason my time in NYC was up. It was this same stairwell; me running down the same stairs while a woman, confused about her life choices, pleaded with her boyfriend to not bash my head in. I did appreciate that. The other part of that memory was the bat swinging down at my hand on the railing, narrowly missing. Had he connected, it would have certainly shattered my bones into a thousand pieces. The bat denting the banister itself, which I found out because my hand ran over the indentation from the last escape attempt.

He was gaining ground. His aerodynamic body added to his physical advantage. I had to take half a staircase at a time. I prayed I didn't miss and sprain an ankle. I really didn't want a sprained ankle to be the reason my life ended that night.

His scream echoed in the stairwell as an audible exclamation, "You're dead meat!"

I don't think even Kiefer Sutherland could have made it sound any more threatening. I leapt onto the second floor. Adrenaline pumped hard through my heart, and so I did something I would never have done under normal circumstances. I jumped all the steps going from the second to the first floor. I somehow, by the grace of God, landed perfectly. No sprained ankle or broken bones.

As I opened the door to the lobby to make my getaway, Patrick attempted the same jump I had just landed. He was not quite so lucky. Both his ankles gave out under him, which caused him to fall forward, face first into the edge of the door. A loud smack of bone against metal caused crimson to splash out from his nose. A second crack echoed as he hit the concrete floor.

"Lucky bastard" slurred from his bloody lips as he looked up at me.

"I wasn't with her. I did heed your warning last time. I didn't know where I was till I was leaving."

I stood a few feet from him, unsure of what he may do as that scene played out in the lobby of the building. The door opened behind me and Patrick laughed. "You weren't lying. Hi, Katy."

I turned to see her standing there. The reason I ran down five flights of stairs in record time. The reason Patrick was bleeding and most likely broken on the ground. At 5'2" and maybe a buck twenty as she shakes off the rain. Waist long, straight dark brown hair. Pouty lips on an innocent face. Katy.

She looked down at him. "What happened?"

"Nothing, babe."

She turned to me for confirmation. "Nice to see you again, Finn. Did this have anything to do with you?" she said, as she grabbed an inordinate amount of facial tissue out of her purse.

"Misunderstanding. Let's help him up. He's too injured."

Patrick applied the tissue to his bleeding nose, then looked at me confused. Why did I help him after not once but twice he had threatened my life? Because the circumstances we find ourselves in in life are ofttimes beyond our control. When confusion reigns and people become reactionary, the ones who are granted forethought are not allowed the ability to forego civility. So, I helped him.

We each helped carry him like a beaten champ away from a fight. Little did he know that battle was with himself.

"Nice to see you again, Katy. This guy seems to be very protective of you."

"Yes, yes he is. And it's much appreciated. So, what are you doing here?"

I looked at him as he ever so slightly shook his head once. I, in return, gave an almost unperceivable nod.

"I was leaving, actually. After I help you to the elevator, I think Patrick can handle himself from here."

I pushed the elevator call button and turned to them both. I saluted them, two fingers to my forehead. "It's been a gas."

Headed to the main door, I turned back around as I heard them enter the elevator. "Katy, take care of each other."

She smiled before they disappeared behind the closing door.

I started walking down the street. Each step covered me a little more in the rain. As I hailed a cab, something made me think. I'd been in New York the better part of two decades. I loved that city. The overcrowded cemeteries that are hauntingly beautiful were always a thought on my mind. They stay with you. The end shot of Gangs Of New York does a perfect job of showing the monster that is this city. How lives that were once so important at one time are lost to the ever-growing entity that is NYC. But they do; they stick with you. However, at that moment, it wasn't the cemeteries. It was the fact that there are innumerable buildings in the boroughs with even more countless rooms within. And I had found a way to start going through them again. It stabbed me right below my ribs, pain that I shouldn't have felt. While it pierced my side, it wanted to give me a high five. A congratulatory gesture on my conquests through the years that had me circling back around. It didn't sit right with me. A mellow, unsettling rumble in my stomach that tried to tell me something. Maybe that was why I hadn't been very inspired. Perhaps it was merely a coincidence.

But anyway it went, I felt this wasn't me. Maybe it was and still is, but not what I wanted. I'm healthy and full of vigor, but nights like that, especially the way it ended, and double for the way it could have ended, weren't giving me what I needed to do my job. What I needed to feel fulfilled.

I needed to know what I needed, what it was that would help make me not feel that way. Make me not feel like my life was missing something, except it was. And it had been missing for so long.

The taxi I hailed down had a rooftop advertisement. Something that I usually wouldn't have noticed, but I did because of its content: an ad for Florida vacations.

CHAPTER 9

T he rain relentlessly beats down on me. I try to keep cover, but conditions aren't letting up and the wind, in all its anger, pushes everything side to side, again and again. As my thoughts turn back to the present, the realization that Viv is out in this weather to pick up my naked ass both warms my insides and has me scared for her well-being. *Why would she do this for me?* Maybe she's just a caring soul. Maybe there's something more to it all that I just don't see. But seeing as she's lived here longer than I, if she feels okay out here, then she probably is.

The past events of the day have been what I was looking forward to for countless nights. Years. There's something in me that is comparing what I thought would transpire versus what actually manifested in her room. There was a sense of romance, the style of romance as we know it. It was amazing, yet somehow at the end of it all, I still wound up outside, naked, and wet. Perhaps even the end of our tryst was how it was meant to end. Our own unique brand of romance, at least for the time being.

The wait for Viv is much shorter than I thought it would be. Either that, or my thoughts of New York take much longer than I realize. But either way, I see her pull up, cutting through the rain, my savior in an old, rusted silver BMW, no topper ads of Florida vacations. Past the furious tears from the sky that pound the windshield and the wiper blades racing back and forth, I see her laughing at me. Open-mouthed and enjoying the fruits of her drive. A good sign in all of this and I am happy she is enjoying this moment, at least for the laugh of it. I run to the car, keeping what I can covered up and hop in.

Inside, I sit on the sandy brown leather seats, stitches that are starting to fray at a few of the seams. Even a knob on Viv's radio has fallen off. Her laughter has picked up and tinted her face a lovely rouge. Her hands motion between herself and myself, unsuccessfully attempting to wave off the hilarity she finds in the moment.

She tries to chime in while wiping away a tear of laughter. "What the…"

But with a childish grin, I quickly interject, "Don't ask."

She notices my eye, causing the laughter to quell a few notches. She reaches out for it, to soothe the redness still present from before.

"Are you okay? It's starting to bruise."

"Oh, that? A fist fell into my face," I say, trying to make light of the situation.

Her laughter slows to a halt, but her mood is still light and enjoyable.

"A couple of times I see." She moves my head around, trying to get a better look. I doubt she's a nurse or anything, but she drove here, so she gets to examine.

She continues, "I don't suppose this has anything to do with why I am picking you up naked?"

"You suppose correctly. Long story," I say.

"We don't owe each other anything," she replies, leaving well enough alone.

"You're not far from here, are you?" I ask, already thinking I know the answer.

"Nah, not too far. I assume you do want to, and need to, come back to my place?" she says.

So

Though I'm not sure if she has any hidden intentions with that question, I don't want to worsen the storm.

"If you have clothes I could wear." I point to my birthday suit.

"Yeaaahhh." She draws out in a negative response to my inquiry. "It's me and my roommate. Her clothes are nowhere near your size. No worries though. Either way."

She says, "No worries," but I do worry because judging by how fast she made the drive here, my place is much farther. And I don't want her driving in this any more than she must. But what should I do? Try to fit into some T-shirt that, while oversized on someone who's 5'4" and weighs a buck fifteen, is going to make me look like some pansexual, unsure of his own pansexuality fitting into a muscle-tee three sizes too small.

She stops at a crossroads. No cars around as the rains punish the streets, flooding the drainage grates. Trees bend in the wind. A congratulatory bow to me and my situation, either that or to her and her kindness to brave this storm. Or both. The streetlights blink yellow. I can't help but think three things at this moment. One, I've been down here for a while now, and I still haven't seen any alligators. Living outside of Florida for all my life, you are made to believe alligators are an ever-present threat, ready to chomp down on you at any given moment. That is wrong and more than disappointing. Two, I want to be with her, though the face of her changes with each flash of lightning that paints the horizon in magnificent hues of yellows, oranges, and purples. Viv one flash; Faith another. My mind is unable to decide. Stuck. Always knowing that I want to be happy but never able to let myself be happy in the now, only in the possibility of what could be. One such option is Viv and me in bed, exploring each other in ways unable behind bushes. And three, the crossroads in front of me, both literal and symbolic. The big what to do, who to choose. Is this night, this moment, the answer to that question or am I overthinking the whole situation?

"So?" She nudges me.

I respond with a raised eyebrow and half-cocked smile. "Got a bath towel I could borrow?"

She makes a left turn and before I can delve deep into thought on anything or even space out, we pull up to a one-level house: gunmetal gray on the outside with what, in the light of the late night, appears to be off-white trim. The black skies make it look more like a house out of a Tim Burton film than a place you'd want to live in, but I can tell in the light of day it has pleasant curb appeal, despite the bushes and trees blowing in the hurricane winds.

There's a tan Ford Taurus in the driveway.

Viv turns to me with an unsure face. "I didn't know she'd be home."

"Seems to be the theme of the evening," I quip.

She catches the not-so-subtle hint at the night's events. "I thought she was at her guy's place."

"No worries," I reassure. "I can keep myself covered until I have a towel. We're all adults."

She laughs and makes a reference to one of the greatest sitcoms to grace television in the last four decades, "Sure about that, Naked Man?"

"I was not doing the Naked Man." I laugh out loud, impressed with her ode to *How I Met Your Mother.*

We dash out of the car and toward the door. About five feet into the rain, she drops her keys and fumbles for them on the ground. There is a look on her face, a mix of frustration and amusement at the moment. And it's the look on her face, as it's being beaten by the rain, that makes her look smokey. Her hair, wet and stringy, lays across her cheeks as she rises up. She sees me watching her. I urge her to finish the race to the door as I do a little dance, a dance that inspires urgency in her and that says, "'Hey, I'm naked here!" She laughs at my short jig and reaches the door.

Inside, the living room has a nice entertainment center with a well-kept, but older, tube television. The opposite wall has an eclectic assortment of framed movie posters, below which, an old plaid couch sits. A very surprised roommate perks up from her zoned-out state, turning from her late-night infomercial. Viv exits down a hall, hopefully to fetch a towel for me. There's a moment of awkward silence as her roommate stares at the naked man who just walked through the front door. She's deer-in-head-lights-frozen, eyes fixed upon my scantily covered crotch. I outstretch one of my hands, which reveals a small spot of well-manscaped pubic hair. She yawns as her eyes widen and shift to my hand for a quick second before shouting. "Viv, did you get a late-night stripper surprise? Cause I'm down for a stripper!"

"Finn," I say, hoping she says something else.

Nope.

"Are you a stripper?" Her excited anticipation causes a slight quiver in her voice.

She is cautious to shake my hand, unsure of what my next move may be. Like I am going to move my other hand and start flapping my penis side to side, shaking water off while singing, "Hello, My Baby."

"No. I'm not but thank you for the compliment."

"Name's Izzy," she replies. "Whatcha packin'?"

"I'm sorry?" I'm taken aback by her question. Not offended or anything, just shocked that she asked.

"Whatcha packin' there, big guy? You walk in covered only by rain and your hands, and now just hands, but you're not a stripper. I see you're in good shape. You groom nicely. So, the only thing that remains is... What. Are. You. Packing?"

I look her up and down. She is a complementary contrast to the rocker chick-meets-Harley Quinn-inspired color and style of Viv. Izzy has smooth Mochaccino skin with dark, almost black eyes, a slight wave to her hair that gives it an "I'm always DTF" look. Her slender, defined jawline, high cheekbones, and perfectly pouty lips give her a natural look that is a balance of sweet meets "*I'll rock your world in ways you have yet to imagine.*" Decadent deliciousness and troublesome temptation all rolled into one.

Before I can get an answer out, a brown, ratty, old towel hits me, causing an instinctual grab for it as it hits the floor.

I grab it and cover myself, though Izzy has already seen the goods.

"Nice find, Viv. Where'd you get this one?" She says this as if I'm not even in the room anymore.

"Hands off, Izzy," Viv demands.

"Wasn't grabbing," Izzy defends.

"She wasn't. I let go to grab the towel, and she got a peek," I add.

Viv returns to the room with another small towel so I can dry myself.

"I found him behind the bushes," Viv illustrates.

"Oh yeah! I was there. Now I remember you. D.B. was talking you up to everyone. You're that producer guy."

"Guilty," I confess.

Viv grabs my hand and leads me to her bedroom. As her skin touches my palm, a thought enters my head. Of the man and his kingdom, of getting what you want out of life. She takes me by the hand down the hall, but my mind is frozen. Something edges in my brain about the machine and its beauty. The incalculable man hours spent building, tearing down, operating, setting up fireworks, selling goods, preparing food, interviewing, managing, bag checking, and more: all to put on a show so glorious that the worries of adulthood slip away. Prejudice, hatred, politics, finances, lost loves, deaths, everything. Gone. And so is my thought.

She closes the door to her room and smiles at me. I smile back, but all I can think about is where that thought was leading. She says something to me as she starts to undress. I really wish I heard her, but my mind is elsewhere, ever searching for the right thing at the wrong time. What sort of man thinks about a theme park when a wonderland is standing in front of him?

This guy. Obviously.

And it's not something I enjoy. It's something that is—a consuming cycle in my mind that won't quit until the answer is found. I hope that I can be here in this moment with Viv. Tend to her needs while tending to mine.

I snap back to the moment as her shirt hits me, covering my head. I remove it and catch the letters G 'n R on it. Nice pick. I flip the shirt around to read the message, "Get In The Ring, Mutherfucker." Double nice pick. And point taken.

For the moment, I shove aside the nagging search for my lost thought and be in service to her.

She is already lying on her queen-size bed, ready to doctor the wounds on my head and whatever else she may find. And I am prepared to let her.

I have never seen her before in all her beauty. We never made it this far behind the bushes, even though we went so much further in other ways.

I look her over as she does me, her beautiful body lying in the middle of her bed. The majesty of her perky breasts, nipples erect. A good sign for me. Her stomach's smooth, soft skin waiting to be gently kissed. I make my way to the bed and slide next to her. Moving in, our lips touch and embrace. Tongues dancing the tango. My hand reaches for her inner thigh, a spot I'd like to still further explore. I slide it up and stop at her black lace panties. I hesitate for a moment for some sort of confirmation.

"It ended this morning," she whispers in my ear.

Good enough for me. I slip a finger between the waistband and her skin. I feel Viv quiver as my nail glides across her flesh the length of the waistband to stop mid-stomach. She takes an intense, shallow breath as I move my hand back to her inner thigh. I rest my hand on her panty line. My thumb wraps upward as the other four fingers lay where her leg meets her dreamland.

As we play with each other, making our naughty nighttime dreams a reality, there is a soft knock at the door. Gentle rasp against the wood, begging for an invite inside. At this moment I am under her, but not yet inside her. She sits up and turns toward the door. The handle rotates, taking care not to disturb us as it opens. Izzy stands in the partially opened door. Her head peers through. Shirt off and bra on, as if she is anticipating a yes. This situation has played out for me before, the woman I'm with and her friend. A fun, frolic of a ménage-à-trois, but as Viv turns back to give Izzy her expected answer, I spy a look in her eye that says she doesn't want this tonight. But before she answers Izzy, she turns to me, sweaty, naked, beautiful. Exposed. She looks at me and smiles a meek smile. Forced but trying to hide the fact she wants me for herself. Not because she is selfish, but because this is more to her than the others. In an instant, I'm back in college, pre-wunderkind of a musician but a whore nonetheless, in bed with that girl. The one who made me realize I'm that guy. Who told me she "wasn't usually like this" and wasn't. And as much as I've still been the same situationally accidental douche since, I don't want to be tonight. I can see it in her eyes. A desperate stare, trying to stay cool and hip. She wants me. Not just for unlawful carnal knowledge's sake, but for all of me. And I find myself taken by that. I shake my head just enough that she knows I'm hers. That tonight belongs to us.

CHAPTER 10

Growing Into You

From the moment I saw Viv in her Van Halen T-shirt, I knew she was trouble. I am twelve years her senior, but there is a connection, a spark that revs my engine in a way I've not felt before, or in so long I've forgotten. Not just sexually. Yes, my loins long for her in ways that make me want to be the white silk shirt hanging off one shoulder man with the wind blowing his hair back on the cover of some cheesetastic mental masturbation novel. But there was something more. A feeling that this phenomenon we call life isn't overrated, is worth sharing with someone. Sure, this could all be the endorphins flooding my brain and making me feel like a high school boy getting an upskirt glance at the head cheerleader he's crushed on all year. I don't care. It feels good. And all that aside, maybe this is what life's all about. The great answer to the cosmic question. The existential relevance all great poets look for. The internal struggle Trent has been singing about since before Nine Inch Nails and *Pretty Hate Machine* when he was working with Exotic Birds and Option 30. Endorphins. Perhaps, just maybe, the science behind this doesn't make the existentialism of it all obsolete.

The hurricane finishes its demolition somewhere between the bedroom door closing for what was left of the night and opening in the morning. All is calm after the storm. The trees are still. The air is moist and silent. Cars drive by on I-4, but the noise seems less than usual, almost too calm.

After a night of doing it like they do on the Discovery Channel, picking me up some clothes and getting keys remade for my place, we decide to spend the day at the animal park, specifically not the park with the caged whales. I like my monkeys, giraffes, hippos, and lions. I see this park for what it is: overpriced food, animals fooled into being happy in the safety of their cages, and countless employees furthering the gilded-ness of the big D. And I don't care. I know the overpriced food helps keep those animals in a clean place and well fed. Yes, they still make a profit, but they never hid the fact they were a for-profit place. I don't care; I love all of this. I decide to put my heart in her hands, metaphorically speaking of course. With her, there is a sense of comfort, of ease. A feeling that things will be okay. It is new for me to feel calm. Calm and relaxed is not something I do well. I tend to feel uneasy when I try to relax, like there's always a sense of something not being right. But here, with her, at this moment, I feel relaxed, and I am content with that.

As I said, the hurricane had passed, and the calm is here. Maybe that's what I'm feeling, the calm after the storm. While I hope it is not just that and something more, I'll enjoy it while it lasts if it is. The storm has passed, and she's still here.

We walk to an area that has Tamarin monkeys. Hell if I know what exact kind of monkey, but these things are the best. Tiny, little guys with puffy white hair on their heads that remind me of an early nineties rock star. These guys are awesome. We sit watching the animals in the cage that the park built, and the tiny rock stars seem content: swinging from branch to branch, grooming themselves, scavenging for bugs in between feeding times. They are a reminder of everything I could have been had I chosen differently back then, everything that most people are. Hell, in a sense, even what I've become. Someone who is comfortable in a routine. While the monkey's idea of every day may not be what the daily grind is to us, it's their little world. Just as we get up, shit, shower, shave, eat a quick breakfast, go to work, come home, and repeat five days a week, these guys do this day in and day out. Hell, I do what I do day in and day out. But this little set-up is a reminder that I am who I am, in spite of that. I wouldn't have met Viv if it wasn't for my own sense of routine and my need to break it.

I turn to her, to stare at the beauty I have quickly become fond of. She stares at the monkeys, a smile on her face. She entwines her arm in mine, giving it an endearing squeeze, a nonverbal thank-you of sorts for the day. I squeeze back, not you're welcome, but a thank-you. Thank you for staying the other night to meet me; thank you for last night; thank you for the sincerity that is Viv.

I know this must seem like I'm some half-aquatic fifteen-year-old redhead who falls in love with a boy while he plays with his dog, even though she has never actually spoken to him and has no idea if he's a complete asshat or not. Spoilers: He (kind of) is, and so is she. But this, right here, is new. And while I'm not falling in love, nor are my feelings close to that, I'm just enjoying it and the feeling it brings. Keeping an open mind about where things could lead.

We decide that tomorrow she's going to take me to the other side, the more grown-up version of what this city was built on. The inevitable follow-up to a park that is perhaps too family-friendly. We find ourselves at Universal. We arrive sometime as the sun sets, not exactly sure, but I don't care either way. All I can do as I look around City Walk, a delightful mix of restaurants and shopping—neither of which screams tourist—is think, *Is this how the other half lives?!* The tattoo shop here actually has some phenomenal artists, not just filler artists to grab the tourist's money. The selection of food is impressive. Burgers, sushi, seafood, and you can even waste away again in Margaritaville. A performer entertains atop a fifteen-foot-high servo driven stilt. A Steampunk restaurant. This place is so inviting without any pretense—if only the town were built on this venue instead.

It is so beautiful. Attention is given to every little detail inside and out, so much more than the gilded land of D. And this, of course, has me thinking, *Is there something I've been missing out on all these years? Have I been wallowing in something that I could have had if only I chosen a different path, a path that seemed, on the outside at least, less appealing?* I don't know, and I don't want to think about it. I try to stop the internal cycle of torment before it grips me too tightly and enjoy the day at a most amazing place.

The more I look around this area that I now live in, Orlando and all it encompasses, the more inspired I feel. The more I want to write songs of substance, not just the pop, (God forbid I say it) generic money-makers I moved down here to get away from. I'm sure Linda Perry can relate. After all, she left 4 Non Blondes, and after years of writing chart-topping songs, she started Deep Dark Robot to write stuff of more substance.

I look around at the Dr. Seuss section and it brings me back to childhood. Bright-eyed and wanting to run from statue to statue and building to building just to be a part of it all.

Viv watches as I do precisely that, the excited eight-year old I momentarily am. "Having fun, are you?" She giggles, enjoying the moments with me.

"Yes! This place is amazing!"

She smiles and lets out a belly laugh. "I'm glad you're enjoying yourself."

And the thing is, I am enjoying myself. At the park for the rest of the day and the following days together, I enjoy myself. I find myself in her company, and not much else matters. I know I still have a record release party to finalize, as well as the rest of the record to help with, but as I've said, I can't do my job if I don't feel inspired. Viv is doing just that, inspiring me and finding new ways to stimulate me.

Great songs, great books, great movies: all of them written by people who were inspired by someone, thus inspiring them to write said medium. No song was written without outside inspiration. So, even the muses need muses of some sort, and that's what's happening right now. She is amusing me. And it is glorious.

It's been a while since the storm, and I find myself happy to be in her company and her happy to be in mine still. Sometimes new flames, like fireworks, die quickly after a huge explosion. But sometimes, flames start strong and get stronger.

But here's the thing. Here's always the thing. The notion that has always been on my mind for years and now more than ever is there, festering in front. An itch I need to scratch but can't reach. A fly that buzzes in my ear that I can't swat away. Faith. God damn if I want to be thinking about her right now, but I am. Not just about our long overdue night together, but about the days since. The fact I haven't heard from her; the fact that in the few attempts I've made to call her in the few moments I've been without Viv, Faith has not answered. The fact that her overgrown man-beast of a boyfriend Ronnie had such a temper with me I don't know if she's okay. But she is an adult and has survived these many years without me; I try to let things rest. But allowing a sleeping dog to lie is harder than it seems. If only in so much as our urge to pet something so beautiful and peaceful, not to stir it but to try and add to its slumber. Except that petting a dog only stirs it. And once it wakes, there's no telling if it will be happy, tired, hungry, or worse, angry that you woke it.

While we currently sit at our favorite day-of-the-week-restaurant-haunt, I feel the buzzing of the fly at my picnic. I don't want this to happen. The restaurant is littered with a few tables of people eating and enjoying their day. The whole environment is in good spirits. Viv and I are just enjoying a few drinks. But I feel the tickle in my ear of the flapping wings and high-pitched biz-buzz sounds: Jeanine.

Entering in through the side patio door, wearing a blue-and-white tie-dyed sundress and sandals to match, she saunters to the bar as if she hasn't a care in the world or a thought in her mind. But I see it in her eyes. She has an idea, and she's waiting for the right moment to release it into the world, to stir up whatever she feels like stirring.

Shoo fly, don't bother me.

But as a fly won't listen, neither will she. Jeanine ignores the expression on my face that displays anything but a welcoming tone. She sits down on my right, once again placing me between the two ladies. I didn't like the feeling before, and I sure as hell don't like it now. The urge to run screaming is rapidly tingling through my legs, an electrical impulse to carry me away from this inevitable disaster for my own safety. But I'm a man, and a man's past, no matter how small or annoying the part, is always his past, and if it collides with his present, the only person to point the finger at is himself.

"Tricky Finn! What an odd surprise to see you here!" Jeanine says in her most pleasantly sarcastic voice as she flags the bartender down for a drink.

Viv looks at me with a raised eyebrow. "So why does she call you Tricky Finn?"

Without me able to get a fraction of a word out, Jeanine chimes in, "Once, a long, long time ago, he did something stupid. Not stupid like idiotic. Just juvenile."

"I was a juvenile. Well, just past that stage anyhow," I defend myself.

"So, what's your excuse now, Finn?" Jeanine chimes in.

"Hey, Jeanine. He seems like a very mature man." Viv coming to my defense is a nice gesture, although I can handle myself.

"Really? Did he ever tell you why you had to pick him up in the middle of a hurricane with no clothes on and only his phone?"

Or not. Maybe I can't handle myself. Abort. Abort.

"Why, Jeanine? Why?" Yes. I'm pleading a little bit, but it seems the once annoying fly at the picnic has matured into a new species of annoyance and is hell-bent on ruining this for me.

"I just thought she should know you, Finn Fairlane. The real you. Like I do."

"You knew me many years ago."

"Judging by the parking lot blowjob and what Faith told me, you are still the same ole' Finn."

Viv is fidgeting in her chair, unsure of what's going on at the moment. "That was a nice moment between two consenting adults."

"Thanks, Viv. But this isn't about you. She is harboring some weird animosity toward me, and I don't know why. This isn't all just about open honesty, is it?"

"Do you have any idea what you've done to my sister?"

"What did you do to Faith? And why were you naked?" Viv chimes in, getting visibly shaken.

Fine. Jeanine wants my life laid out for Viv right here.

"I didn't do anything to Faith. I mean, not currently. We dated. Almost twenty years ago. She broke up with me. All those sappy breakup songs I wrote that played on the radio. All those songs over the years about love that you hold so dear. All for her. All about her. But she left me. Then I moved here, and here she was, is, whatever. And all these memories came rushing back. All these feelings came with them. And things happen. But I met you."

Viv interrupts, "Please tell me I am not just a way to kill time until she comes around on her feelings for you? Not just another woman for you to notch on your head-board?" It hits her, and a look of disgust washes over her face. "Did you just get done fucking her when I picked you up?! Did I sleep with you not hours after you just had your dick inside her? I know we didn't owe each other anything. We weren't exclusive. Maybe we still aren't. But I just fig-ured some shenanigans. Not that you double dipped with me. Or just with me, but with *her* of all people! I honestly thought more of you than that. Hell, I thought you thought more of me! Fuck, more of her! How naïve I must be to assume you wouldn't do that to me? So, tell me it's not true, Finn!"

I don't want to respond. I don't want to lie. I'm an honest guy. I want to stay silent and not ruin this, but the look on my face, a look I didn't even realize I was making, says it all. Well, not all.

"No. No. Yes. I'm sorry." The only words to peep out of my unsure mouth.

Still kicking the dog when he's down, Jeanine interjects, "Finny boy. This is what happens when you avoid your duties. Had you just been writing, producing..." She pauses for dramatic effect that only agitates me more. "You wouldn't be in this mess," she finishes icing the cake that was her words.

"Seriously, Jeanine. That's your moral lesson here? I need to work more?"

"No. But when was the last time you met with Spear Fist? Last week?"

"Why the hell do you even care? What are you getting out of all this?" I desperately want to know. As this situation worsens, I need to find a card to play. An upper hand.

"Gregg is my boyfriend."

"Who?"

"The drummer."

"That's his name!" Not something I should have said out loud, but it came out before I could stop it.

"Seriously? What's your damage?" Jeanine does have a point. I should know all their names.

"Nothing. Just slipped my mind." No, it didn't. I'm just an ass sometimes. Maybe more than I intend.

"I want to see him, and Spear Fist, go far, even if it is because of you. And if it is your doing, I don't want your philandering ways to get in his."

"You couldn't have just come in here and said, 'Hey, the guys need you. Please see them?'"

"I could have, but this is much more a guarantee that now you will. That now you will make sure their record gets the attention it deserves and is due."

I would like to shout names at her. Mean, childish names unbecoming of a person my age, or any age really, but there is a part of me that respects her for doing this. That sees her as a tough, driven individual. As a person who can understand what it takes to get what she needs out of someone, not the annoying child she once was. The fly has mutated into something new. Someone to reckon with, or not to. That phrase never did make much sense. Too bad I underestimated her.

"Finn." The tone of Viv's voice is serious. The anger seems to have calmed down for the moment. "Was I just someone to pass the time? Someone to fill in the space until she calls you back?"

"No. I'm drawn to you. Your energy. Your spirit. I never thought it would go down this way."

"Why did you call me during the storm? Why me? Why not the band? Why sleep with me right after her?"

The answers to those are more difficult than she might think. To say that I don't know many people, and I knew she would answer her phone, seems like I used her for a ride. While there is some truth to that, it's not at all like that.

"I called you because Ronnie just beat the shit out of me, and I wanted to see you."

"For what? A healing BJ?" Viv is obviously not seeing eye to eye with me at this moment. Perhaps I should have been more upfront.

Jeanine laughs as she finishes her drink.

"No. As I said, I like you. Did from the first night." I say this, and it's true, but it's one of those things that will always sound like a line from someone trying to save face.

"I'm not sure, Finn."

"Be as unsure as you want. But I wanted to see you. You. Not anyone else. I didn't call up D.B., bragging to him about the events. I didn't try to lure Faith outside to get my clothes or even my car keys. I called you. It's the same reason…" While lost in my answer, I had almost forgotten that Jeanine was right there. Almost. So, my voice softens. I'm not one to have shame about things, but private things are private. "It's why I said no to Izzy."

Jeanine pipes up in her chair as she sips her drink a la some crappy Audrey Hepburn imitator. "Excuse me? I didn't quite hear that."

Viv turns to Jeanine as she tries to collect her mannerisms. "Please shut the fuck up. You've done enough."

Jeanine stands up huffing as she sets her glass down. "I came here on your side, Vivian. But if you think otherwise, I can leave."

I take this moment for myself to try and preserve my dignity, or what's left of it. "I think that would be best."

Viv whips back around to me. "You've lost your say in this."

The ear-to-ear smile that crosses Jeanine's face is wiped away just as fast as it came as Viv says. "He's right though. Leave."

Jeanine storms off. "You know, Finn, if you put as much time into your clients as you do screwing up your love life, you'd still be famous."

The sting of her words, blunt as they may be, stab sharp, mainly because she might be correct. But be that as it may, wallowing is not my thing. At least about that. So as the silence drowns us for the moment after Jeanine's departure, I try to tread the waters and let my mind clear.

"If you didn't want to screw this up, you sure as shit did a good thing badly."

"So goes the story of my life. But at least I trudge along and try to do it right."

She smiles a little smile. If she weren't trying to hold it back, it would be so much bigger and so much beautiful, but it is this shy smile that caught my eye and heart in the first place.

"What do you want me to say?" It's not a great thing to say, but it's all that comes to my mind. I'm at a loss for words. Honesty wasn't a home run, and neither was withholding the truth. And of course, with the middle ground long past missed, I am at a loss for words. So, I ask her.

But her immediate response is silence. An unsettling silence: the kind that all the fiber of your being knows is not going to be broken with kind words. A silence so tense that dare it breaks may cause nuclear-level explosions. But all I can do is sit and hope I'm not the trigger that sets it off.

Watching her search for her words is not beautiful. It is scary. There are not a lot of women who could have done this to me. There's Faith. And one more in the time between Faith and now. That's it. And now there's Viv. I am not that man anymore. I can't be the one who walks away uncaring, unphased, unscathed. Not from her. I have my scars, and I wear them like a badge of honor. I am who I made me and I'm okay with that. But I don't want to add to her wounds any more than I have this day. So, I'm sitting. Waiting. There is a part of me that hates that I allowed myself to fall for someone so quickly, that I allowed myself to get close. But I did, and a larger part of me does not hate it, does not want it to be different.

The center of her lips begins to open. The silent tension dissolves without explosive effect, more like a torrential downpour that, in an instant, hushes without cause. There is a suspicion in that silent tension that something worse is yet to come.

"I want you to say nothing. You and Jeanine have said enough." She stabs me with her words.

"Then what can I do? What do you need from me?"

I always felt those were desperate words to use, but after asking for the words to say and that being her response, I succumb to a submissive role for the moment.

"Time."

A harsh, one-word response to shut me the hell up and stun me. Not that I can't move. I'm just so unsure of what move to make that my mind won't move my body, which is doubly not fun as I don't even respond to her rising from her seat and walking away. I just stare across the bar as she exits out the patio door and disappears off into the same viewpoint as she did when we first found each other in the bushes.

Still, I'm stunned.

CHAPTER 11

Dream On

E ven D.B. and the rest of Spear Fist feels a stronger connection to Badaboom. The magic power of the hurricane brings everyone closer to what's important to them in some mystical, cosmic way. Neil and Vincent have come together on their riffs in a very coupled way. Gregg seems less distanced from the band, which is nice considering what Jeanine did for him. Maybe it's because of what she did for him. Jeanine is either going to be a proverbial Yoko to Lennon or Dorothea Hurley to Bon Jovi. If she's some incarnation of Hurley, then I welcome it, but if she's a Yoko, then I shall destroy her.

They've had two meetings as a band without me in the time since the storm, and both have accomplished what I hoped: ideas born and breathing on their own. The best thing about their coming together is that both practices have been without me, which, surprisingly, is my end goal. To help things get to a better place. To get a band to a mindset where they want me around instead of needing me. The devil's in the details of the difference between the two.

So far, this third meeting, with me in attendance, is no different. The energy buzzing around the studio is

THE *Fairlane* INCIDENTS

contagious, full of creativity from all sides and a healthy exchange of ideas. This session was the most cohesive I've seen them since I first started working with them. Instead of turning every little idea into an argument, causing backward progress, they are listening, offering insights to enhance ones already given instead of new ones that negate the original. The band acts as a sounding board to better each song as a whole, not trying to force-fit pieces together. To me, at least, this is how people create fun music.

We all sit around, instruments in hand, discussing ideas for the last song to be written, the opener. Without a solid opener and a killer closer, which they already have, the album, any album really, is just a collection of forgettable songs. A strong opener makes the following songs tie together—whether musically, lyrically, or telling an epic story. And the closer brings it all together, an exclamation mark on the album. We need the opener. The record release party is a few weeks away, and we still need to record this one last song, mix it down, and press the albums. As anyone in the industry knows, that's a lot to do in very little time.

Gregg gets up from his drum set and lights a hookah. This is no ordinary hookah either. It has five three-foot hoses, one for each bandmate and an extra for guests. The design of the hookah itself is what makes this puppy special. The blown glass body was fired specifically for the band. The base of the water pipe is a fist. Stemming from that is a spearhead embedded into the top of the hand and spear rising from there, with red glass bleeding out of the wound. The whole thing, except for the blood, collects the resin, changing color until cleaned; that, however, is not near often enough. But always fresh water in the base.

We start passing it around, adding fuel to the already creative fire. We were talking about intro tracks. There were already eleven songs on the album, not counting the opener.

D.B. chimes in, "Iowa."

Gregg retorts, "You want us to cover Iowa?"

"I assume he means do a similar intro. Dark, heavy, and cryptic in sound and voice," I chime in, wanting to prevent a derailing of the past few weeks' productivity.

A ten-ton hammer of an idea smacks me across the face, bringing the searing smarts of Ronnie's fist fresh to the front of my mind again.

Give them "I Will Build My Cross."

There is a school of thought out there that old writings are old and always write fresh lyrics for fresh music. Never revisit old sets. I can understand that mindset. If it's old, by the time acceptable music is written for it, the verses may be outdated, outgrown, or just below current talent levels. But sometimes an old set sticks around. I feel like this is one of them.

Keep it a soft, spoken word intro over music: slow, fast, in between, it doesn't matter. We'll figure that out quickly. But for now, the lyrics. The rising tide of the album. The introduction dripping with sarcasm that starts Spear Fist's latest, greatest album ever.

We are the crucified
Not those who live in
Cold, cardboardboxes,
or who walked into
Shower rooms
turned ovens
We are the crucified.

With roofs, beds, and food on our tables. Our wounds attended to at the push of 911 or 976. They are not the crucified. Those who left their homes being promised a better life, not knowing that was death. We are the crucified because it is our blood that runs red. Our cries that are heard. Not theirs. Theirs run clear because no one is there to see it run red. No one hears them cry. No one cares. Not anymore.

We crucify ourselves.
They do not.
They want the pain
And the hunger.
The frostbite.

Infections. Disease
and the ridicule.
They suffer from
h o m e l e s s n e s s
genocide, mass
incarcerations and
being subhuman
because they are
humble. If this is true,
Then crucify me
And forgive me
for I know not what I do.
For I will buy some
wood. And
commission a cross.
And then
I will crucify myself.

As I finish reading the lyric set, the guitar is already strumming something that resonates of a diminished minor. The sad sound of forlorn, isolated, desperate solitude fills the room. A kick drum starts in, followed by a soft, military-style drum roll on the snare. The bassist sits, listening, mentally writing the bass line. I see him air bass out a minimalist riff, something to drone in the background. It already sounds perfect to me. The drum roll turns into a beat. The guitar picks up momentum.

From my pocket, my phone vibrates and buzzes a few bars of "In-A-Gadda-Da-Vida": my "I don't have you programmed in my phone so why the hell are you calling me?" ringtone. I am hoping for a callback though. The record release party is quickly approaching, and I'm still hoping for news from my contact. Everything they have under their belt is good, if not great. But it's been under-publicized and underrated. I want this album to get the attention it deserves. Maybe it's fate lending a hand.

"Hello. Fairlane speaking."

I listen to the other end of the phone as the guys all stare at me. As of now, the release party is at a microbrew bar in an indoor marketplace. It reminds me of a permanent expo booth set up, but with good shit. Big enough for a sizeable stage. Live sound is always finicky and always a gamble. But it's live music, so I don't much care about that. Fans will hear them, people who haven't heard them will become fans, and all will buy their album and support local businesses. This will be the event. Food enough for everyone to play into Romanesque stereotypes of gluttony and misconceived vomitoriums. Beer aplenty to make sure this brewing company stays on the map and not just makes an appearance.

She talks for a moment and I listen intently. A smile slowly starts crossing my face. The guys all have the same quizzical look on their faces that beg to know why the hell I am smiling. From the pot, perhaps. Yes, but no. This is more.

"Sounds perfect. Original date still?" I ask.

The guys are getting excited and start joyously laughing for reasons they don't yet know.

"Perfect. This will be huge. I'll be by tomorrow with the deposit," I assure my contact. "Thank you so much."

I hang up and find the band staring at me with a mix of "What the fuck" and "Dude, we aren't done yet" carved into their stoned faces.

I yell to the gods above, "We got the amphitheater!"

The guys start in with a chorus of cheers. And I let them enjoy the moment before I bring them back down to reality.

"The opener, guys." A sobering reminder that deadlines approach.

The fleeting moment of joy has passed, and they quickly sober up.

"How do you do it, man?" D.B. asks, presumably of my booking the dream location.

"I make phone calls," I deadpan.

"Not that. The music, Finn. How do you write what you write?"

The look on my face and the pause in my answer must have given away more than I intended. I'm not sure how to answer in one conversation what I've been writing about and trying to explain myself for decades. I don't want to lie to D.B., and this moment isn't here to brush him off. Actors pull from the deepest, darkest emotions they have to shoot hard scenes. This, in relation to musicianship, is a hard scene. I don't want to fake this.

"D.B., you have that girl, the one that got away. I'm sure everyone in this room has that one. But it's more than just a failed relationship," I start.

They have given me their full attention. Vincent has stopped strumming. Neil has put the hookah pipe down and exhales his last hit. No feedback drones in the background. Gregg sets down the sticks he was using to tap out beats on his thighs. Every ounce of attention is on me.

"You have to be willing to destroy yourself in order to make something far greater than just you. You have to be willing to destroy relationships, almost consciously. Like a speeding train toward a stalled car on the tracks. You see it happening, and no matter how hard you pull the brakes, it's too late. There will be blood. There will be pain. And there will be destruction. But unlike the train and the car, our odds of walking away are much better. It's in how we deal with it. It's that we deal with it that makes our music. Makes something much greater than we could ever be individually."

D.B. interjects, "But she's back in your life. Can't you have it all now?"

And while that is a great question, the obvious answer of yes is far too simple to be accurate. Or ever the answer.

"Faith is the greatest love I have ever known. The greatest inspiration for all my writing, in the past and now. A part of my heart has ached since we first went our separate ways all those years ago and still aches to this day. Wanting, yearning to be with her. To be with her, in her presence, is to be in the presence of greatness."

"Then what's stopping you?" D.B. prods for more.

"We hold onto things. Memories. Ideas of what once was and what could have been. Like a high school sweetheart that went astray or crush you never dared to approach. You hold onto manufactured ideas of what you thought the future would be like or who the person was in your mind and of a relationship never had."

Gregg goes to speak up but coughs a bit. A break in the tension. "Hmm. But wait. You did have her. Had a relationship."

"Yes. And we all went to high school, and college, and the memories are there. You can't go back. No one is the same as they were then. No matter what they say. So, the relationship we had then is there, in the past. To start it again would not be to pick up where we left off like no time has passed, and nothing happened in the between."

D.B. lights up, a sobering, buzzkill of a moment. "You would have to treat it as new. Learning to see if it would work this time around or end worse than last time."

A wink at him and tap my finger on my nose. "There it is. And the songs of the minstrels, bards, and lyricists of times past are not actually about the reality of the relationship. They are about the romanticized concept of what the relationship is or was."

Vincent clears his throat, a voice I've heard only a few times in the past month. "And to try again could ruin what you have to write with."

I wish he weren't wrong. He is, but not fully. There's always a part of a writer that doesn't want to ruin the illusion of what he or she is romanticizing. The rose-colored glasses give them the fuel to write. To pull back the curtain and reveal the tiny man behind it doesn't make for a great story. Just a great moment in it. But on the other hand, magic is only cool if you know how they pull off the trick and you can still find it magical.

It's a conundrum for the ages, more so than to be or not. Or being with the one you love or loving the one you're with. It's about starting over with the one you used to love to see if the love is still there. Being open and vulnerable, once again, to the person who, once upon a time, tore your world asunder.

So, when D.B. asks, "Can I have it all?" the only honest answer is, "I don't know." All I can do is try to understand where and how everything fits together.

The events of that meeting bled over into the next few days of recording track after track to get the sound just right. But unlike my first month here, I find myself now wanting to turn up the snare and adjust the low frequencies of the bass drum and floor toms. Tweaking the equalization on the guitar to get the notes ringing crisp and clear before throwing the right amount of fuzz, distortion, and overdrive onto it to give Spear Fist the sound that will push them beyond famous.

Here's the rub, though. I wouldn't be in the mindset I am if it weren't for everything I've been through since moving down to Florida. I would have influenced the band differently if things happened differently. The end sound of the album would not be what it is if I hadn't irked Jeanine into what she did because her mood and perspective on the situation affected Gregg and his input into it. D.B., Vincent, and Neil would also have contributed differently if their lives were influenced differently. Some may say that the whole feel of the album is happenstance, since it's based on the events that preceded. While not entirely wrong, it's not right either. The overall feel of the album is decided long before the events of our lives transpire, but the way it is put together—the dark, sullen tones or bright guitar solos, the use of a droning bass line or something more akin to John Myung, if D.B. is going to have angry vocals or just the other side of vengeful—those are all influenced by the events in our lives.

And here's the funny thing: While what happens to each of us every day may be coincidental, the way we handle them is what changes how these incidents affect us.

CHAPTER 12

Separate

L ife becomes a pattern, no matter where you live. Everyone has a break from the daily grind, but even those become routine and become their favorite haunts. My life is no exception. Wherever I've lived, I have my favorite places. NYC was Sunswick. Chicago was Exit and Neo. In Orlando, it has become this restaurant, our restaurant. There's something about the patio, the way it is set up. It allows for groups to sit together without being segregated from others. The fire pit in the center of it all. This day though, it looks as if they also added fire pits on each end of the patio. Not the round kind on the ground. These are raised, in fish tanks, I would guess. Glass rocks cover the bottom. Propane-fueled. Very pretty works of functional art.

It is little things like that you notice at your favorite haunts. The idiosyncrasies of a loved one that only you know about. If I didn't frequent this place, I would not have noticed. I wouldn't have known it was new. And much like visiting my favorite haunt after a brief time away at a new locale, I'm here again, grabbing a quick drink as a cosmic thank-you for things coming together. Badaboom is finished. The albums are pressed. CDs printed. T-shirts made.

And I must head over to the amphitheater. My contact is already in the middle of setting up, and I need to be too. It's nice right now—early afternoon. The patio is empty, save for one young couple eating fried cheese. A peaceful alternate from the nightly masses that gather.

But perhaps coming here tempted fate to smite me again. Maybe I should have had a drink at home and went straight to meet my contact. But fate has other ideas.

Fate has Faith.

All I want is some sense of normalcy for the day. It's too big a day, too much riding on this. Not just for me, but for D.B. and the rest of the band. Normalcy, for a while in my life. But I guess if you've led the life I've led, my normal isn't the same to anyone else. Normal is this, wanting a day free of drama and not getting it. Ever.

I get up to leave and somehow manage to make eye contact with Faith. Faith, who stands all the way at the opposite side of the bar. Past five rows of booths, tables, a bar, server station, and not to mention windows in dire need of cleaning, plus all the customers and staff inside. It would only be to my benefit if she sat facing away, so the gods have seated her facing me. She is speaking with the bartender. She has no man by her side. No sister. No killer bee buzzing around or walking mountain guarding her against the likes of me. Just her. A small ship in the storm of my life. *Why the hell is she here so early?*

I break eye contact and look back to the young couple sharing a chair meant for one still feeding each other sticks of fried cheese. It's not that I don't want to see her. I do, more than anything. But right now, I have to go to the record release party I set up. I have to call agents, managers, record labels, the people who make names. Get all the affairs in order, so it goes off without a hitch—all within a few hours. So, I can get their careers going up, up, up. I look back at Faith to wave goodbye. She doesn't wave back. She holds up a finger that universally means "Hold on a sec." For her, I'll wait a billion seconds. Always. But this timing is horrendous. I need to leave. I stay though.

It's what I do. It's one of those little things about me. One of my idiosyncrasies, for better or worse.

But this might be what it is all about. What we musicians have been singing about since we first learned how to sing. The moments spent with loved ones, whether family or the friends we consider family, figuring out which people in our lives deserve the title of family, which people deserve to stay in our lives. Moments spent laughing and sharing stories. Raising a toast to memories of the past. To inside jokes. To the little idiosyncrasies that only those closest to that tight knit group knows. Raising our glasses and sharing a drink with those that not only know us best but accept all parts of us for who we are.

Idiosyncrasies. It fits, not just now but always. All places for all people. It is a perfect word. I feel a little like Mr. Rogers, and that's my word of the day. Say it with me, Idio-syn-cra-sies.

I watch her as she heads to me. Every time I see her, thoughts of my past race through my mind. All my regrets that led me to my present. She steps closer. All my mistakes that shaped who I am. She still steps toward me. All my loves. My loss. My ambitions. She steps closer again. My fears. Dreams. Hopes. This point. The now. The "why" that answers why I am here. The curiosity that led me by the hand my entire life. Disregarding the consequences of it all. Thinking only of the possible reasons my curiosity leads. The possible outcomes of the curious situation. That is why I am stuck standing here and not running to save my sanity. And my curiosity is answered.

She exits the restaurant. Her pitch-black hair, the perfect contrast to the lightning, is with her bright smile across her face. Short-sleeved shirt showing off her sleeved arm still vibrantly colored, but also a new work of art on her other arm, a piece that, like her hair, is inked in stark opposition. A black, shaded design of spider web and lace that starts from somewhere beneath her white V-neck T-shirt and trails off just past the elbow. The unscented, dye-free lotion hydrates it enough to glisten in the bright light of day.

It brings about a newness in her. A far cry from the straight-haired, conservatively dressed young woman I first met all those years ago. A notch away from the grown woman I didn't recognize at the burger stand outside Old Town. There is this look in her eye as she smiles and heads my way. I don't know what the look means, nor if I should be excited to find out. Maybe I should be nervous. I am nervous. Anxious perhaps, but still, I know I am not getting out of hearing whatever her eyes have to say. Maybe I don't want to get out of hearing it. Maybe, just maybe, I am ready to listen to what her eyes are not able to speak.

She stops in front of me. We stare into each other's eyes, playing a game of chicken. The first one to speak loses, except I don't know what to say and I have to leave. I don't understand why she came out here to stare at me. I don't mind. There's sadness in this moment that makes me want to cry. *How did she know I'd be here? Did she spot me from inside well before I spotted her?* The look in her eyes moves to her lips, her cheeks tugging up the corners. Just enough that if you are looking for it, you'll see it. A moment later, she purses her lips, drawing in confidence to say what she needs. But as quickly as they tightened, they relax. She squints her eyes—a sign of disappointment in herself.

Without saying a word, she gestures with one finger for me to wait here. I raise an eyebrow in curiosity and nod my head. Off she walks behind the building. I let her do her thing and not spy. I pull out a cigarette and light it up, enjoying the inhale to calm my nerves because I have to leave.

Half a cigarette later, she returns with a reusable shopping bag in hand.

She tosses it at me, saying, '"Here."

I catch the surprisingly light bag and peek inside.

My clothes, keys, and wallet.

"I thought you might want them back eventually," she continues.

"I have to get to the amphitheater. The party's in a few hours," I whisper.

"I know," she says. "I'll be there too."

I may not have spoken first, but I lost the game. I'm okay with that. Faith smiles and stares into my eyes. Her mouth refuses to say what her eyes are screaming. I wish I were better at those eye-to-eye conversations. But I'm not. So, I wait. I wait for her to say something more: something like she regrets the last two decades, something like she's sorry she hurt me. But why would I want her to say those things? I don't regret the past twenty years. I'm not sorry she hurt me. My love for her, the love we had for each other shaped me, shaped my life to make me who I am. It gave me the life I have, and my life isn't a life to complain about—at least the nights and days I can remember.

Maybe she needs to tell me she's engaged. Some desperate attempt by Ronnie to mark his woman: to remind her not to have sex with me, to proverbially urinate all over her to ward off any other potential suitors who would otherwise make attempts to steal her for themselves.

A final goodbye, perhaps. Before sailing off into the sunset, forever lost at sea to me. But I don't want that. One can't simply just turn one's back on their history and pretend it never happened. Faith would have to lose her ink, strip her hair, go back to being the innocent, naïve girl she once thought she was, forget everything she has become.

So, I open my mouth to say something. But my mind is still unsure of what to say, which works out.

"Here comes Viv," she says.

I watch while she disappears back into the crowd at the bar, but I still have one eye on Viv as she sits near to me, all too aware of the peculiar events that just transpired. The look on her face is not kind.

But now I'm wondering what's next. The gods have told me once that I should have just drunk at home. I have to leave, and now Viv shows up. I don't mind that she's here. In fact, under normal circumstances, I would welcome the fact she is here, but I'm not sure why she's here too. And at noon, nonetheless. *Why the hell are people I know here at noon?*

"Thought you were at the theater?" she interrogates.

"Stopped by for a quick drink. It seemed fitting." *Why am I defending myself?*

"What's in the bag?" She pokes at it.

"Seems she wanted to give me back my stuff," I show her the bag.

"Clothes?" She tries not to seem jealous or intrusive.

"Just debris from the storm. Nothing important that wasn't replaced," I reply.

But it is—giving this back to me, not saying anything. Silence speaks louder than words sometimes. Interpreting what the silence means is a whole other story. I want to know why she sat there silently. I want to run inside after her but next to me now is a woman who offers herself openly. Viv drove through a hurricane for me. She is doing her best to be accepting of who I am and the past that has caught up to me.

And all I can think of is how I can't deal with the inquisition starting up right now. I have to go.

I look into Viv's eyes, and they desperately scream to me, "Stay! Don't run. There's so much more for you here than there. I've not hurt you and I won't." But at the same time, Viv is angry at what she thinks she saw. Angry and uncertain in the fact that she knows both her and Faith hold pieces of my torn heart. The silver lining she has in that lies in the fact we still have more uncharted territory than charted. There is no pain here, not yet anyhow. But her uncertainty also lies in the fact I'm not a big enough asshole to get up from one woman I am with to pursue the past and tumultuous present of another, she hopes, no matter how powerful the urge to do so maybe.

I have to leave.

"Why are you here?" I turn the phrase on her.

"I have to use the lady's room," she says, avoiding the answer. "Wait."

"I have to go meet my..." I start to say.

Viv interrupts, "Just wait a minute."

She heads inside and Faith emerges back out, a game of "Let's fuck with Finn" I don't have time to play.

"I left him," she starts.

I fall back in my chair. I stare at Faith with both wide and squinted eyes. A look that says, "You shouldn't have," yet at the same time begs, "Did you do it for me?"

"I didn't leave him for you." Well, that answers that rather quickly. She continues, "Don't even start there. I left him because it was time. He never was who I imagined myself with for long term. He was fun. He was a distraction." The reasons pour forth from her mouth.

I ask, curiosity piqued, "Distraction from what?"

"Life. You. This mortal coil." Her answers are curt.

I gaze at her for a moment. She sinks into a seat next to me as if saying that released the weight of a thousand worlds. But she still doesn't look happy; that gave her no solace to end things with Ronnie. She holds onto a look that foretells of a night ending very badly.

At least she isn't reminding me of every bad thing done. She is bittersweet. Like I may have meant more to her than I thought.

"And you were supposed to be just a distraction. It was supposed to be fun. It was not supposed to be this. What it was. When we met, I was using you. It was supposed to be simple," Faith says, all but confirming I am wrong about her feelings.

I feel like an asshole because I HAVE TO LEAVE. I am getting told everything I ever wanted to hear, and it should feel great—a should-be-joyous, momentous occasion but I HAVE TO LEAVE. The irony of Faith's words at this moment is "I'm not hurt nearly as bad as I thought I would be." Instead of dread or despair, I feel a sense of relief, not quite of joy. Almost relief. A sense of calm. As if my years of worry, my years of wondering, were all for nothing. Well, not nothing but rather unnecessary. The universe had my back in making sure she was okay, but the price to pay was mine.

Then she continues to tell me how it wasn't simple. It wasn't just her getting hers—at least after a while. It became something more than her selfishly fulfilling her needs. It became real. It became something she wanted, something she feared losing. But, like me, she too saw the inevitable end. Saw that our lives crossed but that road was coming to a close. That the departure would be painful and so she started distancing herself. She started keeping her distance before things got bad, I mean utterly bad, so that when they did, she could leave mostly unscathed.

"Did it work?" I keep my response short and simple. I don't want to turn this into a conversation that I fuck up, an honest chat about things that turns into hell because of my mouth.

She smiles, almost. She wants to; I can tell because her face tightens for a quick second, and it changes the look to a hint of happy.

Then she unloads, "I didn't like the fact that I used you. Yes, at first, I was okay with it. I wanted to feel something new. And you were there. I didn't like that I fell for you. But I did. I resented the fact that our paths had crossed at such a shitty time for both of us, but I stayed as long as I could. I didn't like most of what we had because of the situation. Not because of you. I've tried so many times to push you out of my mind. To make me not love you. To demonize you and make you into someone you're not. To believe the tabloid writers as if they spoke gospel because it would have made you much easier to hate. But I couldn't, I can't, and I don't know why our paths have crossed again, but I don't want them to split. Not again. Not now. I know you didn't keep yourself pure for me all these years, and I didn't do that for you. I lived my life after us, and I loved my life after us, but you're here, and I'm here, and we wouldn't be who we are had it not been for the other. So why forget all of that? Why push it all aside for possibilities that may not be? I know nothing is certain, even us, but I'd rather try us than not try at all. I'd rather bank on our past and our history. I can't guarantee this would work anymore than I could have thought back then that I'd be who I am today. But I'm here, Finn. You're here. That's gotta mean something."

I want to run to her through a field of lilies into each other's arms and hug forever. But that's not us, nor is it real. What's real is my muse, the love of my life, the woman who shaped me just confessed the weight she's been carrying for so long. She admitted everything, and she knows that I'm content with Viv. I'm satisfied with my current situation, short and new as it may be. I'm happy. There are no rock star nights of endless drugs and meaningless sex with strangers forgotten in the next day's blur. And I'm content now. Yes. I love Faith. Yes, Faith will always be my one. She will always hold the biggest place in my heart.

She will always be "that girl."

Do I wash away the foundation I'm building with Viv? Do I ignore my short time here, great as it was? Just write it off as filler, something to pass the time until Faith hopefully calls? I have a beautiful woman who accepts me for who I am, for what I am. She doesn't judge my past, but believes in the now and the future. A woman who wants to be with me. A woman who inspires me to be better. A woman whose history with me is untainted, mostly. A woman who seems to want to build a future with me.

But Faith sits before me. *Should I have known that it would have led to this? How could I have known?* As fucked up as it is, all three of us here just past noon, I somehow should have known. It is just this. And it seems that *la fortes del destino* have brought me to this, to this moment.

She stops speaking and her eyes shift to the sky above, searching the heavens for what's next.

She leans forward and kisses me. Not a hot and heavy, "Let's go behind the bushes" kiss. This is a kiss I have never felt before. A real "My hand to God" kiss filled with real emotion, love even. I hold her head in my hands. We share a kiss filled with both solace and sadness, excitement and calm. I feel myself shaking. I shake, tremble, quiver, and it feels scary. I feel like I might explode. The world around me ending in a fiery death caused by my explosion. I hear everything. The sound of her lips on mine. The sound of my heartbeat. The sound of her heartbeat. The sound of Viv saying, "I'll call you back."

I didn't hear the patio door open.

I stop kissing Faith and turn to Viv.

Both women have their attention on me. Four beautiful eyes staring at me, all with a yearning and a burning hellfire if I don't say the right thing.

I am master of my fate perhaps, but I'm a horrible captain when it comes to my destiny. I look at both, trying to find the correct response somewhere inside of them.

"I said what I said. I don't take any of it back," whispers Faith.

Viv looks at Faith, trying to read her said words while stabbing her with her eyes. Trying to piece together what was said between us. Trying to find the words to say that will sway me.

But why are two women vying for my affection, wanting me to be with them?

Viv is new and incredible, and our slate is still without a gash, unchipped. She cares for me as I care for her.

Faith has always been that one. The one. *The* one. The one that got away. Can that one become someone new? Can a man have more than one lost love?

I respond the only way I know how. I stand up. I look at them both for a moment, searching their eyes and their souls for the answer to my life's dilemma.

"I have to go" is all I say.

I grab the bag Faith returned and walk off. The women stand there and stare in silent dumbfoundedness at the audacity of my actions. I get into my car and drive off.

I pull out onto Route 192 and turn right. I watch in my rearview mirror as two wonderful women remain motionless, uncertain of what just happened. Unsure of why I was able to leave them with no answers.

Viv had driven through a hurricane to save me from myself. She's overlooked my past, which seems like that should be automatic. But I find that most people, while they say they are okay with someone's history and they tout live and let live and shit, in reality, their inner judgmental self wins. But Viv, she ultimately seemed okay with it. Because as she puts it, I "came from a time when things like that were cool."

That's the thing about her that has me so intrigued: her ability to separate me from my sins, to see the person I am in spite of all my past mistakes, or despite all my past mistakes. But I am not sure this is one of those mistakes she'll be able to look past. Maybe they will both show up at the party tonight and let bygones be bygones. But that's not likely. Perhaps I screwed the pooch on this one. Though, I was just trying to have a drink by myself before joining the evening's festivity set-up and final preparations. Now I wonder if the fading view from my rearview mirror will be the last time I see either of them.

As Faith and Viv fade from sight, I turn my sights back to the road and traffic. Something in my mind emerges, making me think of the storm. Of Viv and her roommate. Of that thought that escaped my mind. This city of Orlando. The perfect placement of it in the state of Florida. Dead center, as if demanding attention from everything else that is great about the state. I start thinking of the parks, the castle, the rodent, the dynasty, and the man who built the brand. I described it as a machine of beautiful hate. I said that because of the outward beauty it portrays, projects. It fights every second of every day to have every living, breathing member of this world see it as that beautiful creature it wants to be and not as the hateful, mechanized system it can be. The racism thinly veiled in old crow characters, the womanizing and misogyny of the man himself drawn out as a character with a cleft chin. The health-jeopardizing heat the employees must work in day in and day out. The vast amounts of land and ecosystems they destroyed to build their empire on.

And I think of this organism that defines Orlando, and I think of myself. Throughout the years I've cultivated this image, this persona of someone, like anyone in the entertainment industry, you find your crowd and appeal to them. The mass appeal. The journey of getting there, though. That's what makes me think of myself while pondering this place. The pain that I've caused. The months and years lost to alcohol-induced anger, the fights, the bruises, broken bones, the blood, sweat, and tears. All of it to make something that is, in the end, bigger than myself. Greater than any one person. But the hate, the pain that I had to produce to create such beauty, I was the machine. Unintentionally, I was producing the hate that kept the image of me so beautiful. The public image that has people come up to me on the street and give me their praise. It is a realization too many years too late. But I think on this: *Am I starting a cycle over? Is Viv going to stay and be a new Faith? Is there, perhaps, more to this story than cyclical self-destruction?* All I know is that without the chaos of it all, my work would not be what it is. I can't regret that, and I stand by those decisions. Maybe too much. But I do.

I think in each of us there is that beautiful person who causes so much pain without wanting to. Most of the time without realizing it, but we do. And when we finally face the hate we made some people feel, the pain we caused others, only then can we begin to break the cycle that keeps us moving in the same direction.

As I pull up to the valet at the grand event for the evening and toss him my keys, I realize I may have driven around longer than I thought. They are setting up the zones for valet and drop-off. The posters already line the walls and windows. Merchandise booths set up right inside. I exit my car and head through the doors. D.B. and his band have taken up post not far from the exit, talking to my contact.

She tells me that everything is set. I hand her the check that has been in my back pocket. She smiles and assures me that this will be a success.

That everything is going to be fine.

I can only hope.

THE FORTUNATE

Finn Fairlane

DEDICATION

To Kris. You continue to inspire me.

Table of Contents

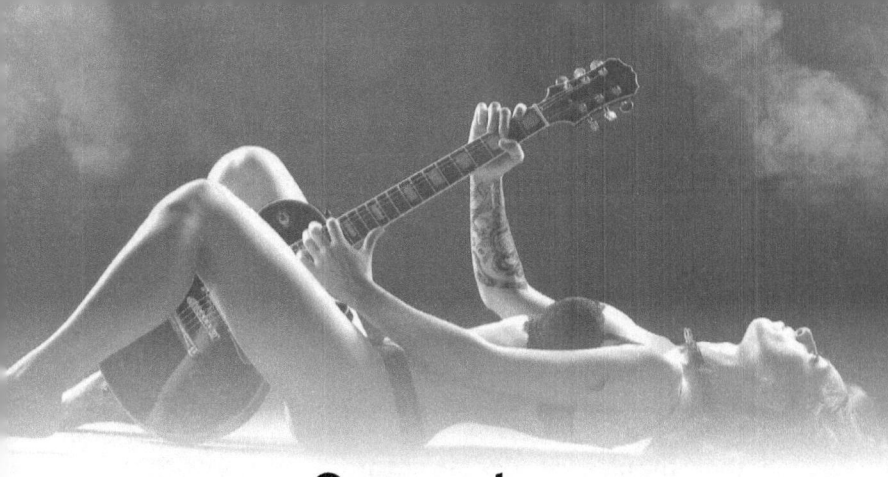

CHAPTER 1

Epic

I've been told if you want to do something, get out there and do it. Don't wait for things to happen. Don't wait for things to come to you. They won't because you have to make things happen. So, I did. It's what I've always done. I create and help others create. Right now, I'm watching this thing I helped create—this living being that breathes on its own, unsteady on its infant legs, is unsure of what direction it wants (or is able) to move. But as it grows and matures, it finds its way. Its legs become steady, and it stands firm. It plays the music it helped to create through the conduit known as Spear Fist—the music from their fourth album, *Badaboom*.

I helped create that entity. I am a very proud parent, but it has grown. It is angry, screaming and cursing—and everyone loves it.

This creature that speaks to society—whispering to listeners' souls and inspiring them—some call it a rock band, others a music group. I call the creature's musical offspring records. I must nurture it and help it get to where it needs to go. Like a baby, it must be hand-held and guided. It must be led through the tour planning and nights of travel. It must learn the steps to the nightly performance: the setlist, the solo breaks, the song intros. That's our next step: the tour.

People may think that without the members, the music doesn't exist, but it does. It has always existed, laying all in wait for the right events to wake it up and usher it forth. Then, once the music is here, it never goes away. It lives on forever, not just through the albums, downloads, and radio waves, but with every impression it creates on a listener: the in-depth discussions about the meaning of a song; the older, lifelong fan imparting musical wisdom that is Rush on some bright-eyed youth tapping the beat as he listens to *2112* for the first time; the long-haired, teenage boy in his Iron Maiden T-shirt, flannel, and ripped jeans learning the chords to "Powerslave" on his new Fender. In this instance, however, people are experiencing it live. The record release party is hugely successful, and I couldn't be happier. The current record label is here enjoying cocktails as they smooth talk possibilities with bigger labels. Potential tour managers, publicists, band managers, you name it ... they are all here. The next step is happening right now.

It is all so beautiful. New life is rearing its head, and people are liking what they see and hear. It's music to the fan's ears. Many, many new fans and old fans are all enjoying the latest child of Spear Fist. Money in my pocket, cash in the band's pockets, but it all comes at a hefty price. There's a piper to be paid in order to produce something that will not be forgotten, to be part of that which will live on as its own. We've all seen it on MTV or VH1, or read about it in *Spin*, *Kerrang*, or *Rolling Stone*, the suicides and overdoses of the greatest musicians to ever live: Morrison, Jones, Joplin, Hendrix, Cobain. The harsh reality is that there's more to that list than just the few 27 Club members rattled off, more that don't belong to that club: Cornell, Bennington, Hide to name but three.

But the price is also paid behind the scenes. It's what happens after the lights have dimmed that lead up to the hotel room destruction, fights with fans, or band member brawls played out on the nightly news or MTV, back when it was about music with the great Martha Quinn feeding it to us, bit by bit. The screaming matches and thrown fists behind the veil, the smashed drum sets, split guitar necks, cracked bass bodies, bloody noses, and broken bones; the snide comment made by someone thought of as a friend that ignited the spark that led to the crimson mess; the loved ones left behind in some small town to move out to L.A., New York, Chicago, or wherever it was that first caused the lonesome trail of estranged family and friends. The overdoses don't start with peer pressure presented to them by some cheesetastic actor from a high school video warning about the danger of drugs in health class.

It begins without anyone noticing. It's some seemingly mundane moment that goes almost unnoticed that starts it all. But a piper must be paid for the way I left Faith and Viv unanswered on the patio. Driving off, leaving behind two women you claim to love doesn't go without repercussions. The rekindling of a flame nearing twenty years old doesn't come without cost, and, much like a cable company, doesn't forget the hidden charges and fees.

Those lucky enough to make it out the other side alive, sanity intact, get to see the music live on and take a shape all its own—actually enjoy the spoils of victory. Even more rare than not being written off as a has-been or never-was, or being crushed under the weight of everything, is the most precious of them all. If we are lucky enough; the loves we destroyed; the people who got left behind; the ones who mattered the most but wouldn't, or couldn't, stand in the way of the train wreck we call "pursuing the dream" are there at the end of it all. They stand with open arms as we crawl out from the wreckage of our success.

The band is on stage now, lights shining down on them. All the guys are in top form as the music blares forth from the amplifiers. The bassist, Neil, is uncharacteristically not standing off to the side, playing in some shadow. His energy carries him from one side of the stage to the next, over and over again, as his long curly hair trails behind like the tail of a comet. The sweat flies off Gregg as he hits drum skin after drum skin after drum skin. The veins in his arm course with as much blood as they can carry to make sure he delivers the boom of the bass drum in perfect timing and that each cymbal crash rings out with as much energy as the first in the set. Vincent rocks out his guitar riffs, showing his baby off to the world, and the world is eating it up.

D.B. is soaking in all the energy from the audience and putting it back out in his performance. The light glistens off the sweat of his brow as it drips onto the stage under him. D.B. screams word after word into the chrome microphone shining under the lights, helping bring this infant to life so the audience will always remember. It's something that the audience will want to run out and buy and listen to over and over again until the song is so ingrained in their heads they won't even need the CD anymore. It will just play in their minds, every note of every instrument in perfect pitch and perfect time.

I smile as I watch the band up there. This is it. The moment we've been working for—Finn Fairlane and his band of metal men. This moment is what it's all about: all the blood, sweat, and tears; everyone and everything we left behind; the parts of ourselves lost in the making of this thing. The countless days of work that's involved, the hours locked away in a studio seeing the same four faces over and over, the lack of sleep or proper food—most people don't see it. They don't know because they can't know unless they're in it. It's not just cool jam sessions with hot girls draped over the amplifier. There's so much more than most people know. But I know. Spear Fist knows.

Standing at the archway to the stadium, listening to them, watching them with her head leaned against the metal trim, is perhaps the only person in my life who knows how hard the music industry is without being in it herself. A melancholy smile hangs on her face as she stares toward the men on stage. A distant look in her eye, searching for answers to her life's mysteries; perhaps trying to figure out if either of our dreams would have come true if we didn't have the end we had. Maybe she is trying to figure out if her dreams have ever come true. But it is the sum of our experiences that make us who we are.

When I first met her, she was a much more straitlaced businesswoman-to-be. Even her admitted growing dislike of that field wouldn't necessarily have pushed her out of it. She may have made more of herself and settled down with a guy. Who knows? Had I not met her, maybe I wouldn't have ever been pushed to do what I have done. She has been my muse, and no one can be certain there would have been someone else. All I can do right now is watch her watch them and wonder what runs through her mind.

She turns her head and looks down the row of seats to this section's other entrance—to me. Her smile grows for a moment as she stares. She gives her head a couple of slow, determined shakes. There's a thought in there. I wish to the heavens above that I knew what it was. No one shakes their head unless they are thinking of an idea that requires a response. But I don't know why her smile grew. I can ponder forever and still not know. But after her smile has grown from ear to ear, her eyes light up. Her slow indication of a "no" stops. Her determined shake turns into a nod, one deliberate nod.

I nod back and return to watching the show. D.B. on stage, mic in hand, sings his heart out. Sweat pours off his entire body. He high fives a few people standing in the front row. I watch as I see our baby come to life up there, in front of a packed house.

A tap on my shoulder pulls me out of the trance and back to reality. A simple phrase is uttered, and the voice belonging to it is not Faith's. No, that would make it simple and pleasant. It's Vivian's (Viv's) voice that indicates her presence. I do love the sound of her voice. Though at this moment, all I want to do is enjoy the show, enjoy the party, enjoy this moment, and enjoy this night for all the work we put into it. I would like to relish in it for a while. But I hear Viv say, "Hey." So, I turn to face the music.

I attempt to force a smile for her, except there's too much on my mind. No smile emerges. The simple thought of not wanting to deal with her right now, not wanting to feel the fallout of recently passed events. I just wish she would see my intentions without me having to tell her them. I hate sounding like an asshole, but I guess if I sound like one while saying what's on my mind, even if she knew what I wanted without saying it, I'd still be an asshole—if only by intention. I just want to relish the moment; savor this moment of perfection, for these moments are few and quickly fleeting. In that regard, I guess it has fleeted. So let the music play. I shall face it with gusto.

"Hey, Viv. Nice to see you here." I keep it generic to not add to her ammo.

A chuckle from her indicates pleasantry, I hope. "Cut the quaint. I told you I'd be here. You think you leaving me with Faith, not answering either of us, is the worst thing that could have happened?" she fires at me.

"Yes," I say, immediately realizing the size of my ego. "No. Well, it wasn't a nice thing to do."

"No, it wasn't nice. But it's done. It also wasn't fair of either of us to corner you like that." Viv smirks.

I don't respond, not because I don't have anything to respond with but for all the shitty things I've done in my life, calling her out on something like that would be hypocritical. So, I nod, as I often do, and turn back to the show.

She leans against the wall, resting half against it and myself, her head on my shoulder as we watch the crowd. I've always enjoyed watching the crowds. There's your usual assortment of headbangers and mosh pit participants, but I like searching for the ones who feel the music on a higher level—not the guy in the pit who's so drunk he sways in there like a 'roided-out bodybuilder. Forget that guy. He's just blowing off steam from the fact he's got anger issues even outside the pit and knows it. Guys like that are just too stubborn to do anything about it. No, the one I want isn't in the mosh. He's close to the stage, protected by the buffer zone after the pit ends.

The fan whose focus is so zoned in on the stage and the sound that nothing else is in the room with them. Those fans are the people who need this the most. The kids in the mosh pit just need a release for anger, same with the head-bangers. Whatever their need for release is, it's justified, I'm sure: bad day at work, problems at home that won't calm anytime soon, relationships, the gamut of issues everyone faces at some time. But those people out there, listening and watching with laser focus, those people need the cathartic energy. They have a spiritual connection with the music that ensures what we did wasn't a passing fad, that it will help those in need now and in the future. Those are the ones who let our spirits live forever through our lyrics, our music, and our songs.

Viv looks at me as the song plays out its final cords. I stare at her, unsure what to say since the fallout was pain-less: no punching, no crying, no thrown sticks or stones. The aftermath felt more like the calm before the storm, but maybe that's the way life works sometimes. The fallout is just there, an afterthought, something that exists in the background of our thoughts and minds. Sometimes, sometimes not.

I feel a hand wrap around my waist from the other side and slide toward Viv, which means it isn't Viv's hand. I turn to see Faith. Both women are not just within touching dis-tance but are touching. Something feels wrong. Where's the other shoe? When's it going to drop and how hard? For the moment, I enjoy the silence among us and watch the event as the next song starts. I feel they understand what I did, what I had to do to get this to happen. The shoe will drop, just not now.

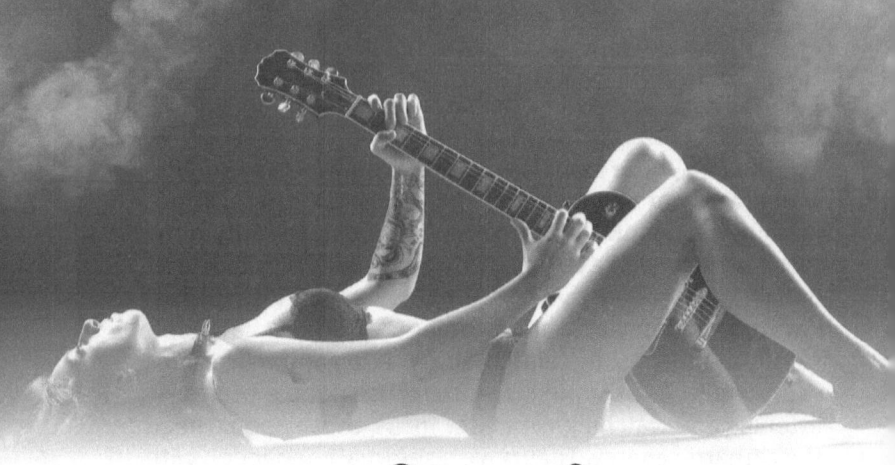

CHAPTER 2

Can't Getcha Out of My Mind

There are significant moments in life that happen, and you have no choice but to feel yourself there, caught up in the moment, taking it all in: moments where you think you understand the impact of what is happening—moments when I stand off to the side, observing, watching, taking it all in, but my idea of the situation, my perceived comprehension of the events surrounding me, is not even close to what is actually transpiring. Sometimes what you see, what you think you are experiencing, is miles away from what is actually happening. The record release party had me basking in the warmth of what I had helped create: the event, the music, the surrounding atmosphere—all seemed calm after the storm as I looked onward to the stage. So, of course, I didn't see what was happening while I had my back turned. I didn't see the storm brewing quietly behind me.

It is a new night out with D.B., Vincent, Neil, and Gregg: no strumming guitars to make girls swoon, nor talks of upcoming albums; no new swooning fans for me to sweet talk into some carnal act behind bushes. The storm of this record is over, and not only did we survive, but we prevailed. So, we celebrate. As celebratory occasions call for, we decide to check out a new spot, to break the routine and start something new—some place called Taps & Corks, an unpredictable location that is, at any given time, either dead quiet or raucously boisterous and loud. But that doesn't matter since the pool table is decent and the tap selection is one of the best in the area. It's something of a hidden, local gem, far enough away from Orlando proper to not get too many weekend warriors but close enough to have the regulars night after night like a degenerate, drunken Cheers.

We all sit outside, under the Edison LED-lined, horseshoe awning at our wobbly wooden table and chairs. We sip on our local craft IPAs, laughing and joking around. The Orlando area after dark is always whispering a welcoming hello with a gentle breeze that whisks away the toils of the day on an otherwise quiet night.

"No, no, no," I say in defense against some half-heard question as Neil takes careful, cautious steps toward us, carrying a round of shots. "I've said it before, and I'll say it again: whether it was a one-night stand or some form of relationship, I've never had sex with a woman I didn't love on some level."

The guys laugh at that and wave me off.

"So, you're telling me," D.B. pipes in, "that you've never just nailed a girl to get your rocks off with no sort of emotional attachment at all?"

"Yes. But I think you all misunderstand what I say," I retort.

"First, take a shot," Neil says, setting down a round of shots.

"Fine," I say, tapping the table with the shot glass, then downing the crappy tequila. "It's not that I've been in love with every girl I've banged. I'm saying I've loved them on some level. It's not some Disneyfied-over and unrealistic romanticism that's been drilled into me from watching one too many princess stories."

"Then what is it?" Vincent chimes in.

"It's why waste your time with someone just to get your rocks off if there's no connection at all. I could use a crusty sock for that. Make connections on as deep a level as you can, every encounter you make, for as long as the encounter lasts," I explain.

"Deep," D.B. thinks aloud.

"Not really, but thanks. Life is too short to waste on anything else," I finish.

I think they all understand my words. It's why they write music. It's why they create what they create—to make connections with people on some level regardless of having met them or not, just connections through music. They're connections on a more profound level than looking cool with an axe in your hands and girls swooning over you as you stand in front of a mic; it's why we all write music.

It feels nice to get back to where we all once were, where we all once belonged, but there's something in the air, in the breeze that gently flows by; an almost stinging sensation whose irritation is just annoying enough to not ignore but whose source you can't trace. Maybe it's the betrayal of our day-of-the-week fried food restaurant to this place that pecks at me. Maybe. Perhaps it is something more.

A red Mustang pulls up. We all turn heads, like paparazzi at a red-carpet event, to see who exits the car and who they might be wearing, except none of us really give a crap about fashion. The source of the subtle, annoying stinging sensation reveals itself as the driver's door opens—Jeanine. She emerges from her car and waves at Gregg. The passenger door opens, and a soothing balm to relieve the sting in the name of Faith steps out.

The week since the release party has been unsettling, not that anything has happened but that's the unsettling part. Nothing has happened. Faith and I haven't talked. Nor have Viv and I. I know we all have lives, but there's an eerie feeling in the air that everything is not all right, one which I will try not to worry about tonight. Alcohol and paranoia are not good friends.

The horseshoe-style patio is great because it is both intimate and open. Small groups can all fit without being on top of each other and large groups can gather while still being comfortable. Faith and Jeanine make their under-stated entrance with a simple hello to everyone and take their seats, Jeanine on Gregg's lap and Faith next to me. She sits close to me as an acknowledgment of sorts but not as close as I'd like. Not that I want her on top of me dry humping away or anything, but a tad closer as an unspoken statement that we have history. Where she sits, it feels like a drinking buddy copped a squat there. I don't want to overthink the situation any more than I just have, so I turn my focus back to the moment with friends.

After an hour or two more of enjoying the night's cel-ebration, Gregg directs everyone's attention to himself. The joyous night turns silent as he stands for an apparent announcement. Raising his glass, we all follow suit.

"This album, creating it, recording it, and releasing it, has been an unbelievable experience. I couldn't have joined the Spear Fist family at a better time or on a better album. It's been a helluva ride! You made me feel at home. Thank you."

D.B., Vincent, and Neil all nod while D.B. throws in a wink of reciprocation.

"And I want to thank Finn ... for his time and dedication to us, to the album, to helping us create something more. And because of this, we are going on a North American tour. I'm very grateful."

He turns to Jeanine and says, "But through all this, I know that you, baby, have been by my side and have helped calm my nerves on more than a few occasions. I know that you have helped push not only me but others as well." He turns to me and nods. I nod back. "In this thing we call life, I could not have asked for a better woman to be at my side." He looks around and gets down on one knee. "I know this isn't the most romantic spot to do this, but ... I don't want this to change. Jeanine Siubhal, will you always stand by my side and be the inspiration in everything I do?" I see the surprise on her face accompanied by an ear-to-ear smile as he pulls out a ring, but I'm not close enough to see if it's a ten-karat ring encrusted with stolen jewels from ancient Arabia or something he got from Hot Topic.

To me, this moment isn't about them. I turned away before I could see, what I am guessing is, her shaking her head, jumping up and embracing him in some Hallmark-fashion. No, I'm no longer watching the happy couple but am instead staring at Faith. There is a distance in her eyes as she watches the moment, trying to be happy for her sister—a fight against the happiness she feels for her sister, knowing the struggle that comes with the life she is about to (hopefully) permanently enter. She senses me staring at her and looks at me, her eyes turning to a sad sullenness. She gives a weak, fast fading smile, the corners of her lips dying as soon as they spring to life. Faith shakes her head no. Not a full shake, though, but enough so that I can see it while sitting next to her. An answer to an unasked question, but what is the question she is answering?

Jeanine and Gregg share a joyous kiss. I hope the happiness they feel now lasts through the nights of late shows, long travel, the frustration of writing, and the complex and sometimes resentful mind of the creative person.

I still stare at Faith, trying to read her mind and hear the question in her mind that she answered. Is she saying no to their engagement lasting, or no to the thought of me ever doing such a thing to her? My attempts at mind-reading are cut short. Faith stands up, says her half-hearted congrats, walks away from the crowd, enters the bar, and takes a seat at the counter. I hear the cosmic voice in my head tell me, "Go get her." I follow suit with sincere congrats and they are wholehearted, for this is a joyous moment. I may not be the biggest fan of Jeanine's, but she wasn't wrong when she blew up my relationship with Viv. Plus, she makes Gregg happy. I head to the bar and grab a seat next to Faith. My back to the outside tells her with body language that I am here for her.

She turns to me as I sit. "Seeing a car crash in Florida is not something you wonder if you'll see, just when you'll see it. When you see it happening, you know it's not going to be good, which means it becomes how bad is this going to be."

"But isn't that life? No matter what car you drive, accidents are accidents. They happen. So, why not have someone in your passenger seat who makes you smile? Someone who makes you feel like a better version of yourself? He's a good guy, Faith. Better than most out there."

She downs an entire double bourbon neat in one gulp. "Damn it, Finn. You know the road they're headed down."

"No. That's the thing; we don't know. We know the metaphorical car they'll be driving and who will be driving. We don't know who will be riding in the backseat or alongside them. We don't know. We can only guess based on our experience. Since no two experiences are alike, it means a different answer from each person you ask," I state.

Maybe she's right. Perhaps she knows what will happen, but that would be just a coincidence. Maybe she can see the future, but more realistically she's worried for her sister. Perhaps she realizes that things could have been different for her, different for us. But as much as I try not to ponder on these things, it's in my nature to wonder. If she is still so upset by the thought of it all, then perhaps there still is hope. That ever-shining light in the distance that we all navigate by praying it doesn't lead us astray: hope.

So, with hope in my heart, I speak. "We could drive together. Hop in the same car and see where the road takes us."

She smiles and points at me with a suspicious finger. "We've traveled that road before, Finn. And it was rough and broke us." She sips a new double bourbon that is placed in front of her.

"But we're different. Stronger than we were twenty years ago."

"See, that's the thing. We might be stronger, but something tells me, hell, shows me that you are no different." Faith's words sting my heart.

I have to try and soothe the pain. "Those were ... a series of unfortunate, and unplanned, events. Things happened. I want this, and something inside tells me you do too, despite your outward reservations."

"Perhaps you're right. But right now, at this moment, I'm not thinking about that. About us. Right now, I'm drinking to not think about my sister or the road she's about to travel down. I'm drinking because you might be right. I'm drinking because of her." Faith polishes off another double bourbon, sets the glass down, and stumbles back out to the crowd. As she does, Viv walks by, giving a friendly hello. Faith, however, makes a feeble attempt to smile and wave.

Of course, this is happening right now. Why wouldn't it be happening now? Every time I want to talk or have a moment with Faith to try and put back together some of the broken pieces of our past, something happens. In this instance, it's Viv. Not that I should be too upset since I do love her. Maybe love is too strong a word. I do care greatly for her. (Isn't that the Hallmark card you want from someone? "Dear blah blah, times with you have meant the world to me. I care for you greatly, but because I'm emotionally stunted, I can't tell if it's love. Sincerely, Ass-face." The card cover will have a rose on it.)

She is an amazing woman who cares a great deal for me as well. She didn't walk out when she learned the whole truth of my past with Faith. She still came to the release party after I left her unanswered on the restaurant patio. She is here tonight. The one thing that I don't understand is why Jeanine did that to her friend. I know why she did it—to get me to concentrate, though doing that to her friend was uncool. But I digress. She's here right now. The reality is things with Faith seem to be stalled on a deserted road with no hope of being fixed (at the moment). I shall see what Viv wants from me.

She plops down on the bar stool next to me, and before turning to me with that unsure look in her eye, she orders a Sailors & Sprite. I wait for her to speak. Not that I don't have anything to say, but I don't want her to feel pressured into some sort of banter if silence is what she prefers.

"We need to talk," Viv starts.

Or not; Viv wants to talk. Now my mind starts racing ... pacing ... wondering. Hell, can you do all three at the same time? I'm not sure, but if a mind can, mine is. Why is it I always feel like I'm in these unfortunate situations that I didn't put myself in? Am I being broken up with twice in the same night?

"I'm listening," I say, sipping my Boom Juice IPA. She doesn't immediately start speaking. Her pressed lips contort as she searches for her words. Her scrunched nose is making her look far more adorable than she wants. She looks so innocent at this moment, like a child vampire in a goth-horror movie right before a kill. It has me on guard.

"We talked. Faith and I, at the Spear Fist show," she says.

I give her a corrective look that sets her on a quick rapid-fire correction, "Record release party, album bash, whatever. We talked." She slows down again. "You're a wonderful person, a good, helluva guy. But you're a wreck. You're a mess of a person." She scrunches her face for a half-second at something she just said. "Helluva guy? I don't say things like that. I don't even sound like myself right now."

I want to interrupt. I want to say something that will reverse this car crash happening in front of me. But I know it might be too late for that. If it is, it is all my fault. I stare at the beautiful nose ring, snake bites, and melancholy stare that made me fall for her in the first place, hoping that somewhere in there is hope for me.

"We've had fun. A passionate, wild start. But this," Viv says, while her finger waves back and forth pointing at me and herself, "can't work. I want it to, though."

"Me too," I interject.

She puts up her hand to stop me from saying more as if, perhaps, my words could sway her. She won't let that happen.

"I know you do. You want it to work with me. But, not just with me. That's what hurts the most. That, despite everything, you still cling to what could be with Faith and not what is with me."

She pauses, the sadness in her eyes stopping her from saying what's next. My mind looks to the immediate future, in search of what could be coming. Is she walking away from everything, or will we still be friends? As if that ever really works. Her lips won't move. They try to open, but some unseen, powerful force keeps holding them shut.

She turns to her Sailors & Sprite and sucks it all down through the tiny, black stir straw. She slides it forward and motions for another before turning back to me. "I could have loved you. Like, truly, deeply, madly loved you, Finn. I was starting to, ya know. See, that's what hurts. Not falling for some rockstar I loved from my teen years. In the end, I don't care about that. I care about you, but you care about more than just me. Here's the rub: I deserve better. What makes this whole situation sad is that without me, you can care just for her. Without her, you'd still care for her. That's what hurts the most."

How am I supposed to respond? Do I tell Viv she is wrong when I know she's right? Do I beg and plead for her to stay when she's already made up her mind?

"You're the fortunate Finn Fairlane." She adds a bit of fake awe to my name. "You really are. Everyone, at one time or another, finds someone they think could love them. You have at least two women who, on some level, do love you. But you are just too stupid to see that and be with that love," she finishes as she swirls around in her bar chair to walk away.

"Wait," I plead.

She stops and turns around but doesn't walk back. "Don't worry. I'll still be around. I'm a glutton for punishment."

"So that's it?!" I say at a high enough volume that might be confused for yelling. We aren't exactly whispering anymore. The rest of the barflies are too drunk or involved in their own dealings to pay attention to our public display of affliction anyway. "That's all she wrote?!"

Viv laughs. "Is that ever all she wrote with you? Someday, after we're no longer intertwined, I'll retell the great Fairlane incidents of 2017, and no one will believe me. Maybe I'll start a journal so for all eternity there's proof that once upon a time this actually happened." She takes out her phone and snapshots a picture of me, stunned.

I watch as she opens the door to the outside world. I can see sadness mixed with overwhelming relief engulf her expression as she breathes in the warm night air. Her shoulders lift a little as if the weight of my world has lifted off her shoulders. "I'll see ya around, Finn."

CHAPTER 3

Majestic

The times, they are a-changin', or at least they are for me. As they change, I find myself back where I started down here, standing in front of the greasy hamburger stand outside Old Town, chomping away on fast food as I listen to the world around me. The sounds of locals hitting on some attractive tourist from some random city, the families seated nearby as they discuss the past day's events, laughter and screams from the rides all surround me—they swirl about my ears and my mind, trying to feed me some ounce of inspiration. I need to hear an anecdote to motivate me. I need to see some pure emotion in someone's eyes or smile to guide me, some sign within the cosmos that grabs my attention and steers me toward greatness.

The upcoming tour, and now Gregg's wedding, need to come together. This tour can't be some chump tour playing basement bars and rural barns. It needs to be bigger. It needs to launch their status in the industry to more of a household name. The wedding has to be something that won't be overshadowed by the impending tour. If the wedding fails to go off, or doesn't happen for some unknown reason, the tour will not happen. Of course, it can't be as extravagant as the tour. I must keep all the tour plans away from Gregg. I must put aside any old grievances I have with Jeanine and work toward a common goal. Not that I'm involved in the wedding. Hell, Faith hasn't asked me to be her date, and I wouldn't just assume to be her date. So, unless the band invites me, I might not even be going. But back to my point: musicians implode. I need to make sure that doesn't happen.

A mental checklist of the things I need to do: realistic tour dates, travel plans, accommodations, band lineup for each stop, marketing the tour, merch ideas. There's a whole list I'm not remembering right now. I can't. My mind isn't focusing. That to-do list seems insurmountable, in part because I can't zone in on any one point. My mind is playing leapfrog, jumping from bullet point to bullet point but never lingering long enough to flesh out any details. Something isn't right at this particular moment. I look around at the tourists and locals in their sandals and shorts. I see teenagers finding young lust. Hell, I even think I hear the same girly-man screaming on the Vomatron from my first night here, but it's just not the same. Maybe it's that the night breeze is a little cooler. Perhaps it's because I've become intertwined, on some level, with this great city. Maybe it's simply that you can't go home again. Home, in this instance, being my first Orlando muse.

I try to find any inspiration as I look around. The giant, neon entrance shines its color at me, but it's coming in dull. The drones of conversations around me ring distant. Everything around me seems far more mundane than my first encounter. The people are all having fun, but it all seems as generic as the gift shops that line West Irlo Bronson Memorial Highway. This isn't working for me, none of it is. It all falls flat and uninspired. Any artist knows when he can't or doesn't feel the inspiration surrounding him, it's time to move on.

Making things happen, making music happen, is what I've done for almost twenty years. It hasn't always been easy, and it hasn't always been fun. But when you want to do something, whether it be making some music or becoming a doctor, you do what you need to do to make your dream a reality. You give it your best shot, all your attention, and things get sacrificed: relationships fall apart, loves that could have been great—groovy kinds of loves—pass you by, family grows distant, friends get left behind. All are a means to an end, but it doesn't happen overnight. It doesn't miraculously fall into your lap without sacrifice. And it definitely doesn't happen without inspiration.

Back at my home studio, I riffle through some old lyrics I wrote. I find a few sets whose words still hold meaning and relevance. Looking over those, I listen to some old instrumental recordings I had saved on my computer. I'm searching for something, anything, that says my time down here will be worth more than the first three-and-a-half months, some notion that gives me direction on where to go next. Anything at all. Again, though, I find myself empty, staring at old, unpublished writings that do not stand the test of time. Looking at some of these, I'm not sure they had a shelf life of even a month. I need something, and I need it fast. Deadlines wait for no man. As such, I do what I do. I get in my car and drive toward inspiration.

There's no better place to find inspiration when your usual wells have dried up than a record store. Now I'm not talking FYE, or any corporate, overpriced, vague resemblance of a Spencer's-turned-CD store. I mean a real record store. One run by a few tatted dudes who have lost and worn out more cassettes and vinyl than most will ever own. A store with aisle after aisle of CDs and stuff that spins at 33 & 1/3. Park Ave CDs is one such place. Now it might not be the size of Amoeba Records in Hollywood, but the selection is still damn impressive. Hell, I haven't been to Amoeba in a while. It may not exist anymore but if it does, make it a must-stop on your next Cali trip. But in Orlando, Park Ave CDs is the place to buy.

It is here I find myself trying to flip through vintage vinyl until I stumble upon something so beautiful, so jaw-droppingly eye-catching, so wonderfully unique that I have to have it. I have to listen to what it has to say to me, and I must ingest everything it has to offer so I can give back to the universe something that can only hopefully compare in greatness. As my mind can't stand the thought of it anymore, I catch out of the corner of my eye something so beautiful, so wondrous, that I couldn't ignore it. My head turns to get a full view. I'd say this beauty is about twenty-five years vintage, dressed in torn, faded jeans, and a baggy, home-torn tank top from an old Skinny Puppy tour, with ombre hair pulled back in a long ponytail. She has on such simple attire, and it is beyond sexy. Before I can even fully take in all there is to her, she looks at me and smiles. My heart pounds within my chest. She wasn't supposed to see me staring. This wasn't a leer, just a view of admiration that went on a second too long.

"So, which is better in your opinion?" she says, holding up two CDs. I set my selection of vinyl against a support column and make my way to her. My mind races about the possibility of the conversation about to happen. I am not falling in love with her at first sight. My reverence for her is far more aesthetic. Beauty can spark creativity. It happens every day in a sunrise somewhere for a poet or a new paint job on an old car that moves a mechanic to tune up his old Corvette. As I walk the twenty or so steps around the aisle to her, my mind is already starting to simmer with new ideas for songs, locations for tour stops I haven't thought of before now, stage setups, new merch ideas, and more. Everything else that has been slumbering away in my mind is waking up, stretching out the sleep that had overcome it, and is beginning to move about.

She hands me *Jungle of The Midwest Sea* by Flatfoot 56 and *Smash the Windows* by The Tossers. A quick glance, I give them both back to her, and say, "Get 'em both."

She looks at me for a second and nods her head. "I like that idea."

"If you like raw energy, check out The Pogues, Pink Fairies, Heavy Metal Kids, or Days N Daze. Those guys all deliver. Not that Flatfoot or The Tossers don't," I offer up.

"Thanks." She smiles. "Any other suggestions?"

"If you really want an experience, pick up Nick Cave and The Bad Seeds," I add.

"Murder Ballads is my favorite." She surprises me with that response.

"Name's Finn," I finally introduce myself.

"Jacquelyn. Nice to meet you, Mr. Finn." She extends a hand.

I gently shake hers. "Just Finn. Finn Fairlane. No mister."

"Alliterative, like a superhero. Peter Parker. Bruce Banner. Matt Murdock. Clark Kent-Man of Steel. Finn Fairlane—man of music." She smiles.

She obviously doesn't know who I am, or was, which makes me wonder why she's talking to me. Maybe it is just for a good recommendation. Whatever the reason, I'm happy to talk.

I notice a look in her eye. She's searching for something in mine. I don't know what it is she's searching for. I guess it must be the same look I give people, and probably just gave her, to see if they recognize me and want to be in close proximity for some superficial reason or if they actually just want to talk. I do know that if she is looking for a music recommendation, she's probably not directly involved in the industry or a rabid fan of any particular genre, which means I don't know her or why she's giving me that look. Could she be just a regular person who happened to stop me in my comfort zone? A welcome stranger to discuss things within my wheelhouse? Wouldn't that be a nice change of pace?

"So, are good music recommendations your only superpower, or are there more?" she continues with a playful laugh.

"That and a great ability to screw things up right before my eyes," I say with an odd hand wave like I'm performing a magic trick.

"Well, Finn. That doesn't sound like a fun superpower." She adjusts the tension of her ponytail as she begins to eye the register.

"It's not, but the demolition is a sight to see." I try to save face.

"Hmm. I see. Well, thank you for the many bands I shall be checking out. You seem to know your way around a music store." She starts toward the checkout.

"I try. Enjoy." I smile back, giving her a two-finger salute and a wink.

I grab the selection of records I had leaned against the column and head to the register. While paying, I look around at the customers in the aisles and the guys behind the counter. These people are why I continue to do what I do. It's nice to be here. It's nice to have met Jacquelyn. Moments like these confirm that all the relationships I have had and subsequently blown up weren't all for nothing. While the immediate result is more often than not a destructive one, the things that grow from the ashes are, in the big scheme of things, even greater.

New tunes in hand, I say a silent goodbye to Park Ave CDs, turn my car's ignition on, and check my mirrors where I spy that next to me, listening to her new, choice picks, is Jacquelyn. She turns down the volume and waves for my attention.

"I have an extra ticket to a show this weekend at House of Blues over at Disney Springs. My way of saying thank you for the help."

"That's a very kind gesture for a simple recommendation. Won't the person you were supposed to bring be upset?" I pry.

"Subtle, Finn, but there's no one in that sense. Assuming that's what you're implying. They were just a gift." A perfect reply from a seemingly perfect woman.

I chuckle and half-smile, brushing back my hair with my hand. "Sounds fun." I grab a piece of paper and pen, get her number.

Before I can roll my window all the way up, she shouts, "Don't you wanna know who's playing?"

"What?"

"The concert. This weekend. Don't you wanna know who you're going to see?" she asks.

Shaking my head, I shout back, "Not really. Any concert is better than no concert."

She smiles at my response, rolling up her window. Between my new records and my upcoming weekend rendezvous, I would call today a success.

I drive away smiling at my fortune, ideas flowing and springing to life. This was just what I needed. Serendipity, if ever there was such a thing. Now, as there are still a few things I need to pick up, I head on over to my next stop.

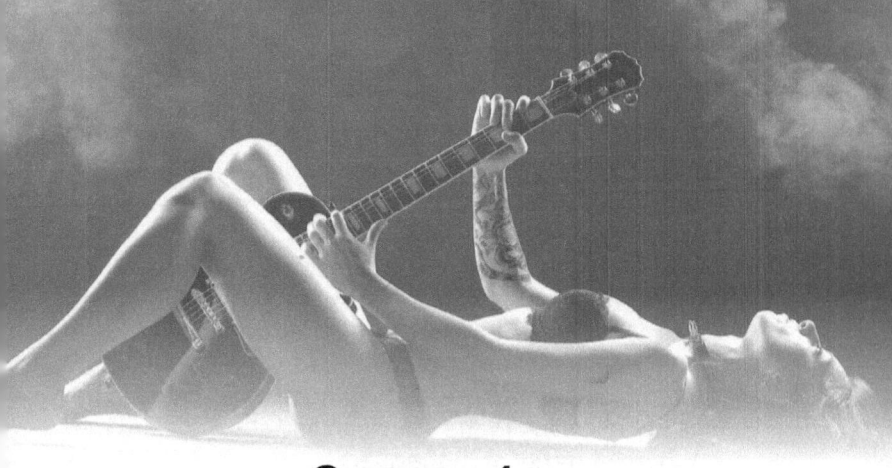

CHAPTER 4

Delirious

T he weather has shifted since earlier, so now the temperature is dipping into the chilly, high fifties. Quite a drastic drop for Florida, but being from the Midwest and New York, I am still warm, though slowly acclimating to the weather. By this time next year, I'll be cold. People, the tourists and the locals alike, don't seem to mind the chilly cold here in The City Beautiful. That's the joy of living in a tourist town. When everyone looks like they are on vacation, the warm tourists, the acclimating local transplants, and chilled local natives alike all blend seamlessly together to make this city always comfortable and the epitome of endless summer.

I step out of the coziness of my Grand Am into the nibbling cold, walk past the replica *Back to The Future* DeLorean and into, in my humble opinion, Orlando's best music store, George's Music.

As soon as I walk in, the walls of guitars off to the right that usually call out my name are drowned out by a loud, rambunctious, pink-and-black-haired girl off to the left, testing microphones at noise levels I imagine Huey Lewis telling her through his megaphone she's "just too darn loud." But there's this raw energy to her voice, one that can both hold a key and sound like she's about to spew blood from grated vocal cords.

I head over to watch as she screams in various pitches, with different vocal effects all emanating from within her. The words she sings I do not recognize, perhaps they are her own. She looks up at me with crazy eyes outlined in haphazard black mascara and clumped eyeshadow. She hands the mic back to the salesman and steps toward me.

"Whatcha starin' at?" she sneers.

"Talent."

She chuckles a bit, but her guard stays up, a feature manifested in spiked wrist guards. "Nice pickup line, bub, but I like innies, not outies."

I give a whole body laugh at her presumptuous response. "Outies and innies. Nice euphemism. Not why I am standing here, though."

She stops her shopping and gives me a moment. "Then why ya here?"

"Were those lyrics your own?"

"Yeah. Why?" she says, epitomizing the nineties image of the overly defensive new adult.

"I liked them. What's the name of your band?" I try to help her relax before she has an aneurysm.

She gives a quick breath out and shakes her head. "Don't have one at the moment."

"What? A band or a band name?" I retort.

"Band," she snaps back.

"Too bad. You've got some real potential." I start to turn away from her, slow and deliberate.

Her brow furrows, eyes narrowing to needle points aimed at me. "What the hell does that mean? Potential?"

"Potential means you have the qualities and, hopefully, capacity to do something greater," I jab.

"Listen, jerk. Don't patronize me. I know what potential means," she jabs back, poking me with a sharp, threatening finger.

"You're the one who asked what it means." I hope for a response.

She doesn't bite.

Before stepping away, I bait her by saying, "I mean, I'm setting something up, and from what I heard, I thought well ... nevermind."

She steps toward me with an outstretched arm. "Wait. I'm working with a band, but we're replacing a guy."

"So, you do front a group." I smirk.

"Yeah. Sorta," she says, averting her eyes.

"Why are you replacing a member?" I keep my tone innocent.

She gets agitated, shifting back and forth on her feet while tapping her hand against her opposite arm. "Look, bub. He didn't understand the metaphor and persisted a little too hard. You got a problem with that?"

I throw up my hands to show I mean no harm. "Hey. Good enough for me. How's the search comin'?"

"Nothing yet," she says, defeated.

"You put an ad out for one?"

"Damn." The defensiveness of her words protects her emotions. "No, not yet. Why the hell do you give a crap anyway?"

"You seem to not be having a good day. Give me your band name, site, whatever, and I'll contact you in a day or two."

"The Shit Machines," she says with a shit-eating grin.

"Seriously?" I try not to laugh. "You're called The Shit Machines?"

A hearty laugh escapes from within her, allowing her to relax for a minute. "Nope. Just thought it'd be fun to fuck with you a little."

I smile. "Nicely done. So?"

"So what?"

"So, what's your band's name?"

"Logan Square."

"Interesting name. How many albums?"

"Two. Working on the third." Her guard drops a little more as she describes her band.

"Do your albums have names or just colors associated with them?" I search her for a little more info.

"*Fistful of Nothing* was our first. *Punching Rosebuds* followed that," she says.

"*Punching Rosebuds*?" I pause between words, clearly missing something here.

The beginning of a sly smile forms as she holds up a fist and, with her other hand, curls her index finger tightly into her wrapped thumb like a tense okay sign. She proceeds to shove the fist through the two-fingered rosebud. "Sex sells. Even dirty sex."

I shake my head in amusement. "What's the title of your third album?"

"*Violent Relaxation*. Figured this one we'd keep less *Deep Throat* and veer toward astronomy references."

I don't want to overstay my welcome with her. Seeing that I do have my own things I need to accomplish, I extend my hand out for a handshake. "Thank you for your time. I'll be listening tonight and be in contact. What's your name?"

"Logan."

A light bulb goes off in my head. "Nice. Logan Square."

She smirks. "Not too dull there, mister..." She returns the handshake.

"Finn," I reply as I turn away. "Nice to meet you."

"Ya, you too."

I leave Logan be to stir in the momentary unsettling that is both her lousy day and potential for something greater. I gather the new strings, cables, the bass guitar I've been wanting, and a few new FX pedals so I can head back to my abode and create some musical genius.

At this point in the game with Spear Fist, I don't actually need to be creating new music for them at this moment, but I find the process of creation to be a cross-platform experience. It helps me figure out show lineups, plan trips from city to city, and create new music for future use. The hardest part for me is helping lineup bands to tour with, as not all groups do more than one leg. Yes, venues have their own booking agents, but I like to be more hands-on than some other people in the industry. I want to make sure things run as smooth as possible, even if it creates more work for me.

I rack up a few more thousand onto my credit card (if only for the points) and start loading up my car. On my way out the door, with the last armload of newly purchased goods, I turn back to Logan who is standing where we said our parting words, microphone in hand. On her face is, what I can only assume, the closest thing to a smile she has mustered in a long time. She's not doing anything either, just standing there in this awkward stare that looks like she's frozen in time. However, there's this look in her eye, a look that screams she couldn't give less of a shit about what she looks like in that moment. Something is going on inside her head that has gripped her and is holding her in that spot. She knows the thought is delicate, and any movement will cause the idea to flee. It is this level of self-comfort, of okayness, that makes for great stage presence.

She's not going to be one of those musicians who's up on stage worried about whether or not their bicep muscles look savage during the raging guitar solo their fingers are bleeding out when, a couple decades earlier, they were a skinny, lanky kid who had talent dripping off their chin. No, she won't be one of those. Musicians like that don't lose talent, just respect. It becomes about looks and sellability to them, not the music. I spent too many years doing that in my own way and losing respect for myself; I won't go there again. I know this Logan girl never will. Watching her stand frozen, oblivious about how others perceive her; that's what music is about, not giving a crap.

Whatever thought is playing out in her head must be a good, deep one. Something has struck a great chord in her head, and from the amount of time she's been thinking, it must be important. Hopefully, it's something to inspire her. Hopefully I helped with that.

Who knows? Maybe she does not know the source of her thought. She could be standing there, trying to figure out where the notion came from and what it all means. Either way it goes, in two days-time I'll be getting a hold of her, and if the thought took root enough in her, perhaps I'll hear about it. But now, I have work to do.

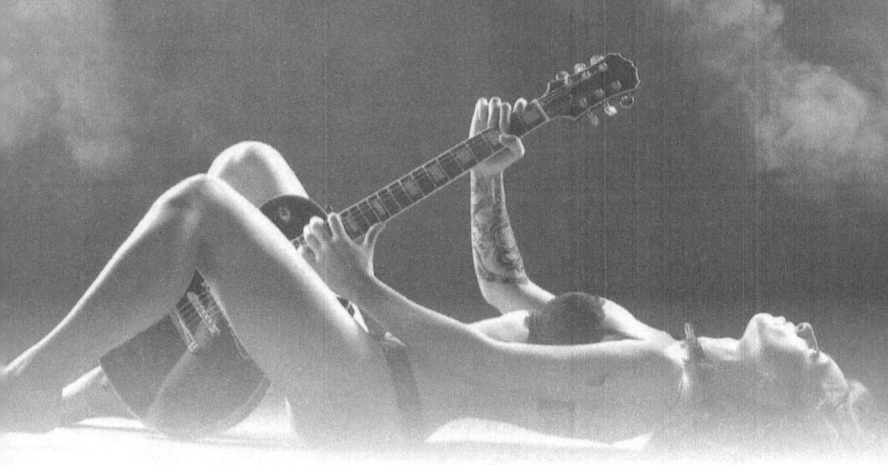

CHAPTER 5

Hazy Shade of Winter

Florida winters are an oxymoronic thing. Sure, from a technical standpoint, we have winter in so much as the season is marked on our calendars. Having lived in Chicago and NYC, I can tell you what we experience in Florida is not winter. It, at best, is a mild cooling off from the scorching summer days. The coldest parts of the nights will dip into the forties or even thirties, if it's terrible, but the days are still comfortably warm in the fifties, sixties, and seventies.

But that's the thing: cold can creep up on you out of nowhere too. What starts as a beautiful day in the high seventies or low eighties can sink down into the forties at night. If you're already out enjoying a night on the town, the cold strikes you unprepared. You're left chilly, without a jacket, flannel, or some piece of clothing with long sleeves to stave off the cold. The beginning of this winter has already been unseasonably cold. To be honest, it might still be late fall. Hell if I remember when each season starts.

I restring my guitars and new bass and get everything else in order. (I'm not wanting to wait three days for store set-up on an instrument that plays well off the wall.)

Instead of picking up an acoustic guitar or bass and fiddling away, I open Bandcamp.com and search for The Shit Machines. I do this out of morbid curiosity to see if some other group of rejects already took the name. Behold, no one has been that brazen, but there are several records named in a similar vein. After my inquiring mind is satisfied, I search for Logan Square and pull up a discography of their first two albums.

I didn't think that the small-framed, pink-and-black-haired Logan, or rather the inner angst that was her, would lead such an interesting, eclectic combination of sounds. Best likened to a mixture somewhere between Faith No More's first two albums with Mike Patton and the sludginess of Alice in Chains or The Atlas Moth. It's an interesting mix that's pleasing to the ear and, at the same time, is utterly dissonant. Lot's of 7th's in the vocal harmonies and suspended chords, but among all that, the thing that sticks out the most, at least for me, are the lyrics: relevant, authentic, and intelligently written. The anger, the pain, the hope that lies within the words all have pointed directions and speak loudly of today's collective feelings.

Yes, I now know who I want on a lineup with Spear Fist on this tour (if only for a small leg). I am not in charge, though, so I have to run it past the guys or, at the very least, D.B. I shoot him a text asking to meet up, if for nothing more than a name drop for him to check, good conversation, and a beer with a friend, perhaps a word or two about Faith or Viv if he's heard anything. I write Logan a quick message via Bandcamp reminding her of our meeting and the usual courtesy of hoping she is okay. Now I wait and see if she gets back to me.

I find myself feeling a bit peckish as I drive to my meetup, so I reroute D.B. to a new destination. This way we can grab some food too. I change our stop to a Florida staple Tex-Mex joint called Tijuana Flats. The food itself is exceptional, with a hot sauce bar to boot. Speaking for myself, it's the excellent paint job of green, dripping goo around the door frames, and a sugar skull facing the cashier, taking up almost the entire height of the wall, that I find impressive. The hair on the sugar skull flows back to the entrance door. A handful of the acoustic ceiling tiles are hand painted by different local artists, making this company an artist haven of sorts. Doubly, it gives me the ability to eat and simultaneously be inspired.

The irony here is that despite my over-glorified intro to such a Florida favorite, my meal today is their signature queso dip and chips; it's a simple, delicious snack food to fuel my evening. As I take a seat at a high top table within arms-reach of the hot sauce, D.B. arrives and orders something much more substantial than I: a double meat steak burrito with extra jalapeños, beans, and rice, sure enough to dwarf my tray of chips—at least to the outside observer. To anyone who's eaten here, both meals are fit for a king.

We stand at the hot sauce bar, surveying the ten or so different flavors, all lined up from mild to hottest. As we gather our tiny cups of varying flavor hot sauces, the idea hits me for tour stops, a few festivals added in for a broader audience. For the single-stop nights, book a few different flavors of metal. Like the hot sauce bar, they are all sauces but at different degrees. We can add bands from hardcore, metalcore, thrash, black metal, doom metal, all different genres, and make a tour stop or two more of a day-long event than just an evening out.

While we wait for our food, we get straight down to business—the tour. "I met a girl named Logan who fronts Logan Square. They'd be great to do a few shows with. Have you given any thought to the tour? Who you guys want to tour with? What cities are a must? So on and so forth." I dive into the conversation.

He takes a sip of his blue Powerade. "Yes and no," he responds.

"Those are the two definitive answers to my question," I quip back.

"Yeah, of course. I have," D.B. restarts, "but we're already running into roadblocks." He gives me a look that is both irritated and annoyed, a look I have given many times before. I have an unnerving feeling I know the source of their newfound troubles.

"Jeanine?" I ask, already knowing the answer.

He nods, drinking another sip. His eyes wander upward, unsure of what to say next. He stares at ceiling tile after ceiling tile, pretending to study each one's artwork as if he's some ceiling art scholar, but I know what's running through his mind. It's the same thing that's run through all the minds of every entertainer at some point. He's starting to think that this guy who's only an album deep with the band, who meshes well with them and is talented on the skins, is now going to make every decision, musical or otherwise, based on how his counterpart will react to it. He'll think about what she would want, what she would say, and what she would tell him to do. D.B. is worried that all of Gregg's judgment will now defer to Jeanine. He's concerned about the guy behind the drums being effectively replaced by the girl behind him.

"What's happening?" I probe. "What's she done?"

"Finn!" a voice shouts from just outside their kitchen. A girl no more than twenty-two, with curly black roots into a faded red ombre, calls out my name. I raise my hand and say, "Here!" As she delivers my chips and queso, another girl of a similar age calls out, "Danny!" He follows suit, and she drops off his food. At last, we both get to eat. Hopefully this will quell him a tad.

"She wants to be married by the start of the tour," he lays it all out. "And a traditional wedding at that."

"Three weeks till they tie the knot? Five weeks total to plan? She's fuckin' nuts," I say, queso dripping down my chin. "She can't do all that planning and us finish planning the tour? Even planning a tour this fast borders on stupid!"

"It's interfering with practice. We're tight and all, but there's more to it than just the music. You know that," D.B. responds in an almost defeated manner.

I sit, eating queso-covered chip after queso-covered chip, eyes wandering around, trying to think: trying to figure out how I'm going to handle this without disrupting the delicate balance of the band, not break up Gregg and Jeanine, and also not further piss off Faith in the process. I know Faith should be the last thing on my mind, not even weigh in as a factor to this equation, but like it or not, she's part of it, at least indirectly.

The next thing out of my mouth is the line every good person in my position says, the five little words that keep clients happy and things moving forward (at least momentarily): "I'll take care of it."

He nods through a bite of his burrito. A muffled "Thank you" escapes his mouth.

"It's what I do. So, bands?" I prod.

"A couple I have in mind, but I haven't contacted any of them yet. We've never done a full North American tour, just regional shit. Even our overseas tours were small in comparison," he rattles off, in an attempt to satisfy my question.

"No worries. I'll contact the bands—just give me their names," I say in an attempt to ease his mind. "Also, what sort of trust do you have with me just lining up some bands without needing to run them by you?"

"That's fine. You know your stuff. As long as you think they'll fit the bill, go for it. As for the bands I have in mind..." He starts rattling off a few bands I've never heard of before: Children of Dismay, Bereft, and Starkill in the Midwest; Spellcaster and Four Stroke Baron on the West Coast. But honestly, my mind is elsewhere. I imagine the talk I'm going to have with Jeanine. I'm thinking about whether Faith will be there as a witness, and if so, how I'm not going to come off the bad guy. I'm thinking about the conversation I must have with Gregg about Jeanine. But a thought occurs to me, one that has nothing to do with the music but still needs to happen before the tour: the bachelor party.

"Who's the best man?" I ask, changing the subject.

A smile crosses his face, hinting to the answer I suspected would exit his lips. "I am."

"So," I start with a deep breath, "tour in under a month that needs finalizing. A wedding that, while out of my hands, needs to happen. And a bachelor party that needs to go down without blowing shit up."

He shakes his head as he takes a massive bite out of his burrito. "Yup" exits his full mouth as food falls out.

"Looks like we've got the makings for something here," I exhale my words.

"The makin's of what is the question," he says, chomping away.

I chuckle, sipping my drink. "Best man means best man responsibility. Any thoughts on the party?" I take a crunchy bite of a cheesy chip.

While we eat and start to think, I text Jeanine, asking to meet up with her later tonight. A strange request from someone who tried to make her go away for a big chunk of her childhood. She responds surprisingly quickly.

[Jeanine: Working on wedding plans for a while. What time did you want to meet?]

Of course she's working on wedding stuff. She's planning it in record time.

[Finn: Whenever works for you. 10? 11?]

An even more rapid response: I'm not liking how quick she's getting back to me. Something doesn't feel right.

[Jeanine: Sure. Sometime in there. Taps?]

[Finn: C U then.]

But here's the thing about this. I invited Jeanine out to tell her she can't be controlling. She's working with my schedule on this. She responded fast. Perhaps D.B. and the guys are just misinterpreting signals.

"Stripper or strippers?" D.B. asks.

With a raised brow, I respond, "Do you even need to ask?"

"Jeanine will never allow any of where this plan is already headed. She'll kill him if she knows he knows he's getting strippers at his bachelor party," D.B. realizes.

"Don't worry; Gregg won't know anything," I say while smiling a shit-eating grin.

"He still has to get married after this whole thing. You can't blow up the wedding because of some grudge against Jeanine," he scolds.

"I'm not going to," I defend. "But I'm also not going to walk on eggshells because of her either."

"Fine. We'll need food. And drinks," D.B. states the obvious.

"Done and done. I know a bakery that sells booze-filled cupcakes and booze-infused ice creams."

D.B. shakes his head at me. "You know places that others wish they knew. You sure we can do all this without blowing up the marriage?"

"Trust me. It will be a night to remember."

We enjoy our meal in a strange silence that only good friends can have. It's an unspoken understanding that our food needs tending to, as if by talking more, the food would not taste as good. So, we sit, enjoying the rest of our meal in silence.

D.B. finishes off the last bite, wiping his hands and mouth on a few napkins. "So, I saw Viv chattin' it up with someone new. You and her through already?"

I nod and search for a better answer, but it's hard to place words about twenty years of mistakes and yearning into a sentence or two.

He returns my nod after a moment. "I understand. Faith," he says.

"Yup" is all I can muster.

"We all have some version of Faith. The hand we couldn't quite hold onto long enough. Just slipped away like in the movies," he says.

"I got the comparison," I say, wiping my hands on a napkin.

"You and Viv seemed tight. She likes you. Or did. Whatever," he says, standing up to get a refill.

"It's all good, brother. Things happen. I gotta go talk with the bride-to-be now. See ya soon."

He bids me farewell with his two-fingered nodding salute and a wink.

On my drive to neutral ground for my meeting with Jeanine, I try to organize my thoughts. I attempt not to think about Faith and all the things I still have left to say. That's if she's even there—there's a small part of me that hopes she joins her sister. Another part, however, prays it's just Jeanine because then I can concentrate on the task at hand. I can help ease the tension the band is feeling over all this. I can also help her understand that a traditional wedding in three weeks' time isn't realistic for many reasons, but a ceremony and reception of a less-traditional sort may be feasible with just close friends and family. A nice chat is possible about how the guys worry about her becoming the proverbial Yoko.

But there's this larger part of me that hopes Faith is there. A piece of me wishes she tags along because she wants to see me; a part of her wants to be with me and that she rode with her sister to profess she was wrong. Maybe she doesn't want to throw away a second chance because of a rocky start, and that she is sitting there because she shouldn't have left things the way she did. But I know I'm not that lucky.

No matter now, though. I pull up to Taps & Corks to have my friendly-yet-professional business meeting with Jeanine and, behold, a sight for sore eyes. Sitting next to Jeanine, drinking a bottle of some craft IPA, is the tattooed, dark-haired raven that is Faith. The almost two decades after our first parting pales in comparison to the past two weeks, knowing that she is here, in Orlando, right down the road, yet still so far away.

I take a deep breath before exiting my car. I exhale, trying to push out all the nervous butterflies that still float through my insides every time I see her. I'll walk inside and say a friendly hello, no undertones of desperation or unconscious hinting at wanting to drag out our current demise. I step out of my car and shut the door. The sound of the door slamming shut as some guy stumbles out of the establishment grabs their attention, causing them to turn in my direction. They both raise their drinks in acknowledgment of my arrival. I see a friendly look in Faith's eyes, where she isn't staring at me with daggers waiting to pierce my heart. It's a nice start, but things can change. I see Jeanine, pointing in my direction and speaking a few words to Joe, the bartender, as I make my way to the door. He glances my way and nods as he begins pouring a Shanghai Tea. A drink on Jeanine is a gracious act from someone who spent a good portion of their younger years trying to drive me insane. Perhaps people do change.

I take a seat at the bar as Joe sets down my Shanghai Tea. I go to take a sip but end up drinking it all in one go. Perhaps I'm not as ready for this as I thought, or I just need a little help from this alcohol-infused friend.

"So, Mr. Fairlane," Jeanine starts, "I trust you've been good."

I try not to glance at Faith. I don't want to see the look in her eyes as she awaits my response. On the same note, I don't want to see if she's not looking or doesn't care at all. "Doing what I do. Which is why I'm here."

I see Faith nudge her body toward us while trying to act like she is watching the television and not listening. She polishes off her drink in the meantime.

I signal to Joe to whip us up another round and watch Faith as she glances in our direction for a moment, surveying the scene to make sure Jeanine and I are dealing no further damage to each other.

"And why exactly are you here?" Jeanine pries.

"The band is my business. Literally. Their future partly lies within my hands. Their business is my business. What affects them affects me. No one is mad here, but some people have some concerns about things," I say, watching Faith roll her eyes at me beating around the bush.

Jeanine twirls her hand, urging the point to come around. "What exactly is this thing that affects you and them that they aren't mad about but just concerned about?" She pauses for a moment. "Did I catch the drift of your vagueness?"

I laugh at myself because, as annoying as I find her, my respect grows for her with each encounter. I can understand why the guys want me to handle this and not them. She can be a little intimidating.

"Yeah, you did." Now it's my turn to pause because I don't want to blow up the band or her relationship with Gregg, but I don't know a gentle way to bring it up. "Five weeks is an unrealistic time frame to plan and execute a wedding. You only have three left. They will go by in the blink of an eye." "Execute" may not have been the best word choice.

I see Faith turn up the outer corner of her lip. A hint of a smile that sides with me, but who knows how far along she'll ride in my lane on this?

Jeanine straightens herself up in her seat, the words she's about to say dancing on the tip of her tongue. "I don't want him going on tour and forgetting about me at the first pair of tits to flash at his concert."

"Wow. First of all, why say yes to a man you think would forget about you over a pair of breasts? Secondly, Gregg's not that type of guy. He loves you and listens to you, which is the second point I need to talk about."

"What? That he listens to me?!" A proverbial defensive barrier erects around her in a flash. She is on full defense. "Like that's some bad thing to listen to your fiancé? Like I'm supposed to be nothing more than eye candy standing off to the side?"

I interrupt as I roll my eyes, "Easy there, killer. Not what I meant." I pause for a moment, hoping she will calm down.

"Then what do you mean?" she huffs out.

"I mean he's a talented musician with thoughts of his own, and some people feel that he's deferred all his judgment to yours," I say, downing the rest of my drink.

"So, I'm some fucking Yoko Ono now?" she fires back.

I take a long, obvious exhale, trying to calm myself and give myself a moment to think.

"Nooo," I say, rubbing my face. "I'm saying Gregg is a musician: delicate ego, not all that self-confident when it comes to the ladies, and, in this case, that's you. What I guess I'm saying is that he needs some reassurance from you that he can think on his own and that you don't hold it against him if he disagrees with your opinion."

"Couldn't have just led with that?" she says, with a small smile on her face.

"Not sure I could have. But now we have to address the first point." I signal for another Shanghai Tea.

"I want to be married, and I want to be married before the tour. In that, there's no leeway," she commands.

I nod my head. I have to think about how I'm going to respond because, again, I can't blow anything up. I can't point out the obvious: that the tour is only four months, and even that is a short amount of time to plan a wedding, or on a more existential note, marriage doesn't change anything in a relationship besides your surname.

"Okay, granted. But give me that the timeline is a little insane," I say, hoping to start a compromise of some sort.

"Yes, it is," she confirms. "But I have all the details figured out. All the big ones anyway."

"Like?"

"Colors for the wedding, besides white. Flowers for the tables. Officiant. DJ. Food. Open bar. Invitation design. Guest List. Rehearsal dinner and everything along with that. Even a list of about ten halls because of the short notice." She pauses with a smug, self-satisfied smile on her face. "Is that okay with you, or am I missing something?

"Time for guests to RSVP and make plans in their schedules to actually come to the wedding?" I retort in jest.

"Done," she says.

One word can sting sharp, but I'll play coy.

"I assume mine got lost in the mail?" I ask.

"No. Just assumed you'd be there. You are the band's go-to guy after all."

That settles that matter. And like that, the sting is gone. "Thank you. What about Gregg's input on the event?"

"We've been together long enough for me to know what he'd want. That way I can leave him to the band. I've been planning my wedding ever since I was a little girl. Everyone thinks about it. I just went a step further."

I see Faith nod her head as her sister speaks—her way of confirming what Jeanine is saying.

"I didn't realize you were that insane, but cool. It works," I kid.

I see Faith tighten her lips and tilt her head at my statement, a motion that says I didn't say the brightest thing just now.

"Not how to calm me down, Finn. There's nothing insane about wanting a great wedding. You only get one if you do it right."

"Wrong correlation, but I know what you mean," I say, not meaning to further stoke the fire.

"Wrong correlation?" she starts. "What the fuck does that mean?"

"I mean that you only get one wedding if you do the marriage right, not the wedding," I respond, hoping she backs off the point and gets back on track.

"Whatever," she snorts back. "I'll be married by the time the tour starts and everything will be better."

"Better?" I ask. I glance at Faith, who is shaking her head no to my question.

"Yes, better."

"Okkayy," I say. "So, three weeks and a wedding and tour finalization."

"Yup."

"You'll let him make his own decision and not hold a grudge if his opinion differs?"

"Yes."

"And you'll deal with the wedding stuff so he can do what he needs to with the band?"

"Sure."

"Sure?"

"Yes."

"All right."

"All right."

I turn to my new drink I have yet to pick up and polish it off in one take. "It's been a pleasure, ladies. Have an excellent night." I turn toward the door and begin to walk out. No begging or pleading in my eyes. No desperate tone in my voice. All business. All business and no Faith.

"C'est la vie," I whisper to myself as I open my car door.

"Wait," I hear Faith call out as she exits the bar. A sight for sore ears if there ever was one: a simple word to satiate my yearning for her to speak to me.

I turn to see her double time her steps toward me. I keep the door open but wait for her to reach me. While I do love the dance we do, I am a bit worn out tonight.

"I like the way you handled yourself in there," she starts. *Not a terrible way to start this off but where is she going?* I wonder. Is this a simple thank-you, then off for the night with her sister? Or is there more?

"Thanks. I had a little help from you," I admit.

"Saw my face a few times, did ya?" she laughs.

I return the laugh. "My mind still can't get over the fact she's not ten and trying to constantly ruin our, um, private time."

"She's grown and everything. Quite the spitfire when she's so inclined." Faith beams with pride and admiration for her little sister. Her sentiment brings a sparkle to her eye.

It is in this moment that I see why Faith was so unexcited for Gregg's proposal. Why she has the worry she does for her sister and that while, perhaps, no one can make Jeanine fully understand the future she has laid out for herself, I may be able to help shed a little more light on it.

But as quick as the sparkle is lit in Faith's eye, it has diminished. She jolts back to reality by the weight of the situation. Faith turns to her sister, who is laughing it up with the bartender as he says something to her, leaning in close.

"I'm not going to beg," Faith starts.

I want to say, "that's not your style," but she knows that, and I don't want to interrupt her either. I want her to keep her flow.

"But say something to her," she finishes.

I shut the door to my car. "What do you want me to say?"

I could point out the obvious; I owe Faith nothing, and that she broke things off with me, again. First, almost twenty years ago and again more recently. I could remind her that we are not an item, a couple, a force against the world. I am under no obligation to oblige her whims to protect her little sister, who, as I've learned, needs no protecting.

But then there's the other side of me. The side of me that will forever yearn for Faith, forever want to make her happy, want to see her smile. I know that my conflicting emotions are nothing new. My inability to take a side and stick with it will always be my downfall. But it's the hopeless romantic in me that idealizes what we could be. And it's that side of me that will always win.

She turns back to me, a sullenness in her eyes that screams please. A look that is begging me to do this for her because she knows I might be able to say something to her sister that will get through.

Damn me and my never-ending desire to see her smile.

"Anything," she says.

I nod and put up a finger for her to wait outside. I make my way back in and cop a squat next to Jeanine.

"Did we forget to discuss some other fun topic for the night?" Jeanine starts.

Joe the bartender sees me sit back down and before he even takes a step in my direction, I motion for another drink. What harm could it do?

"It's not all glitz and glamour," I say, starting with the obvious.

"Oh, God. Did Faith send you in here to give me some cautionary tale from inside the scene?" she says with a snicker.

"Nope," I say, taking a sip of my newly poured Shanghai Tea. "Just wants me to tell you something."

"So? What are you going to say?" she says, sipping her drink.

"I loved it. I wouldn't take it back for anything," I say looking out the window toward Faith. "But that's because she chose to leave me. Had it not ended, who knows where I'd be today."

Jeanine laughs. "So my sister sent you in here, in some last attempt to warn me of the road I'll be taking, and your warning is, 'You loved it'?!" She takes a drink and continues laughing. "How peachy."

"I loved the one-night stands and booze and drugs and fame and everything that came with it," I pause for a dramatic moment. "Because I had to love it all. You don't get the nights after a show goes off perfectly without the hangover and pain that comes the next morning. The angry boyfriends chasing you down the road with a baseball bat in some vain attempt to defend some cheating girl's honor. But that's not Gregg." I pause to take a sip from my tea.

I watch as the look of self-satisfaction and all-knowing starts to disappear from her face.

"I loved the mornings after when some girl I didn't know was staggering out from my bandmate's room in nothing but panties, rubbing the sleep and drugs out of her eyes, searching for the rest of her clothes scattered throughout the apartment or house or wherever we happened to sleep that night. Nights before those mornings were what the music is all about. But it's also about the overdosing and being there when it happens. It's about the downward spiral into addiction from not seeing anyone you love for months at a time. It's about the fights with bandmates because single-serving strangers night after night wears off and gets stale, and the bandmates are the only consistent sights, yet they drive you nuts. The inability to see the ones you love and, even in the day of Skype and Facetime and Snapchat, sometimes not seeing them for days or weeks at a time, because that's how busy life can get for people.

And it's fun, and it's crazy, and it's maddening, and it kills, sometimes fast, but most of the time, it kills very slowly."

"So, what are you getting at, Finn?" she says, straight-faced as straight-faced gets.

"I'm saying Gregg is not like that. But he'll be around it every day he's away. I'm saying that even the happily ever afters in this industry are not nearly as happy as they are made out to be. And most are definitely not ever after. I'm saying this is the way things are, and you'll be on the sidelines while he's gone and that can be months at a time. It will be equally hard for you. Thoughts that you never thought you'd have will form in your head and will haunt you. You'll obsess over them and not know why. You'll rationalize the thoughts, and it will placate them for a while, but they will creep back in and will have grown and gotten worse. I'm saying Gregg is not like that. He's not like me. He's a good guy, and if you think everything I just laid out is okay, then Godspeed. That's what I wanted to say. Gregg's a good guy. But so was I at one point—at least I'd like to think so."

She sits there, barely breathing. I already see the thoughts forming in her mind. Now I have to wonder if I planted them there or if I was just the guy watering the seeds that were already sown, by Faith possibly. But they are there and sprouting.

"I'm saying he's a good guy, Jeanine. I'm saying he needs to be an active member of Spear Fist without you encroaching on that part of him. I'm saying this because it is my job to look out for the band, to look out for those I love. And while yes, you were the annoying little sister always trying to poke your nose where it didn't belong back then, you've grown into someone I respect. So that's it. That's how it is, and what you'll have to deal with. If it's starting to cause issues already, then you're in for a very long road, but Gregg's a good guy. He's not me, or at least not the version of me you remember."

I finish off my drink and salute Jeanine good night. I head out the door to an anxious, waiting Faith.

She waits at my car, pacing back and forth.

She hesitates with the nervous words she is trying to say. "What did you say?"

"The truth," I say. "It's what you wanted, isn't it?"

She nods and grabs my hand. Immediately, thoughts of a thousand different ways this could go start flooding my mind. But I try to quell the thoughts. This has not gone well for me in the past, and I am done getting my hopes up for someone who doesn't want me as I want her.

"Thank you. For talking. With her, with me. You don't owe me. But still, you do these things," she says, keeping eyes locked with mine. "It's these things that keep drawing me to you. These things that make me rethink everything."

"What are you getting at, Faith? I just said a few words to your sister. She proved herself to me. I respect that." I keep eyes locked with her all while trying to throw up a veil between us.

She lets go of my hands. "Finn, tomorrow night there's some of us meeting up at the restaurant. You should come."

That took a sudden and drastic turn. Did she see the veil and not what was underneath? Is she choosing to finally stop the dance we do so well, or is she slowing the tempo down a bit?

I smile because I want to say yes, but I've always said yes. I still want to succumb to my desire to be hers and her be mine. This time, though, I can say no, only because I have a prior engagement. This time it's not for a fan, or for a chance to get laid, or for some situation that will end badly. It's just to make a new friend and see a show.

"Thanks, I'll try to make it, but I'm heading to House of Blues to see a show."

Her eyes turn away from me. "Oh, that's cool. I mean, it was just a whatever. No worries if you can't."

"What is that?" I say, referencing her sudden tone change and verbal garbage. Is she suddenly shy about her feelings toward me?

"What's what?" She fails to be coy.

"The 'oh ... I mean.' Like you're asking me to a school dance, and I just said maybe."

"Nothing, Finn. Damn. I'm trying to be friends, civil, cordial, whatever since we're obviously going to be in close proximity for a while," she says, backing away a few feet.

"You left me," I remind her while opening the car door. "Again. I have plans. I'm not avoiding you. I'm not sidestepping anything. I have plans." I get in my car but leave the door open.

"Is this business tomorrow or a date?" She crosses her arms.

"Does it matter? You left me." I close the door and start up my car.

Faith steps up to my window, tapping on it. I push the button to lower the window.

"I don't want to be enemies." Her words are soft.

"We're not. But you wanted me to stop chasing you. You said that I hadn't changed enough. You said things, and these things all indicated for me to stop trying. So, for now at least, I am." I start driving off and watch Faith in the rearview as she stares at me. I can't tell if she's shocked I drove away or shocked I'm not trying to get her back.

I want her back. I do, but I'm not going to plead and beg. I spent too many years destroying good possibilities all at the thought of her. She's here now and has made it clear that she and I are not a thing. So why should I keep jeopardizing potentially good relationships for the off chance of her and me being an us? Besides that, tomorrow is just a thank-you for good CD recommendations.

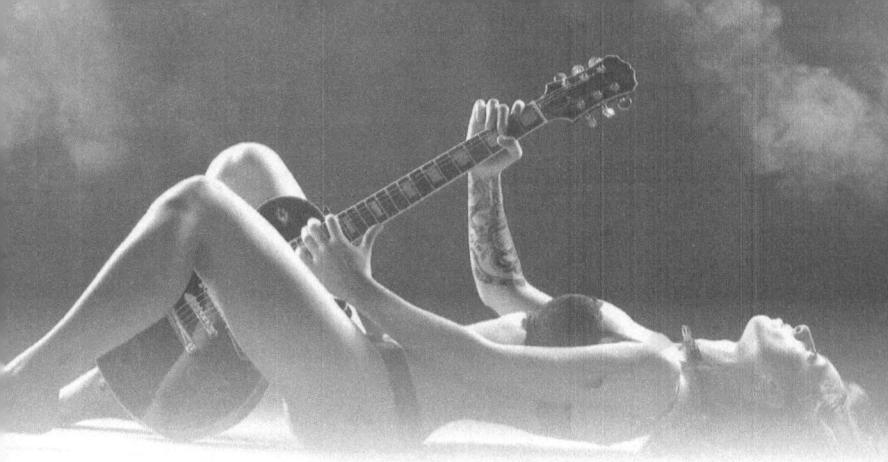

CHAPTER 6

Speak of the Devil

The start of this day is one that has become an all too unfortunate, common occurrence. A quick view of the news that plays out in the background as I eat breakfast tells of another school shooting, another group of kids dead. So goes life. I'm not overly left or right, but the sad fact is the people discussing gun control keep having the wrong conversations about it. Hell, I guess if I knew the proper discussions to have, I'd be in politics. But I can't help think that these kids don't even have a chance. I wonder how many of these kids being buried now even experienced a first kiss, a first love, first lay, or, hell, been in a fight. Seems unimportant now but without these small things, the bigger things like a first heartache or a first bloody nose from that first fight can't heal. It's in the healing that we grow stronger. However, it's the politics in between that kills these kids. What makes me feel more than slightly selfish in this whole thing is that I feel inspired to write.

Long Walk, Short Drink

No one's been perfect in history,

THE FORTUNATE *Finn Fairlane*

But some cross a line into insanity.
Tell us lies that become crystal clear
The thin veil that stops calamity.

Leading us down a ten-mile road
To three ounces of water.
Hundred and five and the sun beats down.
That's a long walk.
Leading us down away from our homes
To three ounces of water.
One o' five. Hell, we all might die
On a long walk for a short drink of water.

Feeding us bullshit they call steak dinner
Just to calm the masses.
We chew it all up and when we shit it all out,
They feed it to the lower classes.

Somethin' should go here, a line 'bout policy.
Somethin' 'bout the way we ship overseas.
Somethin' 'bout labor and cheatin' our own.
Somethin' 'bout jobs and bringin' them home.
Leading us down a ten-mile road
To where there used to be water.
Hundred and five, hell, we're all gonna die
On a long walk for a short drink of water.

Don't get me wrong; these lyrics may seem unrelated, but the point is still relevant. Living in Florida, there hasn't been a school shooting—yet. Who knows what the rest of 2017 will hold. I'm sure, though, that it'll come soon. We already had Pulse nightclub.

I can't let the daily news keep me down, not today. I have to find a way to relate it all to music, since that's what I do. A painter would take it out on a canvas. A novelist would write a book, and a screenwriter a screenplay. I make music. If art isn't a reflection of life, then what is it a reflection of?

After I finish writing the lyrics, it's time to make a few calls and book a few more tour stops. A task that doesn't take a terribly long time, and since I have some time before meeting Jacquelyn, I figured I'd call Faith, see if she's down for a quiet drink before she's surrounded by friends.

I find myself back, sitting at the day-of-the-week-fried-food-two-hundred-grams-of-fat-per-entree-overpriced-restaurant patio that not too long ago was our almost nightly haunt. While I wait for Faith, I feel a set of eyes staring at me. It's one of those things no one can explain, but when someone is staring at you, you feel it. The hairs on the back of your neck tingle. A voice inside your head silently warns you to look up and meet those eyes, which is what I do. I look up and see a heavyset lady in her fifties staring at me. The look on her face is anything but pleasant. I hate to use this term, but if she doesn't have resting bitch face, I don't think anyone does. But she sits, staring at me with her frizzy, sun-bleached hair in desperate need of attention, sunglasses resting on her head. I'm just sitting here with my drink, minding my own business while I wait for Faith, but here she is staring at me. Her judging, quadruple chin chastises me from afar. I smile at her, trying to disarm her razor-sharp stare, but she just snarls and shoves a whole mozzarella stick into her mouth.

As my level of feeling uncomfortable couldn't get worse, my savior arrives. Faith pulls up and gives a quick wave at me from inside her car, acknowledging my presence. I turn away from the bitter, middle-aged lady who stands up and walks in my direction.

Faith takes a seat as the lady stops at our table, eyes still trying to pierce me. "You don't remember me, do you?" she asks with squinted eyes.

From her words, I feel like we may have met before, and it went far worse for her than it did for me. "I'm sorry. I don't."

She nods her head and snorts a self-satisfying laugh. "Of course, you wouldn't! The famous Finn Fairlane, once too big to take the time for the little people. How's it feel to be one of us?!"

I look to Faith, whose look of confusion while shrugging and shaking her head almost makes me laugh.

"Look. I apologize for whatever I've done. I'm no saint, and sorry if you mistook me for one." My apology may be sincere, though I doubt she'll take it that way.

She looks away in disgust. "You left me and a line of people who'd been eagerly waiting hours to meet you. You just up and left with no reason why. You may have been famous once, but that time has passed. You acted like a grade A prick. I hope you're happy with yourself!"

She storms off after relieving years of repressed anger toward me. But she opened a floodgate of unpleasant memories, memories I wish weren't brought up tonight. The news from the start of my day is a foreboding of things to come.

But here's the thing of it: I sat and judged her moments earlier based on what some would call "resting bitch face." That's assuming I saw her before she saw me. Otherwise, she was giving me a dirty look. But I don't know her. Just as she judged me for all these years based on one action taken in bad timing, I judged her. How do I know she is not dealing with the loss of a loved one now like I was back then? If not a loved one lost, some tragic event that is causing her to take out her frustration on a stranger?

That's another thing in itself. People see a television star, screen queen, musician, whoever in real life, and think they have a solid understanding of that person based on a character they played, a song they misunderstood the lyrics to, or an interview or two they've watched on television or read in some magazine. But they do think they understand, so they approach and feel far more comfortable than the celebrity. And people will talk to you like you've known each other for years. Being on the other side of that, it's not always comfortable. It mostly is us thinking that we must pretend this stranger is a welcomed friend when all we really want is to be left to our own devices.

But what happened, happened. Some lady I didn't sign a picture for years ago got mad at me today.

"What was that all about, Finn?" Faith asks in a state of confusion about the whole event.

"Something from a long time ago," I say, finally turning back to Faith. "Fun times, right?"

"Always an adventure with you," she says while laughing.

I just nod at her comment as I sit in awkward silence, my mind still lost in the memories the stranger resurfaced.

Faith watches me as I stare off into the vast distance. I can tell she's trying to read me, read my mind, but this incident she doesn't know about. She never heard because it was after we broke up. I kept it out of the news. But she tries to read my mind as she stretches her neck to reposition her head so she can stare into my eyes more comfortably. It is a welcome distraction from things long past.

"As fun as it is to sit here and watch you space out, I could be doing other things with my time," Faith semi-jokes.

I snap out of where my mind was taking me and come back to the moment with Faith, a smile on my face.

"Sorry. How have you been since...?" I let it trail off. She knows what instance I am talking about. "We didn't get much of a chance to talk standing in front of my car."

"Pretty good. Viv and I are becoming friends." I don't even need to hear the rest of her thought as she begins. I can feel that the rest of it will not end well for me, but on the other hand, if it doesn't end poorly for me, maybe it ends well for Faith or Viv, or both.

"She's quite the funny person," Faith continues. "I can see why you feel the way you do."

What the hell does that mean: "Feel the way you do"? I can sense her undertone. The subtlety of her fishing for me to confirm that she used the wrong tense: that my feelings are passed, gone, and dead. Why Faith needs such affirmation on this, I do not know. She's made her stance clear. Perhaps it's an "if Faith's alone, I should be alone too" thing.

"She's a good girl, but she saw too much of you when she looked into my eyes and not enough of her." I tell her that because it's honest. I don't expect Faith to run into my arms for some happily ever after moment, but if she needs solace, I can offer that.

Speak of the devil, and she shall appear. As if summoned from the "Finn doesn't need more crap today" section of my life, Viv enters through the swinging metal gate.

Faith turns as the door slams shut, acknowledging Viv with a head nod. Something about this moment actually seems a bit more relaxed than the last time we three were sitting on this patio.

"I know you don't have too terribly long," Faith says, turning back to me. "So, I told her to come early. Sitting alone on a restaurant patio can give off the wrong impression."

Viv grabs a chair next to Faith. "Finn," Viv says in a direct and almost unfriendly manner. The smile on her face contradicts her tone.

I return her greeting in the same manner, which causes her smile to widen. She does have a sweet, beautiful smile. Her snake bites beautifully accent it. I find it ironic and slightly amusing that here the three of us sit again, though this time on better terms.

There is another strange, extended moment or two of awkward silence. Three grown adults sit in this uncomfortableness of knowing each other and each other's recent pasts. It's this silence of not knowing what to say but not wanting to engage in small talk about the weather because small talk would seem petty. So, Faith and I sit, sipping our drinks, while Viv just kind of watches us, adding to the uneasiness of the moment.

After what seems like an hour of silence, but was probably more like forty-five seconds, I decide to stop the junior-high charade. "Drinks?" I ask.

A unison "yes please" from both ladies sends me inside for refreshments. I stand at the bar, waiting for my drinks, while a bartender who looks like he belongs in a dads-only rockabilly band pours them for me. No visible tattoos or piercings but he's got the pompadour, chops, sly smile, and softer-sided rockabilly attitude, and he seems kind enough. I turn around and watch through the windows as the two women I love are sitting on the patio, side by side, engaging in some sort of conversation and, judging by their faces, a pleasant one too.

I find strange happiness standing at the bar, watching them talk. Faith seems happy, or at least not weighed down by anything at the moment. There's a part of me that is at peace watching her. Faith laughs at something Viv says. A smile crosses both of their faces. For a second, it makes Faith look like a mischievous cherub. She used to be my mischievous cherub.

The clink of the drinks being set down behind me is my cue to pay the barkeep and return to the world outside. I toss him a ten spot for his efforts. He thanks me with a two-fingered salute against his downward tilted head as he nods and winks. Very befitting of him. I'd expect no other sort of thank-you.

I head back out to the uncomfortable silence, but that time has passed. Instead, I am greeted not by a "Thanks for the drinks," but a "What's her name?" by Viv.

I set down the drinks, completely confused by the question.

"The bartender was a dude, and I didn't ask," I say, turning back to look again at the bartender. "At least I'm pretty sure that's a guy."

Both Faith and Viv laugh at my expense. "No, no, no," Viv clarifies. "The girl you are seeing tonight."

Now that I know the direction of the question, I can feel that no matter the answer, my balls shall be busted on.

"I see you two were laughing at my expense while I was inside." I sample my drink.

"Actually, Finn," Faith starts, "laughing at the poor girl about to be sucked into the loving disaster that is you."

"Thanks," I say as dryly as I can but somehow still sound far more sincere than I intended. "What makes you think I'm seeing a girl tonight?"

"Your vagueness about the whole thing, for one. Like you have to hide your life from me." Faith pretends she's all hunky dory.

"Well, it wasn't too long ago it seemed I should have, even though I tried not to. And by too long ago, I mean…" I defend.

"I know what you mean. Things can change in a few weeks-time, Finn," Viv chimes in.

"Yeah," Faith confirms. "Look at the two of us all buddy-buddy when a month ago, we didn't know you were banging both of us."

"What the hell are you doing? It was at that same time you were banging me back and still with Ronnie. We don't owe each other anything like that. And you, Viv…" I let myself trail off because, with her, I don't really have a leg to stand on.

The ladies both stare at me, waiting to finish my thought on Viv. "I'm sorry. I didn't realize that things were where they were." I should have realized that after her roommate Izzy walked in ready for a three-way, but Viv's eyes told me she didn't want one. Maybe she just wasn't in the mood. Maybe I read too much into it. Perhaps a part of me knew what I was doing and wanted to blow things up. I could list a hundred different reasons or justifications why I did what I did. Excuses and hindsight reasoning don't matter now. Now, all that matters is I made presumptions and ended up here.

"Relax, Finn." Faith jumps in while lighting up a smoke. "We're all good," she says, gesturing to the three of us. But in my experience, anytime anyone uses the phrase, "We're all good," it usually means that, in fact, things are not all good.

"I'm glad the three of us are on such good terms." I gulp down the rest of my drink. "That's relieving. But now I must be off."

"So soon?" Viv asks. "Everyone should be here shortly."

I shrug and point to my imaginary watch. "Show starts soon. I'll be by afterward, I think."

Viv feigns a playful pout. "See you soon, Finn."

"You too, Viv." I turn to Faith, whose silence has been noticeable the past few moments. "You okay, love?"

She looks in my direction but stares past me, lost in thought. Something is simmering beneath the surface. It's a look I've seen on her many times, so I know I just need to wait a moment for her to find her words.

"I'll walk you to your car." She has found some words.

A silent walk to my car finds me leaning against a closed driver's door as we stare at each other. She forces out small, quick smiles of regret.

"You know I've never stopped loving you, Finn. I tried to convince myself otherwise, but it never worked," she says, now staring at the ground. "I don't know why I'm saying this or what I expect from you in return. I just thought ... it just felt like it was something I needed to say."

"I know." I lift her chin up. "Tonight, it's just a show. I'll come back afterward if it's not too late."

I lean in and give her a hug. We look at each other with the same regret-filled eyes we've stared at countless times past. Our lips hold their position less than an inch apart, begging to touch each other, wanting to feel their warmth smushing against one another. She smiles, then plants a proper kiss on me. Nothing in her kiss is deep or passionate in a way that lends itself to us ending up on the blacktop next to my car, grinding on each other. Her kiss feels like she's telling me I'll always be her number one, but now is not the time. There's no other way to describe it, and if you've ever been privy to either of the above, you know, without a doubt, you've felt it and which one you've felt. If you've ever felt both kisses, then first, you don't need an explanation. And second, my condolences on having felt that tinge of pain. If you have never felt either, the feeling is further ineffable. The latter kiss is filled with so many emotions, all ready to boil over ... if only the timing was better, but no physical sensations can accompany its description.

She walks away, back to Viv, who I see shaking her head. I smile a half-smile, knowing that after all these years, Faith and I still drive each other crazy. I grin not because I enjoy driving her crazy but because no one can drive you that insane without equally feeling that much love for them.

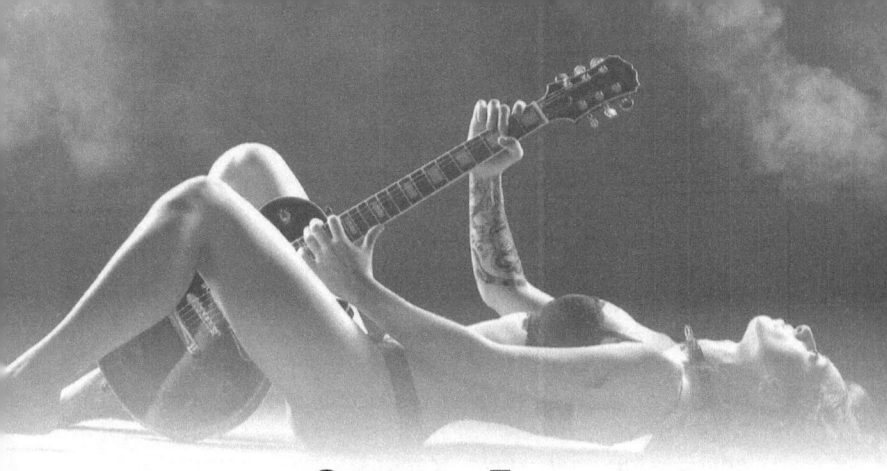

CHAPTER 7

Take the Time

After getting through security, I stand right outside the lobby to House of Blues, looking around for Jacquelyn. After a small flood of people pass by and clear, I see at the other end the bitter, middle-aged woman who had finally gotten her chance to let me know how she felt all those years ago, bringing back once more a flood of memories I wish I didn't have.

My old band was doing a record signing at Empire Records or Tower Records or some such place in Bloomingdale, Illinois, or some suburb around there. We had all our tables out and set up. Our new release, Tweaker, was overflowing in the display setup, waiting to be purchased by many enthusiastic teens and adults. We had our piles of Sharpies® at the ready to sign copy after copy and guitar after guitar. The crowd outside had grown immensely and had been waiting for who-knows how long. The store employees were laughing with us over some stupid joke, and everyone was happy. It was set to be a great day for everyone.

Then my phone rang. The caller ID lit up, letting me know my mother was ringing me. I sent it to voicemail, figuring I'd call her back the next day or whatever. But it rang again. Again, I sent it to voicemail. She dialed one more time. This time I picked it up.

She sounded hysterical. From the moment I said "hello," all I heard were tears. I stepped away from the table to a quieter spot in the store. Through her tears, she told me how my childhood best friend, Marty, and his family, had been in an accident. I could only make out every few words. They had been friends of my family for years. We'd spent holidays together, a few vacations, weekend excursions, etc. We drifted apart here and there but were always close. It was one of those relationships that no matter how long it had been, once you were together, it seemed like it was yesterday we were together. Now I was listening to the tears of a grieving woman tell me about a drunk driver, a crushed car, a flipped car, a lamp post, a semi-truck, all four something, but I was able to gather the gist of what she couldn't say distinctly. The next, unintelligible word was not one I wanted to hear.

All I knew was that a whole family was gone. Three generations of blood lay mixing together on a highway somewhere off 294 near Chicago. It was a moment that gets ingrained in your mind. A moment that forever will be painted crystal clear, like when Kennedy was shot or when the Twin Towers fell. It was a moment of disbelief so intense that all reality was pushed aside, as my mind tried to rationalize how this was and could not be.

But in the end, it was. I had to be there. I had to meet up with my family to see their family one last time. I turned to the rest of my band. They saw the look on my face, and the color was gone. I was pale; I know it because of how nauseous I felt. My stomach churned and tried to keep down my lunch. All I wanted to do was get there, get to where I needed to be, to be with them, with family. But I had to run to the bathroom. And, of course, in true record store fashion, the bathrooms were anything but sparkling. I knelt onto a sticky floor, under a flickering light, onto something that I could only imagine was a combination *of unrinsed floor cleaner and drying urine. I didn't care. I started heaving and vomiting into a toilet that had even grosser brown and red stuff caked onto the rim under the seat. I couldn't stop. My body was trying anything to make it not real, anything it could to deal with the news. But it was real.*

I don't remember how long I was in the bathroom. At some point, I remember leaving out the back door and the band telling me they'd take care of the rest. But I was their front man. I was supposed to be there, signing away and making music fans giddy at the excitement of meeting me and getting my autograph. Instead, I was on my way to say a final goodbye to a family that was my family.

The drive to the hospital was numb. I was in a trance, trying to play out the scene in my head and how it happened: how a person could drink so much, they no longer cared about the safety of others; how a person could drink so much that they no longer think they can't safely operate a vehicle. I tried not to imagine what the moment was like. Did Marty and his family see the accident approaching? If so, did anyone try to warn the driver? Were they blindsided? Did they feel the impact, or was there no pain? Did they die on impact? Then the worst possible thought on this situation hit me. What if Marty or his wife or his mother didn't die on impact and watched helplessly as the rest of their family bled out, as their own blood drained from their bodies as car after car drove past, apathetic to their distress? I tried to shut my thoughts down and not think about the accident. I decided to concentrate on driving so I could make it there safely, so that I wasn't the cause of someone else's loss of life.

By the time I arrived, the rest of my family was there. The room I was taken to, just past the emergency room entrance, had its door closed. I remember the nurse who had handled the situation since the others arrived leading me to the room and stopping outside the closed door. She turned to me and put her hand on the door. She didn't turn the knob but asked me if I was ready. I could hear the others in the room crying. The sounds of their pain and loss muted through two inches of wood. It was real, and I had to face it. I nodded my head. She turned the handle. My mother was inside sobbing as my father stood with silent, stoic tears streaming down his face. There were gurneys lined up next to each other: one each for Marty, his wife, his child, and his mother. So much loss in one room. I just stood there. I couldn't cry. I couldn't feel anything to cry for. I was trying to rationalize it or block it from hurting again. Stop it from being real.

To see tubes sticking out of a child's mouth from resuscitation attempts, same with his wife; their lifeless bodies still begged for help, silently calling out to be saved. I remember they didn't look dead. They looked like they were asleep or lying in wait to yell, "Got ya." I didn't see injuries. Their faces had scratches on them. Otherwise, they all still looked like themselves. I couldn't wrap my head around it. I was told they died from crush injuries. His wife and child died more slowly from internal bleeding than he or his mother did. Their deaths were far quicker, near instantaneous. I found little solace in hearing those words about them.

Death is still death. It's why we scream into microphones. It's why poets take a pen to paper. It's why oil and acrylic get brushed and thrown onto canvas. It's our way of trying to grasp the concept and deal with the loss, a demon in our lives we must find peace with. I thought I had found peace with this event until it decided to rear its ugly head in the form of a bitter, middle-aged woman who ripped those old wounds wide open again, twice in a night.

So, I'm forced to sit and stew in the memories of the faithful departed. A crowd of people walks by me as I stand in my thoughts just outside the House of Blues, but the commotion of the present event flings me forward in that fateful night.

A rush of first responders poured into the emergency room as a man who knelt on the gurney did chest compressions, one after another, until they halted and got the man intubated. I looked at the man on ventilation. Some nurse saw me staring through the curtains of Marty's room as they all passed by, talking over the patient's body.

"They had to use the jaws of life..." The rest of the sentence was lost on me. I didn't know this guy. He didn't know me. But I saw him clinging to life, struggling to hold on. I wouldn't have remembered the man, except for the next thing that my ears picked up was implanted in my mind forever. "He was the driver who caused the crash."

At that moment, all compassion left my body as it was replaced by a deluge of hate and vengeance. Here was a guy who couldn't stop at a couple of drinks, a guy whose lack of self-awareness, lack of self-control just cost four people their lives. I did not care for this man and, had I not had more self-control, would have made sure his life ended right then and there. But I knew it wouldn't bring them back. I knew that my desire to serve vigilante justice would only make my life harder than it would be without my friends we called family.

So, I watched as his life teetered. Each time his heart rate changed on the monitor, my eyes grew wide with hope that the numbers would fall and drop to zero. I hoped that the defibrillators would do no good, just zap away at his remains. I hated myself for feeling those emotions. I hated myself at that moment for wanting one more life to end that night, as if it would be some sort of cosmic balancing to even the score. Except you can't even a score like that. Yes, he was at fault. Yes, his actions had consequences, dire consequences. Had he lived, he would have had to live with those consequences, but he didn't.

After an hour or so of sitting with my deceased friend and his family, I watched as the drunk driver's heart rate shot up to over 200 beats per minute and then dropped to zero. Flatline. Something in the crash caused a strain on some heart vessel. It perforated, causing him to bleed out internally. I don't know if he felt any of the pain that *my friends felt. I don't know if that matters. There was no cosmic scorecard. There was no karma to balance there. The only thing there was death. And a lot of it.*

The crowd disperses, pulling me from my memory, leaving the angry, middle-aged woman to see me. Snarling like some feral dog, she walks up to the threshold of the inside and outside. No re-entry, so at least she can't touch me. She squints at me, ready to say some anger-filled jab to make this day more downtrodden.

I speak first; I don't need more from this lady. "Listen, I don't know why you held onto that sort of anger for all these years. It's not becoming on you or anyone. If you think my life was or is something close to perfect that you must knock me down a peg, then I'd suggest looking in the mirror to see what's really bothering you. I'm sorry I had to leave that night. I didn't want to and wish the events that made me duck out didn't happen. But they did, and I'm sorrier than you will ever know. Now please, let go of the anger and try to enjoy the show."

She stands there, mouth agape and motionless, dumbstruck as to what she can say next. So, I turn around and look back into the Disney Springs grounds for Jacquelyn.

CHAPTER 8

Galactic Brain

There Jacquelyn is, passing through security and picking up her belongings from the tray, dressed to the nines for the occasion in a strategically torn midriff top that came from somewhere between the late 1980s and early 1990s, executed with a bit of both side and under-boob showing. But she has the carefree attitude and confidence to pull it off without it looking like an attention grab. Just someone who is comfortable in her own skin. Her hair is pulled back into a ponytail so loose, it's a wonder it is still held back, with perfectly executed video vamp makeup to finish the look.

She strides over to me, stopping less than a foot away, and hands me my ticket to get inside.

"Nice jacket." She puckers her lips in some half playful, half sensual way, grabbing my sports blazer that is downplayed by my T-shirt and torn jeans.

"Just a style I like. Love your outfit. Very throwback," I say with a smirk.

She grabs my shirt and pulls me in for a quick, surprise kiss. My eyes widen from the blitzkrieg, and I look down at her eyes as she locks lips with mine. She too is staring up at me and finishes her kiss with a smile.

"Now that that's outta the way, wanna buy a girl a drink?" she says, prancing off to the bar.

The shock of her kiss and the boldness of her actions leaves me dumbfounded for a moment. She looks at me with a tilted head, surprised that I was, well, surprised.

"Cat got your tongue?" she says while laughing, gesturing for me to follow her.

"How do I know you don't have the herp or somethin'?" I spew off the first thought that comes to mind.

"How do I know you don't? Now, come on!" She sets off to the bar at the opposite end from the venue entrance.

I shake my head to bring myself back to the moment and follow her. After ordering a couple of whiskeys on the rocks, I turn to her.

"Thank you for all those recommendations. I'm really digging them, especially Flatfoot 56." She smiles, looking out over the crowd.

"No problem," I respond. "Do you always thank strange men by taking them to concerts?"

She shakes her head while drinking her whiskey. "Not usually. I just like to have fun. Be in the moment, ya know?"

I nod because there's something about her, something I can't quite place my finger on. I watch her turn out to the crowd on the floor. She's watching them as I watch them. She's looking for those people who aren't just here for a few beers and a night out. She's looking around to see whose life needs some musical therapy.

I was curious. I didn't read any marquee on the way in. I didn't see the ticket she handed me but just pocketed it. I pull it out to see who shall be gracing the stage tonight— Nirvanna: A tribute to Nirvana. Interesting. We shall see how it goes.

I was going to ask if she was even a Nirvana fan, but she's staring out at a father and his pre-teen daughter standing in what will surely become the mosh pit. Not far off from them, next to the security railing against the stage,

I see a tiny woman dressed like she's straight out of a nine-ties street-workout video but was probably born in 1993. She yells at some shaggy-haired guy who hovers at least a foot taller than her. He stands there frustrated but, judging by his sloped shoulders and defeated posture, is used to the abuse she's doling out. While I can read lips a little, she's talking at him so fast I can't get much. I do read out a "You don't own me" phrase, to which he replies something that elicits an eye roll from her.

Jacquelyn and I watch this go on for a few more moments before he storms off in our direction. Poor guy: who knows why she was so mean just now or why he stands by, taking it. The evident frustration on his face signals this is not a new occurrence. He stops at the bar a few feet from us and orders two beers and a double shot. The bartender puts down the shot first, and the abused boy-friend shoots it before the bartender can say, "Here ya go." It's that kind of night for him.

We stand at the bar there watching more of the crowd for a while. Stagehands set the stage with banners that indicate a Blink 182 cover band will be up first: fun times of corporate, pop-punk with an easy-to-digest flavor for the masses. It's everything that Nirvana was not, but three-quarters of this crowd is too young to know the difference. The sign of my times goes forward in reverse. Most of these kids think the two bands come from the same mental place. Rebellion, outsiders trying to find their voice—Nirvana, yes. They were on the forefront and helped create a genre that spoke to so many. The other band just played fun, punky music for teenage girls to lose their virginity to. But whatever, I have a new friend standing next to me.

"I wouldn't have taken you for a people-watcher," I say, leaning into her so she can hear me over the blaring house speakers.

"I am," she says, shaking her head as she continues looking out toward the crowd. "My job doesn't really allow for much watching."

"What do you do, Jacquelyn?" I ask, hoping to learn something about her.

"Nothing important," she evades. I let it go. "What do you do, Finn?"

"Drink a lot and make things happen."

She stops watching the crowd and turns to me. "I see how it goes. I avoid, so you avoid. This could be fun."

A guy closer to my age stops next to me at the bar. He orders a few beers and turns to me. His face lights up like he's seeing Santa Claus in person. He grabs a pen and coaster off the bar and takes a step to me.

"Dude. Bro! Holy shit!" he starts off. Yes, I've heard those four words in that order a few times before. At least he's friendly. "This is so awesome!" he continues as he looks around for a familiar face to show me off to.

I look at Jaquelyn, who's suddenly very interested in why this guy is geeking out over me.

I grab the coaster and pen. "What's your name?"

"Ben. Ben! My name is Ben!" He starts shaking with excitement.

It's been a while since someone got this excited to see me. I look at Ben. "Think we can keep it between us?" I whisper in his ear, while signing the coaster with a personalization.

He nods his head with such vigor I am afraid he may herniate a disc. Then, he walks off, pocketing the coaster, a 360-turn-around in coolness.

"What was that all about?" Jacquelyn asks with a raised eyebrow.

"Nothing. Just thought I was someone else."

She shakes her head in utter disbelief of my excuse but lets it drop for the moment.

The house lights dim as the show starts. The flashing red and blue lights from above the stage make their figure eights as the Blink tribute band goes through the usual suspects of radio hits. The crowd eats it up. I must admit it is a relatively entertaining show. I just never understood the allure of pop punk outside of the catchy hooks. Or is that it? Escapism in its most capitalistic form. Just some-thing for the masses to eat up and consume so someone else can profit off their struggles? But now, for the moment at least, I know why I am here. I watch Jacquelyn bob her head to the tunes as she sings along, escaping from what-ever hell has a hold on her during the daylight. There's a part of me that wishes I could be like them. Just bobbing along to the music, but pop punk had always felt so empty to me. I need more from it. I need to be a part of it, part of its creation, part of its exhibition. Even here as I watch her, I can't get into it. Maybe I am just angry that I can't be one of them, so easily able to escape their problems in this music. Maybe.

Maybe I am just not a fan.

Either way, Jacquelyn looks good. She seems happy with a smile on her face as she urges me to sing along. I want to sing along. I want to be happy, but all I can think about is the woman I left behind tonight to be with this one, this woman who knows less than Viv did when she and I first met. Jacquelyn doesn't even know who I once was. Perhaps what I find so appealing about her is that she thinks I am just a regular guy. I smile at her as she gets me to sing a line or two about how it ain't so and how I won't go.

The show goes on and on. I try to enjoy the quiet moments with this enigma of a girl, who apparently just wanted someone by her side tonight. But the Blink 182 tribute band exits the stage, causing the house music to come on the speakers. The house lights get a little brighter. If she wants to talk to me, she has some time. And it looks like she does.

"Having fun there, big guy?" She watches me look around.

I turn to her and smile. "Yeah. Fun show."

She scrunches her face, not really believing my words. She looks me up and down, searching for an answer written on me somewhere. She stops at my hands, which are hanging out my pockets by the thumbs.

She leans into me. "What's her name?"

I keep close to her but turn to her ear. "No her."

"Not anymore, huh?" She grabs my left hand, examining my ring finger for a sign of a long-worn ring recently taken off. "Maybe. Maybe not." She puts my hand down. "I'm smarter at these things than you'd think."

"Perhaps." I grab her hand in turn. "I don't see a ring on your finger either."

"God no. Did that once. Not happening again." She twists her face in disgust of the thought of marriage.

"You're what? Twenty-five? Divorced or widowed?" I pry.

"Kinda personal there, Finn, don't ya think?"

"A bit, but no more than your presumptions. Turnabout is fair play." I let slip a smile, hoping it lightens the mood.

Jacquelyn nods in agreement, smiling back. It's funny because on stage are two pretty decent-looking ladies in cheerleader uniforms straight out of a Nirvana video, entertaining the crowd and I couldn't care less. This is partly because both of the cheerleaders have a look on their faces and body language that cry out desperately for some sort of narcotic/upper fix, but mostly because Jacquelyn has me intrigued.

"I'll answer if you'll answer why that guy geeked out back there," she asks.

I think hard about it for a moment while I purse my lips in thought. "How about we enjoy the show?"

She nods and turns back to watch the sedated cheerleaders lead on. She leans into me and wraps my arms around her. It feels nice but also friendly. I wonder what it means. I'm not clinging to some notion that this may lead to sex or the love I've been waiting for all my life or some trite thought. I mean, I'm just thinking about if she is interested in more or feeling her way around those parts, or just a touchy-feely kinda friend with no intentions of anything more. I don't try anything. I don't let my hands wander. I refrain from whispering sweet nothings into her ear, not that I was tempted to do such things. I just try to enjoy this night as much as I am able to, relax, and take in anything that happens to me.

I look around at the crowd as the house lights lower once again and three guys dressed precisely like Nirvana, down to the iconic white sunglasses and bleached hair with overgrown roots, take the stage. It's like reliving the days gone by of discovering grunge music and the religious experience that went along with feeling the music on a spiritual level. I see it happening again. I look around and see a bunch of kids, some still high school-aged, mesmerized by the music pouring off the stage. Even Jacquelyn has relaxed a bit in my arms because she likes to sing along to all their pretty songs.

I am enjoying this night out, away from my life in music while being surrounded by it. This evening is a nice break from the norm without straying far from it, but there's a thought running through my head. *What will I tell Faith when she inevitably asks about tonight?* It doesn't mean anything more than this moment: a new friend is resting in my arms. On the same note, if she wasn't a "she" and just some new guy I friended, I wouldn't be doing this, but she already got past the first kiss and she didn't seem impressed. So, what will I tell Faith? What is there to say to Faith? Not much, I suppose. But then again, how do I feel about this whole thing? At the moment, I don't know, and I don't really care. I'll deal with whatever may be brewing in the back of my subconscious when I need to deal with it, a proverbial bridge I will cross once I get there.

Right now, I need a drink.

I pull my arms out from around her and whisper in her ear, "Gonna grab a drink. Want one?"

She turns around. "I'll come with."

I start through the crowd of people standing shoulder to shoulder. Jacquelyn grabs hold of my jacket, so she doesn't get separated. We bob and weave our way to the bar. Once again, I see the shaggy-haired guy who was earlier accosted by the pint-sized woman. His mood doesn't seem to have improved. It makes me wonder why someone would stay in a relationship like that, what someone could see, or think they see, in someone else that lets their own self-worth be sacrificed.

The same bartender from earlier sees us and makes a circular motion with his finger at us, asking if we need another round. Impressive that in a crowd of well over a thousand he remembers us; a talent that lands him a ten spot for himself.

Jacquelyn gets close to me, if only to speak. "You keep looking around."

My focus turns to her. "It's what I do. I people-watch."

She shakes her head. "Naw, I people-watch. You're looking for something."

"I don't know," I answer because I really don't. I look around at everyone, everywhere I go. It's a habit I picked up after Faith first broke things off back in 2001. Maybe I'm always looking for her.

"Well, whatever you are looking for, I hope you find it. You seem very intense and yet very laid-back at the same time."

My focus shoots to her to look her in the eye. "You do know those are contradicting descriptors?"

"Exactly. But that's you. You need to relax and listen to the world," Jacquelyn says, shouting at me over the music. "Stop looking around. You can't see the details when you keep looking at the big picture. You need to listen to what the world is telling you. Even in a loud place like this, you can hear it, if you listen."

She might be right. Who knows? I think after my start down here, I'm still in the mindset of trying to fit into the lifeline of the city, intertwine myself in some way. What I fail to realize is that after what I've been through down here, after the people I've met and involved myself with, I am intertwined. I am in the city's lifeblood.

The rest of the show is spent with us at the bar side. We aren't drinking a ton, one or two with waters to make sure we stay soberish, but we found our spot here. We found a place where we both feel relaxed and enjoy the show for what it is.

As the masses exit and make their way back to their cars after the show, I swim with the current, so to speak. We first stop at Jacquelyn's car. I seem to be doing a lot of standing outside vehicles lately. Maybe it's just a thing that happens in clusters, like celebrities dying in groups of three. But, either way, here we stand, outside her bright yellow BMW. I notice a few key marks running along the driver's side of her car. I run my finger along them as if I am inspecting them for some microscopic clue.

"I gotta get that fixed." She waves off the key marks.

"Lover's quarrel?"

She lets out a hearty, throated laugh. "Ha! No. Just some guy who wishes we were lovers. Some men just don't understand boundaries."

I take a step back, not that I was even that close to her at the moment. She notices and smiles at the gesture.

"You're safe. If you weren't, you'd know it. However, if you were hoping for an invite back to my place..." She trails off.

I shake my head. "Oh no," I start with a dog-sly smile. "I actually was hoping for an invite to the back seat. Figured the theme of the concert and all."

She gives my arm a quick jab. "How about a goodnight kiss where we stand?"

I nod my head as she moves closer to me. "I like that."

She rises on her tiptoes as I lean my head down a bit. Our lips get close to each other. We hover for a moment as if some unknown chemical reaction may occur if our lips met. This time is different from the first, surprise kiss. For a moment, she hesitates as our lips gently caress. I can hear her breathing slow down, but there is a nervous quiver to her that, after tonight, I would not have expected.

I pull away for a moment and look her in the eyes. Her carefree look has changed. Her face no longer reads of the woman I met earlier. There's a vulnerability in her eyes that is new to me. From the shakiness in her breath, it might be new to her as well.

"You have done this before. At least once. I know you have," Jacquelyn says, looking into my eyes. The corners of her lips begin to pull upward.

I move in and lock lips with hers. The feel of Jacquelyn's well-moisturized lips as they press against mine sends a shiver down my spine. Our kiss starts slow and not too shallow but grows into a deeper, more passionate kiss. Our lips move in sync, and our tongues dance around.

The first time you kiss someone, starting with your very first kiss at some young, tender age, and leading to your latest kiss outside a car reliving the glory days of grunge, a million thoughts fly through your head, and all in about the ten seconds it takes to lead up to a first kiss. *Are we going to connect? Is she a closed-mouth kisser? Will she use tongue? Too much or too little? Will I use too much tongue for her? Will our rhythms match? Do I have bad breath? Will she have bad breath?* And about ten thousand other questions fly through your mind, hoping you can make all the necessary adjustments before she cuts the kiss short and bids you goodnight. But all those thoughts, all those worries disappear the moment your lips connect. The instant you are finally in the moment, everything falls away—if the kiss is magic. And the good thing about most winter nights in Orlando is they can still be warm with the enchantment from those summer nights. And if her thoughts are similar to mine, there's magic right here.

She pulls away from me, biting her bottom lip. "Mr. Fairlane," she playfully bats her eyelashes, "that was ... thank you."

"Thanks is all mine." I pull at my shirt collar, cooling myself off. "I think now is the perfect time to go our separate ways for the night."

Her face scrunches a little, as if she's holding back either a smile or tears. "Is this it then?"

"Only for the night," I say, realizing that I just sounded either really romantic or like a stalker.

She opens the door to her car and takes a seat. A shiftiness in her movements has surfaced in the moments since we just kissed. Perhaps I am not the lip-locker I once was. Did I do something to make her uncomfortable? That would not at all be my intention, but if she took something I said in jest as a serious statement, then I may have ruined potential. Making off-color remarks is never my intention.

"See you soon, Finn." She shifts her car into drive and starts to idle forward. I shut her door and watch her drive off.

I stand for a moment and make sure she's okay as she drives away. I'm not really sure what happened at the end there, but something changed. Something shifted in her. I can only help but think that I did something to somehow ruin what was a great evening. My evening, however, is not over. Now I must return to the woman for whom I will always be a slave.

My drive back to the patio section to see Faith, and whoever else might be lingering there, wasn't long; still, it gave me time to think. And think I did, about what this night could mean or could have meant, what I could have done or said to have suddenly put her on edge. Maybe it wasn't something I said or did. Perhaps it was her, but if it was her, then there was nothing I can do about it and nothing I can change. I can only control what I do. So, I ponder what I did, what I said to have possibly caused the sudden shift, but I come up empty, which means I wait a few days to give her time to cool off and hope she returns my call.

But with those thoughts aside, I can turn back to the task at hand: the balancing of the fragile relationship I have with Faith and not doing anything to screw that up any further.

I pull into the back side of the restaurant and park my car. As I approach the hedgerow where I first explored anatomy with Viv, I see a rustling in the trees. I laugh to myself to think that not too long ago, it was myself and Viv

THE FORTUNATE *Finn Fairlane*

back there reliving our pasts' moments of innocence lost. I must have laughed a little too loudly as I hear hushed whispers and a pants zipper. I slow my walk a little to see who it might be that will be doing the same walk of shame back to the patio that Viv and I once did.

A moment later, out from the bushes, pink-and-black hair peeks out and I laugh as the head attached to that hair is Logan. She stops, frozen by the sight of me, as a shit-eating grin crosses her face. I smile and nod at her accomplishment of the night. This makes me wonder that since she's into innies, not outies, who it might have been that ducked behind the foliage with her. Here's the thing I've learned in life though: never wonder a question you aren't prepared to hear the answer to because when the answer is spoken, it's there and you can't unhear it or unsee it. I see Logan reach back into the bush and grab a hand. The body that follows the hand is one I recognize. One I care for. One I was behind those same bushes with a few months back—Viv.

Except now I am Faith and Ronnie rolled into one, both proud of Logan for living her life and scratching an itch that obviously needed scratching, but also hurt because this is someone I care for and somehow, even though it was me back there with her, disappointed she would sully the place that was ours. Though in all realistic thought and reasoning, that place was probably hers and a few others' before it was ours, but it still hurts. Maybe sting is a better descriptor. But any words that I may use here, it's strange to be on the other end of the scene this time.

Logan takes a few steps toward the patio when she realizes that Viv and I are eye-locked with each other, unsure of what to say. Logan stops and turns toward me, quickly reading my face. She sees a palpable awkwardness in the situation but can't quite place her finger on it.

I try to be polite about it as Viv and I owe each other nothing. Well, at the very least, she owes me nothing. But what do I say? At least it's not a cup of male tears? That's just barbaric and dumb, but then the fact that that specific thought popped into my mind makes me wonder, when Ronnie saw her and I pop out from the bushes, if he too had once been behind them with her. Regardless, I'm not going to say that. So, what will I say to break the awkwardness of the silence among us?

"Good times," Viv says to break the silence as she walks toward me.

"Indeed." A laugh escapes me. "I see you know Logan."

"You know him, Vivian?" Logan interjects, extending a pointed finger my way. "Do you know who this guy is?"

"Yeah, babe. We're friends. Met a few months ago," Viv says, calming Logan down. Viv turns to me and says, "Logan and I used to date. Reconnected when D.B. invited her out tonight."

"I take it he's here then?"

Viv nods her head.

"Hey! Wait a minute!" Logan's excitement is uncontainable. "So you're in charge of Spear Fist?"

I scrunch my face and tilt my head side to side. "I wouldn't say 'in charge.'" Yes, I just used air quotes. "Just providing a guiding light for them in their current tour. Did you get my email?"

She shakes her head. "I didn't think... I was going... Sorry I didn't get back yet."

"Calm down. It's all right. I see D.B. took me up on my advice to contact you so here we all are."

Viv looks at me with a look in her I have felt on my own face before. She's waiting for the other shoe to drop in this situation. "You okay, Finn?" she asks.

"D.B. mentioned you started seeing someone." I nod my head at Logan for verification.

She shakes her head. "That was nothing. A short-lived mistake."

"Shorter than me?" I try to make a joke.

She forces a smile. "Yeah. Nothing to waste more thought on. So? You okay?"

I smile and look up to the night sky full of stars. I inhale a deep breath and let it out before looking back to her. "Perfect. Come on."

I am perfect though. As much as it stung moments ago, the sting is now gone. It feels like the waters have calmed down and things are somehow falling into place, at least for the moment.

We all take a seat next to each other on the patio, and as if no time has passed, D.B. is surrounded by a small crowd of people hanging onto his every word. Vincent and Neil strum their hollow body guitars to an acoustic version of Slipknot's "Snuff." Per expectations, there are three girls all ooh-ing and aah-ing over the musicianship of the two. The rest of the patio is filled with familiar faces laughing and enjoying the warm night and cooling breeze.

The one face I don't see outside is Faith. I look around as if I may have passed over her and not noticed, but she is not there. I peer through the windows to the bar and see her in there staring out at me, a smile on her face. She points at me, then pantomimes a drink. I nod yes and wink. She salutes me and turns back to the bartender.

D.B. excuses the current conversation that has the surrounding crowd entranced and turns to me with an extended fist that must be bumped. So, I do. Our fists explode back as we make explosion noises … cause that's how we roll.

"What's the word, good sir?" I ask after our fists settle down.

"Making friends," he says, nodding to Logan.

"So, this will work then?" I ask, tossing a glance to both D.B. and Logan.

D.B. nods with a wink as Logan shakes her head with enough enthusiasm for everyone—an answer I assume is yes but is actually everywhere in between, to which I nod back. "Good to hear." I turn to Logan. "You need to decide how long you want to be on tour together. That's something I can't decide. Only you, your guys, and Spear Fist can."

She nods back to show she understands but doesn't say anything. "Any luck in finding that new member?" I ask.

She snickers at my use of the word member. "After I met you, I did my research into you and decided to make a few calls and such."

"And?"

"I have a few leads," she imps out her words.

"This tour is much bigger than anything you've been on before. Leads won't cut it, and the tour launches in under a month. Make something happen and soon." My words come out like a lecturing father, but the need calls for it. If she wants to take her band farther, now is the time.

Throughout this whole exchange, I can't help but notice that Viv has been silent and staring at me the entire time. I'm sure something akin to guilt has been haunting her, taunting her, or tugging at her since our eyes met as she emerged from behind the trees. I figure I need to soothe whatever it is that irks her.

"Viv, you all right?" I start.

She nods her head, though the look on face says otherwise.

"Just making sure. Your quiet is kinda creeping me out," I joke.

She laughs, relaxing her face. "Been a long couple of days."

I see Faith say something to her sister and Gregg before walking out with a couple of drinks. She seems to be in a much better state of mind than before I left for the Nirvanna show.

Faith hands me my drink and says she'll be back in a moment. She steps away to a familiar face who I've never talked to before. They have a few laughs, making her settle down on the arm of the patio couch. I smile and turn back to my group.

"Strippers?" I say to D.B.

"Strippers? For the tour? That could be fun," he says, obviously not keeping up with my random thoughts.

"For the bachelor party. Gregg's inside so we can talk, no?" I ask.

"Yeah, we can talk," D.B. confirms. "And it sounds good to me. I can always have a few extra good-looking ladies around."

"What else are you planning? Strippers are fun and all, but you'll need more," Viv offers her unsolicited input.

"Did you ... want to go?" I hesitate.

"I mean, I'm not his closest friend, but we are friends. Plus, a cause for celebration is a cause to celebrate. So ... yeah," she says, then quickly adding, "if that's cool."

"Yeah, that's cool," I chuckle. "Logan, I know your chosen preference, and since you'll most likely be touring with the band, you can join us if you'd like."

"Ass and titties, hell yeah!" she says with the excitement of a twelve-year-old boy who's never seen either before.

"So then, Viv, what else do you think we need for the party? Isn't the point of a bachelor party to get drunk in some hotel room with a stripper or two doing unmentionable things to you that you'll never speak of again?" I ask, sipping my drink.

Lighting up a cigarette, Viv offers further thoughts. "An event. Something other than sitting in a strip club, or hotel room, shoving ones and fives into G-strings."

"Like what? Stripper paintball or something?" I try to figure out how to fit strippers into another kind of event.

"I'm with Finn," D.B. interjects his thoughts. "Bachelor parties are about boobs and booze, baby! I've never been to one that wasn't."

"Straight-up strippers is just so passé. You gotta do more. Like maybe a road rally or something, then strippers," Viv mentions, straight out of the early nineties.

"A road rally? Like a scavenger hunt in a car?" I attempt to clarify.

"Yeah, sure. Something other than a strip club. Unless that's what you want is just booze and boobs," Viv finalizes.

"Wait. Wait," D.B. says, waving his leather wrist-banded hands. "What's the end goal of the road rally?"

"The strippers, duh," Viv starts. "You don't tell him anything about what you have in store for the night. You start the road rally doing offbeat findings. Like a G-string for a guitar instead of the underwear. Stuff like that."

"Oo! Oo!" Logan interrupts, the proverbial lightbulb above her head lighting up. "Then in the middle of the rally, you stop off for a steak dinner. Something with a pink center. Or a side of chicken breast!"

I laugh out loud at Logan's excitement over a bachelor party for a guy she met only earlier tonight. She has the same look on her face as she did when I saw her decide to buy the microphone at George's Music. I can see why Viv used to date her and, as they put it, reconnected tonight.

"A road rally might be cool, but it will have to be epic." I set that conversation aside. "That bit of planning aside for the moment, how's the night looking, D.B.?"

"Same ol' same ol,' my man. Just waxing intellectual about the existential," he says, chugging the rest of his beer.

I lean back in my seat, nursing the drink Faith had bought for me. I zone out of the conversation that continues around me as I focus on Faith. She's still sitting on the arm of the plastic wicker patio furniture, talking with that same girl she settled in with after handing me my drink. I want to go say something to her, not to bother her or start anything but just to say hello, though I don't want to interrupt the conversation she looks so content with carrying on. I sit back, watch her, and listen to the ambient noise that surrounds me on this patio. I feel the light, cool breeze pass over my face and neck, and I can feel every little hair blow in it, every inch of my skin cooling off in the night. I feel very comfortable just sitting, a hard situation for me to feel comfortable in.

I don't go say anything to Faith, as she is happy. I don't want to be overbearing, though something in her conversation has her look my way. She stops talking as she sees me. She raises her drink to me in a silent toast and takes a sip. I watch her as she stands up and pats her friend on the shoulder before walking back to me.

She doesn't stop at me though. No. As she passes, she motions with one finger and an upturned hand for me to follow her. I excuse myself from our current conversation and head out of the patio. I follow Faith around the corner to the trees, but she doesn't go behind them. She stops at her car parked in front of them.

"We could go behind the trees and make out a bit?" Faith jests.

There's something in that joke, though, that is both sad and true. The tone in Faith's voice is a bit sullen and desperate, not desperate in a pathetic way but in a "Please don't say yes to this" way. This is all fine and dandy because I am not going to. Going behind trees isn't characteristic of Faith, and I've been there before. That's not something I wish to relive with Faith as my substitute for Viv.

"What's on your mind, love?" I say, keeping a close distance but being careful not to touch her. I want to. I want to grab her tight and run away, hand in hand, like some stupid fairy tale but it's not what she wants.

She turns her stare to the ground like some shy highschooler asking a boy out for the first time. We've been there, we've played that part, so I can't understand why she's playing it again.

"How was your date?" And there it is, the million-dollar question of the night.

"I'm here. Aren't I?" I take my finger and lift her head. She nods in adolescent-like, guilty admittance of agreement. "It was a thank-you, not a date." At least I think that's true. I could be wrong, but I'm sure I'm not.

"Is everything all right at work? Do you need money or something?" I am still confused as to why we walked back here.

She pushes back from me a little bit. "No," she huffs out. "Everything is fine. I just thought ... I don't know what I thought. Maybe I wanted to go make out behind the trees. Maybe I wanted some company back here." Her voice takes a drastic turn to sarcastic. "I thought you might want to hit this." She pulls an already packed glass bowl out of her cigarette box, a lovely blue-and-green, blown glass piece with resin built up to give it a tie-dye look.

I let the subject of what's on her mind drop for the moment, as whatever it truly was has disappeared. So, we sit smoking a little weed away from the rest of the company.

The smoke circles around us as we exhale, dancing in the thoughts we both want to say, though we sit silently for a moment as we partake. I can feel the tension build as she wants me to say something. I just have no idea what it is she wants me to tell me, which gives me no ideas of what to say. We sit, passing the bowl back and forth, letting the THC mellow out our minds and relax our souls.

I look up to the night sky and see what stars I can see through the pollution of the streetlights and buildings surrounding us. Faith leans into me as I look up. I wrap my arm around her and pull her hair back behind her ear with the other hand. She, too, looks up to the sky to try and steal my sights.

"Is she cute?" Faith continues staring skyward.

"Cute? Like a five-year-old? No," I respond.

"Not like a five-year-old. Cute as in, would you do her?" Faith asks straight-out.

"That's a strangely inappropriate question." I shift my gaze down to her.

She pulls away and faces me. "God, you already did, didn't you?"

Not the most relaxing weed she's ever smoked; either that or if this is relaxed for her, she needs to unwind some more.

"No, we didn't. She did kiss me though. But I think she did it more out of curiosity than anything else." I pull Faith back in toward me, but she resists. I stop.

"What the hell does that mean? Out of curiosity?" She takes a deep breath. "Damn it, Finn. Whatever. You don't owe me anything."

I nod. "I don't, but you asked. I'll always tell. I think she just wanted to see if it would be any good or if I had something on my mind. Like she wanted to get the awkwardness out of the way so we could both enjoy the show."

I look into her eyes as I speak because I want her to know. I want her to know that other women will always be nothing compared to her. I will always put Faith first. That is something she needs to know.

"Why?" She scrunches her eyes.

"Why what?"

"Why tell me? Why still carry a flame for me after all these years? Why hold me up to some standard that is impossible? Why all of it?"

There you go. The world around me has stopped spinning. All guitars in my mind have stopped playing. The feedback from the amplifiers screeches out the deafening, high-pitched timbre. The cymbals ring out as everything around silences. The music has died as I have been asked the impossible question. I must now try to answer what I could not answer for the past nearly two decades in song. I must now try and find a way to verbalize feelings that have controlled and guided virtually every action I've taken since the day we split, if not since the day we first had margaritas. But what can I say? What is there to say that hasn't been said before? What words are there to summarize in a few sentences everything I have done over the last 6,205 days of my life? Which, for all you *Rent* fans, is 8,935,200 minutes. I only know this because Katy—of Katy and Patrick—had me watch that movie and that song stuck with me in a weird way. So, I calculate the years from time to time. Strange, I know, but back to the moment.

The thing is I want to answer. I want to tell her how I feel: how I've always felt; why I've always felt that way; how my feelings aren't just about my idealization of what a relationship should be. Tell her that my emotions are not about my Magical Kingdom-addled brain thinking a prince has a right to kiss a sleeping stranger, and everything will be happily ever after. I have no false conceptions about relationships; that is not where my feelings for this woman lie. My feelings lie in everything she does, everything she says to me, that has ever made me feel like more of a man than I should feel like or would have otherwise.

My feelings are about her and how she treats others. They are about the amazing woman she was back then that pushed me to become something more. They are about this fantastic human being that wants to better herself so she can perhaps help someone else in her own way, right now, and for the past decade, has been through boosting confidence with a great cut or color. That's what cosmetologists do, but when she does it, it puts a smile on her face as well. I know this does because I know her. I see the way she cares for her sister and doesn't want to see her end up in her shoes in ten years. The fierce loyalty. All these things I can say about her and why I love her.

But here's the catch. These things that make someone fall in love with another person—they are moments in time, instances that happen without much notice or fanfare, but I noticed. I saw what happened and why they happened. I can't sit here with her, both of us flying high, and cite examples from her life that are the reasons I fell for her. To state all the individual times over the years I can remember that added to the overall feeling—call it love, call it what you will—would sound like a stalker guy watching her from up in a tree. But the years that made her so endearing to me were so long ago. Yes, since we've been back in each other's lives, I've seen those moments, which is why I know she hasn't changed. Perhaps I am holding onto the past, and there is no present or future. Maybe I am wrong, but to operate under such assumptions would make for a life full of hesitation, and that is not fun. Rock 'n roll isn't about thinking about sex, wanting to try drugs, and almost putting on a record. No, it's about doing all these things and doing them to the fullest.

I look Faith in the eye. "I can't answer that in this state of mind. It wouldn't do my words any justice. It wouldn't be fair to you to hear them coming from me while I'm not totally sober. But I will tell you. Just not at this moment."

"Finn..." she starts, but I pull her in and plant my lips on hers.

I do this because she needs to know I love her. She needs to understand my feelings. My advance is not uninvited. She reciprocates my move, and our lips dance like soft waves of the ocean crashing on the shore. Our tongues swim in each other's mouths, ever searching for the meaning of life. Our eyes are closed, as I think about all the time I have to make up for, all the time I have missed and the things she has been doing. How I want to hear about them; I want to hear about everything. I want to be there for her, but I can't make grand gestures. We have to take it one day at a time, one moment to the next.

I gently place my hands around her waist and hold her. I feel her body pressed against mine. I know what lies under her clothes and how amazingly beautiful it all is. Now is not the time for that. That moment must wait. Now is all about the kiss, a kiss to rival any kiss throughout the ages, a long-awaited hello that says we both made it; we are both here.

She pulls away, and as I open my eyes, I see her eyes slowly open. An ear-to-ear smile on her face. "Ronnie called me. He wants to work things out."

And my newly found cloud nine has dissipated. I am free falling to the earth below with no parachute, no safety net; only the hard ground below to stop me. My body feels like it is spinning in a free fall, no control over anything. I am just waiting for my demise.

"Just being honest about things?" I am now very confused about the moments prior.

"Tryin'." She is looking everywhere but at me.

"Was this a final kiss? One final way to say 'I love you' but please move on? Or a welcome home of some sort?" I say, bobbing my head around to try and catch her attention.

"I don't know what I am going to do. It's not that easy to turn your back on five years," Faith says with a frown.

"I can wait. It's what I've done for seventeen years," I say, her eyes finally reconnecting with mine. "Is that why you wanted to get together earlier tonight? To tell me this?"

"I didn't get the chance. Finn, this isn't easy, ya know?" She looks me dead in the eye. I don't flinch. I don't want to flinch. I don't want this moment to end. I don't know if I'll ever get a moment like this again. Looking at our history, past and current, it is likely I am, but if I were to assume I would and never do, then I would hate myself for cutting short this moment. If we do get to do this again, then this is just another beautiful memory I will have.

"But I thought you said he wasn't the one. Or that he wasn't right. What you told me before." The desperation in my voice is subtle but there. I can feel it creeping in and slowly taking over.

"I know what I said. But he's a good guy, Finn."

"Strapping, young lad if ever there was. Great punch too. But you don't need someone to tend to you like a pet. So, do tell." I was able to hold at bay my never-ending desperation for her until the last three, little words.

She caught it too. She looks on for a moment, watching my face, my eyes, my mouth, every inch of me for something. What she's looking for I do not know, perhaps the answer to life or another kiss goodnight. "Finn. I don't know. I love you both, and it's hard to let go of either history. Of either past. I don't want to. I just need time."

She turns away from me and gets in her car. I watch, unable to move, as my body is unable to gain control of the free fall and smacks against the blacktop below. But, since I'm not actually free-falling 20,000 feet, I live. The pain in my heart swells. I can't move to not watch her drive away. Perhaps had I been able to answer her question, she would have stayed. If I had given her whatever sign she was looking for while searching my face, maybe she wouldn't have left. But she did, and I am once again alone.

CHAPTER 9

Light Me Up

Fuck inspiration. Fuck the tour schedule and planning. Fuck it all. It's not that I want to be angry; I just am right now. There's a feeling deep inside my mind that nothing I am doing is right or will be right; that everything I'm doing will all be for nothing, and it tears me up to think like that sometimes. This isn't the first time I've been caught in these thoughts, and the sad truth is it probably won't be the last time, but right now I have nothing. I don't have the girl I've been thinking about for all these years. I don't even have the new girl who has added to my confusion for the other girl. I have myself. I have the money I've made. I have my toys. However, none of those last two things provide any sort of consolation over not having the girls.

Once you start this line of thinking, it's hard to leave, not because you want to stay wallowing in this self-pity or whatever it might be. No, no one actually enjoys wallowing in self-pity; it does nothing to better yourself. What makes it hard to leave is that once one lousy thing creeps into your mind, it opens the door for every bad thing, big and little, that has been patient and quiet, waiting in your subconscious, to race to the front of your mind. Every little fight you had where you said something you came to regret or did something that wasn't becoming of you, every time you spoke in a volume that became hostile, is fresh in your mind again.

Every. Little. Thing.

It just sits right behind your eyes, playing over and over like commercial ads reminding you of everything that you were and still might be. The frustration from the reminders only angers you more because you know you aren't that person. You are better than you were and even when those things happened, you weren't proud. But you can't take back what you said and can't undo what you did.

Maybe it's my thinking that's flawed. Perhaps it's me. All I know is that right now, nothing feels right. Nothing feels real, and all I have to help me feel better is a six string and whiskey. One of those things is a long way to the bottom. I don't want to drive down that road again.

The fact is, though, as angry as I am right now, and as much as I feel unproductive and want to watch the world burn for a moment, I'm getting places lined up. Maybe productivity even when it stems from negativity is still good. At the very least, it's still productivity.

It's been a few days since Faith told me she was going to try and work things out with Ronnie. I know it's only a matter of time until that blows up again, but I don't have the power to move things along for them. I accidentally did that once, and it hurt … my face. I don't dare think about how much it would hurt if the situation somehow repeated itself. Not that it would. In the past few days, I've taken care of a lot of the tour arrangements for the following months, and things are looking good. From hotels and motels to even the no-tells that we'll be staying at and the venues they'll be rocking are almost all lined up. Once I start making one phone call, the rest just seems to happen. The label is doing radio ads for the local region and poster ads for the farther reaches of their fandom and to draw in new ones.

But that's just it: this is what my life has been for so many years, and it feels empty. I want to share it with someone who is as excited about it as I once was. Someone who can breathe life back into me and make me feel like I have meaning and purpose. Wouldn't that be a great cosmic joke? We're all full of piss and vinegar about life until we find our purpose. Then it becomes dull and unfulfilling, repeating itself over and over, draining the life and will to live out of us until we die. *The Grand Irony of Life*. Album title of the moment right there.

There's a part of me that hates thinking like this, a piece of me that knows I am being petulant and unreasonable, a part of me that knows I have friends that would take a bat to somebody if I asked them to. But even those friends are only my friends because of the industry and what I've done for them. So yes, I feel alone, and there's a part of me that knows I may have done this to myself. There's another part of me that wonders if everything I'm feeling right now is just stress-induced anxiety. Will it all calm down after the wedding and after the start of the tour, or will it continue until I can find someone who doesn't care about the material things I can offer them and wants to be around me for love of the game? For love of being around me?

I am almost forty and still struggling with feelings of inadequacy and inferiority since as far back as I can remember. The sad thing is, even when I point out to myself, or someone points out to me, all the things I have accomplished in my short stay on this planet, all I can do is listen and sing along to "Bohemian Rhapsody" playing on my iTunes, about how anyone can see that nothing actually matters and nothing matters to me.

But on the other hand, I know what I do matters, maybe not in the cosmic sense spanning galaxies and clusters but it matters here, on Earth. On this rock we call home, what I do matters. People listen, and they are affected. And that is something. But of all the people I may or may not have changed with my music, how come I can't find something to affect me like that? Or is that the missing muse I'm now once again lacking in my life? Damn, I hate this feeling. I want it to go away.

The fates answer my cry to the universe with a text message, a simple sign that things may not be as bad as I feel they are right now. Jacquelyn apparently is the sign I was looking for, as her text reads,

[Jacquelyn: You around?]

Short, simple, to the point. The point though is what I don't get. I know this isn't a booty call. Booty call? Is that phrase even alive anymore? No matter though, it's not that.

[Finn: Yeah. What's up?]

I reply, not wanting to come across like an excited puppy waiting for his new home.

[Jacquelyn: Wanna come over? I'm off work tonight.]

I don't really need to think about it. Yes. Yes, I will go over. I take a moment to text back. Not that I needed it, but I didn't want to respond too quickly. I am relishing in the fact the universe listens sometimes.

[Finn: Sure. I'll need your address.]

I grab my wallet and keys and head to the liquor store. I figure a nice bottle of whiskey since it's what she drank at the show. She might like more than whiskey, but I don't want to bring something she doesn't like. Thing is, I don't know what she wants, of course besides hanging out. Maybe she doesn't have an agenda, just looking for a friend. What could be more friendly than a friend with whiskey? I don't want to seem like I'm asking her to go steady with me by bringing a bottle that's too nice, so I figure I'll just grab some Gentlemen Jack©—quality enough to not get sick but not expensive enough to give mixed messages. Maybe it's just whiskey; I shouldn't over-think it.

As I pull into a parking space for the liquor store, Jacquelyn texts her address and tells me to bring a swimsuit. I'm already out, so I figure I won't swim. At least now I feel like she's inviting me over when there are going to be other people. I mean, who invites one person over to go swimming? That just seems a bit … I don't know … strange.

I make my way through the light traffic on I-4 and end up at her house a short time later. As I pull up, I realize I either missed the life of a short party, or she has other things in mind. I'm about to find out which.

"Those don't look like swim trunks," she says, opening the door.

"Didn't get the message till I was at the store buying this," I respond by holding up the Gentleman Jack.

"It's cool." She smiles, grabbing the bottle. "We don't need suits anyway."

The mystery that is Jacquelyn confounds me each time we meet, but it's not a bad thing. Seeing her brings a sense of calm to my otherwise chaotic mind, a sense of peace that only Faith used to bring but now only adds to. I look around the otherwise empty house, scanning for signs of life besides her and me. I see nothing and hear no one.

"Who all is coming by?" I ask, following her to the back lanai.

She looks back at me for a second while she continues walking. "In case you can't tell, I don't have many friends."

"I find it hard to believe that someone like you doesn't make friends easily," I say, trying to be smooth.

She opens the sliding door leading to the pool, sectioned off from prying eyes by a privacy fence. "It's not that people don't want to be my friend. Don't make that mistake. I'm just selective. Too many people want to be friends with me for the wrong reasons."

I chuckle because I can understand her sentiment. There are moments when the single-serving stranger by my side is nice, but it's not real. It never is. The connection isn't with me; it's with what I do, but I don't know what she does. The elusive being that is Jacquelyn hasn't told me what it is she does, but I can gather it is something that doesn't yield many close friends. Given her looks, I bet she's a model. I chuckle, and that causes her to turn back to me.

"What's so funny?" she asks, dipping in her toes to test the waters of her hot tub.

"I can relate," I mutter, looking around her pool. The in-ground hot tub spills over into the long pool, whose circumference waves along the sides. The pool lights within the waters change color every ten or so seconds, adding to the allure of the evening. Next to the hot tub is a wine glass with old wine stains at the bottom—a sure sign of nights spent alone in contemplation about something she'll never tell.

"I'll be right back," she says as she disappears back into her house, still carrying the bottle of Gentleman Jack©.

I wonder what it is she wants tonight. A friend to hang out with or someone to help her forget something? Whatever it is, I am not going to overthink this. I'll enjoy it for what it is, and much like the Nirvanna concert, listen to what the universe is trying to tell me.

I slip off my shoes and socks while she is inside. I carefully test the waters on the first step into the hot tub. Hot, but not scalding, a gentle heat to complement the chill air tonight. From behind me, I hear the door slide open and the clink of two glasses against a bottle. I turn back around to see a bottle of Cabernet Sauvignon and two glasses in one hand and two towels in the other.

"About the other night," she says, setting the glasses and towels down on a table next to the pool.

"No worries," I interrupt. "You don't have to explain yourself to me." I do find it interesting I bring over Jack and she pulls out a Cab. Maybe she plans on me coming back. Perhaps she just wanted wine.

She gives me a half-smile of appreciation for the interjected words. She pops open the wine and pours a glass for each of us.

"I'm glad you came by. It's hard to find good people when you work in an industry where they have the wrong idea about you based on what it is you do." She hands me my glass. That was a long-winded response, if ever there was one.

"My objective tonight is not to find out what you do for a living," I say, raising my glass. "To new friends."

She clinks my glass and takes a sip while keeping her eyes locked with mine. "So, you didn't bring a suit?"

I shake my head, eyes still locked with hers.

"We're adults here, right?" she says, looking to the hot tub.

"It would appear so," I reply with a curious mind.

"Since you don't have a suit, neither will I." She takes off her top.

And in about the most confusing three seconds of my life, I try unsuccessfully not to stare at either the most perfect set of God-given D cups ever grown or the most natural-looking fake boobs ever. I don't want to be staring like some high school boy at his biology teacher that he's lucky enough to finally nail against the classroom blackboard, but I am. Not even so much in the fact that she just so nonchalantly took off her top, but the fact that she did it without the implication that this is going anywhere.

She sees me staring and smiles. "Eyes up here, big guy."

I snap out of it and nod in agreement with her words. "Yeah, yeah, of course. Yeah. Didn't mean to."

She turns around and starts unbuttoning her shorts. "It's just flesh, my good sir. We all have it."

And there it is: no more thinking that Jacquelyn is some mystical, mysterious, mythical creature. Oh my. No. She is just someone comfortable in her own skin and sees no reason to be modest about it.

She grabs her glass of wine off the table and slips comfortably down into the hot tub. She takes a sip and waves the glass at me. I know she is wanting me to take off my clothes, but I freeze. It's not like this is even the first time I've gone full monty in a hot tub. It's just my first time with her. The thing about this moment isn't that a female wants me to get naked. It isn't even that an attractive woman wants me to get naked. The notion that nags at my brain, making me feel like a redheaded mermaid falling for a guy who doesn't know she exists, is that I do feel something for her. It's the ambiguity of my feelings for her that makes this moment so nerve-wracking. I know I can't place it precisely, and that inability to do so is causing me to freeze.

"Scared there, champ?" she calls me out. "Or ya gonna get in?"

I snap out of my brain fog and come back to the moment. "Yeah, I'm coming. Just a little chilly." I set down my glass of wine and start to unzip my jeans. She lets out a "bow-chika-bow-wow" like cheap music from bad porn.

I kick off my shoes toward the table; one hits a leg of a chair, jarring the awkward moment into a little more awkwardness.

"Did that on purpose," I say, trying to play coy.

"Sure ya did." She laughs, calling my bluff.

I take off my top and fling it over a chair back. The cool air of the night sends shivers down my spine and goose-bumps form across my chest. Sure, I shiver a bit from the cold, but more so from the nervousness of the moment. I know I must get down to what God gave me, but the sudden cold breeze is doing nothing to help my cause with the little man, my special guy who is getting smaller and smaller with each passing second. So, I drop my jeans and take one leg out, but as I go to take off the other pant leg, I stumble a bit on the damp concrete. A few fumbled steps, and I grab a patio chair. The chair is so lightweight that it slides with the leverage from my body, sending me to the cold ground.

She claps her hands while saying, "Bravo! I give it a seven out of ten."

I look up from the ground and smile through my wounded pride. Standing back up, I know this is the last step before there is nothing between Jacquelyn and me. This is the final moment that separates men from MEN.

I drop my drawers, having no shame left after the fall. Maybe it's the pride that has abandoned me. Maybe it's that I'm standing here buck naked, and my little man looks like a turtle who's retreated into his shell. Either way, I drop them. I stand before this gorgeous woman in nothing but my birthday suit.

"Well, hop on in. The water's nice and hot."

I start to step down into the hot tub, the temperature of which might be able to slow boil an egg, but it feels so nice against the cool air of the night. As I take another step down, my whole body starts warming up. I sense the heat of the water climb my legs and radiate throughout my entire torso and down my arms. My red-eared slider starts coming out of his shell.

"Your wine," she says, gesturing behind me.

I turn around, having forgotten my glass from the moments caught in my head. I grab my drink and return to the waters. I sink down opposite her. As I settle in, I watch her as she looks around the night sky to the stars above. The ambient color of our surroundings changes with the underwater light in the pool, as it cycles through deep red, blue, green, and white, and back again, over and over. The wavy lines that shape the pool add a sense of calm to the evening.

"I find it hard to believe that you have no one else you'd rather be with tonight," I say, calling her bluff.

"Believe what you will, Finn. I like the time I've spent with you so far. Figured I'd see what you're like just hanging out." She sips her wine, then continues looking to the skies above.

I relax some more and slide down in the tub till my neck and head are the only things above water.

"It's amazing what you can find on people when you search their name online." She brings her gaze to meet mine.

"Some more than others, I presume," I say, sipping my Cabernet.

"The real question is why do you want to hang out with me? There must be someone else you'd rather be with?" she says. She starts to creep her way toward me.

I could be honest. I could just blurt out that I'm here because I'm momentarily angry at my life choices and back in college, I should have stayed with the girl I was with.

I should have made the conscious decision not to be an asshat. I could tell her that I am here because the woman I want to be in this hot tub with is working things out with her current guy; that this girl that Jacquelyn has never met is trying to erase the image of me being balls deep in her from her man's mind. But let's be honest, that would not exactly be the nice thing to do. So, a comforting spin on the truth it is.

"I too choose my company wisely. Someone as selective as you must understand." I pretend not to notice her inching my direction. I look around her backyard at the chaise lounges under an umbrella and the small, round four-seater table with painted PVC chairs next to the loungers. I scan my way around the flower garden with what I assume is an attempt to grow some kind of foliage.

She stops about halfway to me, reaching out to grab the bottle of Cabernet, refilling her glass. She doesn't inch closer after setting it down. The thought that maybe she was just slowly going in for a refill does occur to me, but the pacing of it seems a bit peculiar.

"I've read some interesting things about you, sir. May I inquire if they are true?" She asks her question in a tone of voice that is both very straightforward and not lacking politeness. The question to me shows that she has not had any real run-ins with anyone who ever once was, or still is, famous. Bringing up particulars of one's past is sort of an unspoken taboo, but there is also an innocence to her question that makes me think perhaps she's just making conversation. I mean, I haven't heard her phone buzz or ring at all tonight. Maybe she isn't one who has a cornucopia of friends waiting to get shwasty at a moment's notice.

"If you read it, it must be true," I say, smirking. "Otherwise, why would it have been said?" I start inching my way to her. I figure it seems to be the thing to do, so why not do it? She doesn't give me a look of disapproval, so I continue.

"Well, I mean, I'm sure some of it must be false." She shuts down her words. "I guess, asking you about these things violates our first-date clause of no questions."

I stop close enough to her for a feeling of intimacy but not close enough to be intrusive. Just close enough that if my hand falls an inch or two too far, it may gently caress her leg. However, before I can even get to test that strategy, she pulls my move. I feel her hand casually pass over my leg, sending shivers up my spine. The subtleness of it, as she pretends nothing just happened, has my heart pumping just a little faster than it just was. Then again, maybe it was an accidental graze.

"It would be a violation of those rules. At least for now. I'll answer a more specific one if you answer a question afterward." I offer up an exchange.

She purses her lip toward her ear and scrunches her nose in quick thought. "Depends on the question," she rebuts.

I nod at the quickness of her counteroffer. "Okay. Here's the question." As I am about to say something, I feel her hand rest on my thigh—intentional and well played, though I am not exactly sure what it means. She's comfortable and maybe she's just friendly, or this could be going exactly where it is meant to go; where, now at least, I hope it goes. I forget my question for a moment as I think about her hand on my thigh, slow-moving it closer and inward. The thoughts swimming through my brain have taken the turtle entirely out of his shell. He's starting to lift his head and neck in search of his surroundings.

"Cat got your tongue?" she says, as her hand strokes my inner thigh in small, deliberate motions.

"The ... question .... is," I say in between breaths being stolen from me, "what is your occupation?" I try to word it as carefully as possible so she can't weasel her way out of an answer.

Her hand stops. She looks at me with eyes that are flooding with disappointment. Not my intentions at this moment. I did not mean for this ship to change course, but before defeat overflows from her eyes, a devilish grin takes over. She moves closer to me, turning to face me. I can feel her skin connect with mine under the water and can't help but look at her lips at this moment. A little bite of her bottom lip tells me this is going to go exactly where I now think and hope it will go. There is also a part of me wondering why it is going where it's going. Is it because she wants me or because she read about Finn Fairlane extraordinaire in some e-zine? As much as I should care about her motives, I like her, and no matter the reason she wants me, she wants me. I choose this life and can't really be too snub-nosed about why she wants me. On top of it all, it's not like Faith is knocking at my door. No, she went back to Ronnie. She went back to years of not feeling like it is actually what she wants. Whatever. Right now I have things to concentrate on.

Her hand slides over and grips my rock-hard manhood. She gently moves her hand up and down, just enough to tease me a couple of times.

A smile crosses her face. "It's nice to see you are a grower and not a show-er."

A slight chuckle escapes me. "Told you it's cold."

I wrap my hands around her and run my fingernails up and down her back. She leans in for a kiss as she climbs onto my lap. I feel her perfect breasts press against my chest. Her soft flesh against mine as the hot water flows around us causes my arousal to heighten. My man is now standing at high alert, code red, the alarm that says you must be ready at less than a moment's notice because the shit's about to get seriously real.

This kiss she gives me, it is not disarming, not like the first time. That kiss was to get out of my head any mis-interpretation I might have had that first date. It worked, and it put her in control. She is still in control as her kiss explores more than just my lips. There is a deepness in her touch that pierces my soul yet is gentle enough to say that this night might be more than just the things we do for unlawful, carnal knowledge.

I pull back from this kiss and lock eyes with her. She waits in anticipation of finding out why I pulled away, not a look of disappointment but more of a yearning to know why I stopped.

"We are on uneven playing ground," I say, slowing the mood down a bit. It might not be the suavest thing I can say to control the pace of the mood, but it's all I have.

The wind picks up for a moment as she shifts back from me a tad. It sends a chill across my warm body, causing quite a jarring feeling. It takes me out of the moment for just a second. I shake it off the best I can as the wind dies back down. The clear skies above grow cloudier by the second. A distant thunder roars; no lightning though, just the clap of thunder.

"I promise I'll tell you. Don't ruin the moment," Jacquelyn says with a slight grimace.

I nod in silent understanding.

Her grimace fades away. "I just find that once people know what I do, it's the only reason they want to be with me. You understand?"

"I do, and when you tell me, then you can ask any question you want about my past," I tell her. I can't help but think that if she genuinely understands being in that situation, she wouldn't have Googled my name. Or at least she would have respected the violation enough not to have brought it up in conversation in some attempt to lure me in. But I want to enjoy the moment. I want to enjoy this encounter and this being with her. The violation of our initial agreement aside, I enjoy my time with her, and much like Viv, she doesn't seem to mind my past, or at least what she read about it.

I look into her eyes and push aside my other thoughts. I pull her close to me and connect our lips. She lets out a little exhale as she climbs back on top of my lap. I feel her skin press against mine as I become more and more aroused. She reaches down below the water and grabs my rock-hard, little man. Forget the foreplay; as Rilo Kiley sang about talking and touching, well, it leads to sex, leaving no mystery. Well, there will still be some mystery left, at least for me. Jenny Lewis may have left out kissin' in those lyrics, but their fans get the point—and right now, so do I. Jacquelyn wants it, and she wants it now.

She maneuvers herself right on top of me. I feel the warmth of her lips between her thighs as they wrap around my man. Jacquelyn is met with resistance as she tries to slide me inside. She scrunches her face as she wiggles my stick, trying to fit me inside her. There is no happy ending, at least for the moment. She flops down out of momentary frustration. I can feel myself sitting between her, my sausage snuggly wrapped in her warm, tender bun.

"I seem to be having trouble." She lets out a timid laugh, squirming around as she rubs her squeezebox on my ... well, inappropriate musical metaphor for my penis. I'd come up with one, but blood isn't flowing to my brain at the moment.

I smile at her troubles. Sex is not why I came over here tonight. It has just turned into a huge bonus ... if we can make this happen.

"No worries. If at first you don't succeed ... but you know this isn't why I came here tonight," I say, clearing up any misconception she may have.

Her voice quiets down. The look in her eye is shadowed by the underwater light changing to a dark blue. It gives her a menacing look, like she is about to tell a scary campfire story. She is still so beautiful in all her apparent maleficence. Her right hand is below the surface. She moves my sausage aside to play in her own playpen. I'm not sure what she is doing but who am I to stop her? "I know. It's what I wanted. I don't get to do this as often as you might think. But I want this. People look at me and see a piece of ass and a big set of tits."

"I don't think that's all true. You are very gorgeous but... " I try to say something that will boost her waning self-image, but my mind erases all the words I've ever known, making me unable to finish the thought.

THE FORTUNATE *Finn Fairlane*

She smooshes her lips against mine as my thought escapes me. The tightened eyes and raised cheeks tell me she has had this conversation before. Her left hand grabs my hand and places it over her right. I feel three fingers emerge from inside herself. She places two of mine back inside. She uses her hands to silently direct mine. I am her sex toy for the moment.

I. Am. Happy.

"It can be. But you didn't. You were respectful at the store and the concert. It impressed me," she says, pulling my hand out and going for a second attempt at insertion. "Now shut up and get inside me before the mood is ruined for good."

If there is ever a time to know when to shut up, now is it. I don't know what the hell the finger play was for, but it did something. The approach is still tight but manageable. The runway is cleared.

I. Am. In.

A thought enters my mind—no glove, and yet I am still getting love. The first thoughts that always go through a guy's mind race through mine. Is she on birth control, or are we using the ever so unreliable pull-out method? Does she have any STDs? Hell, do I have any STDs? I know I don't, but it's still something to think about. How can she trust that I just won't bust a nut inside her and have little Jacquelyns or Finns running around in nine months? I can't really answer those, but I sure as shit don't want to ask them either. One of those questions put an unwilling look on my face. She stops. She leaves me inside of her but comes to a standstill. She rests a hand on each side of my face, holding her stare with mine.

"I am on the pill, and we've been over the herpasyph," she finishes with a deep, full-tongue, passionate kiss. While those words aren't exactly a mood-setter, they do set my mind at ease. She is sharing something with me tonight; I am here for her pleasure.

The look on my face relaxes. I can feel my tension wash away as Jacquelyn gives me her reassurance on my unspoken thoughts.

She slowly moves her hips as I fill her up. The light of the moon and the underwater colors set the mood for a much more passionate encounter than I would have imagined. The occasional slight breeze further cools down the chill of the night.

Our hands caress each other's bodies, exploring wet skin as we try to find where and what pushes the right buttons. I discover some of hers in the small of her back and the inner thigh. Not too close to the fun zone, more midway down her thigh; the area that is too intimate for public, and generally the start of where you try touching to test boundaries—like the previews at the beginning of soft-core porn. This is what turns her on. No complaints from me. My fingers run behind her neck, gently touching where her hairline starts. I can feel her shiver for a moment and stop breathing. Just for a second, then she catches her breath.

"Finn," she whispers ever-so-softly in my ear. The feel of her breath on my skin sends shivers through me.

The bubbling jets of the hot tub drone out their watery approval as we stay intertwined and connected beneath the surface. But even above the roar of the jets, I can hear Jacquelyn's heart beating fast and, if beating hearts could beat in emotional tones, nervously excited. I'm sure she's done this before. She knew exactly what she was doing to get me to this point, but still, the sound echoing from her chest has newfound excitement in each rapid beat.

Her grinding against me starts to quicken. She digs her nails into my back as if she needs to hold on or else be sucked away in the vortex of a black hole. The piercing pain adds to my arousal. She bites her lower lip as I feel her tighten around my member. Her nails release as she keeps increasing her speed and pulls close to her, smashing our bodies together in an attempt to defy the laws of physics. And I say kudos to her efforts. But I am a man, and the sensations are too much. She holds me tighter as I try to pull away. I am trapped in her wild, sexual embrace.

"I can't hold..." I start to tell her, but she stops me with a deep kiss. I feel her muscles pulsate around my rock-hard sidekick.

She continues her climax as she pulls on my hair yet keeps me in for more kissing. My arms fly down to my side as I can't hold out any longer. My pelvis thrusts upward as I cum hard inside her.

She rests down on me for a moment as she writhes around, playing with my man still in her. She smiles while looking around at the patio furniture behind me and the yard and space beyond the lanai.

"You're not as ... vocal as I thought you'd be," she says, still scanning the surrounding area.

"Same can be said of you," I reply.

"Private moments are meant to be private. You don't always want to be the main attraction, do ya?" she says, returning to me. She slides off of me and stands out of the hot water.

As she wraps herself in a towel and heads on in to clean herself up, I can't help but think about what she said. *Do I always want to be the main attraction? Could that be my issue? Faith, Viv, now Jacquelyn.* In some way, could there be something inside of me that craves to have every girl helplessly fall for me, like some nineties song about love letters in the sand?

I do know that tonight wasn't about rekindling some long-lost love, nor was the excitement with her about the possibility of being caught by restaurant patrons or throwing a bone to a long-time fan. It wasn't even about her fulfilling some long-time teenage fantasy. It was about the moment; it was about us.

I sit alone in the hot tub as I watch the few clouds above pass by, covering stars as they do. The infinite abyss above me, and bubbling water around me, and all I can think about is the girl a couple dozen feet away from me cleaning herself up. I don't know much about her. She only knows slightly more about me. But I do know that until this thought, Faith had been out of my mind.

Maybe that's my problem. I always have and always will come back to Faith. Every thought, every action, everything I do, eventually, for better or worse, will be done with her in mind.

From inside, I hear the unmistakable organ notes resonate and the lyrics that immediately follow suit as she hits play on her stereo. A girl who, in this day and age, still uses a real record player and stereo set-up, not some iPod dock connected to what now passes as quality desktop speakers. As Madonna sings outs from inside, I know that this girl, Jacquelyn, is a mystery, one that apparently stands alone. The problem is that when I hear her call my name, it doesn't feel like home. But the sadness that flows through me right now is that I want it to feel like home. There is this woman who has given herself to me, if only for a night, and seems so sincere and real in what she does, even if she does seem a bit apprehensive about letting me into her world.

So now, in a matter of months, I find myself caught twice between my undying feelings for Faith and another woman. This one doesn't seem to mind my past and wants to be with me for other reasons than who I once was or how much money she thinks I have. But unlike Jacquelyn, Faith doesn't seem to want to be with me. Maybe this time I won't have the opportunity to mess this up with my lovingly disastrous ways.

I open my eyes to the harsh light of day. As the world comes into focus and my mind clears away the fog of sleep, I remember I am not in my own bed. She is gone: up, awake, and somewhere that is not within eyesight. Clear in my mind are the events of last night that led into today: the hot tub, the wine, the sex, and the bedroom afterward.

Everything that is running through my mind right now are thoughts I've had at one point or another about one woman or another. But now, I am comfortable thinking these thoughts: feelings of uncertainty and being okay with that—true desire for someone other than Faith. It is strange not to fight these thoughts and hold onto the possibilities of what my mind thinks could be with Faith, to let go of those, at least for the moment so I can ponder the possibilities with Jacquelyn. You know, before I unconsciously and inevitably mess things up here to leave open the possibility there.

I cross my arms behind my head and stare at the MC Escher mounted on the wall across from her bed. I think if art says anything about the character of a person, this piece is pretty much my life. The stairs that are leading everywhere, with no real direction to any one place yet, while boggling the mind to comprehend the spatial reasoning does make sense in the chaos. If I can relate to that, then maybe she does too, and that's why I feel the connection to her.

The chaos of it all hits me. One week until the wedding and only an extra five days until the tour starts. So much to do still and here I lay, in a new girl's bed, trying to figure out the meaning of life. It brings a smile to my face because no matter how many times I've been in this exact situation of lying in some girl's bed the next day, contemplating the meaning of it all, it is never the same. The meanings I find in the previous night's events are never the same. No two women are ever the same, and thus why my next day's contemplation is never the same. So, I lay, trying to figure it out but there is a nudge in my mind, a nudge that makes my subconscious speak aloud to me, that this time I shouldn't overthink it. The voice inside my head whispers to me that I should just let it be. Perhaps this is what she was trying to get across to me at the concert.

But here's the thing, I can't just let it be. Everything I've done since I met her has been for her. Her being the capital H. The F A I T H. Everything since we've broken up has been because I've had thoughts about her, thoughts about what could still be, or what could have been, to put it more realistically. Ideas put into lyrics about regrets of things said and done, songs about my, and the great human, inability to move on because we know how wonderfully fantastic things could be if we could just get it right—like an artist continually tweaking the hairline of a portrait to make sure the resemblance is absolutely perfect—we strive and strive to make things right so they can be everything we ever hoped to be. But more often than not, things are not what we expected. Things do not turn out like we thought they would. They turn out how they turn out and, more often than not, the way they turn out is well below our expectations of where we think it should be. I look around at how it has turned out for me.

I look around this room at the MC Escher and to the antique dresser with a vanity mirror connected to, what I assume, is some sort of makeup lighting concoction. I look up to the ceiling at the off-white color needing to be repainted and think about how my life turned out exactly like I always wanted. I wanted the music. I wanted the fame and the fortune, the weeks in and out of hotels and long nights on the road, all of it. But when you want all these things, and you are working toward these things, you don't think about, because you can't see, what will get left behind. You can't foresee what will get damaged in the process; the things that get hurt that, one way or another, leave you scarred and a little less human.

The smell of bacon and coffee waft into the room from under the door. I take a deep breath and enjoy the aroma. I reach over the side of the bed and grab my shirt and pants. I figure with the tour mostly planned and ready to go, I can take care of smaller details after eating a filling, late breakfast.

As I pull my shirt over my head, I hear the sound of footsteps and the door to the bedroom open. My top pulls down over my eyes to see Jacquelyn standing there, looking radiant and far too awake no matter what hour it is.

"Thought maybe you worked up an appetite." She extends the tray my direction.

I straighten myself as I pull up my jeans. She walks the tray to me.

"Thank you. Smells delicious," I note.

She places the tray on my lap and takes a seat at my feet. I dig into my food and coffee.

"I don't care about your past. It's what you do now that I care about. It's what you do today that makes you a good man or a bad one." She doesn't mean to, I'm sure, but she sounds like the beginning of a motivational speech in some coming-of-age film.

I stop eating and raise a brow to her words, waiting for her to say more. "I had fun," she continues. "I have fun every night we are together, and I'm not sure how I feel about that."

Not the most promising way to end what I'm guessing is her attempt at some sort of confession. I wait some more to see what else is on her mind.

"I mean, I'm not normally the dating type. Life's led me down a more 'love-em-and-leave-em' path." She hesitates, as if I may cringe at those words. "But with you, it's different. It feels different. More comfortable and yet uncomfortable at the same time. I'm not sure how to put it into words, really."

I swallow the last bite from my pile of bacon and set the tray aside. Before I say anything, it dawns on me that she generally doesn't cook, either for herself or others, as my entire breakfast tray consisted of about half a pound of almost overcooked bacon and coffee. No eggs, no pancakes or waffles, just bacon, which leads me to believe she was happy I stuck around. This is her attempt to do something nice, which also leads me to believe that whatever she does for a living, it is not cooking.

But back in the moment with her, I find some words. "New. The word you are looking for to describe your feeling is new."

She shakes her head in short bursts of agreement without breaking eye contact. I grab her hand. "Whatever you find you need out of this thing we have going on, it's okay. You don't have to figure it all out right now. I'm not going to ghost you or cut you out."

I feel my phone buzz in my pocket, and I know she hears the quiet commotion too because the look in her eyes shifts out from wherever she was lost in and back to her bedroom. Her eyes almost look sad for a moment as she is brought back to the reality that we can't lay in bed forever.

I pull out my phone, figuring it's some email confirmation on one of the hotel/motel stays we have on the tour. But no, this moment with Jacquelyn couldn't end uneventfully. It has to be interrupted by a text from Faith—cryptic and vague.

[Faith: Meet me at the patio. I'll have a drink waiting for you.]

[Finn: I have a few errands. Tour shit. Be there this evening.]

[Faith: I'll be there.]

Life can't ever be easy. I have come to learn that's the way the universe works, at least for me. I can't enjoy this moment of newfound feelings Jacquelyn has for me. I can't be relishing in it with her because now I have Faith on my mind, poking away at me. Jacquelyn knows it too. She sees it on my face—a tenseness that wasn't there before I read the text.

Jacquelyn stands, distancing herself from me. "Let me guess: you have to go?" She hammers that nail dead center on the head. Her face falls as all happiness she just felt is washed away by the cynical beast resurfacing. Her immediate composure starts to shut me out as she stands there, trying with failing effort not to cross her arms.

"Yes. But there's nothing to worry about. I have to go meet someone, probably about the tour or her sister's impending doom with irrational, preconceived notions of love and marriage," I say, trying to calm her growing nerves. "Want to meet up tonight sometime?"

Her arms uncross, and a new sort of uncomfortableness clouds over her. "I can't tonight. I have to … work."

"Ah, the elusive work topic. I see. Well, if you want, call me afterward. We can have a late dinner or early breakfast, if you'd like," I offer up.

A smile crosses her face for the first time since she heard the rattle of my buzzing phone. "I'm sorry. I get that way sometimes. Comes with the territory."

"You don't have to apologize for who you are. You don't owe me an explanation. I'm just happy you like me enough to get jealous over suspicion," I say, calming her nerves. "May I use your shower before I go?"

She nods as she walks me to her bathroom. "Of course. You don't mind if I join, do you?"

The hot water ran over our bodies, causing scenes from last night's hot tub adventures to replay in my head. My eyes were focused on her, bringing my mind back to the present. Her toned abs, an outline of a six-pack starting to shine through. She definitely gets her exercise.

She presses her perfect breasts against me as she moves in for a deep, passionate kiss. I love the feeling of her skin pressed against mine. The water makes small pools where it can, cascading down our bodies in little waterfalls.

Now, in any standard shower sex scenario, I'd turn her around, smack her ass, and fuck her from behind, watching the shower water bounce off her perfectly sculpted ass, but there is passion in the air, a new flavor of romance dancing on my tongue this moment that says, "not facing away. Not doggie style." I want to keep it more personal. There's a long-lost emotion that has awakened in my mind that wants something more.

Right behind her are built-in shelves for soap and shampoo. Perfect footrests for me to try new shower adventures. I turn around so the water runs over her. I don't need the warmth right now, and cleanliness can wait till this is over. I run my hands down her back as she strokes my ego, making it bigger and ready for action. I place one hand on each of her ass cheeks and firmly grip down, hoisting her up. Her feet catch on the makeshift footrests now behind me. She is either a quick learner or has done this before. She holds onto me with her left arm while aligning our fun parts with her right.

I slide inside her, smooth and easy. I hear her take a short, deep breath and tense around me, the familiar feel of someone being pleasured by me. The sensation only adds to my growing feelings for her.

As she slowly wiggles and slides around on my (what Lady Gaga so eloquently refers to as) Disco Stick, I realize that my feelings for Jacquelyn might be growing faster and have a farther reach than I feel I am ready for. Only once before have I fallen for someone in such a short amount of time, which brings me back to where I am supposed to be heading—Faith.

"Shit," I say out loud, thinking I am going to have one pissed-off ex on my hands if I take too long.

"It's okay. Like I said, I'm on the pill," Jacquelyn responds to what she thinks is me about to send my little guys marching on.

But I take the misinterpretation to try and speed things along. I concentrate on her moist warmth that surrounds my member. I look down as she thrusts her pelvis back and forth, forcing me to fill her up. I look at her to see her staring at me, which excites me in new ways. She speeds up her grinding as I feel, even in the showering waters, the spilling of her juices all over me. I feel them run down my leg, intertwining with the shower water. She bites her bottom lip as she tries not to deafen me with her screams. I can't hold it anymore; her permission to land has been received. My body tenses for a moment before it all involuntarily relaxes, including my grip on her bottom. She slides off my rock-hard erection as I accidentally drop her; an accident that shoots massive amounts of unwanted pain in my special place.

She makes quick work of her feet and pads her fall as I try to regain my grip on her. It works just enough that her somewhat gentle landing leaves her unharmed on the shower floor. I, on the other hand, manage to hold myself up just long enough to make sure she is safe before sliding down in searing pain.

She has this look on her face as she giggles like a forest nymph. She is not laughing at my pain but at the comedy in the situation. It makes me start to chuckle, which does not help relieve any of the pain, but she is just too beautiful as the shower rains down on her to not laugh along.

"So much for going out with a bang today," she says through her laugh.

I crinkle my nose, nodding at her statement, as I collect myself as much as I can. She stays down there, looking at me, even though I turn off the shower. As she smiles, I see in her eyes someone who looks content. I always said contentment is next to godliness. So, I'll take the happy look in her eye as I dry myself off with the towel that was flung over the shower door.

And yes, I know what you are thinking. Cleanliness is next to godliness, but if there is a god and you stand next to him, I think contentment would be the first feeling that comes to mind, not, "Boy, do I feel clean." That's what showers are for.

"Can you turn the shower back on for me, Finn?" Jacquelyn asks as I step out. I oblige, leaving her happy and content in the indoor rainstorm.

"Call me later tonight?" I ask, heading out of the bathroom.

"I'm out late. Is that okay?" Jacquelyn shouts from under the stream of water.

"Of course." I make my way down the hall.

I don't want to leave right now. What I want is not to have a throbbing penis that is hurting because it was just bent close to a 45-degree angle while rock-hard. What I want is to be with her in the shower, holding her or, at least, pulling her hair. But as I said, I have to go to the woman to whom I will always be a slave.

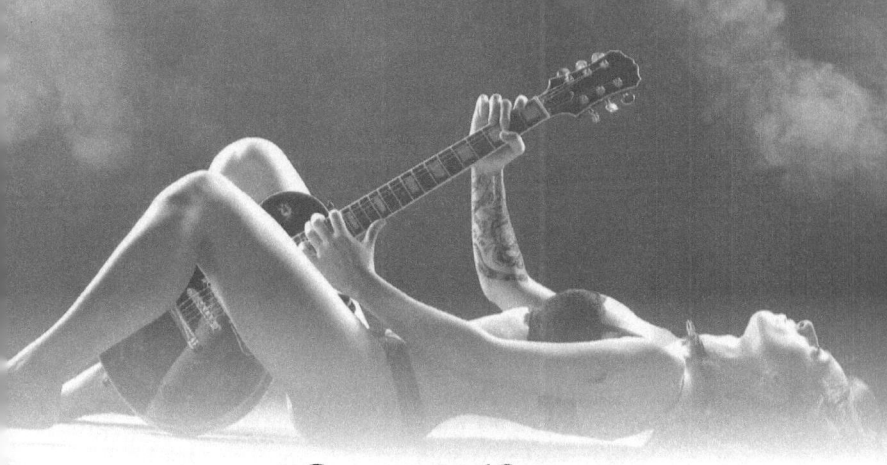

Chapter 10

Broken Things

T he night air is calm as I enter the patio section of our old haunt. I see Faith sitting there by herself, away from any crowd. Her only company is the drink she has waiting for me. None of the usual suspects are around. Sure, there are other people, non-players in my world taking up space around me: the regulars we know only from here but never see anywhere else and the usual staff. They laugh, talk, drink, and go about their world without concern for what is happening in mine. I don't mean anything contemptible by that. I go around every day without more than a general concern for what happens in other people's lives. I think we all wish people well in a unified notion that humans are, by nature, not assholes. We just don't go out of our way to make sure every stranger we encounter is happy and taken care of. If we did, homelessness would be much less a thing. But I digress.

Faith sits there and connects eyes with me as I approach. There is something I can already see simmering just below her surface, waiting to come to a boil.

She hands me my drink as I get within arm's reach. I start with a sip of the now watered-down libation, before taking it all down to save the integrity of what was once a good drink.

"Took you long enough," Faith starts. "Everything all right?"

"Perfect. I'll tell ya, if anyone asked me ten years ago, hell, even three months ago if I could ever be truly happy with someone who wasn't Faith Siubhal, I would have laughed in their face. This new girl. There's somethin' there. I can't explain it, but it's there. I would never have thought you pushing me away would actually work out for both of us. You back with Ronnie, giving it the good ol' college try. Me, happy and content for whatever it is we have. I didn't know I could feel that with someone other than you."

As I finish my last sentence, I realize that everything I just said either sounded way too manic, like I'm losing my mind or, more likely, like some backhanded way to brag to her about how I feel right now. From the look on her face, she is not as joyful about my newfound happiness as I am. She forces out a smile to hide the truth I just saw. I'm not purposefully sounding mean or trying to dig at her. She asked; I told. Then again, she is the one who pushed me away and said she was getting back with Ronnie, so I shouldn't feel guilty over my happiness; maybe I feel bad that my happiness seems to make her less happy right now.

Whatever the reason for the way she feels, I need to give her a chance to speak. So, I bring it around. "How are things with Ronnie?"

She smiles a quick smile and stands up. "Let's take a walk."

"Where did you want to go?" I inquire.

"Anywhere but here," she says, starting off the patio and toward Highway 192.

Where we are on 192 is part of the main thoroughfare. A seafood restaurant is across the street, next to a hotel and discount gift shop. Next to where we are is a jungle-themed miniature golf course. I've not played it myself, but that's not saying I won't. And, of course, next to the mini-golf course is yet another staple of the greater

Orlando area—another discount gift shop. The sidewalks that line 192 are sprinkled with tourists and locals making pilgrimages to various destinations around the area. It does remind me of Reno. The streetlights and neon signs of the surrounding buildings guide our way as we stroll down 192.

We stop at a parking lot exit as a crowded SUV pulls out to make a right. Faith looks at me, "So, you really like this new girl?"

I let out a smile, one that comes so naturally just thinking about the mystery that is Jacquelyn. "Yeah. I do. She's ... uncomplicated. Or at least that's how things are right now. It's nice. Comfortable."

Faith lets out a quiet chuckle before walking on.

"Maybe not uncomplicated," I backtrack, causing a raised eyebrow from Faith. "Well, yeah, uncomplicated but mysterious."

She continues staring at me with a hint of a smile trying to cross her lips.

I know she needs a little more so I say the only thing I can think of. "It's complicated."

She shakes her head at my unraveling of the whole thing.

"Not the relationship. Understanding it is complicated." A feeble and failed attempt to clarify.

She only shakes her head, looking upward into the night sky.

"It's funny," she says.

"What is?" I respond.

"The universe, life, everything," she says, the weight of her words causing her to sigh.

I am enjoying this little moment with her, even though I'm not sure where she is going with this. I too look up toward the sky and the infinite beyond, trying to see what she is looking at.

She continues her ponderance. "The vastness of it all. To think that within the scope of existence, we are not in the same spot of the universe we were when we first met. Not just that Earth travels around the sun but that the sun moves throughout the universe, on a straight path forward." She pauses for a moment, just staring into the night. "But we don't realize we travel. To us, we feel like we've not moved. But try to imagine how far we've come." She looks forward again and continues walking. "Did you ever think we'd end up here?"

The gravity of her words hits hard. I'm searching for the right thing to say, but I'm not sure there is anything to say. I think her words are things to ingest and let take over your body. It's thoughts like those that made her my muse. The ideas, dreams, and notions of life she has can still instill inspiration without even trying. She is magical. So, I enjoy this walk with her.

"Hell, I always thought it would turn out differently," I admit in a moment of raw truth. "Did you think it would have led to this?"

She smiles and gives me a soft huff. "Had you asked me that back in college, I would have thought I'd be living in a subdivision somewhere. I'd be working somewhere, marketing probably. But that changed. Had someone asked me after I finished cosmetology school what I would be doing, I would have thought I'd be some hotshot salon owner by now, rakin' in the dough. But as it turns out, I make a good living doing what I do and don't have to deal with owning a salon."

"Never thought about the end of you and me?" I put out there.

"Sure. Once, it was all I thought about, especially right after we broke up. I wanted to turn around and see your smile that told me everything would be just fine." Faith turns to see me smile. She points to me. "That smile. Right there. I dreamt a thousand times of that smile saving me. But it never came around. I never heard from you. I only kept up on you through magazine interviews and radio shows. So, I moved on. But I always figured in the end, if it was meant to be, it would be."

The words she speaks do not bring much relief to my soul. I don't feel saved or redeemed. I feel like those words told me that everything I did between our break-up and now has been misguided. Maybe that's life—just a series of foolish steps trying to do the right thing. Hell, I don't even know how to respond to something like that.

"I wish I knew. I would have run back," I say.

"But it's that you didn't know that made me able to move on," she says. Those last words slay the demon that has been taunting me, and possibly her, for two decades.

We continue to walk in comfortable silence for a few moments as we make our way farther down the street. We feel ourselves being sucked into the tourist-trapping lights of 192. I am not sure if it is the proverbial flame of the neon lights pulling us in like moths or something more, but she has yet to speak on whatever the subject is she wanted to talk about. I'm not going to force her to speak either. When she wants to chat about it, she will. It's just pleasant being with her: no big news or life-changing event is happening; no sexual tension waiting to snap; no anger aimed at either of us; no animosity brewing beneath the surface. All cards laid out. All our chips cashed in. Just two friends who are enjoying a moment together.

"Ronnie's coming to the party, right?" I finally break the silence after a few, long moments.

"What party?" Faith says, watching traffic whiz by.

"The bachelor party. I figure the past is the past, and if you and him are good, then I should be good with him." I know it sounds cheap and tawdry. I don't care; it's not. Our lives are intertwined and have been, even the years we were apart. If this guy's going to be in her life, then he's going to be in mine. I might as well make the best of it.

She thinks for a moment, making a few contorted faces as she gathers her thoughts. While I didn't think my original question or clarifying statement that followed was confusing or misleading, something in my words set off something in her mind that is causing a sort of internal confusion.

After a few, short moments of her face finding its way back to normal, she manages to say, "Yeah. I think so. I'll ask him. I thought you already invited him."

"I don't know. I may have. I'm just making conversation. Not really sure what else is going on in your head and thought words needed to be spoken." That's crap, kind of. I wanted to be nice and make sure he's coming. A friend of my friend is not my enemy, so why not embrace it? She might be right though. I may have invited him already.

"So, the tour is all laid out?" she pipes in.

"Yeah, looks like Logan Square will be doing at least all the East Coast stops with Spear Fist. Maybe more, but that can be played by ear for a bit," I offer up, trying to add some sort of enthusiasm to the quiet that surrounds us.

"I'd suggest clearing the air of any lingering whatevers that might still be hanging around between you and Viv," Faith says in an all-too-wordy response.

"I don't think there's anything to clear," I say, looking across the street at a couple of random teenagers meandering about a parking lot.

"No lingering emotions? Nothing to say to her about the turnabout in the bushes with Logan?" Faith pries.

I shake my head. "Honestly, nothing going on there."

"If you're sure," she prods.

"I'm not sure what you want me to say. Admit some lingering feelings of hopeless romanticism toward her and how I wish we were still together? She broke it off and for good reasons." I try to shut her down, but still she pokes.

"What reasons were those?"

I stop walking on the sidewalk near some parking lot entrance. The lights of the stores behind Faith turn her into a silhouette. "She said that if she stayed with me, she'd be with me, but I would be with her and you, at least emotionally. Is that what you want to hear?"

"It's not about what I want to hear, Finn. It's about the truth." She turns back to continue walking. "So, is it true?"

I stay silent for a moment, thinking about my words. Rare moments allow me to choose them wisely. I think because in these rare moments, my mind knows I am most likely going to have to eat them. "True? Yeah. Always. But you know that, so I don't know why you need to hear it from me."

She laughs a hard but honest laugh. It's a laugh that starts in the stomach and works its way out to help save the brain from the pain and aggravation of what you are about to say. "Do I? When we were together back in the day, how many other girls were there?"

She pauses and looks at me. The look in her eyes demands that I do not answer. I just take a deep breath, indicating that she should go on.

"Even now, after we … reconnected or whatever, how many girls? How is it that you love me? How is it that you have all these feelings for me? Feelings that place me so high on some holy pedestal, making me untouchable and infallible in your eyes? I need to know. These aren't rhetorical."

A car obnoxiously blares its horn as it whizzes by, the music that raged out of the open window partly drowned out by the loud blast of the horn. The dark, with all the surrounding artificial light, silhouettes the car and hides the mysterious driver. But it takes me out of the moment, if only for a second.

"Well?" Faith says, further prodding me for an answer.

"Of course. But I don't hold you on some infallible pedestal. Make no mistake of that. I know that you, just like me, are fully capable of fucking things up without trying. I love you not even in spite of that great ability but love you more because of it. I never needed a perfect woman. I've made my mistakes, but you were always the right thing. You were always the one choice I made that I knew was right. You, Faith. No one else. But you asked me to stop. With no uncertain words, you said, 'it's over.'"

"Is it ever really over between us?" she says.

Those words make the universe stop. Every planet and star have stopped in their paths. The question that, if answered, would give me the answer to life itself. Is it ever really over? Only time will tell. But knowing that it won't be answered here and now, the universe moves forward.

I look at her. In the reflection of the neon lights, I can see tears running down her face.

"I don't see why you needed to know all this anyway," I say. "You got your guy back. But here's the thing. In the short few months I've been down here, I've made a family. D.B., Vince, Neil, Gregg, Viv, you, hell, even Jeanine. You guys are all my family. So, I might always love you, and that's fine. That's for me to deal with. I won't pursue you. I won't bug you. I won't bother you or remind you of what could have been. I got your message. But you are part of that group, and we are all on the same path in the same caravan. I can deal with that."

She starts walking through the parking lot toward a Baskin Robbins/Dunkin Donuts shop. At this hour, I'm not sure if she's looking for a sugar fix or hit of caffeine. I'm just along for the ride.

She turns to me and stops just outside the door. "It all matters, Finn. It matters more than you know."

We both reach for the handle at the same time, causing our hands to touch. Nothing we haven't done a thousand times before, but there is a spark. She pulls away too fast, like a reaction to static shock.

"Wasn't there something you wanted to tell me? Isn't that why we went on this walk in the first place?" I ask, letting go of the door.

The same honk from moments ago sounds again from a car entering the lot. This time, the lights of the buildings illuminate the racing stripe on the blue Camaro that is undeniably Ronnie's.

"Hey, you guys!" he shouts from the window, unintentionally sounding like Sloth from *The Goonies*. I might not have anything against the guy; it's just that he sure makes the shots easy to take sometimes.

He pulls into a parking space with the force of a stunt driver testing the limits of the car's brakes. He hops out and lumbers our way.

Faith turns to me and smiles a tiny, half-smile. "Yeah, I do. Another time though."

"Thought I was s'posed to meet you for beers?" Ronnie says in a way that conveys his less-than-intellectual mind.

She smiles for him. "Yeah, just decided I wanted some ice cream. Thought I'd make it back before you got there."

He nods at her—an indication her answer was acceptable to him, though I'm not sure what would have happened if it wasn't. He turns to me. A quick thought enters my mind that I should either run, run so far away or start round two of a losing battle, but a more mature idea dominates my actions. I extend my hand out in greetings.

"Nice to see you, Ronnie," I start.

He looks down and half-heartedly shakes my hand, "Finn. Keeping your paws to yourself."

I casually let go of his grip. I don't want to come across as defensive. I also don't want to maintain a handshake with a man who still holds a grudge. It might be a legit grudge but still a grudge, nonetheless.

"No hard feelings, I hope." An earnest response, hoping to diffuse any further momentum.

"Nah, man. I won." Ronnie sneers his lip while flexing his pecs beneath his white tank top.

There's a part of me that wonders what Faith doesn't see in herself or what she does see that makes her feel so inferior or so undeserving of someone better than him. I'm not saying that someone better is me. I can hope it's me, but I'm just saying anyone better than the oversized neanderthal that is Ronnie Frown. And while I can understand how he got that nickname, I can't help but wonder if that's the surname he signs now.

"I trust you're coming to the bachelor party?" I ask, trying to bring the conversation around to something slightly more comfortable for Faith, and to help this brute move beyond the image of my little guy in her behind.

"Hell yeah. It'll be..." Ronnie pauses for a moment, and at that moment, all I can think to myself is, *Don't say it. Please don't say it.* A small hope that he has some original thought in his mind, but he says it anyway, "Legendary." For the love of all that is holy, a phrase that has been well established and now wholly unoriginal in usage just spewed forth from this man's mouth. The only person among the more than seven billion people on God's green earth that can say that phrase and not be called unoriginal is NPH. On the other hand, Ronnie's right. Legendary it shall be.

"Good. Then let's get some ice cream and head back to the bar," I say, holding the door open for them.

"Ladies first." I wave my hand for Faith to enter first. Ronnie follows behind her with a quick slap on her behind.

She jumps from the unexpected slap and shakes her head, presumably at the juvenileness of his action. Though, the look on her face reads, to me at least, that this is the man she has consigned herself to. We grab a quick couple scoops of ice cream. She orders orange sherbet and I peanut butter and chocolate. Ronnie buys some monstrous sundae topped with everything they have behind the counter. The good news for me is that if he eats like this on a regular basis, I won't have that many years to wait until he drops dead of a heart attack.

For now, however, we climb into his monstrosity of a muscle car and cruise back to the patio bar we love so much. The quick two-minute ride is filled not with any sort of intellectual or enlightening conversation, but instead, our ears are graced with the gravely sounds of some Lamb of God-style vocalist. Not bad music by any means, but not the mood-setter to end what lack of conversation Faith and I didn't have.

Our short trip out for ice cream is enough time to fill the patio with the usual suspects: D.B., Gregg, Jeanine, Vincent, Neil, Viv, and Logan, all relaxing around the red-cushioned, plastic wicker furniture that makes this spot so homey. As if walking into a scene from month's past, D.B., dressed to the nines with his leather-studded wristband, is swaying a beer around in exaggerated motions as he tells some story to a crowd of mesmerized onlookers. Again, I think to myself that these people could probably not care less about him if he weren't who he is and who he is going to become shortly. Then again, he is who he is. So, enjoy the moment, good sir, for they are fleeting and few as the years go by.

D.B. sees us enter the patio and his storytelling stops as his eyes turn to the three of us. He wets his throat with the rest of his beer as he stands up, waving us over.

I hear D.B. say to the crowd of spectators, "This is who I was talking about. The man, the myth: the one, the only Finn Fairlane."

Some girl from the crowd who reminds me a bit of Faith from our heyday pipes up, "Wait a minute, bruh. All of that over a girl? No way would a girl ever go through that for some dick."

D.B. turns to the young woman, who after saying "bruh" makes me think her driver's license was purchased from a frat boy for fifty bucks, and retorts, "Ask him yourself." He then turns to me, slinging his free arm around my shoulder. His beer breath makes me slightly intoxicated. "Finn, I was just regaling some tales of yore. These fine folks don't believe me when I tell them of your exploits!"

I excuse the fact that he sounds like a pirate onto his second or third bottle of rum and turn my attention to the crowd for a moment.

I give the crowd a humble smile. "I'm sure whatever D.B. said is either oddly true or wildly exaggerated. Your choice as to what to believe." I turn to the man that has helped me stay relevant and whisper in his ear, "You get the stripper lined up?"

"Just one?" D.B. laughs. "No, my friend. I got three!" He pats me on the back while laughing. "The stories from the party will need to be epic enough that they live on in the hearts of all men!"

"Gregg! Come here," I shout while waving my hand.

He gets up from sitting next to his fiancé and, after planting a huge kiss on her lips, walks to us.

"Nice to see you, Finn," Gregg starts. "Very excited to see what you all have in store."

"Me too. It seems that D.B. has made some adjustments to the plans," I say.

"As long as I have plausible deniability, Jeanine can't be mad," Gregg clarifies.

"All good, mate. You know nothing!" D.B. sounds even more like a pirate than moments ago.

I turn to Gregg. "Has he been watching a lot of pirate movies?"

"Had a marathon earlier today. He's on a kick," Gregg replies.

"Well, then. Yo ho ho and a bottle of rum!" I shout, flinging my arm around D.B.'s shoulder. "Next round on me!"

As we all sit regaling stories of yesteryear, I can't help but notice that Faith, as happy as she says she is with Ronnie, giving their relationship another shot, doesn't have the look on her face of someone who is ecstatic to be with their significant other. The look on her face might be signaling something more. I would go talk to her and find out what's bothering her, but she told me no. She said she wanted to be with him. So, who am I to fix her problems? Of course, if she said anything, I would in a second. But she hasn't, and quite honestly, I can't get Jacquelyn out of my mind.

The hours pass, and the restaurant finally closes down. We all sit in quieter moods as our last drinks have been drunk. The winds from the day have all but stopped. Hell, even the traffic seems not to be as noisy. The staff has come to terms with us sitting on the patio after closing, with locked doors restricting our access to bathrooms. It is the point of the night that as people find the need for the facilities, they find themselves in their cars heading to wherever the night leads them. As the numbers dwindle down, I am surprised to find it down to just Faith, D.B., and myself. D.B., though, is passed out across one of the red-cushioned love seats.

I watch Faith as she sits almost uncomfortably, like a child who wants to speak up but doesn't know if talking is allowed. I don't want to be the first to speak on this. I do wonder where her man ran off to. This late at night, leaving her alone doesn't seem like the gentlemanly thing to do. Not that anyone here is a threat. However, in this area, you hear stories, and I wouldn't want my lady, whether it be

Jacquelyn, Faith, Viv, whoever, to be on the nightly news in some tragic story.

A buzzing in my pocket interrupts my less-than-pleasant thoughts with a welcome invitation from Jacquelyn: *Come on over if you'd like*. No need to ask me twice. I nudge D.B. to wake him, but he is passed out cold. I decide it best to let sleeping D.B. lie and save the goodbye for those in the land of the woke.

"I gotta get back to Jacquelyn," I say to Faith, as I turn from D.B. "You just gonna stay here all night?"

She smiles her sad smile and shakes her head. "I was hoping to talk to you about something."

"I remember. It's why we took our walk that got interrupted. Then you said, 'another time,'" I recap. "I've been here all night. You have said nothing." I realize that may have sounded like an attack. It is not meant to come off like that. It's just that she has been avoiding me all night, and now that I get up to leave, she suddenly remembers.

"It's not when I meant to make this happen," she defends.

"Whatever it is, I'm sure it is great news for you and not going to be such great news for me. Anyway it goes, news that must be told to me directly by you doesn't have the glow of something that is going to overcome me with joy. So, can this wait for when I'm not tired and can handle stabbing news with a bit more aplomb?"

Faith nods and smiles. "Yeah, Finn. I gotta figure out where my man went off to anyway." She gets out her phone and starts texting him.

I lean in and give Faith a friendly kiss on her forehead. When my lips meet her skin, I can feel her shiver just a tad, not too much but just enough to say there is more to explore. However, now is not the time to pry or read too deep into things, so I leave it, and her, to the remaining night.

CHAPTER II

Life Is a Highway

L ife's got a funny way of working out sometimes. You see someone, and you don't know why but something is nudging you deep inside that says you have to say hi. You don't know why, but you do. You follow that instinct. A friendship is formed, or possibly two lovers have just said hello. Life sometimes points things out to you like it pointed out Florida for me, signs that keep popping up over and over again, like the number twenty-three. It's nothing you can place your finger on, but it seems so right that anything else is just wrong. You can feel it anywhere you are, at any time, without notice. Here, in Florida, on this peninsula of impossible weather, it happens more often than one would imagine. This phenomenon is not just about meeting potential lovers or friends. It's about the number of small businesses that flourish here against all odds. It's about Florida Man and things that could only happen here in the land of alligators, meth, and sunshine. The invisible hand of fate that guides you along the path of life seems to favor this state and its residents.

But that's how it's been for the last few days. Every moment spent with Jacquelyn seems to be those moments guided by the hand of fate. *La Forza Del Destino*. We haven't been doing anything that would seem paramount. We haven't even left her apartment in three days. But every moment since I exited the patio without news has seemed to be guided by a force not of my own. I am okay with that.

The plans for the tour and the bachelor party are all in place. I am left with next to nothing on the agenda. My to-do list is down to having a talk with Gregg and no other deadlines. Jacquelyn had a few days off, so we decided to make the most of it. Our time was divided relatively evenly between her bedroom and the kitchen. There is something very relaxing about lounging in bed, holding the person you are falling for. And I was falling ... fast. It's not been that long since I met Jacquelyn, but still, I find myself more and more fascinated by her. My thoughts are continually leading back to her in the moments between making love. Ideas of what-if and could-be situations all seem happier if she's in the picture. The thought of her not being around darkens all the colors of my mind. While rock 'n roll is known for black clothes and dark makeup, those shades just don't seem like colors to describe us two. Jacquelyn is definitely a door I don't want painted black.

But here's a hue that does darken Jacquelyn and me ... Faith. The nagging feeling in the back of my mind—the what-if. The should've, could've, would've that is my history both real and imagined with Faith. We are two intertwined souls on this life that is a highway, and yes, even now while I am with Jacquelyn, I want to ride it with Faith.

All. Night. Long.

It's a struggle, a war within my head, a devil on one shoulder and angel on the other. I try pushing my thoughts aside, the little voice inside my head that tells me Faith is the one, the cosmic intertwining, but I can't. Even though when we are together, I've become better at playing the role of uninterested, I still am. I've started treating her like I've treated so many one-night stands over the years, as if she's disposable. That's not what I meant to do, but I guess it's what we've boiled down to for now. And for now,

I really do love, or what mixed emotions can be confused for love, Jacquelyn.

Day three of our mini-staycation, and we once again find ourselves exploring each other's bodies. This round, we decided that making cake while making love seemed like a fun way to multitask.

We both face the bowl of unmixed flour, sugar, egg, butter, and vanilla. Jacquelyn stays bent over in front of me, trying to hold the electric mixer in the ingredients, while I glide in and out of her from behind. She turns the beater on high, causing a bit of flour, egg, and sugar to splash out of the bowl. I help her steady her hand and get the beater deep inside all the mixings. We slowly mixed the batter, hand on hand, as we continued making love. The eggs blend with the flour and sugar, forming a paste that the butter warms up to and begs to be a part of. The vanilla swirls around, slowly enveloped by the rest. All the ingredients merge into one tasty, decadent treat. We continue mixing it together as we both reach our own climaxes, a perfect finish to making the batter.

As my endorphins calm down and the fantasies of the past three days dim in my head, reality sets back in. A few different thoughts rush in my mind as I stare down at her beautiful, perfect, heart-shaped ass. I have to leave this moment; I have one last duty before the tour—the bachelor party. But another thought enters my mind, one from years prior. A thought of buying my car, of being on that lot and test-driving the car before I bought my current one. I know where this thought is going, and I don't like it.

My beautiful Grand Am almost wasn't mine. I saw the green shine in the sun a few cars down from where I had currently been standing. The car in front of me, keys in hand, ready for a test-drive was a Porsche Boxster, and it was beautiful. By all standards, the Porsche was a superior car to the green Grand Am that glistened for me under the sun, so I had to test it out. The salesman seemed to want me to want this car. I wanted to want it. So, we took it out. It was beauteous. The engine purred like a kitten.

The leather seats were as comfortable on my ass as any pair of breasts I had ever rested my head on. We took off out of that lot like a bat out of hell. It cornered beautifully and stopped on a dime. I had no reason not to buy that car. It was priced reasonably for a Porsche. It had no visible damage. Now I'm not a mechanic, so I didn't know what to look for under the hood that indicates wear and tear that will need replacing sooner rather than later.

So yes, I should have walked off that lot the proud new owner of a Porsche Boxster. She was a beauty. But when we pulled back onto the lot, we drove by the green Grand Am, and my undying love for Pontiac shouted inside me that I needed to test-drive one more car that day. The green Grand Am wasn't perfect, but she was comfortable, ran smoothly, and I know Pontiacs. There is comfort in familiarity that had me leave behind the Boxster for what anyone would say is an inferior model. But I did and had no regrets about it. I love my Pontiac.

And so, I stand in my birthday suit as Jacquelyn stands in hers, scooping cake batter into a pan. She uses her finger to scoop out a little bit of batter and feeds it to me. I eat it off her finger and smile. She deserves better. I have no chance with Faith, and Jacquelyn indeed is a Porsche Boxster if I need to make such a vulgar comparison. But Faith always shines brighter in the sun than anyone else ever will. Jacquelyn deserves to be with someone who she shines that bright for.

Hopefully, one day, she will shine that bright for me; I want her to. While the past three days seem to have dulled Faith a little, only time will tell if this shining down is temporary. It shouldn't be like this. It shouldn't be that someone needs to come along to make dull the shine of someone else. It should be that the person who comes along shines brighter. *One day at a time, Finn. One day at a time,* I tell myself, because any other way will just cling onto hope that is gone.

A quick shower and brush of my teeth later, and the cake is ready. We sit at Jacquelyn's dinner table that is straight out of the late seventies or early eighties: white laminate with gold trim, white metal legs that flare out at the bottom to make it look luxuriously laughable. But it's what she has and surprisingly beautifully contrasts the rest of the decor. Table and matching chairs aside, the cake is pretty good.

"I don't think I'll be able to see you tonight," I say, sipping some milk to wash down a bite of cake.

She smiles and swallows the last of the cake. "It's okay. Tonight is going to be a late night. I think a night away won't kill us." She winks at me, and it sends butterflies fluttering about my stomach.

"I still don't know what you do for a living," I pry. It's not that I care so much as the curiosity over not knowing has grown greater.

"I haven't told you yet." She reaches for more cake. "No questions, remember?"

"Yeah. I remember. I also thought the past three days might have earned me a little something," I say, finishing my milk. I stand up and head to the door. I have to leave and am not starting an argument over something so trivial right now.

"All in due time, Finn." She meets me at the door and wraps her arms around me. "Have fun tonight, and don't do anything I wouldn't do," she says through a little chuckle.

"After these past few days, I struggle to find what that might be." I go in for a deep kiss. Our lips connect, and tongues dance for a moment. I pull away and look into her eyes. I sense a bit of sadness inside them.

"Did I say something wrong?" I don't want to offend her. It was not my intention.

She shakes her head. "You're fine. Have fun. See you tomorrow, maybe?"

I nod as I walk out the door. As I reach the end of the walkway up to the door, I turn back. Jacquelyn watches me as I walk to my car. I smile and wave. She puts up a hand and casually shuts the door.

Life Is A Highway

With the scenes from the past few nights playing out in my head, I think to myself that this night is going to be unforgettable. I need singles. Lots of them.

CHAPTER 12

Tattooed Dancer

I walk up to the place, the only place around that would let me set up what is sure to be a truly epic event, a bar in the theme-park district that holds itself to the highest standards. Tonight, we test that standard.

From the outside, the doors and the first ten feet of windows are blacked out. A way to protect their reputation, perhaps? Or to protect the eyes of innocent bystanders passing by? No matter the reason, it gives us more privacy. The bar inside is fully stocked with only top-shelf liquors, none of that Barton's or Montezuma shit. Only the best, like Cabo Wabo®, Herradura®, Casa Dragones®, Ciroc®, Belvedere®, Grey Goose®, Bombay®, Hendricks®, Havana Club®, Brugal®, and then more scotch, bourbon, and whiskey than I can even think to name. They all line the shelves for tonight's event. Opposite the wet bar is the food bar, set up with only the best Florida has to offer, which isn't a whole lot. I'm not saying there isn't good food down here. But there's no real Chicago-style dogs, Italian Beef, or deep-dish pizza. No authentic New York pizza or Cajun food.

What we do have in Florida are the best burgers in the South and possibly the country. (Some will argue that Kuma's Corner® has better burgers, but they've also been around longer.) We have Adler's Burgers at one station. From the first bite to last, these burgers put a smile on my face. The food alone creates an atmosphere of relaxation and conversation. A must-have for the night. Next to them is the Fish & Chip shop. Hands down the best in the area, and greasy food is excellent in helping break down alcohol. And of course, Tijuana Flats is set up buffet style. But what good would all that food and drink be without a dessert station? And because it's a night of lust and gluttony, we have alcohol-infused ice cream, and yes, the alcohol will add to your drunken buzz this evening. From Raspberry Limoncello to Chocolate Caramel Whiskey, Bourbon Stout Vanilla and more, there is something for everyone.

But if I am to mention all the food and drink, I can't leave out the highlight of the evening—the center stage for which all of this was set up, twenty by twenty, and stabilized with a top section to support the stripper pole. Chairs line the stage. And all of this is for us tonight. The only strange men here tonight will be us. No random creeper to make the dancer uncomfortable. Tonight, we are the random creepers. Tonight is for Gregg, to celebrate his life and his decision to tie the knot with the one girl I never thought I could respect: Jeanine.

Before any of the night's events can begin, I must do something I've been putting off. Once this night is over, even having the discussion would be counterproductive. So tonight it is. I invited Gregg out for a drink. Not here. He's not allowed to see the venue beforehand. He has no idea what is in store for him. I invite him for a pre-game drink on The Porch of Bad Decisions. I figure this is as good a place as any. Plus, we get to look out past the lake in the center of CityWalk to Toothsome® and Hard Rock® Cafe. I want to make sure that this talk I'm having, borderline too late, with him is as nonconfrontational as possible, something I am generally not one to consciously avoid. I figure though that, in this case, such precautions may be called for.

"Jeanine told me to expect this," Gregg says.

"I knew she would. She loves you. Or at least the idea of being in love," I say. So much for nonconfrontational.

"I'm gonna put a pin in that remark for a minute," he starts. "She's not Yoko. And do you know why your comparison is crap?"

I know why. But I'm gonna humor Gregg anyway. "Why?" I ask.

"'Cause by the time Yoko came along, the rest of the band was already starting to turn on itself. That piece of information is not some dark secret. Just the simple truth behind the myth that is the Yoko effect," Gregg rattles off.

"I know all that. But it's the myth that has been the root of band destructions. The band needs you, your decisions, not someone else's. Jeanine said she wouldn't interfere. I need to know that is the case and will be the case when you're on tour and she's not with you. She'll need to know you are still there for her, still with her. And I've seen it more than a few times where the female inserts herself in controlling ways as a way to delude themselves that the band member still loves her," I start.

"Jeanine's not like that," he defends.

"Maybe not now. I'll grant you that. But I need to know that a month into the tour, you won't be asking the band to change the setlist and record it as a way to show her you love her," I continue. I need him to understand and be sure.

"I wouldn't do that. Even if I did, why would it matter?" Gregg asks, starting to get defensive.

"Because it interrupts the flow. The groove that you will fall into. Change the setlist, change the groove. Friday's setlist is different from Saturday and Sunday, but they stay the same for a while. It's your first long-legged tour, and you need a groove. You need a clear mind and nothing weighing on it. No guilt from her or the band. No feelings of inadequacy because someone has injected themselves so deep in your life that you can't make your own decisions," I say, trying to wrap it up.

"Things will be fine. Once the wedding is over, all this stress will vanish, and I'll be able to concentrate on the tour," he says. "Let's pull the pin out for a moment. You said she was in love with the idea of being in love. What the fuck is that?" Anger swells in his voice.

"Let's slow down a moment. Jeanine said something about everything changing after the wedding. It came across very naïve," I explain, hoping it quells him a bit.

"So, she's a little naïve? What's the harm in that?" he asks.

Out of the mouths of babes—a thought I'm glad does not escape my lips. But I do need to respond to that question. Hypothetical, it was not.

"Look, I ran this course with Jeanine, and I'm here to make sure stuff doesn't blow up. She thinks that everything, all problems, all future problems, and any thought you might have to unzip your pants for another woman will magically get cured after the 'I do's' and refused to be told otherwise," I say as the look on his face drops. It's a look you see on someone the first time they discover something about their paramour that is less than appealing.

"I didn't realize," he says as his thoughts escape him.

"Look, I've known her since she was knee-high to a leprechaun. She's grown and matured as a human. In many ways, she's one not to reckon with." I pause for a second to make sure I said that right. I can never remember if it's "to reckon with" or "not to reckon with"; either way, I think he understands.

"But the two little words don't change anything. I'll still be on tour. She'll still be home. There will still be girls trying to cash in on some rock 'n roll fantasy," Gregg says in harsh realism.

"And I told her you're not like that. I told her you are not who I used to be." I let out a small laugh.

He looks at me with a half-smile, shaking his head. "No. Thank God I'm not. No offense, while who you were was awesome, that's just not my scene. After a show, I want to shower, maybe grab a drink at the bar with the band or crew, then crawl into bed to watch some TV."

"Have you told her these things?" I ask.

He nods his head. "I'm sure of it. I love her to death. She's my everything. I wouldn't do anything to her like that."

"Then tell her. Tell her you are the man she knows you to be and not the man she's scared you'll become." That's as honest a statement if ever there was.

"At the end of the day, Gregg, I have to look out for the band and its members. That includes you. The well-being of Spear Fist is my job," I assure.

"She's told me so many stories about you from back in the day," he starts.

"And it's stories like those that have painted all musicians to be like me. Caused her to believe that anyone in this profession must naturally act as I acted. Show her that you're not like me. Tell her what you told me and don't do what I did. You have a chance to have something great, but don't try to get there by ignoring the issues simmering below the surface." I try once again to wrap things up.

"Thank you," he says.

"Don't thank me. Just be good to the band. They're your family, at least until this tour is over. Then if you want to reevaluate your standing, you can. But the guys like you and you fit in. Don't ruin a good thing," I finish as I stand up. "You have a party to get to."

Most of the guests have arrived. The music is pumping, the alcohol is flowing, and two of the three dancers are dancing. I stand next to the bar, watching as D.B., Vincent, Neil, and Gregg are all stage-side, laughing and making it rain money down on the girls. The other attendees, friends and family of Gregg and the guys, are relatively evenly split between the stage, the food, the alcohol, and the ice cream. Hell, Ronnie's making his way through all the food as if it's about to run dry. The lights around the bar are flashing their various hues of reds, blues, yellows, and all the blended colors between.

As the song ends, one of the dancers slides off stage, picking up her bikini on her way out so the other girl can do her solo show. She heads my way as though she had been spying me while performing. I take a sip of my watered-down bourbon as she finishes dressing; a feat that done while walking must be quite tricky.

"Enjoying the night?" she says, breaking the ice.

I try to be a gentleman as I figure she is around enough sleazebags, but I do find my eyes wandering a little bit.

"It's okay," she continues. "You can look. It's why you paid us tonight."

I smile because I know that as much as men would like to think women don't notice, they do. They always do. Women don't have ESP or anything, but men harbor this illusion that women can't see their eyes wander as they look around, as if there's some law of nature that says because men can't see their own eyes, neither can anyone else. But they do; women see.

"And if you were up on stage, I'd be looking," I respond. "But you're trying to talk with me. That puts you in a different setting."

She waves her hand haphazardly through the air. "If only others were as enlightened as you."

"If only," I laugh. "So, you need a drink? Well, wait. Are you allowed to drink?"

Her eyes are still on me as she turns her body toward the bar. "I dance naked on a stage and grind on random guys' laps, and you think drinking isn't allowed? As long as I can do my job, I can have a drink." She waves down the bartender. "Vodka tonic rocks. No lime," she orders with a confidence that says this is the only thing she likes to drink. She turns back to me. "Love the tonic but never understood the old crooners and their gin. I just can't do the juniper taste."

"To each their own. If you're hungry, grab some food too," I offer up, still trying to figure out if she came here for me or for the drink.

She nods. "I will. How about a private dance? You are the one who put this all together, no?"

"Yes, I am. But I'll have to pass on the dance. Not that you aren't attractive; you are. Just that..." I start.

"You aren't sure where you and your woman stand on this sorta thing. No worries. I've seen your kind before. Your kind usually doesn't have the dough to put something this size together though," she says, sipping her drink the bartender just set down.

"If only my life were that simple."

She raises her glass. "To simple things."

I raise my glass, and we toast.

"Not to be a buzzkill but aren't there supposed to be three of you?"

She nods. "Running late. She'll be here shortly."

"She's not the only one running late," I say, feeling my phone buzz in my pocket. "Excuse me for a moment." I slide right on my phone as I make my way to the exit. "Viv! Where are you?!"

I manage to make it outside and away from the establishment to a not-much-quieter spot to try and hear her.

"I need someone to come get us! My car broke down! I can't get anyone to answer their phone!" she says in a faux panic.

"No worries. Let me tell someone who is sober enough to remember, and I'll be on my way. Do I need to call a tow truck or anything?" I say, easing her worry that she might not be able to see some strange tonight.

After finishing up the details of the where and how with Viv, I head back into the venue to find D.B. I figure letting someone know I'm leaving is better than just cutting out. D.B. is on stage, and the third stripper has arrived. The other two are dancing on the side of D.B., who is lying flat on his back. The third is squatting over his face, with her back to us, as she picks up a twenty off his nose without using her hands. I watch as she slowly lowers herself down, her wonderfully shaped derriere on display for all to enjoy. There's a familiarity to it though. A body part as ambiguous as that has a familiar look to it. I watch as she wiggles over his nose and slides on down, just enough to keep the twenty secure in her lady parts. She stands up, grabs the twenty, and turns to face my general direction.

I think of all the moments in my life that I've been shocked, awed, amazed, disappointed, dumbfounded, kerfuffled, and speechless, this one takes the cake. The face that accompanied the strangely familiar behind is one I have spent much time with as of late, and one I didn't expect to see up there—Jacquelyn—though this does explain her secretiveness about her profession. Her eyes meet mine, and in an instant, I see them go from empowered woman in control of herself and her future to ashamed girl whose father caught her doing the naughty in his home office while working out her daddy issues with some random guy.

I'm not sure what to think. There's a sense of betrayal that I feel while her eyes are locked on mine. Did she think I would belittle her for her job? Is she so used to men running away from her when she tells them she's a dancer that she felt some need to hide it? Or am I the one being naïve? Did she hide it so she could use me to get her rocks off? Please, I'm in the music industry. Hell, there's no difference between what she did to me and what I did to others. In paraphrasing the immortal Sir-Mix-A-Lot, "use and abuse me cause Finn Fairlane is not your average groupie." But still, she played me, if it was all an act like she was Little Miss-Understood. So, I gave her space and time, knowing she did her research on me and that violated the rule she set into place of no questions. She played me and played me well. Hard feelings? We shall see.

Most of the guys here are too caught up in the display of flesh that they don't notice the events transpiring around them. Most of the guys didn't notice, but Ronnie notices. I see him sipping a beer, silently watching this unfold with a sense of empathy in his eyes.

The internal thoughts that just played through my head gave Jacquelyn enough time to walk this way. Now it's time to test her mettle.

"It's hard to tell people. They all judge. You see it in their eyes," she says, standing full monty in front of me. I guess if there's ever a time for vulnerability, naked is it.

"Do you see it in mine?" I ask as bluntly as I can.

She stares at me for a moment, trying to find her answer within me. "Finn..." she starts but doesn't finish.

"You broke the rule. You knew who I was," I interject, not exactly sure where I'm going with it. "Did you think that little of me? Or was this all some game?"

I see the defensiveness overtake her. Her eyes lift up and narrow a little, like a hawk searching for prey. "A game? A game?!" she repeats a little louder. "Yes, there are those of us who think of this as one giant game and are out for themselves. Those of us who see a mark and schmooze them up to get as much money as they can without regard for what they do to get it. Is there anything I've done since we've been together that would make you think I'm after your money?!"

"I never said you were money-grubbing, and it's not my fault you've been doing this long enough that that's where your mind automatically goes. I meant our time together. Did it mean anything, or was it all just a way to pass the time between nights on stage?" I notice Ronnie inch his way toward us.

"Isn't that what you've done? For all those years, all those girls, isn't that what you've done? Isn't that what life is? Trying to find someone to help pass the time?" she retorts like some late teen trying to wax existential while sitting in a late night coffee shop. She's well into her twenties and should be smarter than this.

"There is not a woman I slept with that I wasn't in love with, even if it was just for the night. But this isn't about them. It's about you and me. Do we actually have something or not? It's a simple question," I ask as the look in her eyes calms down.

"Yes. But I didn't tell you because I didn't want to see that look in your eye that I saw." There is a steeled calm in her voice as she looks back to the stage.

"I only had that look because you never told me. I have to pick up some people. I'll be back." I find myself trying to prematurely wrap things up again this evening.

"So, I just hop back on stage and do my thing?" Jacquelyn tries to play the moment off as if nothing happened.

"Yeah. Otherwise, I'll have one disappointed bachelor on my hands. I'll see you soon." I turn to leave, and she heads back on stage.

Ronnie, who's witnessed the whole event steps over, beer still in hand. "You okay?"

I nod my head. "I think."

"Interesting girl you got there," he says, sipping his beer.

"Harsh light to see her in," I say.

"I know what you mean," he says with far more maturity and subtlety than one would expect from him. "I'll come with you. Keep you company."

"Didn't know we were good like that." I am honestly surprised at his kindness.

"We're finally even," he says, gulping down the rest of his beer. As we head out the door, he leaves his glass on a window ledge. "Let's go."

CHAPTER 13

End of Days

I feel like Orlando is listening to me, empathizing with me at this moment. The confusion, pain, and frustration the city and I feel are manifested in the chaotic rainfall and gusting winds that sweeping across I-4. The city is telling me it understands. It knows what I feel, and it feels the same. While rain is not an unheard-of occurrence in Florida, these rains are harsh for this time of year. Not a true tropical storm, nor a hurricane, at least not that anyone has told me about. This storm brewed quickly. The skies showed no warnings while I talked with Gregg earlier, but now it rages on. Even on high, my windshield wipers can't keep up. At least the traffic isn't at a standstill. The sounds of Okilly Dokilly playing from my phone connected through the auxiliary jack keeps us company in the storm.

"Not a good feeling, huh?" Ronnie says. I will give him this; he might not be an intellectual on many levels, but he gets straight to the point.

"It's … not pleasant," I respond. The last thing I want to do is piss off a monster who has finally called a truce. "I perhaps let my past take control of my better senses. It wasn't the proper thing to do."

"That's over, bro. You have new problems." He again shoots the bullseye.

"Yeah. I do." I try to smile. The thought of Jacquelyn hiding this from me is really what strikes a nerve. God knows I've done enough in my life not to judge her for her career path, but hiding it, even after she broke the agreement and researched me, that's what irks me.

There's a small part of me that says, "So what? She's a stripper. Get over it." I want to get over it and be fine. But if she knew who I was and am and still decided to hide it from me, then there must have been a reason. First thought would be shame, but I didn't see any in her eyes. I didn't hear any in her voice. So, I have to figure out what I am missing. I have to find the disconnect in my mind that makes everything all right.

"So?" Ronnie asks as the rain continues its relentless assault.

"So what?" I say back.

"So, what ya gonna do about it?" He lays it out.

I have nothing to tell him. I don't think my mind has gotten past the initial shock and anger of finding out in such a manner. I'm a grown adult and hold no illusions about the fairer sex. I know she's had sex and other sex-type relations with people before I came along. Hell, who hasn't by her age? I don't judge her by her past or present as she doesn't judge me for mine. But despite all that, the sight of her sitting on D.B.'s face is burned fresh into my mind. It's not an image that holds any amusement or humor for me. At least not right now.

If I force myself to stop and reason for a second, I don't care that she's a stripper. I don't even care she hadn't told me yet. I care that circumstances were as such that I found out what she did for a living by seeing her wrap her crotch around my friend's nose to pick up a ten spot or whatever it was. Then again, if I was a Dancing Bear and she found out while some lady was swallowing my sword to the hilt, I'm sure she'd be upset too. So, I guess, in the end, it is kinda funny. At least it was D.B. and not some creepy stranger. Of course, now I'm imagining her surrounded by a bunch of wrinkly, old men, all half-chubbed and dry-humping themselves while tossing five spots her way. But I push these images out of my mind and turn my attention back to the road and conversation.

What am I going to do about it? Hell, I don't know, but I do know that while this might seem like some big, defining moment in our, or any, relationship, it doesn't need to be. This isn't going to ruin a good thing, not something like this. It'll take something much more significant to destroy it for us.

"I'm going to be okay and move forward with us," I say most politically. "You can't expect people to change once you already accept them for who they are."

"Not to play the devil's advocate but you didn't know that about her to have chosen to accept it before you guys … whatever…" Ronnie lets his thought trail off, as if that many words strung together at one time, and using the phrase "devil's advocate," overheated his brain.

The music playing through my phone is interrupted. I look down at the caller ID and, for the first time since the night we met, wished she hadn't called. The rain has kicked up a few notches, rendering the high-speed wipers useless. I don't have time to reach down to my phone and reject the call before Ronnie swipes answer, putting it on speaker.

"Hey, Faith. What's goin' on?" I say, trying to keep it casual.

"Oh, hi," she says, sounding startled that I answered my own phone. "I was expecting voicemail. Aren't you at Gregg's bachelor party?"

"I'm picking up Viv and Logan. Viv's car broke down," I reply.

"Well, I guess in person is better than voicemail anyway," she starts.

"Okay but…" I try to tell her Ronnie is with me.

Faith interrupts, "No. I gotta say this."

Ronnie and I exchange glances. I raise my palms in defense for a quick second, then return them to the steering wheel as the car starts to pull right. He raises an eyebrow.

Faith continues with her thoughts. "I tried telling you the other night, but Ronnie interrupted."

Again, Ronnie looks my direction. This time, the raised eyebrow is replaced by gritted teeth, a look I've seen before and don't want to feel the end of, especially while driving.

"But Faith," I try again to interrupt.

"No, Finn. I'm not going to be brushed off or interrupted. I have something to say, and I'm going to say it."

I pick up my phone to take it off speaker, but before I can, she speaks.

"I'm pregnant." She finishes her thought.

I drop my phone onto the floor. The auxiliary cord tugs a bit as my foot kicks the phone farther out of reach. As I reach down to grab it, I swerve into the left lane. I grab the phone and return to my lane. A smooth recovery for such roads.

Ronnie throws his hands to the air. "You're what?!"

A startled Faith can be heard stammering on the other end of the phone. "R-R-Ronnie?!"

The traffic ahead all slam on their brakes. A jagoff in the right lane thinks this is the opportune time to cut in front of me so he can be ten feet farther in the dead-stopped traffic. The wind and rainy conditions exaggerate my swerve to avoid the collision with said-jagoff, and I find myself starting to hydroplane into the left lane. I steer into the skid but pull halfway into the lane next to me. I unwillingly force the car next to me onto the shoulder, but the conditions are too much for the sudden merge. His car hits the median and bounces back. As I regain control of my vehicle, the bounce off the median causes the other car to collide with my driver's side front tire.

"Faith!" I call out as my car spins, smashing the passenger side and Ronnie into the jag that cut me off. I hear a smash of glass as Ronnie's head shatters the passenger window. My car continues spinning another half circle. Ronnie slumps forward.

I try to catch my breath through the pain of the crash. The dead-stopped traffic in front of us is unscathed by my hydroplaning spinout. But the car that got run off the road isn't as lucky. I see out my windshield as the car gets hit, causing the start of a small pileup. A large passenger truck jerks his wheel to avoid the pile-up but is headed dead for me. The only thing standing between the inevitable impact of the truck and myself is Ronnie.

I look to Ronnie. He is still leaned forward, unconscious. A stream of blood flows down from the right side of his head and down his chest. The passenger door window is shattered.

My eyes are fixed on the truck barreling toward me. My ears take in the sounds of the rain and blaring horns. Somewhere, buried with the sounds of the chaos, I hear Faith crying out my name. "Finn! Finn! What's going on?!"

But I can't call out to her. I hear her call my name over and over. All I can do is watch as the truck helplessly slams into the passenger side of my car. In a split moment, I see the metal crumble, and the force of impact pushes Ronnie almost on top of me. His head falls toward me. My car shifts a few feet. I can feel it slide on the wet pavement. I only stop sliding because the car on the other side of mine is pressing its bumper into my back.

I know I can still feel my legs. I know because I can feel Ronnie's blood run down them as it streams out of his head. My chest hurts. Each breath is a struggle for air.

"Faith!" I whimper out. My voice gets drowned out by the sounds of the highway and rainstorm.

"Finn! I can't hear you! What's going on?! Where's Ronnie?" Her frantic yells fill the air.

I look down and see the phone. As I reach down for it, a stabbing pain grips my ribs. I cry out in pain. I can't reach it. I must have broken a couple of ribs. My back hurts. I can still feel all my limbs, which I assume is a good thing.

Ronnie is slumped toward me, blood still trickling out of his head. The crimson puddle below him and sprayed all around tells me he's lost a lot of blood. I look to what remains of the passenger side door. The metal and fiber-glass are crushed. His seatbelt suspends him in position. He needs help, if it will still do any good. I need to get help.

I force myself to unlatch my seatbelt and reach for the phone. As I do, I hear a loud cracking sound and feel a ripping sensation from my rib cage. My scream echoes through the phone to Faith.

"I've called 911, Finn! Stay with me!"

I look down to my ribs and see a bone jutting through the skin. Blood starts to trickle out of the wound. It doesn't appear serious, at least not compared to Ronnie.

Each word I say is a struggle. A fight for the air to speak. "Faith. It hurts. So bad. Ronnie's. Not moving. Bleeding. Everywhere."

"Help is on its way. Finn, I love you! Stay with me."

The pain is too much. The world around me starts to fade. I try to concentrate on the sights and sounds, but all my mind can do is think that Faith said she loved me. That has to be something. That has to be enough. I think about Ronnie, the guy next to me. The guy who is actually with Faith. Why isn't he moving? What happened in the initial impact that's causing so much blood? I guess, in the end, it doesn't even matter. His bleeding has slowed down. I no longer feel the blood running down my leg. I don't see it dripping off his head.

She said she loved me. I heard her say it. She loves me. It shouldn't take harsh realities like this to bolster the courage to say such vulnerable words. Three little words. She has told it to me before, and every time there were always excuses that followed. Reasons that even though she said she loved me, we couldn't be together. Anything to run and hide from the way she felt, from the fear that gripped her of the possibilities of what is and what could be. She always ran. Here, now, she has given me a reason to hold on. A reason to "not go gently into the night," as Dylan Thomas said but to stay here. Hang on to everything I have as long as I can. I know help is on the way. She told me it was. She wouldn't lie to me.

I concentrate as the world continues to fade. The noises that surround me start to grow distant, like a fading carnival as you drive away. The rain seems to beat down softer than before. The searing pain from the snapped rib has dulled down. I hear sirens in the distance. Maybe all will be okay.

THE FRAGILE

Finn Fairlane

DEDICATION

For all the women I've loved before, thank you for helping to make me who I am today.

And for Kris, the one woman who has never left my side, I love you more than I can ever say.

Table of Contents

CHAPTER 1

Welcome To This World

I keep having the same dreams: dreams of a better time; dreams of a time when things were simpler; when I was younger and, perhaps, stronger than I am now. They are haunting dreams from when Faith and I were new and discovering each other in every way possible. Dreams that feel more akin to memories being played back, like a movie in my mind, while I lay in slumber.

Dreams can mean many things, but I like to believe that they show us what we miss or what we wish we could change. Some dreams show us the life we could have had, the world we secretly wish we had. Maybe that's why my dreams always seem to irk me so. Perchance this life that I lead isn't what I truly wanted in my heart of hearts. But if I know this now, I have to wonder if it is too late to have everything that I desire. If that is true, then I need to find a way to the life I should have had. Perchance, the life that I have lived was the life better off left a dream. It's that unattainable goal that provides ambition, but ultimately leaves you where you needed to be—not where you thought you wanted to be. Maybe that's the rub and I am too late. I may be left with nothing but dreams I never realized I had.

This dream playing right now takes me back to New Year's Eve 2000: the Millennium, the big Y2K, the supposed end of it all. Most of us knew things would turn out just fine but jumped on the hype to make the most of a night meant for parties, drinking, and being with friends, the memories of years past and the good times to come. The Auld Lang Syne, so to speak.

We were at a house party somewhere in the Lincoln Park area of Chicago, either on the outskirts of the DePaul campus or just beyond. I guess the location isn't the critical detail here since my mind can't pinpoint its exact location, but there we were. It was Faith, me, and two of her friends from back home. It's been several years since that New Year's, but their names were Henry and Wanda if I correctly recall.

The funny things about dreams are the oxymoronic-sounding, vague specificities of them, like trying to recall a time when you were really high or stoned on something. You know the environment and approximate surroundings from the moment. In hindsight, though, the details are foggy, and the chronology is wrong. The dense, hazy aura surrounds the events you know you were at, but try as you may, you can't recall them as well as you'd like. The missing moments between the significant events that stick out in your mind are gone.

I know leading up to the party we were at some guy's house who lived above some family business in a three-flat on Fullerton. We were in his house, kicking each other's asses on Goldeneye 64 and smoking some most excellent weed. I remember that and taking my third hit from the joint. The next thing I knew, we were all walking west on Fullerton to finally hit up that party. All my THC-riddled mind could see was my legs. I remember thinking that what we smoked wasn't just weed, so I had to concentrate on each step and tell my brain to lift my leg, swing it forward, and repeat. I remember the laughter from next to me as Henry, Wanda, and Faith were all entertained at my inability to walk like a capable human being. Weed had never done that to me before or since. The next thing I remember was that we were at the New Year's Eve party. That's what I mean, though—vague specificity. There are distinct moments surrounded by the nothingness of time lost during that night.

The party looked good, at least from the outside approach; way too many people huddled together on the wood-planked balcony overlooking the alley behind the building. All of them puffing away on cigarettes while keeping warm in the crisp, early winter air. Once again, we found ourselves walking up to the second story of the dark grey brick, three-flat apartment—a most common sight in the Windy City. After paying the five-dollar cover charge for the Red Solo® cup and unlimited refills of whatever was left of the second-rate beer they bought by the keg, we stepped inside the building.

As all memories of parties go, whether high or sober, the faces of anyone that doesn't end up playing a vital role in the night's memory are faceless. Not faceless, like the children from Pink Floyd's *The Wall*, but anonymous, like blurred background extras from an eighties high-school movie party scene. Generic. I am sure this party had their fair share of husky, pseudo-intellectual young men trying to wax existential about the meaning of life and the pointlessness of it all, while their only real goal herewas a feeble attempt to nail whatever girl (or guy) they were philosophizing with. Luckily, those guys aren't the point of this dream.

After the time lapses from walking through a crowd, the next thing I remember was the bedroom. The walls were decorated with framed prints of Kant, Nietzsche, Chomsky, and other philosophers. This bedroom probably belonged to one of the pseudo-intellectuals lost in the sea of people on the other side of the door. On this side of the door, though, was where the real fun was about to go down.

Now I know why I'm having this dream—it was also the beginning of the end.

We could hear the chatter beyond the door, the usual chitchat from drunken college kids as they sauntered by the door, the occasional knock and turn of the knob to see if the room was occupied. Even the noise from the balcony drifted through the curtained and closed window. None of us minded; it was auditory camouflage for our carnal activity. The only light coming into the room was a mix of moonlight and streetlamps diffused by the curtain. It made Faith look beautiful; Wanda too. But at this point in the dream, I'm not looking at either Faith or Wanda. Nope. I'm looking at Henry's rock-hard junk. It was a meager five or six inches, with a head that mushroomed out far enough to where it looked like it might get stuck, like a barbed arrow, once he slid inside a girl. That's where my dream picked up at this moment. That's the moment my mind decided it needed to etch into its eternal memory of things relevant and essential—me staring at some dude's oddly shaped, one-eyed purple people-eater.

There I was standing next to Henry. Both of us were facing the ladies with our fists on our hips, elbows out to the sides, and chests puffed up. We looked like some display of reject porn stripper applicants, waiting to be told they weren't good enough for the main stage. Meanwhile, the ladies were comparing notes on the similarities and differences between our (insert not-yet-used-euphemism) ramrods. But we stood there like champions, also comparing notes on our ladies, breast size and shape, vaginal differences, and so on and so forth. But the party was fun so far. There we were, drunk, consenting adults doing what they do in the exploratory phases of life. We proceeded to rail our girls right next to each other on some stranger's bed. A glorious sight it was, watching two pairs of breasts bounce all about as we slid in and out of our respective partners. Four breasts, twice the usual amount one gets to look at while having sex; it was wondrous!

But for the life of me, my brain can't figure out why this moment was the beginning of the end. How could this be the moment it all started going wrong? I'm sure on some level it already was going awry, but this was the catalyst to bring to light that things were not as glorious as Faith and I perhaps thought they were. This moment is what was needed to ultimately push us away and toward the life that we needed and wanted to live.

The next thing I knew, we were all sitting on the bed post-coitus in uncomfortable silence. Henry and I were wiping our manhoods clean while the girls toweled off our self-made love lotion from their chests. It was at this point in my dream that I remember why this was the defining moment. The beginning of the end, if it hadn't already begun—Henry wanted to swap. I was conflicted, not because I didn't understand the concept but because I wanted to do it also, kind of. My alcohol and THC-riddled mind wanted to stick my dick in the girl next to my girl. I craved to double-dip into the girl with slightly larger breasts and a few more freckles everywhere, which would have been okay if Faith wanted to sleep with Henry.

Nope. She didn't even say it out loud. The disgust on her face at the thought of him was enough to tell everyone she was not down for any swapping of any kind.

I wanted Wanda, but Faith just wanted to enjoy the moment we had and not take it any further. So there I sat, too drunk to think about what she wanted and too stoned to realize what was really going on. So, we two guys were trying to pull a partner swap that neither partner truly wanted. Hell, I didn't want Henry to bang Faith, and Wanda's expression was clear she sure as hell didn't want me tossing one in her. We were caught in an awkward situation in which Henry had an idea that I didn't actually want to go through with but would not back down from because of some stupid, misconstrued sense of machismo, or lack of being adventurous, or coming off as a lame-o, or some silly crap.

But to the point of the moment, Faith made a joke at my expense. For the love of my memory, I can't remember what she cracked, but I made an off-color joke back at her. (It wasn't so much a joke as it was a sarcastic comment that was meant to be funny but came off as one of the most asshole-y, rude, inappropriate things I've ever said in my life.) But Faith made the joke, and she laughed. Henry and Wanda laughed, but I didn't laugh. I knew she said it in jest and was meant to be cute, but I was inebriated. I was an asshole, an asshat, immature, and not nearly as clever as I thought. As I was putting on my shorts so I could go take a leak, I turned to her and, dripping with the thickest sarcasm I could froth in my mouth, screamed, "Fuck you!"

Here's the thing about it though, I don't know what I was thinking. Maybe I thought I was some sort of sublime comic genius fresh off from watching *Man On The Moon*. Perhaps I should have just stuck with music and left clever to the comics. In that instant, the smiles wiped off their faces. The noise outside the room continued on but, inside that room, the silence was deafening. There was a sick feeling in my stomach. It was quickly overtaking my senses, drowning out my ability to comprehend the reprehensible nature of my words and numbing my ability to feel anything but the growing pain in my gut. Before I could even try to defend my indefensible actions, the swelling pain shot forth from my mouth, landing all over my shorts, the top of the dresser, and inside a few partially opened drawers.

Maybe it was the liquid form of Mike Tyson uppercutting my insides till it was outside that caused my off-color remark. Perhaps I wasn't the nice guy I deluded myself into thinking I was. Maybe I did mean something by it, but just can't, or don't want to, remember what it was. It doesn't matter; excuses are for the weak. Anyone who tries to preface lousy behavior with some bullshit reason isn't much of a person. Any way it went, I was standing there covered in my own puke.

The thing about Faith is that she didn't hold my words against me. To her, this moment might be just another flaw she overlooked in some misguided adoration for me. She hopped up, still in her birthday suit, and made her way to me. In the 3.5 seconds it took for her to reach me, another spout of bile and alcohol spewed forth from my mouth, further covering my bare torso. She was such a kind soul and didn't care that she was still naked. She didn't care about the numerous strangers on the other side of the door. She opened the door, with her arm around me, and headed into the sea of onlookers gawking at the sight of her breasts and my chest hair matted in vomit. She led me to the bathroom, the good girlfriend that she was.

I remember clearly that I sat dry heaving into the toilet while she held my hair out of the line of fire. She sat there, rubbing my back, trying to calm my nerves with quiet whispers. Now, the full-chest heaving (whose low-toned sounds could summon ancient, primordial demons) had possessed my diaphragm in full force. All I wanted to do was calm down so I could try to give Faith some false, off-the-cuff explanation as to why I failed so spectacularly back in the room. But I couldn't. All I could do was sit there and listen to her tell me we'll talk about it later or that everything was going to be okay. All sorts of pleasantries were said to ease the tension of the moment, only to prolong the detonation of whatever explosive the bomb held.

The sounds of Faith's voice continues to echo through my ears, the quiet tones of her calming me down from the nightmare of the moment. I hear her whisper to me that "Everything is fine. It's only a dream." Over and over, the sound of her voice invades my mind more and more, making it seem more real. The dream in my mind that is caught on loop, as I dry heave into a stranger's dirty toilet, becomes more vivid as she keeps whispering over and over the same words that solidify into my mind, "It's only a dream."

The reality of my dream fades away as the waking world starts to come into focus. The blurred lines of dreaming and being awake stay discombobulated, though Faith's words stay brick solid. My eyes flutter open to clear away the cobwebs. I hear new words from Faith. "You're finally awake."

The world comes into focus as the blinding light of day dims. All I can see is Faith, her Mona Lisa smile painted onto her face in a never-ending attempt to pretend that everything is going to be okay.

I don't remember the ambulance. I remember the rain and the crash.

"Did anyone pick up Viv and Logan? Her car broke down. They probably think I'm such an ass." I watch as Faith's face twists at my words.

"Viv and Logan are fine. You don't remember, do you?" Faith starts. The only sounds I hear in between her words are the steady electronic beeps of hospital monitors.

"I remember a bit. What happened?" I am wholly stumped by Faith's words.

The air around us is thick and heavy. The tones of the room have disappeared, leaving only the silence to be broken. She points a hesitant finger at me. "You happened. You've been out a while longer than I think you think."

"What? Did I miss the rest of the party?" I try to add some levity.

Her grimace lets me know that not only is the bachelor party over, but also that jokes are anything other than welcome.

I try to sit up in my bed as a pulling sensation tests the stretching limits of the stitches holding the hole closed that my rib stuck through not too long ago. I lay back down and reach for the bedside remote, slowly raising the back of the bed like some invalid mastermind ruling the world from my internal prison. Well, at least that's what it feels like right now.

I am up.

A little more aware than a few moments ago. An awareness springs to the front of my mind that the bruises are healing and still painful (both to touch and just for being).

The blunt, throbbing sensation of a healing bone that feels like it is going to snap back in half at the slightest tap is a new reminder of what I can't clearly remember. And now that I am upright, I will wait for Faith to speak.

"You've been in a drug-induced coma. The rib wasn't the worst of it. The police say there was a multi-car collision, then a secondary hit. That hit took Ronnie, they say. Then a third hit," she says while fighting off tears that well up in her eyes.

I shake my head in disbelief. "Took Ronnie? Where's he at? How's he doing? I don't remember the second hit. I remember the one that knocked Ronnie out."

Her tears break. Faith starts sobbing quietly as tears stream down her cheeks. "He's gone. That second hit messed you up, too."

I try to lean into Faith to give her a hug, but the pain is telling me otherwise. My eyes search the room for anything to help ease the hurt. I find a morphine drip in my left arm and hit the button a few times to help mitigate the sensation, something to make me more comfortable. I extend the better of my two arms and place my hand on her shoulder. She bends her neck to snuggle my hand as she wipes away her tears.

"What do you mean he's gone? And don't tell me he died." I deny what I know is true.

She sniffs up a round of tears, then blurts out in a moment of hysterics. "I thought I was going to lose you. The doctors didn't know how long you'd be unconscious. I was so worried."

"How long? How long was I out for?" I start to remember that I have a tour to manage for Spear Fist. I have a wedding to attend and a career that has people relying on me.

"Five days," she starts as she tries to calm back down, "but the doctors said if you wake, woke, whatever, you should be fine." Faith holds her stomach like an invisible fist punched her square in the gut.

"You all right?" I ask, forgetting the news that catalyzed the crash.

"Doctors say I need to keep calm." The meekness in her voice hopes I remember what she told me. "All the stress is threatening my pregnancy."

"Five days isn't so bad." I realize I missed a few significant milestones in such a short time. "But the tour is starting in less than forty-eight hours, and there's all the final touches, the wedding."

"You missed the wedding. Five days you were out. The wedding was two days after the bachelor party." Faith shakes her head at my narrow-tracked mind. "You're not doing the tour with them. You need to heal; otherwise, you won't be around to do any more tours with anybody."

I move forward as if I had the strength to jump out of bed, but the pain overtakes my body, sending me right back against the mattress. The morphine has either already worn off, or I am in far more pain than these drugs can handle. I hit the feel-good button a few more times.

"Get some rest, love." She bends down to kiss my forehead. "I'll fill you in on everything when you are more awake."

CHAPTER 2

Dance

My first waking night in the hospital is a lonely one. The ambient buzzing and beeping of machines from my room, the noises from the staff as they walk by doing their nightly duties, all seem to be so distant and uncaring. I drift in and out of sleep, constantly waking from pain. The push of my morphine button helps me fall back asleep for a few minutes at a time. I guess five days does not heal broken bones and hard bruises. The endurance of the morphine button to be hit as many times as I have this night is an impressive feat. However, I am pretty sure most of my pressing is an exercise in futility, as I've met my hourly limit of fun drugs at this point.

The few moments I am awake are spent staring at the off-white, acoustic ceiling tiles, as headlights outside cast their shadows in a silent, abstract show eerie enough to scare a small child. The moments between, when my eyes were shut, I drift into a twilight haze where my brain tries to figure out if I am sleeping or awake. I start to dream a few times, but those are quickly cut off as my sleeping mind wants me to adjust, then the pain jolts me awake for a few moments to once again stare at the shadows.

The shadow plays are only a distraction from the thoughts that plague my mind while I lay awake, hoping for sleep. The idea that Ronnie is gone hits me harder than his fist when it first connected with my face weeks ago. While his fist connected quite nicely, I did deserve it. In the end, he was actually a pretty good guy. In the end. I may just be the one to blame for his demise. Had Faith not said over speakerphone what she said while Ronnie was riding shotgun, I wouldn't have dropped the phone and swerved. But I recovered from that; I remember that. His end can't merely be nothing more than the sad conclusion to a series of unfortunate and malicious events. I'm not one to ponder on things. . . oh, who the hell am I kidding? Of course, I am. If I weren't, I would have been able to move on from Faith eighteen years ago when we first split up. I wouldn't be holding onto this notion of who I think she is, or could be, and who I could be that caused all the events to unfold the way they did, causing Ronnie to be riding with me to pick up Viv and her new girl.

Fate is a funny thing.

By the time daylight arrives, I've given up on any sort of sleep. The exhaustion only makes my pain tolerance plummet, exponentially increasing the need for my little morphine button. The thoughts of doing any type of physical rehab or even walking to take a leak are unwelcome.

Lunchtime rolls around faster than I thought. I could have sworn I just woke up and was looking around, but here sits a tray next to my table. My sore muscles and bones lift the lid off my plate to reveal the light brown, wafer-thin patty of mystery meat on an unseasoned, flavorless bun they pass off for a hamburger. Not even a slice of cheese. The side dish of orange juice fortified with iron to give it the taste of a metal spoon is also less than satisfying. But there it is. I must have gone to the bathroom between dawn and now because I don't have to go. I must be more exhausted than I thought.

I close my eyes to take a bite of my sandwich I hesitantly call a burger. A few chews later, and with a swallow, I open my eyes. I repeat this a few times. On my last swallow, however, I open my eyes to a tray-less room. No remnants of my burger or orange juice are left. It's not even daylight anymore; the twilight hour is upon me. The hospital room is lit by the orange-and-purple light of the evening sky. Again, I find myself pressing the morphine button. I'm not sure if my loss of time is due to my pain, some undetected brain injury, sleepiness, the drugs, or a mixture of some or all the above.

For the moment, I am okay with it. I don't have to think about the dead guy I was driving with. I don't have to think about the tour I am missing or any possible impact this may have on my future with Spear Fist or any other band. I don't have to dwell on the pain that Faith must be feeling over her loss. I don't have to think and don't want to remember.

Introspection is bad.

I rest my eyes for a moment just to relax the pain away, but when I open them, the morning is upon me. Next to my bed is last night's mostly untouched dinner I don't remember nibbling on and the food attendant giving me a fresh meal that I'll avoid as long as possible. As he exits the room, a sight for my sore eyes enters with an exhausted smile and a bag with some clothes.

"I have been talking to your doctors. They're a little worried about your pain level. Still, there's physically nothing wrong with you, besides the expected." Faith smiles a little more, extending the bag my direction. "You were out of it last night. I helped myself to a bite of your supper."

A doctor strolls into the room. At least I'm assuming he's a doctor, and my doctor at that, since he has a white coat on, stethoscope around his neck, and a tablet he's tapping away on.

"Good morning, Mr. Fairlane," he says without looking up from his tablet. "I'm writing you a couple of prescriptions for the pain. And your lovely fiancée says she'll fill them so you don't have to."

I give a raised brow to Faith. She shrugs her shoulders, giving me a playful smile. "I'll take good care of him, doctor."

The doctor turns to Faith. "The meds are as needed, but they can be addictive, so use with discretion. If he gets worse, if his energy doesn't pick back up, any of the things we talked about that you said you would rather do from the comfort of your home, you page me and get him back in here."

I huff in amusement that the doctor is giving my fake fiancée a list of things without even acknowledging me.

"Thanks, doc," I interrupt. "I'll be fine. Rest, walk, sleep, repeat until healed," I say, forcing myself to stand up. The pulling pain of the healing stitches catches my attention and shoots any sleep left in me clear out of my head.

The doctor turns back to Faith with a smile. "Have fun. And as I said, page me if you need anything or have any questions." He turns back to me. "She's a good lady to take care of you like this. She could've just let you stay here to recover as recommended. Take care of yourself. I'll see you in six weeks for a check-up."

He exits and, after the nurse removes my morphine IV, Faith helps slide a clean shirt over my head. "Been a long time since you had to take care of me like this."

She shakes her head at my nostalgia. "I remember. Almost eighteen years you managed to not need me to help you." She grabs my pants and starts sliding them up my legs. "That was an interesting night. Let's just get you outta here."

As the drug-addled haze wears thin again, I find myself at home, lying in my bed. I hear Faith in my kitchen and assume she is attempting some sort of dinner.

"Faith!" I call out, trying not to put any strain on my diaphragm.

I hear what I assume to be a metal pot dropping onto the tile floor, "Shit! Coming!" She picks it up, clanking it on the counter.

"How far are you into cooking?" I inquire.

"Not far enough that you can't ask if I'd like to go out for a bite instead." She smirks, gesturing to the door.

The spot we find ourselves in is a Flo-grown burger joint called Adler's, a little place that started off as a food truck and has grown into a brick-and-mortar location. While the burgers aren't as thick as Chicago's own Kuma's Corner, the tastes definitely rival each other. Anyone who's been to a big city like Chicago, New York, San Francisco, or New Orleans knows that big cities have good food, some iconic dish or two that makes it renowned. Florida, especially Orlando, is the opposite of the rule. Food in Florida sucks on a level that you can only understand if you aren't from Florida but have stayed here for an extended period, or inversely, if you grew up here and did extended travel outside of Florida. Orlando is all chain restaurants of mediocre-at-best foods. However, Adler's dares to break such conventions and stands miles above the rest when it comes to Florida food. But that rant aside, we sit in silence as the food is dropped off at our table.

Faith waits for me to bite into my burger before filling me in on the events since the accident. I know she is waiting because her bottom lip keeps ever so slightly twitching, like she is about to speak. I don't know if she is waiting because it's bad news and wants to make me think, chew, and swallow before I respond, or because receiving bad news on an empty stomach makes it that much worse. Whatever her reasoning, I'm okay with her consideration.

"The paramedics or coroner or whoever said that Ronnie was killed in the crash," she slowly starts. "There was nothing anyone could have done."

I try to listen, but she wasn't there. She didn't see the light fade from Ronnie's eyes. Hell, maybe I only think I saw the light fade from his eyes. Conceivably, he was already gone when I saw him. Maybe what I thought was fading light was just him slipping into unconsciousness. The thought of it all sends pains through my broken rib.

Either way, she wasn't there. She continues telling me something more about the accident. My mind shifts attention to the song playing on some local radio station, forcing itself not to remember any more than it already does. I listen to the lyrics as Faith tells me all about the others involved; that it wasn't just Ronnie, but that the police think the driver who killed him was also killed. However, in my mind, none of that matters. Had I only not answered the call, had she not told me she was pregnant, had Viv's truck not broken down, had any of those things not happened, then Ronnie might still be alive. His life wouldn't have been stripped from him. Yes, there's an enormous part of me that thinks it's my fault. I guess only I can take another guy's death and turn it into a moment about me feeling regretful. I am an asshat. Then I hear Faith's words.

"It's not your fault, ya know. It was a bad night," she says, eating another bite of her burger. "It's not like you were trying to get anyone hurt or anything. It just sucks. I lost my Ronnie."

"I'm sorry." What the hell else am I going to say? It's not like I can bring him back. I can't snap my fingers and turn back time. Even Cher can't do that.

"I know you're sorry. But it's not that. When I first arrived at the hospital. . . I didn't know Ronnie had died. I didn't know. I ran to you first." A thick coating of self-hatred covers her words.

There it is: the moment that I have been waiting for since I ran into Faith again. Since our lives have reunited, I have been waiting for some admission or acknowledgment that I am who she really wants to be with. But for the love of all that is sacred, not under these circumstances. Now a seed is planted in the back of my mind, a seed that whispers to me that I did kill him to be with Faith. In all logical thinking, it can't be true simply because of the chronology of the events. But it's planted there and whispers to me, my sweet demise.

A second voice whispers in my other ear that she is only with me now because Ronnie is out of the picture.

That had he survived, they would still be together, that I am some sort of morbid consolation prize. A bigger part of me knows these thoughts are some forms of residual Catholic guilt from my childhood, but still, they whisper.

She continues. "Once I found out he was dead, I hated you. I hated you until I realized that I hated myself for running to my ex before running to my fiancé. I didn't know how to process it, so I hated you. I hated myself. But it's not your fault. There's no one to blame here. I wanted to be mad at you. I wanted to loathe you and despise you. I can't, though. I have to forgive myself if I can. But how can I?"

She stops talking, leaving me to wonder if I am supposed to answer that, or if she is speaking rhetorically. If I don't answer and she wants me to, then I'm an ass. If I answer and she doesn't want me to, then I am self-absorbed or self-satisfying, or whatever the appropriate phrase is that I can't think of right now. But even if I choose not to decide, I still made a choice, right?

"Time. Everything in time," I offer up a humble response. But the Sweet Blood song "Dance" on the radio reminds me that it is most likely too late to be forgiven, or will even that change with time for her? I take a pain pill (or two or three) out of my pocket and toss them down my throat.

She laughs, shaking her head. "Only you can sum up something so complex and gut-wrenching with such a simple answer and expect others to suddenly be okay. Life's not that simple."

I chew a bite of burger. "Never said it was simple. Just because I say something that sounds simple doesn't mean I expect it to be taken so simply. Everything takes time, including the digestion of those simple words."

Her eyes squint as if looking deep into her own mind for a moment before biting into her burger. We sit in comfortable silence for a few, long minutes.

"The day after it all happened, I had a long talk with Jacquelyn." Faith hesitates as she treads forth.

"Comparing notes?" I jest.

"You could say that. From how Jacquelyn made it sound, you really seem to like her," Faith puts out there, hoping for a negation of her suspicions.

"She treats me well. Not as well as others, but I haven't seen her since the bachelor party," I say.

A smile crosses Faith's face as she takes the last bite of her burger. "Heard about that, too. Must have been an interesting sight to find your girl straddling D.B.'s face for a five-spot."

"It was a twenty note, thank you very much." I laugh. The ludicrousness of it all sets in.

"It could have been a fifty, but the way she felt when she saw your face made it all worthless, she said," Faith continues.

I swallow the last bite of my burger. "That's good to know. So, why hasn't Jacquelyn come to visit?"

"That's what we talked about, after the funeral," Faith ventures onward.

"What? You had his funeral without me?" I snap.

She puts a hand up. "Woah. No one knew when, or if, you were going to come to, wake up, whatever. So yeah, bodies can only be preserved well for so long."

"Point taken," I concede to another missed milestone.

"As I was saying, after the funeral, we got things in order for the tour." She pauses, knowing damn well I'm about to say something.

"Who, how, when?" I throw out a few words to chew on.

"Well, Mr. Fancypants. I went into your place and got your datebooks, notes, notepads, etc., etc. Viv and I figured it all out. Made a few calls and changed some things."

"I needed that money from the tour," I say in a moment of ungraciousness.

"You'll get most of it still. A thank-you-for-doing-my-job-for-me-when-I-was-in-a- fuckin'-coma-or-whatever-even-though-you-don't-know-what-you're-doing would be nice," Faith reminds me.

"Of course. I don't know why I said that. I'm sorry. Thank you very much for all that," I apologize. "Viv helped?"

"Viv's actually on tour with them, acting as the manager while you rest here. She and Logan wanted to be together anyway. Logan says Viv is her muse," Faith continues.

"And D.B. and the guys? They're okay with this?" I ask.

"Of course they'd rather have you. Hell, Viv would rather it be you, but she's there because you're here. Now all you have is me." Faith smiles. Her eyes search for a glint of gratitude in mine but only sees the searching within. My eyes scour my thoughts on what I need to do next, for whatever the thing is that will help me forget my life is fig- uratively over while the guy who was kind enough to ride with me—his life is over.

Again, I know in my heart of hearts it's not my fault, but damn if it doesn't feel like it should have been me. Ronnie should have had the happily ever after with Faith. With me out of the picture, there'd be no nagging devil on her shoulder, poking at her to do the Finn Fairlane thing instead of the right thing. But he's gone, and she's left with me. I hardly call this the beginning of a happily ever after, but it is what it is. God, I hate that statement. It is what it is. It couldn't be vaguer and more general if it tried.

I sit, trying to take in everything she told me, the fact that my life came to a sudden, and possibly permanent, standstill. How someone who has no experience with tour management is handling my tour solely based on my ledgers and notes. Ronnie is dead, and somehow, I end up rewarded for it. Not cool. Can't be good karma. Then a thought hits me. Faith never finished telling me what happened between her and Jacquelyn. "So, is she mad at me?" I ask.

Faith shakes her head. "No. No one can ever stay mad at you. That's the great enigma of being Finn Fairlane. No matter what childish, stupid, or immature thing it is that you do, somehow, it's never actually your fault. You have the gift of always being in the wrong place at the right time. The smile on your face is so disarming that it just washes away the anger people may feel at the moment toward you. Jacquelyn, though, I think in the end, she wants what's best for you. Or at least she wants you to want what you want. If that makes any sense."

I hear her words, and in some convoluted way, her words make perfectly clear sense. But she said, "in the end."

"What do you mean, 'in the end'?" I press.

"It means we talked. We came to an understanding," Faith says.

When someone says those words, it can mean only two things: one, they actually did come to an understanding, or two, Faith forced Jacquelyn to come to the conclusion she wanted Jacquelyn to arrive at—Faith's conclusion. With Faith, both options are entirely plausible.

"By the time we were finished, I think she understood my needs. Not my needs as a woman or any crap like that. My needs as a human. I can't be without Ronnie and without you. I need someone there for me, someone who understands," she confesses.

Now I know I shouldn't feel like she is using me as some sort of healing salve to rub on her as she feels the need, but I kind of do. Perhaps, this is the karmic payback I must settle in my own way. Or maybe she should talk to and spend a week with her sister.

"Where's Jeanine in all of this?" I coldly ask.

"Fuck, Finn," she says, the tone of my words stabs at her. "After the wedding, she and Gregg decided she should go with."

I shake my head a little. "So, that quickly now she already has him on a tight leash."

I should be careful when I cook up my words because I know I am often forced to chew and swallow them.

"God, you're such an asshole sometimes. She, Gregg, and the almighty D.B. actually thought it'd be nice to have someone along who can help with everything. She's there to make sure Viv is good. That the bands are good. She put her life on hold for you," she scorns, deservedly so. I am an ass.

"How was the wedding?" I steer the subject a bit to the left.

"Short a groomsman. The guy wouldn't get out of bed," she jokes.

"I needed my sleep. No objections or trashtastic fights?"

She lets out the first real laugh since I woke up. "No. Nothing like. . . God, whose wedding was that anyway?"

I laugh through the pain in my ribs. "Wally and Lynn. Back in, like, 2000," I remind her.

"That's right!" she says, waving her hands. "Some guy saw his girlfriend dancing with. . . what's his name?"

"Yup. He found out they had slept together a few weeks earlier. He was pissed," I continue the story.

"And a fight almost broke out, but everyone stood up for the homewrecker, not the guy who got cheated on," Faith finished up.

"What a night!" My exclamation aggravates my chest pain.

"Who would have known that evening would have been a foreshadowing of things to come for us!" she tries to say with enthusiasm, but the sad reality of her words sinks in for both of us.

So here we sit, in Adler's, our bellies full of great burgers as we wonder what the future holds. And yes, it is a scary thought for both of us.

I feel the pain flaring up. The intensity quickly rises, so I grab a few more Vicodin and fling them down my throat. Anything to make it all go away.

CHAPTER 3

Times Like These

The harsh light of day rears its ugly head. The early morning light that sneaks in between the curtains stabs me directly in the eyes. I look over and squint so the lovely woman lying next to me can come into focus. For a moment, the pain is gone: no broken ribs, no deep bruises, no healing cuts or scrapes. I can't even feel the persistent, throbbing headache I've inherited since I woke from the accident. All of it disappears when I see her. My love, my Faith. She's come home. Perhaps she's always been there, and it's I who have finally returned. No matter; we are together.

As much as the pain disappears when I see her, I know it is still there. Faith is but a safe place, an oasis in the desert, a pill to further numb the pain. But like all things, the pain returns when the release ends. I reach for my diminishing supply of pain pills, ever standing at attention, awaiting my return on the nightstand, much like my late dog, Lt. Dan, used to wait for me. How I miss that mangy dog. The pain floods back in, filling every cell of my body. I could say it seems a little less this time around, though that's like saying 215-degree water is colder than 300. It's boiling and can still kill you or, at the very least, scar you for life. But that's where I am right now.

I peek over to the old alarm clock radio next to my bed. It's the clunky radio from back in the day, the one with the oversized red digital display, yet has the durability to be thrown across the room when you just didn't want to hit snooze for the twentieth-somethingth time. It reads 7:30 a.m., way too early for the likes of a night owl such as myself to rise and shine. Faith, however, shall be answering the call of the alarm in a few. Her work in the salon is never done, which means I'll have to fend for myself until she gets home. That means having to get from point A to point B, if needed. I order an Uber as I crawl out of bed. Rise and shine I must and deal with this day. I think the best way to do that is to swallow the pain pills I've been holding onto. A hazy Uber ride later, I find myself at a car dealership, as it is a day to fend for myself and a day spent buying a car. A short search leads me to a Pontiac not too far removed from mine that was recently totaled.

A slightly less hazy ride home and I head back to bed. Faith is already at work, and I can't even fathom how long I've been up. The next thing I know, I hear the sweet sound of Faith telling me it's 6:00 p.m., and I need to wake the fuck up. Ever the gentle soul she can be.

"Come on, Daddy. Taking care of your ass while growing this thing inside me ain't the easiest thing, ya know." She hints at my impending fatherhood.

The jolt of that reminder wakes me from my fog but only further seats the realization that I am neither fit for Faith nor fatherhood. I don't want to be Abel to her Cain. It's not fair to her or the unborn. Plus, it didn't end well for Abel. I know the pain is waiting to creep back in at the most unexpected moment, so I want to get ahead of it. Get a jump on keeping it at bay before I get knocked down. I'll get up again, though. No pain is ever gonna keep me down. I know that because of the two pills I just swallowed. Here I go, 6 p.m. and my day is beginning, again.

While the pain has subsided since waking, it's still a thick fog hovering just below sight—noticeable in the peripheral and kicking up with movement. The thoughts of the tour, venues, hotels, and stops along the way all kick up a bit in the fog. I know they are taken care of and know Viv is probably doing a stellar job with my tour, but it's my tour. My career. It's the nights like those that I live for: the stage lights burning my eyes, the sound of the feedback bleeding my ears, the adrenaline racing through my veins with such force that I think my heart might explode. What I am doing right now, sitting at a dinner table eating Chinese take-out while reruns of *How I Met Your Mother* sound off in the background, is not my idea of what I want to be doing tonight. It's not my idea of what I want to be doing any night. Being on the road, you grow accustomed to eating cigarette-smoked bar and hotel food, sleeping in beds you never want to look at under a black light, and driving in a car, van, or bus more than living in a house. It's a lifestyle, and it's the only one I've looked forward to since I began touring. It is my time, and it was taken from me by some jackass who can't understand braking distance in the rain, and the second and third jackass who also can't drive.

That is Orlando, the place where dreams are swallowed by the highway system that leads to the only place here allowed to dream. The destination that makes dreams come true, if only they did come true down here. At least I'm pretty sure Florida isn't filled with people who wished for a fourth-rate educational system, meth addiction, and inadequate employment opportunities. But it is what it wants to be: gilded for anyone staying less than two months, a snowbird escape for six, and a twisted reality for anyone who lives year-round, and definitely not how I envision any future I may have with Faith.

"Whatcha thinking about?" Faith slurps up some lo mein.

"Whaddya mean?" I twirl my noodles.

She chuckles a bit. "Your mile-long stare is a neon sign of unspoken thoughts."

"Thinking about the tour. I need this rib to heal, and whatever internal swelling might still be swollen to go down so I can catch up with Spear Fist. I need to figure out what's going on with you and me, I, us. You know. We got this thing growing inside you, and I haven't had any time to process the news. I haven't reacted to it myself yet. I don't know how you want me to react. It's just so much in so little time," I say in a moment of blunt honesty.

Faith drops her fork, the clanging sound of which sends jolts of pain through my left temple. She tilts her head and squints her eyes. The razors shooting out of them cut right through me. "How I want you to react? I want you to react however you react. I don't want some lame, forced reaction of joy if the thought of fatherhood makes you want to run for the hills."

My neon sign of thoughts is shattered into a million pieces by Faith's words and the growing pain that runs through me. It's not like the thought of being a dad makes me want to run a one-way marathon out of town that only Forrest Gump could be proud of. It's just an idea that I never put much thought into. I make music; that is it. I know it's not like musicians are all childless heathens who shun the idea of reproducing. Some of them have wives and children they see regularly and are part of their lives. Some are good parents. I just never was one to think that the title of father would be mine one day.

"I don't want to run for the hills." I laugh. "I'm actually excited, I think. Nervous maybe. I don't know exactly, but I'm definitely in it."

"In it? As in not running, not leaving me behind, not forgetting we exist?" she says with an unreadable facial expression. "I guess that's a start."

"Did you think I was that guy to do something like that?" I tease.

"What guy?" she plays coy.

"Don't give me that 'what guy?' bull," I say with a pointed fork. "You thought I was that guy. The guy that disappears when he finds out his penis works properly. The guy that sticks it in anything wet, without any thought or regard to the consequences that may follow for the fairer sex. You thought I was him."

She laughs through a bite of food. "Maybe a little, sure. But can you blame me? Look at your past. Our past."

"Why? Did you read somewhere that I have a love child running around somewhere I've never been told about? Or love children?" I inquire.

"No," she chuckles. Her laughter helps my pain subside a little. "I mean, over a decade of rock 'n roll decadence doesn't exactly extol the virtues of a housewife, husband, whatever."

"That's a blanket statement if ever there was one." I laugh through my bite of food.

"Hey, at least I know you want to be on board," she defends.

"Plus, there are good family men among the rock crowd. Bon Jovi for one," I say, semi-jokingly.

"Come on, Finn. You can't expect to stay the man you were," she throws out a curveball.

"And you can't expect me to change. You know who I am and who I was going into this," I defend.

"You know, Finn. You don't make things easy. I'm doing this for more than some, still hypothetical, baby. I'm doing this for you, and yes, for me, too. Maybe I need you. Ever think of that?" Faith fires off.

It has crossed my mind. I just don't think I've given it as much thought as I should have if I'm back to thinking about the entirety of the entity known as Faith and Finn again. *Damn, so what's a boy to do? I have obligations. I have a life. I have the woman I've wanted more than any-thing else. I have a to-be child in that woman. How can I make this work? Oh, what's this boy to do?*

Here's what I do know: I love this woman. I've said it before, and I'll say it again. I love this woman and always have. No matter how bad the times got back in the day or how good they were, my love for her never waned. It never faltered—my love, that is. I am sure I fucked up in many ways many, many times, but that's one of the many reasons I love her so. No matter how many times I faltered, she was always there. Well, until the end, of course, but a man can only be given so many opportunities. Apparently, though, after eighteen years, my chances have replenished like the seven-year abstinence thing that makes you a virgin again...so I hear.

"I didn't. There's something in me that hoped you still needed me or had feelings or whatever you wanna call it. But after the years had gone by, I figured I was just another mistake." I finish off my meal.

"My favorite, if one can have a favorite mistake." She smiles back. "So, what do we do?"

She stares at me, a little lost in her thoughts and, possibly, a little scared while waiting for an answer. I know she doesn't want a repeat of our past. I guess neither do I. It's just that I find myself in unfortunate situations. Fun, sure, but unfortunate, and I think that's what she's afraid of, more of the same from the man known as Finn. My rib is starting to throb while watching her wheels turn. I don't like it. I reach for my pills and swallow one, hoping it helps this time. I'm still waiting for an answer from her, though I don't think I'll be getting one anytime soon.

So, it boils down to her question. . . "What do we do?" I don't think something that universally profound can be answered while eating take-out lo mein. I'm not even sure if it can ever be answered, but I must try if I don't want her to leave me again, if I want this thing between us to work. If I am ever to get this crazy little thing we call love and life right, it has to be now. This is my second chance. While most people never get one, no one ever gets a third. So, this is it. I'm not sure exactly what needs to be done or how to get there, but if this is ever going to work, now is the time to get it right. Here's the thing of it all—we have to figure out the "what do we do" of it all. I have to decide if I can leave the life I love behind for her, but I have no idea about anything.

CHAPTER 4

Going Out Strange

There was something about my old lady and me sloppin' down food, trying to figure out second chances, that made me think of a guy I met once upon a time. My meeting with him had nothing to do with Chinese food, but with the need for a second chance with no clear way to make it work. We were both in the psych ward for different issues. He had been there for close to two months while I had just gotten admitted. I guess if I am going to tell you this story, I need to tell you how I ended up spending seventy-two wonderful hours in the Lutheran General Psych Ward.

It was at the end of the final leg of my band's Tweaker tour, right after Marty and his family died. It was supposed to be the happiest of times; it was not. No matter how many girls flashed their breasts at me while I was on stage, no matter how many fans showered me with some sort of adoration, no matter how good everything was at the time, all I could think about was my friend and his family. Marty was a guy who flowed in and out of my life, but no matter how long it had been since we had seen each other, we picked up like no time had passed. He knew my songs before anyone else, even helping with lyrics on a few random occasions. He could spin a story on the spot just for the entertainment value but tell it with such unparalleled conviction that everyone in the room would eat it up like it was fact. At the end of the story, he, and everyone else, would have a good laugh over the thing.

Even though they were just suckered into believing whatever tale he spun, they'd still laugh. He had that sort of disarming smile, dimples and all.

But back to the point, the tour was over. The rest of the band and road crew were celebrating on the record company's dime. I was sitting on the floor, leaning against the wall in some Chicago suburb bar. I wasn't looking at anyone; I wasn't enjoying the moment. There were no trees that made a forest for me to see. No flowers to stop and smell. Just a dirty bar floor in need of a good mopping and a bar that could use a power wash.

The thing about it is that when everything seems fine, or at the very least, should seem okay, it rarely ever is. All the fans that pass by spraying misguided love on you feels empty. Sure, it's quaint, the gesture anyhow. But it's empty. They don't know you. They don't know what's going on in your world, not outside of what they read in magazine articles or listen to on the radio or in podcasts. So, they give you a compliment and continue on their merry way, thinking the words they say somehow lift you up on a cloud and carry you through until the next praise. But in fact, all it does is shine a light in your eye that feebly attempts to blind you from reality while the metaphorical shit is still hitting the fan. That's what was happening in my life at that moment; the shit just kept hitting the emotional fan.

I was sitting there, sipping on some drink, or three, or five, and I heard a voice. I don't remember who it was, or even if it was male or female, but I heard a voice, "You doin' okay?"

"I wish I was with Marty right now." It's what I said. It's what I meant, but not in the way it was taken.

There was never a moment where I thought I was better off dead or didn't want to be alive anymore. Never did I want to leave it all behind or take a permanent solution, but I did want to be with him. Though, in hindsight, the wording would have been better had I said I wished he was with me at that moment—at that bar with us is what I meant. All I meant was that I wanted him here celebrating with us, but it came out wrong. Maybe I said it the way I said it out of grief. But no matter the reason I said it like that, I did.

The next thing I know, the guys in the band are all hovering over me, drinks in hand. Someone off to the side has their face partially concealed by their cellphone. I hear them talking on the phone about someone making suicidal threats and being clearly depressed. I know they were talking about me, but every sentence the phone person said was carefully constructed to be as non-threatening toward me as possible, as if I was going to stand up and chug down a 1.75 of tequila in one glug to end it all.

I tried telling the mysterious phone person that I was okay, and nothing terrible was going to happen. Still, some sensitive soul had already decided that the world may end if they didn't do everything possible, and over the top, to try and diffuse the situation. All they were doing, in their righteous obliviousness, was making things worse. So, I thought, *Hell, maybe I did say something more than I remember.* It was so damn long ago.

The furious sound of the sirens and blinding reds and whites of the ambulance lights filled the room, muffling the chatter and music of the bar. Two guys in full uniform, ready-to-be-single-serving-friends sat by my side, trying to determine if I was suicidal or not. I wasn't in a great mood, and when you're not in a great mood, the last thing you want is to be bothered by inane questions. I was pissed but not at the EMTs. They were just doing their jobs, paid to be concerned for the welfare of strangers and then take them to a place that can take better care of them than they can themselves. (Did you stay with me on that word mess?) So, questions they asked and answered I did—in a most sarcastic and hostile way. They should have questioned the person that was on the phone. Anyone who is excessively over concerned for another human, unable to tell the difference between suicidal state and mourning depression, needs more serious help than I ever did.

As the fates will have it, it was I that ended up in the ambulance on my way for a minimum of seventy-two-hours of observation. The ride to the ward itself has no place in my memory. I can only assume it was mundane and insignificant in the bigger scheme of things. After I was checked in was when I got a chance to meet Christian. This was a kid—he said he was twenty-three—but the nurses always shook their heads "no." I managed to get one worker to tell me Christian was only twenty. Not sure who was telling the truth or why someone felt the need to lie about it, but stranger things do happen. Age aside, this was a young kid with unkempt, thick, wavy hair in need of proper washing. He was allowed to carry a dry erase marker around with him so he could draw spirals and Fibonacci sequences. Christian had a strange obsession with those two things. I'm not sure if he was schizo or something, but he talked about the irrelevance of time and the meaninglessness of it all.

Maybe that's why this memory has sprung forth in my mind, to remind me of the talks of time and its irrelevant meaninglessness. Or my brain has finally realized that the discussions I had in a seventy-two-hour psych ward window needed to surface. That way, they could point out to me some long-lost lesson that is now relevant in my life, still yet unseen to me.

That's the point, though.

Christian and I sat there in the psych ward's common room while the television droned in the background as Angelina Jolie accepted her win for *Girl, Interrupted*. That's the only part of the award show that stuck in my memory. It could be something about an actress winning an award for a movie about being in a psychiatric institution while sitting in a psych ward, watching her accept that award. Thinking of the chronology of it, it may have been a rebroadcast for some other show, but I stand by my point. There were others in the room, mostly drug addicts slowly detoxing. They were the ones sitting quietly on their best behavior, praying they got out in another day or two. Then, they could score another hit since they were getting no real help there. A few others in there were actual psych patients with severe social disorders, bulimia, anorexia, or whatnot. Others, the real lifers, would just sit in a stereotypical fashion mumbling to themselves while swaying back and forth.

Back to the point, Christian and I sat, talking about time and how, from our perspective, we sit on a rock beneath blue skies. Still, the blue skies are actually infinitely expansive space. The rock we sit on actually travels in a forward motion, spiraling through the universe while spinning in a circle. This means we are literally always in a different spot in the universe every moment of every day. So, what does this all mean concerning Faith? I guess it means we were never in the same place as we were from the first night we met. We were always moving forward, just like this planet of ours, ever-changing and refining ourselves, just like our place in the universe.

What we didn't see, or at least what I didn't see, was how strangely we were going out while we were ending, who we were or had become. Not that anyone ever thinks they've become something so drastically different than who they were, but we do. We all slowly change and metamorphose into these new beings, much like our place in the universe is ever-changing. We look around the world in which we live, and the surroundings all look the same: the forest still has trees, the roads are filled with cars, and the drive-thru windows are staffed fully with uninspired teens working for video game money. In the bigger picture, though, we are in a completely different spot than we were a day ago, and more so than a year or ten years ago. We shoot through this universe at 1.3 million miles an hour, so we are continually changing at that rate.

It's hard to comprehend, but it's there. Truth from the mind of a paranoid schizophrenic or whatever he was. The problem isn't trying to understand the theory. It sinks in after marinating in your thoughts for far too long, but it eventually clicks. The sad part of it all is what you miss in between the introduction and the end, how life all transpires and how strange it all is.

It started as me finding someone who intrigued me. Something about Faith hit a funny bone, so I stayed to explore why it tickled me so. She was intrigued by me for God knows what reason. Hell, looking back, I'm not even sure why she stayed or how I fascinated her enough to stick around, but she did. And for whatever reason, no matter how we grew, evolved, changed, whatever, we still stuck around until the bitter end.

The end, much like looking at your immediate surroundings, is never as simple as it seems. What was the end eighteen some years ago is now just a paused moment in our relationship. And here we are now, some 204,984,000,000 miles away from where we were in the universe back then. But if you looked at our surroundings, we appear to be only 1,700 miles or so away from where we were. Perhaps a little older and wiser, but not that far, except we can't go back. We can only go forward. I think that's what that crazy guy in the psych ward was trying to tell me. No matter what happens, you can't go home again. There is no going back, only the forward motion. That's not to say things can't work out. Life can be happy and have a happy ending, as long as you don't try to travel back in time. And so the pause button on our relationship has been un-paused in a big way.

Paused relationships proved Christian's theory of time's irrelevance. Much like my friendship with Marty was able to pick up right where we left off, no matter how long it had been, my relationship with Faith seemed to do something similar, as if all the time between our first big breakup simply never happened in that sector of our minds. For when that fateful night occurred, not outside Old Town, but the restaurant bushes, we were all those billions of miles back with just each other. And yes, it was just as awkward as where we left it. But time marches on and so did we. So when we met, even though the feelings were still there and she did not forget what happened, she had moved on, at least enough to forgive and grow. So, all that time between didn't matter. It was meaningless to a point, and irrelevant in the big picture, because here we are.

To think, all of this is because of Chinese food and noodles. Hell, the mind works in mysterious ways. So, you're probably wondering how the hell all this actually relates to Christian. I'll tell ya, it wasn't like me and the cuckoo exchanged numbers while in the ward, but a good conversation can burn someone's face into your mind. After all our talking, I was twice convinced he would never see the outside of a psychiatric institution, except for maybe in transit from one hospital to another.

A good five years or so later, I was out at some bar/ saloon in a far outlying Chicago suburb. I can't even remember who the hell I was with at the time. It was either an old bandmate from years earlier or some girl who reminded me of a celebrity. No matter to the story, though. We were surrounded by a few hundred people dressed in their best hair metal band attire, singing along to a Bon Jovi cover band called Bad Medicine. I look over to the bar and see, sitting off on a corner stool with no one around him like he was some pariah, none other than Christian from the ward. He was eating lo mein out of a Chinese to-go container. That must have been why this memory surfaced.

Christian's hard lines and sunken cheeks told me that his time out of the ward had been anything but good to him. I watched as he looked around the bar like some ninja was stalking him. However, no ninja was to be seen. Either he was crazy, or there was a highly skilled ninja skulking about. He had a few empty shot glasses in front of him and a mixed drink of some sort he was nursing in his hand.

The band had just finished playing, "Wanted Dead Or Alive" and started that song from *Young Guns*, "Blaze of Glory." It was about that time I saw Christian get up from his stool. The dim lights of the venue and flashing strobes made him look all the more ominous. He finished off his drink and looked out the windowed doors to a small group of leather-clad men standing next to a few motorcycles.

Now I've seen some strange shit in my life. I saw a guy gorgeously crash his motorcycle and slide a good fifty feet on his face across hot asphalt. No, he did not live. It was a sad sight to see. But a motorcycle crash, while never a way anyone wants to go out, is not a strange way to go. Another time, I was walking through some back street in L.A. and saw a guy get jumped by a group of people. While I didn't see him die, the gunshot I heard gave me a pretty reliable clue that he did. Not sure why they didn't try to take care of me as a witness, but they left me alone. Maybe it was the fact I was stumbling drunk and couldn't identify them for all the money in the world. But this night, at the show, I was debating whether or not I should say something to Christian.

I'm glad I chose nay.

As he approached the door, I saw him squat down and take a quick look around. He didn't see me, or if he did, he recognized me but figured I'd not interfere. He then pulled up his pant leg a little bit and pulled something out. I could only figure it was a gun based on where he was fidgeting around. I just figured it was. I knew he was crazy but didn't think he was that crazy. As soon as the door shut behind him, he headed straight to the leather-clad bikers. They didn't even get a chance to see who approached when he started shooting them in their heads. They dropped to the ground like rag dolls. I could feel the jolt of bone against solid blacktop shoot through my head as each victim slammed down. After the last of them fell, the bouncers were running at him, fearless for what would happen to them. It didn't matter though; he turned the gun on himself. A quick fraction of a second and the gun was against his throat, pointed toward the sky. He pulled the trigger, without hesitation, and was gone. Just like that. Gone.

Here was a guy with theories on time and space that were utterly mind-boggling but ended up a blurb in the weekend post. A late-night news story for the masses until the next radar blip. It makes me wonder about his time in between. I pondered where he was in the big picture of things from the time in the ward till that night. While my time between Faith and mine's first departure and our second meeting is irrelevant to the big picture (as far as I can tell), this guy's time between the psych ward and that saloon seem quite relevant to the story. Whatever story that might be, I am sure someone was supposed to take care of Christian. The things that must have happened to make that go awry. The details of his therapy, the trials, the tribulations of this wretched guy's life, everything that ensued led to that point. All those things are anything but meaningless, so many questions to answer to figure out how he ended up where he did. The end of his life was more tragic than our introduction.

Any way you look at it, that was going out as strange as one could go, which finally brings me back to Chinese food and Faith. If I am leaving the music industry, I have to decide how I am going out. If I am to make it work with Faith this time around, I need to figure out how it is going to work. I may need to let go of the past two decades of debauchery and decadence. I will need to devise a way to keep my clients, lest I'll have to hand them off, or at the very least, hand off Spear Fist to someone else. I'll have to decide if someone will take my place in the industry. Pass the torch, so to speak.

However, I am not sure I can leave it behind. I want Faith, sure. She is pretty convinced that I won't make a good father if I stay in the industry. Hell, I could have stopped at father, as in she thinks I won't make a good father, but she has implied she thinks I will magically be a great dad if I leave it behind. Thinking about the convolutedness of it all is maddening. However, the industry is what I love. It's what I know. There's a self-righteous part of me that thinks the world needs me. I can't abandon the world that I helped shape. I would be a selfish person if I left it all behind. One who wants happiness, sure, life on the road seems happy, with late-night, coke-binge, alcohol orgies that blur into each other. But that cannot be true happiness. The equation can't be as simple as fun=happiness. Once upon a time, I would say yes. But I was so much younger then. What I need to figure out is if there is a way to have both. Perhaps that is the pipe dream.

All I know is that right now, at this moment, my body is calling for relief. I reach into my pocket and pull out a bottle of pills. One of the few great joys in life is a good friend and a bottle of pills. I think that thought and immediately know I am deluding myself. But there's a small part of me that thinks maybe I'm onto something. Maybe artists like Amy Winehouse were onto something besides live fast, die young, good-looking corpse bullshit we all daydream about. But a good-looking corpse does not make a good companion for the living. In the long run, I haven't the slightest clue as to what to do. So, at this moment, I'm going to swallow a couple of these little guys to help ease the pain.

CHAPTER 5

Last Dance With Mary Jane

The incessant nagging of my cellphone tugs at my sleep like an impatient child waking his parents for the day's first meal. I crack open an eyelid to meet the harsh light of day breaking through the drawn shades of my bedroom. I realize I must have been out a little longer than intended from last night's pill-popping.

I pick up my cellphone, but voicemail answers once again. I open my other eye to see a notification for twenty missed calls. Before I can check who they are all from, the phone lights up again, followed by the loud, petulant whining of the ringtone. I swipe up to answer and notice a note that was placed under my phone.

"Hello?" I say to the caller, as I lift up the note.

"I've been calling you non-stop! Why haven't you picked up?!" the voice on the other end shouts.

Rubbing the rest of the sleep from my eyes, I ask, "Viv?"

"Yes, Viv! Finn! We need you! You need to come to New York!" she pleads from hundreds of miles away.

"Yeah, okay. Let me just hop on the first flight I can find," I joke.

"Cool! Let me know the info." She starts to calm down.

"Woah. I was kidding," I say, waving my hands like Viv can see me. "Slow down and start from the beginning."

The hangover from the pills drags me back down. I slump into my pillow.

"So, I had a meeting with some record company guys. They want to work out a deal, like now." Vivian starts from somewhere in the middle of her story. "We're in New York currently. The guys were doing a show when I get a tap on the shoulder."

"Okay. I'm following so far," I say, trying to keep Viv on track.

"It was one of the labels who was at the release show. They want you," Viv says.

And there it is. The words that shall draw me into the scene I know so well, and so far away from where Faith wants me to be. Now to figure out what to do. I have obligations. Viv needs me there to push this deal through—if it's as good as her excitement leads me to believe. Faith needs me, and I need Faith more. I can make this work, though.

"No, 'how are you?' No, 'how are you feeling since being in a drug-induced coma?' Nothing?" I jab at her.

"Faith has been keeping me in the loop in case a situation like this arose, arises, whatever. And it rose. So?" she rapid fires back at me with a sudden stop.

I take a deep breath because she already knows the answer. I turn to sit upright in bed and grab the pill bottle on the nightstand to down a pain pill or three. "I'll text you the flight info."

After booking my flight for later that day and packing my bags, I make the surprisingly uncomfortable drive to Faith's salon. Not that traffic is any worse than usual; it's just that my bones don't seem to be healing as fast or as well as they should. Two decades of decadence might be catching up. I pop four ibuprofens before heading into the salon, hoping the grimace on my face is wiped clean.

The front desk girl is dressed edgy but cute, a compliment to the decor and atmosphere of the salon. It's as if a bar that played rock 'n roll decided to cut hair. I approve.

"Welcome to Medusa's Cut & Color. Do you have an appointment, sir?" The overly excited girl greets me with a smile.

"Is Faith here?" I ask. "I need to speak with her."

"Is this about an appointment? I can help with that." She seems far too eager to be chill.

"No," I say, shaking my head. "It's personal."

A change shifts in her look as she makes a realization. "Oh! You must be Finn! I've heard so much about you! She's in back. You're good to head back there."

The lack of any negative tones in that sentence has me wondering what Faith leaves out of her stories.

"Thank you," I say as I make my way around the reception desk and wall that hides the interior of the salon.

The inside is not what you'd expect for a salon. Instead of bright or even more neutral colors, the owners have opted for deep reds in varying hues and brown trims. A very goth look, but one that is well lit so the stylists can see their work. Seven stylists are working on either cuts or colors, all of whom are in torn jeans and dark-colored shirts. Of course, they have aprons on to protect their clothes. The casual dress style makes this place seem like a place I'd like to get a cut. I wonder why she never told me about this place, perhaps to keep me away from a safe spot for her. Maybe something else. I see three empty chairs and assume one of them is Faith's.

At the far end of the cutting chairs, I stand at the entrance to the back room. I see Faith sitting at a table, her face buried in her phone. I knock on the doorjamb to get her attention. She looks up at me and immediately knows that the news is not what she is wanting to hear.

"It's not as bad as you think," I start.

She laughs to keep herself from getting frustrated. "What?"

Too short to be sweet.

"Viv called me. I have to tie up some loose ends with the band. Add to our future securities," I start with a smile.

"Don't smirk at me, hoping I can guess what you need. Just tell me," Faith says with tightened lips.

"Can you drive me to the airport when you are done for the day?" I respond.

"What?! Why the fuck are you flying anywhere?!" She jumps my shit at that, but I guess I could have eased in with more caution. I mean, who doesn't like a little lube?

"Viv never called you?" I ask.

"Nope." She shakes her head.

"Jeanine?"

"Not about whatever the hell this is." She shakes her head some more.

"Spear Fist is in negotiations. They want me to help iron out the details," I start. "Honestly, shouldn't be more than a week or two max."

I can tell she's pissed. The look on her face tells me so, but she doesn't want to say anything. I sure as hell am not gonna start a fight at her work. Even I'm not that petty. I think we are beyond that stage by now.

"I don't have any more appointments today. Let me see if I can cut out early," Faith offers.

"I don't have to be there for a while," I start.

"It's a slow day here anyway. Shouldn't be an issue," she says with a restrained voice.

I stay toward the back as she walks up to a stylist who's slapping color onto a middle-aged lady's hair. A few words are said back and forth. I try not to stare, so I turn my head to watch them in my peripheral vision. I see her point to me, and her boss laughs. She nods, giving Faith the okay. Faith quickly closes up her station before we head to her car.

"We'll drop my car off at home, then I'll take you to the airport," she says.

On the drive back home, I stay behind her. Not out of caution or to make sure she is safe, but to let her lead and control the pace. I figure if she needs to take some time to think about things, I should give it to her.

"I wanted out early anyway. I was hoping to get some extra time with you today," Faith says in a better state of mind as she steps out of her car back home. "Didn't you get my note?"

I shake my head. "Didn't get a chance to read it. Got distracted by the call. But as I said, I still have a little time. What did you have in mind?" I ask, a little curious about her thoughts.

"Wasn't sure exactly. I just know that you haven't really had any quality time out since leaving the hospital. I thought it'd be fun to hit up a park or something," Faith says.

"I'd like that," I say.

"But now there's not enough time because you have to fly out," she says, disappointed in the day's events.

"I can do CityWalk or Springs if that's okay," I offer up.

She smiles a bit, seeming unexpectedly happy that I want to spend time with her. So, we head on out before the flight.

She decides to stop at the Springs, an incredible outdoor shopping extravaganza with House of Blues at one end and a mix of mouse-themed and other brand stores throughout the rest. Not to forget the plethora of restaurants littered throughout. The slight Florida wind adds a pleasant coolness to the little time we have here. Ambiance aside, it's nice to be out and about with Faith.

I slow down a little as she walks, so I can watch her. Her eye was caught by a window display. Her faded jeans and fitted grey shirt with black lace print are perfect complements to the determination in her walk. She is exactly where I want to be if it weren't for having to fly to New York. At least now I know what I'll be returning to.

We spend the next few hours window-shopping and watching people walk through life. Our conversation is quaint and light, nothing clouded with past memories or future possibilities. I think she needed an evening out to just live in the moment without having to ponder the difficult decisions of life. Just enjoying the moments of our outing for what they are. It is comfortable, and I feel content.

On our way to the airport, the light air of the evening starts to weigh down a little more. A fog begins to settle on our otherwise clear venture.

"One week, huh?" she says, as the fog on our evening settles in a bit more.

"Give or take. I have to negotiate the deal. Layout the terms of royalties, etc., etc.," I attempt to summarize.

She gives me a look. It's the same look I saw in her eyes when she was talking to me at Taps & Corks. A look that says she feels like she's about to travel back down an old, familiar road she'd rather not travel.

"Just business. Nothing more," I say, leaving it short.

I can understand the lack of trust, sudden onset as it seems. It's not like our past is filled with moments that instill a sense of calm and serenity in either of us. Faith senses in me the need to not kick the sleeping dog—as much as she wants to, she leaves it alone.

"I have a few doctor's appointments while you're gone. Nothing big. Just prenatal," she changes the conversation.

"Please let me know what he says," I respond.

"She," Faith throws out.

"What?" I ask.

"What she says. My doctor's a woman," Faith corrects me.

"I didn't know. After I get back, I can start coming along," I offer up. I do want to go. I don't want to fall back into our old habits of waltzing in and out of each other's lives as the mood strikes.

"Only if you want to. I can do this myself." Faith throws all confidence in me out the window.

"I want to come along. It's my baby too. I'd like to be there, alongside you," I respond, hoping she can get her self-assurance back.

"Thanks" is all she says back. I think a part of her knows she came unhinged for a split second and is now keeping her head low.

The things the universe throws at us are never easy. It's never an overnight success without the years of struggle that lead up to it. It's never like getting back together, trying again, giving it a second chance, whatever you call it, is as simple as an unchanged replay of the first run, hoping for a different ending. It's years of gained life experiences mixed with changes in who we are versus who we were, all being paired against the other half of the second chance. It's hard and never easy, but that's the universe throwing curveballs at me while I try to make things right. But all the curveballs thrown—Viv, Jacquelyn, Ronnie, the baby—are going to make the payoff of being with Faith all the sweeter. Assuming I can leave the music behind. Assuming it all works out, and it doesn't self-destruct.

A short plane ride later, I land at JFK. Waiting for me curbside at the airport is Viv. No Logan, no Jeanine, no Spear Fist. Just Viv. The look on her face immediately turns to relief as her eyes connect with mine. The visible worry and anxiety drain from her face with a smile. I return her wave with a nod and a wink.

I honestly didn't think I'd be back in New York so soon after leaving. Hell, I didn't know if I'd ever be back. No real thoughts on the subject, but here I am, breathing in the familiar smells of my time spent here and trying to remember the good from the bad, like an old friend trying to rehash the past while sharing a lager at the local dive bar. This is no time to get whimsy and reminiscent. We have goals to accomplish and deals to make. I toss my luggage in the backseat of her rental car and ride shotgun.

Viv takes me through the streets, avoiding the parkway. I'm not paying much attention, so I'm not exactly sure where, but at least I'm not driving.

"So, when's the meeting?" I ask, trying to get straight to business.

"They weren't sure when you'd make it, so they set aside a few times over the next few days. I'll take care of setting up the time. Let's just relax for the night. I know a good place," she assures.

I look out the window at cars driving by and the buildings we pass. There is an uneasy feeling clawing at me as I look around the city I once called home, a notion whispering in my ear that I don't belong here. Not anymore. For now, though, I must be here if only to settle my affairs.

Before too long, Viv pulls into a parking lot. It's a familiar sight, though I can't place it; perhaps it is just passing déjà vu. As we enter the watering hole, the familiarity hits me. We stopped in Queens. Last time I was at this bar, I was three sheets to the wind, laying against the kickplate on the bar, screaming along with Andrew W.K.'s "I Love New York City." Ah, old memories do haunt us at peculiar times.

We cop-a-squat at the barstools. Viv holds up two fingers, and the bartender gives her a nod. It seems that she's been here more than a few times on this leg of their tour.

"How much longer you got?" the bartender shouts over the music.

"Couple o' days. Then onto the Midwest. Chi-town, Twin Cities, St. Louis, and a few more," Viv says with a smile. It seems that she has found something to smile about.

"How's Logan?" I ask out of both personal and professional curiosity.

"Nice small talk we're starting off with here," Viv laughs back. "Logan's fine. Chilling with the band before their show."

"It's already getting up there in time. Don't you need to be there?" I inquire.

"Eventually. Wanted a quick drink first," Viv says as the bartender places our drinks in front of us.

The music of the bar provides a pleasing ambiance to the night. The unique sounds of Volbeat's "The Devil's Bleeding Crown" soothe the nerves of the coming meeting. The night couldn't be going any smoother.

"Finn!" a voice shouts.

I turn to see her. The sound of the voice is accompanied by he-who-almost-pounded-me-into-oblivion-not-once-but-twice. Of all the gin joints in all The Big Apple, they walk in here. Patrick and Katy. At least the big smile on his face is a nice change of pace.

Katy waves at me as they spring on over to us. Viv tosses me a curious look that I smile at.

I whisper to Viv, "Old friends."

She whispers back, "Moreso her than him, I presume."

But it isn't Katy to shake my hand first. Patrick, dressed in clothes that hide his skull-crushing, almost surfer-dude physique, extends a hand. As I return the shake, he wraps his free arm around me. The hug, while meaning well, presses on all the wrong spots of my bones. A need for pills whispers in my ears, but the pills are packed away in my luggage. For now, alcohol will have to dampen the pain.

"Long time no see," Patrick says with a chipper sound in his voice. "Thank you for everything."

"How're the feet? Healed up all right?" I refer to our last encounter.

"A few days of limping but nothing bad. Worst of it was the face. And the swallowed pride." Patrick smiles. "Sorry about that."

"Completely understandable. I woulda done the same thing if I was in your shoes." I smile.

Katy decides to join in. "Nice to see you, Finn. Who's this lovely lady?" she says with an elbow nudge and a wink.

"Katy, Vivian. Vivian, Katy. She's taken over the tour while I was in the hospital. I'm just here to tie things up," I answer.

"Viv. Just Viv. Nice to meet you, Katy," Viv jumps in. "How do you know Finn?"

"He saved our relationship," Katy beams.

Even Patrick is nodding his head. "It's true. Finn may be a lot of things to a lot of people. But he always does the right thing."

Viv gives me an amused nod before turning to Katy. "That he does. And it sounds like a story I need to hear."

"Funny story, but before I tell ya . . . hospitalized?" Katy changes the subject.

"Bachelor party, a little alcohol, stormy night, and a multi-car pileup," I summarize.

"Doesn't sound good," Patrick says.

"Wasn't as good for the passenger in my car." I carry a tone in my voice that answers the next unasked question.

"So sorry, sir," Patrick says, ending the topic.

They both sit next to us at the bar and order a drink. We spend a short while chatting up and small talking about Spear Fist and making a call to put them on the list for tonight's show. It's nice to sit and relax, sharing a drink with no drama. No hidden agendas to bring up at an opportune time. No ulterior motives to guide our actions. Just old friends making new friends.

"So," Viv chimes in, "Finn is a relationship savior? How did he pull that off?"

Patrick finishes a sip of his bottled beer while raising his other hand. "By helping me after I almost pummeled him to death," he says, wiping beer foam off his chin.

Viv looks to me for confirmation.

"It's true," I say. "Mistaken case of wrong place, wrong time. But in Patrick's defense, the presumption wasn't unwarranted."

Katy pipes up with a finger wave for another round. "I walked into some misguided shenanigans, but Pat and I talked."

"Talked?" I raise a brow.

Patrick sets down the empty bottle and starts his second beer. "Seriously. After you helped me back up, I sat in the elevator, riding back, just thinking. Thinking about why I acted like I did and why you did for me what you did. I knew both our actions were because of this girl." He wraps his arm around her, bringing her in for a quick hug. "We talked about everything. All our mistakes. All the reasons we did what we did. And it was great."

Katy takes the proverbial mic. "It's true. Ever since that day, things have been great. And we have you to thank."

I nod in appreciation for their kind words. "I was just a catalyst. You already had a boiling pot. Just needed things stirred the right way," I add.

Things are nice. We sit and finish our second rounds while laughing and making jokes on my behalf, all of which are well deserved.

I feel a sense of serenity because despite all my actions and childish behavior, something good came out of the incident. Which I guess is why we repaid them with the backstage access at the show, a show which is going as well as can be expected.

The night itself is going better than I hoped. No complaints from former lovers. No men chasing me with baseball bats or hitting me upside the face with a hammer of a fist. Pleasant, a word generally not used to describe a heavy metal show, but pleasant the mood is.

I stand watching the show from a similar vantage point as I did at their record release. I half expect Faith to grab my hand or some cheesy notion of romanticism. But no. No fingers are gently interlaced with mine. No arms wrap around my waist or shoulder. I stand, watching them, thinking about all the events that led up to this moment.

I try to think about this life. The nights like this one and the days that lead up to these nights: the work and sacrifice, the ecstasy and the agony of it all. The life that I have created, yes, much of that was inspired by Faith. But I watch it all play out before my eyes. The culmination of everything I have worked for and done being given back to the audience, note by note and lyric by lyric. I love it all. Every moment that I remember: the good, the bad, the ugly. The nights where songs come together in such gloriousness that the excitement keeps you going for another eight hours. The days spent alone trying to remember why you wanted this life because you haven't seen friends or family for so long, your mind starts to forget what they look like. And of course, the moments where you exit from behind a bush from just having done what was done to see the love of your life cast soul-crushing judgment with only her eyes. I look at it all.

I am not sure I can leave it all behind. I cannot fathom what my life would entail without this. I guess now, because I never had to before, I need to think about how I can do this and be a father too. Be there so Faith can be a mother. Kids can be raised on the road. I am sure of it. But for some reason, Faith won't do that. She won't follow me and be with me while I do what I do so well. I can't imagine who I would be without all this. Possibly some remnant of a guy who watches old reruns of a television show while keeping an eye on the baby so his wife can cook a meal or take a bath or whatever.

All those thoughts play so fast that my mind can't focus on any one moment or any one scenario. They just get pushed aside by the never-ending deluge of new situations and thoughts constantly entering my head. It's not a bad thing. It's just that in moments like these—a crossroad if you will—your mind won't focus. To reminisce on it all is too much. So, the universe sends something your way to make you focus or, at the very least, stop the flood of thoughts and memories.

A tap on my shoulder is what pulls me up from under the current. I turn, expecting to see a fan around my age with upturned lips, ready to tell me of his or her love for my work. Some sort of single-serving compliment to carry me through to the next one, but it is not. No. It is not some simple gesture that will be forgotten by me long before the encounter will ever leave the person's mind. Such a simple meeting would be welcome. Instead, I turn to see an expectant, smiling face. The face, though, that is the surprise.

"Funny seeing you here, Finn." Jacquelyn smirks as she sips her beer.

Jacquelyn. I am not sure what to think. Faith said they talked. Faith said Jacquelyn understood. Or did she say that? My mind has been in a constant state of low-lying fog since waking up in the hospital. But I guess the bigger preponderance at the moment is finding out why the hell she is in New York.

I shake the thoughts from my mind. "How are you?"

She extends an arm, her upturned eyebrow questioning if a hug is appropriate. I move in and wrap my arms around her. It is nice to see her, after all. She holds me close for a moment. The feeling of her pressed against me isn't as unwelcome as I suppose it should be. But comfortable places are comforting.

"I wanted to come see you in the hospital," she whispers in my ear. "Faith didn't think that would be such a good idea. Baby and all."

I give her a tighter squeeze before pulling back. "Sorry I never made it back to the bachelor party. I didn't plan on leaving you like that."

"But you did plan on leaving me?" She scratches her cheek.

I shake my head. "I meant, I wasn't going to leave things like that. Stripping, dancing, whatever, just took a moment to digest. I'm sorry I reacted the way I did."

"I think it's all water under the bridge now." She smiles.

Jacquelyn stands for a moment, peering into my eyes. I don't know if she is looking for something in them or just seeing if I am still me. She shifts her gaze to the stage.

"How were you going to leave things? Ya know, had the whole crash not happened?" She continues to stare at the stage.

There's a part of me that understands why she is staring at the stage and not at me. I know it is for the same reason that I can't look at her right now. If we were to look at each other, it might change what we want to say. Damn. What the hell is she doing in New York?

"You're a little far from home." I don't respond to her question yet. I still have to figure out what I would have said.

She turns back to me, sipping her drink. "Needed a little break, and I heard this great band was on tour. Figured I'd become a groupie or somethin'."

That might have been a guarded response, but after everything, I can understand it.

"I was falling hard for you, ya know," I say, a little under my breath.

"I know," she says, taking in a quick breath.

Apparently, it wasn't under my breath enough.

"I was all in for you. It was why I was hesitant to tell you that I danced," Jacquelyn continues. She turns back to the show. "So, you're giving all of this up for her?"

There are the words. Spoken. Pointed. Sharp. And they cut deep.

"It would seem that way." I run my hand through my hair.

"You don't have to. It's your choice." Jacquelyn's eyes are still glued to the stage.

"I don't think it's that simple anymore. Unborn and all," I gently remind her.

"Sure. But this is your life. This is what you are. The music, the stage, the venues, the road. Are you ready to give that all up for her? Your child can travel. You can have both." Jacquelyn has become a devil on my shoulder. But she might be the angel. Hell, I am not sure anymore.

"Faith," I start to say.

"Oh, I know. Faith told me all about you two. Who you guys were back in the day. How it all was before the fame. How she followed your colorful career from afar, reading about your exploits while standing in line at the grocery store or some street-side magazine stand. She told me about her and you and Ronnie. The torch you still hold for her and her for you, apparently. I know the tumultuous tale of torrid trysts." She suddenly stops as if I was cued to interrupt.

"So..." I urge her to continue.

"So, she's not the only one who carries a torch for you. If I am to be honest, I don't think she's the only one your torch holds a flame for." She steps closer to me.

Her eyes dive deep into mine. Our breath is soft. The feel of the bass pounding through the concrete floors seems to slide us closer and closer. Our lips hover just out of reach.

"You don't have to decide anything tonight, Finn. I wouldn't do that to you. But I won't wait forever. I'm not a consolation prize," she whispers in a tone that is somehow both sexy as hell and stern to the point of making me feel ashamed, a little aroused, and a little ashamed for feeling aroused. I think this might be the first time in my life I'll take the shame over the sex.

She leans in, planting a kiss on my cheek. "I'll see you soon. Don't be a stranger. You still have my number."

She leaves it at that, walking away. My mind is spinning—spiraling out of control and plummeting toward Earth. All I can think is that a pill sounds good right now. I thought I was somehow passed all the temptation, passed all the choices being thrown at me like I am some sort of sacred prize for someone. I am not. And no matter, no woman deserves to be a consolation prize for someone else.

I reach down for my pills, and the bottle rises with one last reprieve. Damn. One pill. It makes me wonder how many I have been taking and how often. I thought I had a relatively full bottle when I flew up here. No matter now, though. The bottle gives me one last dose to ease the pain.

Further downward my spiral plummets, though a little slower toward the ground below. Faith and my baby trying to catch me. Jacquelyn and the life that I love trying to shove Faith out of the way in some attempt to be my salvation. These strange thoughts fill my head without any semblance of organization. I want Faith. I've always wanted Faith. The honest truth of the matter is it never would have worked out between Jacquelyn and me. To make it as simple as possible, it wasn't in the cards. Perhaps she just never saw that. Maybe I am wrong. What she does present is an alternative. A chance to have Faith and the life that I love. A life that Faith has only witnessed from a safe distance—cities or countries away. A life that has given Faith pause on giving me a second chance, but a life that is misunderstood by those not directly in it.

I guess now I must deal with Jacquelyn and what-ever emotions and unfinished business still lingers in the universe.

"It's funny that you like these weird places to watch the show," Viv shouts as she hands me a beer.

I take a sip in hopes that it can ease the pain, both emotional and physical, that I feel. One pill just doesn't take the edge off like it first did.

"It's peaceful back here." I sip again.

"But the party is down there. Hell, you're farther away than anyone in the seats," Viv says, grabbing my hand, leading me away.

"The distance gives me a viewpoint to take it all in. A place to reflect on things." I offer up a rare dose of honest vulnerability.

"I saw what happened, Finn." She lets go of my hand now that she knows I am following.

"You have to narrow that down a bit," I joke.

"You and Jacquelyn. I saw her." Viv's tone isn't even subtly leading. It's in my face pointing it out with half of a smile on her lips.

"We were talking. Jacquelyn never came to visit me, ya know." I sip my beer.

"She never came because Faith told her not to. Faith needs you, now more than ever. At least that's what I'm told," Viv offers up.

We walk for a few moments, listening to D.B. interact with the audience—some shit about being in New York and how great they all are.

Viv slows her pace. "You're a regular 'Mr. Self Destruct'."

"Is that what the long silence was for? To think of a Nine Inch Nails song title?" I chuckle.

"Yes. No." Viv scrunches her nose. "It's true, though. The name fits. We could have had something."

Viv turns to me and looks me dead in the eye. She doesn't move closer, keeping her distance as she stares. It's weird. I can see in her eyes that there's no lingering emotion, unlike with Jacquelyn. Hell, Jacquelyn told me I had options. With Viv, though, it's matter of fact. She looks at me and our past. She stares at what could have been without the yearning to try and rekindle it.

I am impressed with her state of mind and slightly jealous that I've never been that guy, never been one to let smoldering fires die out. I always have to suck the last bit of life from each and every ember.

"But you're with Logan." I test the waters to make sure my assumption is correct.

She shakes her head and laughs at me. "Not what I was implying. You cared for all of us, and I'm betting that you cared, on some level, for every woman you've ever been with."

She flashes her all-access pass to a couple of security guards so they'll let us pass. The old familiar halls of the backstage area. The grit and dirt that makes the magic happen all hidden back here.

"I like to think so," I say with a hint of uncertainty to her end.

"And I bet that every single one of those women, or at least a good number of them, could have ended up as a long term, or a permanent relationship, had you not been stuck on Faith." She finger-jabs me with the last of her words.

"Not at all. You left me. . . remember you said one day you'd tell the story of us? 'The great Fairlane Incidents' as I believe you called them." I chuckle. "And Jacquelyn was ended by Faith and other circumstances."

"And what about every other girl before us? What about Jacquelyn? What are those 'other circumstances' you mention?" She stops walking as she opens the backstage green room door. "Do you ever wonder why all your relationships have failed? Why they keep collapsing on themselves?"

The room is a little quieter than the halls once the door closes behind us. The inside is simple with two couches and a coffee table topped with finger food and sweets. A fridge off in the corner is stocked with an assortment of beer, malt beverages, and sodas. Engaged in conversation are Jeanine and Logan. The rest of Logan's bandmates are huddled in the far corner, beer bottles in hand, laughing over something they find amusing.

"There are moments I've tried to answer that for myself, but I only come to one conclusion: right place, wrong time." I grab a fresh beer from the fridge.

I twist the cap as Viv motions Logan over. Jeanine decides to join in the conversational fun. My defenses want to go up like some sort of force field around the Starship Enterprise. The sight of Jeanine and what she blew up bar-side makes me feel a little tight, but she is here. She is hundreds of miles from her home, far from any comfort she knows. Yes, she did it for her husband, to make sure his success wasn't entirely dependent on my lack of any sort of contingency plan in case I was injured. She also did it for me, and for that, I keep my guard down.

Logan shoots out her hand and gives me a hearty shake. Her freshly dyed pink hair is much less tweaker than when I first discovered her. Even the style is not as hectic and disheveled.

Before Logan can say anything, Jeanine grabs me and wraps her arms around me. "It's nice to see you."

Kind words are hard to digest sometimes. The feeling that everything you just felt a moment ago was wrong puts a whisper in my mind that I'm a jerk for feeling that way. So, I respond with the only thing I can think of. "I'm sorry I missed your wedding."

Jeanine shakes her head and gives me a sad smile. "We're all just glad you are okay." She turns to Viv, who is whispering something to Logan, "So, what has he done now?" Jeanine jabs at me playfully.

"We were just talking about him and his great ability to self-destruct his relationships," Viv fills them in.

As if rehearsed in some off, off, off-Broadway production of "The Finn Fairlane Story," Logan and Jeanine both nod their heads with a thesaurus of confirmations to Viv's statement. The almost-forced laughter, while trying not to hurt my fragile ego, comes across like they rehearsed this very moment in some sort of elaborate and slightly cruel prank. Except they didn't. It was organic, a real moment where two people's gut reactions about me confirmed the third person's—that I self-destruct. Now, as much as I would love to move the conversation onto a new subject, something a little less about me and more about anything else in the universe, I have a feeling that is not going to happen. What I am about to be part of is the education of Finn Fairlane and everything I have done, why I made those decisions, and what I should be doing about it all.

"Now I know that you and I don't fuckin' talk outside of music and tour shit, but I do talk with my lovely girl." Logan starts the class for me. "From what it sounds like, I might be way fuckin' off base here, but it sounds like you can't let go. Don't get me wrong; it's not a bad fuckin' thing. Your inability to let go, hold onto whatever it is that lingers inside your brain, is what spawned the music, the career that was fuckin' Finn Fairlane."

I nod my head. "I think that's pretty well established."

Logan huffs and nods in agreement. "Then why can't you fill in the blanks, the space between then and now?"

Jeanine raises her hand slightly, as if to politely interject. "It's what happened back then. The romanticization of what could have been. Of what you wanted it to be. All she did was solidify the end to you and her long after it had already expired. You may have gone on to bigger things, venues, tours, foreign countries, but your heart and your mind are still on campus back in freshman year."

Wow. I'd say from the mouths of babes but a child she is anything but anymore. Once again, she has proven herself to me. I am glad that this time, at least, she is on my side. At least I think they are all on my side, just trying to help me along this path we call life.

Viv turns to Logan with an apology in her eye. "I hate to bring this up, but it's to the point."

Logan nods. "Baby, you ain't the first to play in my sandbox, and I ain't the first to play in yours."

"Sandbox?" I joke. "Kinda a dry place. I would've gone with 'splash in your pool,' 'wade in your waters,' something with a little more moisture."

Logan chuckles. "You've only ever played in them during rainy season."

I nod, smile, and turn to Viv.

Viv smiles as she shakes her head. "Even as I was looking you in the eye, balls deep on your dick, I saw it in your eyes. Of course, at that moment, I didn't know what to think. I thought maybe it was me. I wasn't doing something right; you weren't enjoying it."

I throw up a hand. "Oh no. You were . . . wonderful."

"No need to play coy around me, Finn," Jeanine interjects. "I've been privy to your illustrious escapades for a while now."

"Just trying to show some couth," I defend.

"Even I know it's a little too late for that shit," Logan tosses in her two cents.

"Back to my point." Viv gets her floor back. "I saw it then. Only now I know what it was. It wasn't some unknown greatness floating through your head. It wasn't some moment of musing that you'll write about in some future song. It was thoughts of Faith. Thoughts of a long passed 'what if.' Had that little notion not been biting the back of your mind, some constant reminder throughout the years of what you once had, who knows what you could have had? What we could have had."

Logan tilts her head toward Viv, a gesture not unnoticed by Viv. "Not that I'm complaining. I quite like where the adventure led me. I'm just saying that, present circumstances unknown, it could have been something."

I chuckle. "No need to worry, Logan. She has no residual embers still clinging to life and smoldering for me. Her fire for me has died and been reignited in a luminescent lesbian flame for you."

All of their heads turn to me. Viv says what they are all thinking, "Luminescent lesbian flame?"

I shrug my shoulders. "I wanted something colorful."

"You're an ass, Finn," Logan spits out with a chuckle.

"That I may be. But I'm the reason this night exists. So, ass or not, you all are glad I'm around," I respond with a little unintended narcissism. "But where it led was worth it all, was it not?"

Viv looks into Logan's eyes, a gesture the defensive Logan is not used to. Her shifting posture broadcasts it for all to see. "Of course, it was. No offense, Finn. But this is where I belong. So for me, yes. But have you ever asked yourself that question?"

And immediately, as if the uncomfortableness that Logan felt was cued to jump into me, I start smiling that unsure smile. The smile of a child caught with his hand in the cookie jar. The swaying back and forth, shuffling my feet as my body is attacked by those words, words that I guess I never have faced myself, no matter how many times I thought I have.

Viv continues her inquisition. "I mean that Katy girl seemed to be all hunky-dory with her boy, but what if you were that guy? Hell, we had a great time together, and from what I can tell, I made you happy."

I nod at her words.

"Even Jaquelyn seemed to make you happy. You had no reason to stop seeing her. It's not like she's the first girl you ever saw pick up a dollar bill with her lady parts," Viv continues.

Again, I throw my hands up. "Why does the bill keep getting smaller? It was a twenty."

"Not the point, Finn," Viv continues. "The point is, is that any of those girls, and I'm sure there were a few more between, you could have had a successful future with. A girl who was a clean slate. Someone who you didn't have a checkered past with and old preconceptions wouldn't weigh into every decision."

"I'm losing focus," I admit. "What's the point?"

"Why Faith? Why throw all those things out the window? Why self-destruct every good possibility that has come your way since the day you two finally went your separate ways?" Viv's words hit me hard.

Have I ever actually given any thought to those words? I have in that stupid coffeehouse, existentialism way, pondering the greater meaning of life, love, loss, and the purposelessness of it all. Or whatever college-age bullshit I deluded myself with to try and move forward while really just running on a metaphorical treadmill. I mean, you turn it on, the ground below you moves, the digital readout says that you've been running for forty-five minutes, and you've run four miles. The thing is, though, you haven't. You step off the platform and you are right where you began. You haven't moved in any sort of way that anyone can see. Sure, you're out of breath, and your clothes are soaked with sweat, but you are in the same exact spot you were in forty-five minutes ago. You are in the same exact spot you've been for the last forty-five minutes.

You were running in place. That's all I've been doing. It gives you a workout, sure. I'm not saying it doesn't. But exercise aside, we've stood still. Mentally, I've been standing still, too scared to move on and too afraid to make anything real. I am not sure if it was because I was too frightened to let go of Faith or some other reason. Perhaps I was too afraid to repeat the same mistakes. The irony of it all is that my own fears caused me to repeat the same mistakes over and over again, time after time.

I look up to see Jeanine texting on her phone while trying to hold in a smile.

"Everything all right?" I ask her.

"Just telling sis about all the fun she's missing right now." Jeanine laughs.

"Thanks. Glad we can get more people in on this. I think after all this, I'm going to go get some sleep. You kids enjoy yourselves." I turn to leave and wave bye to them.

As I exit the door, Viv squeezes through before it closes. "I'll walk you to your hotel."

"I still have to find one," I say a bit sheepishly.

"You bought a plane ticket but didn't make a hotel reservation? Dumbass," she playfully scolds.

"Had other things on my mind." I shrug.

"I bet. You can crash with us," Viv says, as if there is no other acceptable option. "Let's grab your bag from my car for the just in case."

The walk is quiet for a minute or two, just two friends keeping each other company. There is a feeling of unease that crawls around my skin, like little spiders gently tiptoeing over my body hairs. They try not to disturb me, but I can feel them all. The unease of it is my fault, I think. Perhaps all the events in my life that have led up to this moment are my fault. Not my doing. Not some grand cosmic plan. Just my fault, like a series of crappy events that all led to here. It has to be this new understanding that I have been scared of. Otherwise, it wouldn't bother me so.

"Sorry if that was too uncomfortable back there." Viv breaks the silence.

"Wasn't your fault. Just brought up some long-needed realizations," I start. "I should probably be thanking you."

Viv lets out a laugh. We both take a few steps, breathing in the night air. I take a look around the Big Apple and think about how it differs from The City Beautiful. There's nothing here to steal you away from your adulthood. Nothing here to make you grab for your lost childhood. Just the living entity that is New York, the nightlife that breathes soul into the morning that resuscitates the night. The never-ending cycle that is New York. And it is wonderful. Nothing jaded. Nothing to make you believe in fairy tales. Just unrestrained, in-your-face-city life from the most brutally honest group of tell-it-like-it-is people—New Yorkers.

A few more steps of our ten block journey stops us at a red light, waiting to cross to the hotel. Viv turns to me. "There was a part of me that wanted to say, 'I can think of a way to thank me.'"

I let out a short laugh as I look toward the night sky.

"I just didn't want you to take me too seriously," she amends her statement.

"I wouldn't have thought you were. Even if I did, Logan kinda scares me, ya know," I offer up.

"She has a defensive side to her. I'll give her that," Viv responds.

"Don't let that scare you off. She's loyal. Guarded."

We both cross as the light turns green. The night air stays welcoming as we enter the lobby to what is now my hotel.

"What about Faith?" Viv asks.

"What about her?" I say, pushing the elevator button.

"I made a joke about you and me. You said Logan scared you off. So, what about Faith?" Viv asks for clarity on the subject.

"Faith. If there ever was such a sweet subject." I let it trail off while I think of the answer. As the elevator dings to open its doors, the answer chimes in my head. "She wants me to leave this all behind."

Viv lets out a laugh loud enough to turn a few random heads. "Yeah, like that'll happen." But the look in my eyes as I turn to her cuts her laughter short. "You can't be serious?"

I shrug my shoulders. "Why not? I've had a good run."

"And you're still running. You are still in the game. You are still great," Viv defends. "Why cash in your chips while you're still hot?"

I laugh. "Hot? I haven't been hot for a long time. Warm, sure. But the days of rock 'n roll like I knew are long over. The sad reality is my time in the limelight ended long ago. Now I'm just living on borrowed time, hoping to make one last great hit and cash it all in, again."

"So, that's it?" Viv scorns. "What about Spear Fist? What about Logan Square? What about all the people, like me and Jeanine, who actually enjoy you being who you are?"

"There's the rub." I tap the side of my nose. "The pro-verbial what-to-do."

The elevator doors open, and the walk to her room is drowned in silence.

We do find an amicable middle ground to comfortably relax in, laughing as we talk and pass the time till sleep sets in.

The funny thing is that Viv and I had great sexual chemistry, but Logan's disclaimer sounds in my head—innies, not outies. So, the night ends without any sexual escapades or events that will lead to an awkward next day, which just leaves the meeting with the record company.

CHAPTER 6

The meeting room is pretty nondescript. The table is your typical laminate office table with a hole in the middle for phone cords and such, and a few generic-looking, black cloth office chairs so we can stare at each other while figuring out the details of the contract. At least the floor-to-ceiling windows overlook the Big Apple. It's a beautiful sight to see the hustle and bustle of the tiny cars and even tinier people below, all moving about their day, trying to make deals, deadlines, and whatever else the city needs from them.

But the executives don't seem to want to stare at the life below us. The suits they wear mean business while my jeans, T-shirt, and suit coat give mixed signals. But here we all are. Even Viv is more professionally dressed than I am. But it's me they want, so it's me they get.

The thought of the push and pull of the contracts, wheeling and dealing to make things happen, starts to irk me. The gnawing sensation of being told counteroffers just to land where I know we are going to land eats away at my bones—my finally healing bones. But now they are starting to hurt. I pull out a bottle of painkillers (or muscle relaxers, or whatever remnants of prescription and over-the-counter drugs happen to be left) from my front right pocket and dump a couple into my hand. A quick look to make sure there aren't too many (though the number for too many has changed recently), and then I toss them in my mouth. A quick head tilt back, dry gulp down, and I turn back to the record execs.

"So? I had to come up here?" I start.

"Spear Fist is yours, are they not?" one of them says.

"Sure. But they are hers too. Viv took over the tour after my accident," I tell them. They should know this. They do their research. I am not sure what game they are playing here.

Ah, the games, the subtle push and pull of words designed to try and get you to give up as many of your rights to the music as they can get without you realizing it. I've done this for far too long to play this game over and over, but over and over is how the game is played.

In all honesty, the meeting is the last thing on my mind. Even as I sit here at the table with the execs and Viv, my mind is thinking about New York. It is thinking about the life I left behind to move south, just to end up here tonight. I remember the radio commercials and taxicab advertisements that whispered to me. I remember why I moved. I remember wanting to get away from moments like this, not the meetings and making futures happen. That's part of the business. It's the game of the business. I wanted to get away from the young bucks. The new adults fresh out of school that happened to be in some position of limited power, even though if you sniffed hard enough, you could still smell dorm room sex on them. They are the hotshots who think that because they remember sixty percent of the crap they read about while getting their bachelors and have minimal field experience, they know it all. It's that position of naive arrogance that I wanted to get away from—that I was tired of dealing with. But here I am, sitting with two guys who are precisely that.

What I'd rather be doing is wandering the city. I'd preferably be visiting the places I left behind: a stroll past my old apartment building; a walk past my favorite restaurants or a chat with the bartender I used to know, assuming they are still there. I'd sooner be talking with Faith about this bullshit I have to do right now. I'd rather be chatting with Jaquelyn about the future we could have had if only the car didn't smash into me and kill my girl's ex-fiancé. (That's a lot to chew on right now.) But no, I am here and about to hear something stupid come out of one of the guys' mouths.

"But you are the man in charge," the other one says, as if to remind me of my place in all this. As if I will jump up, shove Viv aside and declare that, yes, I am the man in charge. Screw him.

"I don't think my penis has much to do with my authority," I joke.

They turn to each other and pull their papers close to them. The first one turns to me. "We don't have to do this if you can't be civil."

"You wanted to meet with me. Viv could have handled it, but you wanted me. I told her no. She nudged and insisted until she got me here. So far, I'm more impressed with her abilities than yours," I say to them.

Why do I say such harsh words to two guys that can offer me lots of money? Cause I don't care about them. I don't give a crap about their student loans or their car repairs. I care about Spear Fist, Viv, and about my future. If I show them I care about them, then it gives them the upper hand.

The one I seemingly offended more stands up and looks toward the door before glancing down at his colleague. The two don't say anything. I can sense Viv's eyes locked on me, trying to telepathically call me to her. She wants to see my eyes. She wants to know I am not going to fuck this up. The irony here is that if I turn to her, I will. So, I don't.

The second pushes his chair back from the table. He rises without looking at me. A wise move. Show me you don't care. The first guy, though, he glances at me, and I can see his fear.

"That's fine. Your bosses won't care that you lost Spear Fist. There are others out there," I start as they take a step toward the door. "But how are your bosses going to take it when you tell them that you mucked up a deal with Finn Fairlane?" I wait for a reaction as they continue to the door. A hand reaches the handle. "That Finn Fairlane won't deal now or any time in the future with them because you decided to walk away?" The handle does not turn. The first one glances back at the other. Some silent conversation plays out, and though I have no clue what they are saying, I know they are both realizing that scare tactics don't work on me. "Walk away if you want. I can call your boss right now. He'll be happy to hear from me. How happy will he be to hear from you?"

They sigh simultaneously, both returning to their seats.

"Fine," one of the suits says. "Let's move on."

They start to explain their want for Spear Fist, their desire to have them on their label. They both spout the same crap I've heard time and time again about where they see the band going and all the same scripted bull they've spewed before. They have their usual demands, which will be whittled down considerably by the time I am through, but my pills kick in and kick in hard. Did I take any right before the meeting? I don't remember. I may have. I must have. My wandering mind only does this when the pills are making my pain go away. And the more pills, the less pain.

I try to stay focused on their words. I want to make sure that anything I respond to isn't giving away any of our rights. I want to respond appropriately, not because I give a crap if they know I am stoned on some pills right now but because they will exploit the fact I am high right now. A mistake that has cost many dearly.

I don't know how long I was lost in my thoughts. It only seemed like a few seconds. I think I only said a few words to myself, but I hear them repeat my name.

"Finn? Finn?" the second suit says.

I look up at them. I didn't even realize I was staring down. I quickly rub my left temple and wince in feigned pain.

"Excuse me, I need to step out for a moment," I say, rising from my seat.

One of the suits speaks up. "Um, we have to get through this. We were in the middle of something."

I turn to him. "And I'll be back shortly. It's not the end of the world. Talk with Viv while I'm out. Order some pies, pepperoni and sausage. Just give me a minute to take a leak."

I exit the meeting and walk to the bathroom. Surprisingly enough, I find myself actually needing to take a leak, after which I find myself staring back at me in the mirror. I need to get my head in the game. I called a timeout. Never a good move to do first, but who am I kidding? These kids are new to the game and only have playbook experience and minimal field time. I don't care that I called time; Viv is still in there making sure the deal doesn't go south.

I pull out my pills to do a quick inventory count but find the well has run dry. No rattling sound as it exits my pocket. No little pill, whole, broken, smooth, or jagged to help ease the pain. I need to be able to concentrate, but it's just not happening right now.

I flip the lever up and turn on the faucet. I splash some water onto my face a few times. I know that it doesn't actually help sober you up from whatever chemicals that have taken control of your brain. It does help slap some cold sense back into me for a moment though, a quick jolt to grab my attention, and hopefully hold onto it long enough to finish this shit.

I grab a paper towel from the automated, touch-free dispenser and begin to dry my face. The door opens, and one of the suits walks in.

A self-deprecating smirk crosses his face. "You were right. A bathroom break was a good idea."

"Sometimes I have good ideas," I joke. "I'm heading back now."

"Pizza is on its way," he says, unzipping his pants.

I head back to the meeting room to find Viv sitting by herself.

"Where's the other guy?" I ask, looking around.

"They decided to take advantage of the break," she starts. "One's in the restroom; the other went looking for a vending machine for soda."

I pull out a chair and turn it toward Viv as I take a seat.

"You've done an impeccable job with the tour, handling the band, and everything that I was supposed to be doing," I begin, making sure I have her attention.

"Thanks?" she says, raising a brow. "I had help."

I nod in acknowledgment. "I know. But you have been the front of it all."

Her attention is still locked fully on me, waiting to see where the ship is headed.

"You have been able to pull this off with just my notes and a love for the music. Is this something that interests you?" I ask.

"What?" Viv asks, the confusion evident on her face.

"What we are doing now—meetings, tours, life on the killing road. Is this something that interests you?" I continue.

"I guess, but I don't know what I am doing. I still feel like I need a crutch or training wheels or whatever. This is like brand fuckin' new, Finn." The hysteria in her voice grows as the realization of where the ship is heading becomes clearer.

"I know. I'm here. But you're at the helm now," I start.

She interrupts with a hint of panic, "Why now, all of a sudden?"

"It's time for something new. The whole reason I left New York was to get away from meetings like this." I pause as I look around the meeting room. I walk to the window and look down at the ground. The cars zooming about on the street below in anonymity make me almost happy to be here. I find a strange comfort in the overwhelming size of this city. "I love this life. I love the music. I love it all. I am just done. There is something in me that is ready for something new."

Viv looks at me, searching for what that "something new" is. "Is that something new Faith or Jacquelyn?"

I turn to her with an unsure look in my eye. She knows that is the answer I am searching for.

"My waters run much deeper than just Faith or Jacquelyn. I'm not sure I can even express the thoughts running in my head right now," I admit as I walk away from the window.

"Try me." She smiles.

Before I can even attempt an explanation, our conversation is interrupted by the opening door and the suits returning with sodas for us all.

They both sit down at the table. "So, Finn, we were about to discuss where we see Spear Fist heading."

"Yes, you were," I butt in. "When I stepped away, I realized something."

The suits look at each other before looking back at me.

"What is that?" one of them replies.

"You asked for me by name," I begin.

"That is correct," the suit confirms.

"Your label knew I was out of commission. It's why they sent you and not someone with more experience. It's why, even after I am sure Vivian explained my situation, you demanded to have me here," I continue.

As I continue, I see the sweat start to build on their foreheads. I can see the nervousness grow as each word exits my mouth. To them, this meeting is as much about landing a deal for themselves as it is meeting me. Fanboying out is not professional and not part of the agreement.

"Viv works for me. I run Fairlane Records, and she is my proxy. You are her account," I ad-lib.

"Fairlane Records? We were unaware you started your own label," the suit says, his nervousness growing more and more.

"The details are being hammered out," I continue to bullshit them. "I started it while I've been recovering. Viv and her team have been more than sufficient in handling my affairs." Luckily Viv is smart enough not to say anything and go with the flow.

"We understand," the other suit interjects.

"And as you understand, Viv is who you will be addressing for the rest of this meeting. Not me. I am invisible. Deaf, though, I am not."

I watch the gears turn in their minds. Each of the suits wonders how they are going to handle Viv. I can see the silent conversation between the two of them as they figure out how to handle this change. My words continue to echo loudly in their heads, "deaf, though, I am not."

I roll back in my chair and stare out the window toward the Big Apple, the city that made this meeting possible. Had I not worn out my welcome here, had I not needed to get away and reinvent my career, had so many little factors not fallen into place, I wouldn't be here right now. But I am here, back in the city where this chapter of my life all started.

Yes, I got picked up and noticed in Chicago. But my behind-the-music aspect of my life and career didn't start until New York. So, here I am, sitting in a meeting while facing the behemoth of a city and looking at the same sidewalks walked by Neil Diamond and Mike D, Cyndi Lauper and DMC. So many great musicians of influence beyond their years, and I am somehow a part of that. Looking out over these streets, it feels good.

I listen to Viv and the suits talk, the details of everything being hammered out. It feels nice to sit back and let the worry fall on someone else, someone who has the eager eyes of innocence and the gusto for diving into the industry. To think about how our relations started versus where they are now. I believe that sometimes the happenstance of life happens for a reason.

My ears pick up on something that is said. To be honest, I'm not sure exactly what the suit said, but I hear a pause in Viv's voice as she responds. I lean in and whisper to her, "Whatever you feel works. Go with it. Just don't sign anything until I give it a read. They are more than authorized to leave you with unsigned contracts. Nothing of importance is that imminent."

She gives me a slight nod and takes a deep breath. I can see her gather herself and regain her initial confidence. For the rest of this meeting, I sit in blissful reminiscence about my years in New York, my time before in Chicago, and the months in Florida. I trace all my moments, all my decisions, and connect the dots that ended up taking me here; it's the start, apparently, of something new—Fairlane Records, or whatever bullshit name I spewed off the cuff. The thing is, though, it worked. Whatever happened, whatever the words I said, it worked. Viv is in charge as I watch from further behind the scenes, tears welling in my eyes—a smile on my face.

I never thought that for a kid who wanted nothing more than to be on stage, soaking in the adoration of fans, that being the furthest behind the scenes possible, and still be in the scene, is where I would find happiness in it all.

At least for the moment, but tomorrow is another day.

CHAPTER 7

I Give As Good As I Get

Ｔhe night is invigorating. The meeting went well. In some ways, it went better than I could have expected. Viv has taken the reins which my hands are tired of holding—calloused and worn thin from years of tugging and abuse. New ideas flow through my mind in waves, as broad strokes of forming plans take root. And as plans take root, they need sustenance to make sure they grow. There is no better nutrient for the seeds of music than that of alcohol. Luckily hotels have long since taken to the notion that travelers like to imbibe while away from their regular domiciles, thus I do not have far to walk. I turn down the lobby and follow the walkway to the welcoming room that has a bar and bottles upon bottles of various poisons to soothe a weary traveler. I am one such traveler.

I cop a squat center bar. Before I can even wave a finger to grab the barkeep's attention, his rag is already flung over his white button-up and black suspendered shoulder, and he is picking up a glass to pour me whatever my heart desires.

"Widow Jane, neat," I say.

I Give As Good As I Get

Before I can even fully settle into the quiet reverie of victory, I feel a tap on my shoulder and turn to see a brunette smiling at me. The purposefully grey streak just off-center from the front of this mystery woman's forehead is an unusual choice for someone with otherwise jet-black hair. Perhaps she is a fan of the mutant comics. Her olive skin and soft, rounded facial features, accented by the dim lighting of the bar, emphasize her Far East beauty. There is a familiarity in the way she dresses—a casual uncaring coupled with a finish that is sure to turn heads.

I am not sure why this stranger is so eager to talk to a man who just sat down, but I am not one to reject such a fascinatingly beautiful woman.

"A man who knows his bourbons." She smiles, batting her eyelashes as the bartender places the bottle back on the shelf.

I give her a nod. "It goes down smooth."

I glance at the bartender as he slides the glass in front of me. He notices my eyes shift to the lady next to me; it is a subtle glance that tries to ask if she is just a lady or a lady of the night. He casually shrugs his shoulders as he shakes his head no. If he hasn't seen her here before, then odds are I won't be dealing with any sort of financial transaction, not that anything will transpire either way. I have Faith anxiously awaiting my return in Orlando.

Her look shifts. I've seen the shifting look countless times before. The look that at this moment in time—this moment in my life—is wearing thin, getting old, and becoming a bore. It's not that I don't appreciate the gesture or the meaning behind the look—the glimmer of recognition that I am someone they recognize from a magazine or television interview. I do appreciate it. It's just this night, this moment, is supposed to be mine, a moment of self-reflection for what was accomplished tonight. But privacy and moments of being alone are things that I chose to possibly forfeit long ago. So, here I sit, next to some exotic beauty who I believe is most likely not a hooker.

"I know this may sound strange," she begins (always a preface to something I've heard before). "I've heard a lot of good things about you."

"I'm sure they aren't all true." I turn to her, taking a swig of my bourbon.

She smiles and chuckles a little. "Esther." She extends her hand to me.

I set down my drink and shake her hand. "Nice to meet you."

I am not sure if it is really nice to meet her or if I am just being cordial, polite, giving an empty pleasantry to fill the moment. It doesn't really matter, I guess. Hell, the company can be a good thing.

"What's your poison?" I gesture to the bottles behind the bar.

She puts up her hand to catch the attention of the eavesdropping barkeep. "Old Grand Dad, neat."

Those words make me choke on the air. "You must have something you're trying to kill inside you."

She lets out a hearty laugh. "It was the first drink I ever had. Something about it stuck with me. It's the only whiskey I drink."

The bartender places a coaster in front of her, followed by the spirit. I motion to her glass, then to myself, and then make a writing gesture to put it on my tab. He nods and leaves.

"I hope you don't mind the company. You have a look about you..." Esther trails off.

"I do have a certain look to me, so I'm told." I'm not sure where she is going with this. Maybe it is her way of asking if she could sit. Maybe I should say she can. So, I extend a hand at the empty seat next to me.

She slides over one and turns my direction.

"Something good happened tonight. I can tell," Esther says, as if she's some sort of seer.

I sip my bourbon. "It did. Contract negotiations. Things are looking good."

"Thus, your reason for celebration." She turns to the otherwise empty bar (save one table in the corner), then back to me. "But there's no one else with you. A party of one is so lonely."

I hear it. A hint in her voice. A whisper of sensualism. I do appreciate the attention, everyone does, but I also much enjoy my time to myself so I can sort out my thoughts.

"What exactly are your intentions with me?" I bluntly get to the point. I wave to the bartender for another round as I polish off the current.

"Only the best of." She sips her drink with a little slip of her tongue. A little on the nose, but I don't think Esther beats around any sort of bush, so to speak.

"You know what they say about those kinds of intentions?" I ask, hearing the bartender laugh a muffled laugh.

"The road to hell and all. But Finn, may I call you Finn? Navigating those roads doesn't have to be all that tricky. As they say, it's about the journey, not the destination." She caresses my arm, not in an obvious way. Subtle, gently, as if she was casually moving her arm and her fingers happened to brush against me. Except it was obvious and not as delicate as she had hoped.

"It's a journey I've been on for many, many years," I begin.

"And one he's looking to end, unless I can change his mind," a third voice calls out.

I didn't hear her footsteps. I didn't detect the click-clack of her heels echoing on the marble floor. I was engaged in a conversation I've had one time too many, and yet I didn't hear them. I didn't see Esther look to her, nor did I notice her stop a few feet behind me. But the voice is undeniable. It is a voice that has confused me—that has tempted me (and won on a few occasions)—a voice that apparently is still fighting for me—Jacquelyn.

"I see you met my Esther." Jacquelyn smiles.

"He has," Esther interjects, "and everything you've told me rings true, so far."

After giving Ether a friendly hello kiss on both cheeks, Jacquelyn wraps her arms around me, regardless of whether I wanted to hug her or not.

I do reciprocate—a little out of common civility, and a little out of the joy I still get from seeing her. There is a part of me that begins to hurt as I hold her. It's a bone-deep pain where the pain had started to recede, a pain that causes shortness of breath for a moment. I reach into my pocket, but the bottle is still empty. No magical refills have occurred since the last time I pulled it out. It looks like I'll have to grin and bear it this bout as I slip the bottle back in my pocket.

"Still on those from the accident, I see," Jacquelyn notes out loud.

"Pain is acting up. I think my years have started taking their toll on me." I shrug.

Jacquelyn opens a hand purse, clutch thingy and pulls out something. She holds it in her fingers, bringing it to my lips. "Say 'ah.'"

I open my mouth as she pops in a pill. I swallow with my bourbon (always doctor recommended) and nod a thank-you to her.

"I didn't realize you were a walking wealth of pharmaceuticals," I jest.

"I'm a lady of many talents." She winks. "Speaking of ladies of many talents, you and Esther seem to be friends."

"Only for the moment. I should be getting back to my hotel." I start to stand as I pull out my wallet.

Jacquelyn pats the seat I just rose from. "Come on, sit. It's not like you're going to just kick back watching TV in your hotel room all night. This is New York City."

I let out a forced, exaggerated, loud sigh as I resign to sitting back down. "What is on the agenda for tonight?" Yes, there is suspicion dripping off my chin in those words, but I am here, so I'll play along.

Jacquelyn gives Esther a dog-sly smile. "Whatever the mood strikes."

I down the drink in front of me. I figure either this evening is going to go exactly how I think they think it should go, and I am going to need far more mental lubrication, or it is going to need to become something I'd not remember anyway. So, either way, I'm just getting a jump on what needs to be done.

Both girls lean toward me. It's a moment that should never make a man in my shoes uncomfortable, but this moment is. Jacquelyn knows I am trying to work things out with Faith. Maybe she just doesn't realize that the drunken sexcapades with randoms are coming to an end. Then again, she might realize just that, and that is why she is doing this, one last sexcapade to send me off. I mean if that's the case, then who am I to deny someone a send-off party?

Softly breathing into each ear is Jacquelyn and Esther, a veritable global sampling of things to leave behind. Esther exhales softly in my right ear, "Are you ready for the real celebration?"

I turn to my drink. It's moved a bit from where I left it last, at least I think it did. That shouldn't even matter, though it sticks out to me for some reason. I take a big gulp. The taste is off, like the barkeep used a dirty glass and poured a different bourbon, something different that offsets the flavor just a little.

"Ladies. This isn't why I came here tonight. I was just enjoying the moment," I say.

The pain in my bones fades, as a gentle flush through me relaxes my muscles. The pain is gone. I think that pill she gave me finally set in. That was one quality pill. I feel like I could be sitting on a chaise lounge, poolside at some resort, sipping Mai Tais while sucking down shrimp cocktail. That is if I wasn't here. But damn, this calm sensation is taking over me. All the cares in my head are neatly nestled away in a dark corner to be forgotten for a while.

Jacquelyn leans in to say, "And we are here for you. We are what you really want. A reason to stay."

I can feel my brow furrow. Jacquelyn's words make sense, pointed and sharp. Mean, almost. Stay here in New York or stay in this life? Stay.

"How did you know I was here?" I ask Jacquelyn, my brow still furrowed.

"This is your hotel. It seemed as obvious a choice as any." Jacquelyn smiles.

My mind grows a little foggy. All the objects around me grow distant even though I am here, in the moment. My glass seems out of reach. The girls on each side of me float like butterflies. I see money land on the bartop. The bartender waves at me as he fades into the distance.

Ding. I hear a dinging noise.

I am not in the bar anymore. I see lighted numbers in a small space as whispers float around my ears and butterfly kisses land on my neck. I feel like I'm floating upward.

Ding. There it is again.

I close my eyes to steady myself, only for a moment. I need to stay in this moment—keep a hold of myself. All I can think is that I drank something more than a couple of whiskeys and a pill. I clench my eyelids shut hard. I need to push it all away from my eyes. Push it down and flush it out somehow.

The sun beats down on me, reflecting off the white sands. I watch the sea as the waves silently and softly crash onto the shore, licking my toes. It sends a shiver up my legs. It relaxes me with each wave that caresses my feet.

I try to look at the endless beach around me. There is nothing but sand and ocean water. No other people around. No other sights. Just the endless white sands, gentle waves, and burning sun overhead. I am okay with this. The solitude is nice. I haven't had such time to myself in decades. I'm not sure if I've ever had this sort of alone time, time for just me and no worries about others. About the . . . whatever it was I was working on that was so crucial. All me and no one else. No one to set expectations on whatever it is they expect from me.

The tingling works its way up my leg. It tickles but also feels exciting, a feeling out of place where I am. I look down to see a hermit crab crawling on the inside of my thigh. I try to wipe it away, but I can't move. My arms won't move. I see them next to me, lying there like two lifeless flesh logs. Useless. It doesn't matter. The hermit crab is gone. But the tickling is still there. The feeling that something is crawling farther up my thigh, stopping at my manhood.

I am enjoying the thoughts that wade through my mind: feelings I can't place; ideas that I know are there but don't make sense; thoughts that are nothing more than lumps of clay waiting to take shape. The pieces know what shape they will end up taking, and that I am the one to shape them. I, however, do not comprehend what the clay thoughts want to be sculpted into. They are just there, in my mind. They are like I am—free of any responsibility, free of any burdens. Free from myself.

I feel no pain because this sensation tickles. Tickling isn't painful. Sure, it can be when someone gets a hold of you and doesn't stop while your breath starts to run short, and you can't stop laughing. That is a painful tickle, but this, this feels freeing. It reminds me of a playful tickle fight that ends in a deep, back-curling kiss leading to more.

I enjoy this moment. A moment when all worry slips away. A moment that seems as if it will go on forever. Just the sand and me getting licked by the waves of the ocean.

I wonder how I got here as I look around at the endless beach with nothing on its horizon. I try to recall why I can't move. Nothing comes to mind, just the peaceful lull of the waves and the warm, moist feeling of something wrapped around my special part.

I can't move.

Shit.

This feels too good to be true.

I am dreaming.

My eyes shoot wide open, knowing that what felt too good to be true is true. And the person making those feels in me is not Faith. The blinding light shooting through the window obscures her hair. I turn my head away from the light and see Jacquelyn sleeping soundly next to me.

Esther.

I shove her off and jump out of bed. I fumble for my pants that were luckily on the floor next to me.

I zip up and look to see her standing at the foot of the bed, wiping her smile dry.

"Good morning. I hope that was a fun way to wake up." Esther steps toward me.

I take a step away. "No, it wasn't."

She cocks her head.

"I mean it was, but it wasn't. I'm spoken for. You can't just start sucking off any man you think might enjoy it. There are boundaries. Clearly, something you struggle with," I try to clarify.

Jacquelyn starts to stir from the commotion.

"Come on, Finn. All the flirting last night. We hit it off pretty well. I mean, really," she shrugs, "what's a little blowie between friends?"

Something in Esther's words caught Jacquelyn's attention. She sits upright in the bed, still clothed from last night, a hopeful sign that nothing happened.

"I barely know your name. Calling us friends is stretching it," I shoot back. "And while I appreciate the gesture, you can't just suck someone's cock without their permission."

"What did you do to him?" Jacquelyn enters the conversation. The sleep that was left hovering over her has been pushed away by the force of my words.

Esther steps back, throwing her arms up. "Nothing that last night wasn't leading to. You promised me a good time, Jacquelyn. All I was doing was trying to make sure a good time was had."

Jacquelyn's face scrunches up tightly in disbelief of the words she just heard.

As the three of us stand our ground, waiting for Jacquelyn's words to form in her head, my phone rings. Of course, my phone rings. Nothing would add a little more tension to an otherwise already tense moment like a ring from Faith. And of course, the universe has responded with such a call.

"Good morning, love," I start the call with.

I try to wave my free arm to silence the commotion around me.

"You never called me last night," Faith says with a tinge of sadness and suspicion in her voice.

"Tell me you did not fucking mouth-rape him, Esther?!" Jacquelyn yells.

I don't know what I missed in the two sentences I had with Faith. I'm not sure why my wonderful and glorious arm wave of silence did not work. Hell, I really want to know what was said that caused Jacquelyn to shout like that while I am on the phone with Faith. I just hope Faith somehow didn't hear that.

"Finn! Tell me that what I just heard wasn't about you?!" Faith reprimands with a cold sternness in her voice.

"Jacquelyn, you promised he'd be down for all this!" Esther shouts back.

So, yes. Yes, Faith heard what Jacquelyn shouted. She knows that something happened.

"Yeah, and I was wrong," Jacquelyn snaps back. "That doesn't mean to just take what you want anyway!"

"Did you hear that, Faith? I was a good guy." I try to save face.

"Yeah, real good guy, Finn. Is that why you didn't call last night? You were too busy being a good guy?!" Faith's voice quickly rises in volume.

"I don't know." I start to respond. Probably not the best way to begin defending yourself. "I don't remember last night. I only had a couple drinks," I finish before shoving the rest of my foot in my mouth.

"You don't remember!" Faith yells. "I can't stress myself like this, Finn! I'm fucking pregnant with your child, but you have to run to New York for a record thing. Fine. 'It should only be a few days or so,' you tell me. Fine. Convenient you forgot to mention to me that you might embark on some all-night bender for one last hoorah before settling down into such a boring life with me, the mother of your child!"

Jacquelyn and Esther fade to the background. I know they are yelling back and forth right next to me, but all my mind can hear are Faith's words. I can see her black, curly hair whipping about at a hundred miles an hour as she yells. Her furrowed brow that bursts with anger yet looks so beautiful. I can picture it all. Perhaps I deserve her wrath. But in truth, I do not remember.

"You can't drug people just to get some party started! He isn't some lap dance club trick!" Jacquelyn's words resound in my ears, and I'm sure Faith's as well.

"Lap dance!? Finn, what the fuck happened last night?!" Faith demands.

"I didn't get a lap dance. Jacquelyn said I wasn't getting lap dances!" I plead.

"God damn it, Finn! We need to talk, and it's not something that we can do now. Just call me when you end your stripper session or whatever it is that's keeping you in New York this long," Faith finishes as she hangs up.

I know hanging up a cellphone is just a tap on the screen. Still, I swear I heard it bang against the base like old rotary phones. The sound and fury of hardened plastic slamming down over and over on those two little buttons that hopefully disconnected the call—I heard that in the digital tap on her screen.

But she said that we need to talk. Those words never predicate some great news. No one ever blurts out the ominous "We need to talk" and follows it up with something like, "Here's a new car I thought you might like." No, it's never good. But now I can concentrate on the morning BJ and why it happened.

"Hold on one second, ladies." I throw my hands out. "What the fuck did you say about drugs?"

Jacquelyn's lips tighten for a moment, knowing the revelation she has to enlighten unto me.

"She fucking drugged you! She thought it would make the night more fun," Jacquelyn says, with raised brows and scrunched lips, as she flings her wrist toward Esther.

I turn to Esther, who is standing there like some child who got caught putting a slice of turkey into the DVD player to see if something would happen. As innocent as the child might have been, her actions were anything but.

"Did you fucking drug me with GHB?" I ask, far more shocked than awed.

"And Rohypnol," Esther says, as if that is somehow better.

"Not any better, dumbass," Jacquelyn informs her.

"Why would you think that is okay? What, you listened to some love songs I wrote? Are you a deranged fan or something? I mean, deranged I get. Obviously. But seriously, you can't just go around drugging guys you want to sleep with." I grasp my head, trying to comprehend the intentions behind her actions.

"Okay, first of all, Jacquelyn said you'd be DTF. I was just adding a little spice," Esther tries to defend.

I swing around to Jacquelyn. "You said what?! You know what? It doesn't matter. Did you know she likes to drug her partners?"

Jacquelyn takes a deep breath and long exhale. "It's something we've done in the club if a big spender gets a little too handsy. It's not supposed to be a night-out-on-the-town trick to get laid by."

I shake my head in utter disbelief of the night's events.

"So, what the hell happened last night? What did we do?" I ask, still ignorant of what transpired.

"Nothing," Jacquelyn is quick to respond. "I wanted to. I thought it would be fun. I thought if Esther and I were able to do what I had hoped we'd be able to do, you would see that you didn't want to leave it all behind."

"I've done my share of drugs. Hell, I'm dealing with this shit still right now. But in all the years of doing dope and coke and whatever other narcotics passed my way, I

have never been fucking drugged by a crazy-ass stripper!"
I pause for a moment to quickly recall the two decades of
foggy nights. "Nope! Not once!"

Esther steps forward. She begins to open her mouth to
say something, but Jacquelyn holds up her finger to stop
her from speaking.

"Leave, Esther. We'll talk later," Jacquelyn demands.

Esther hangs her head and heads out the door.

Jacquelyn turns to me. "Come on, Finn. We had something. It was fun. We had fun."

"What happened last night?" I stay on the subject.

"You were out of it. I figured it was too much alcohol or
your pills or whatever. But you were out of it. You didn't
want to do anything, much to my chagrin. So, we put you
in bed, and we fell asleep," Jacquelyn pauses, looking for
a reaction out of me.

I hear my phone ring again. I look down, hoping that
Faith is calling back—even if just to yell some more. At
least she would be speaking to me. But it's Viv. I let it ring
to voicemail.

"Isn't this life the life you built? The life you wanted and
worked for since you first picked up a guitar?" Jacquelyn
continues over my ringing phone.

I stare at her, wondering what deranged person thinks
that last night's events are anything like what musicians
plan their lives for.

The phone rings again, and again it's Viv.

"Bad time, Viv," I greet her. "What do you need?"

"Contracts need your signature. You need to read over
them and sign them. You fly out tonight. Come sign them
before you leave," Viv demands in a most authoritative
tone. She is no doubt taking well to her new role. A smile
crosses my face.

"I have to go, Jacquelyn. Perhaps we'll talk later," I say
as I turn to leave.

I open the door as she starts talking, "Do you really
want to give up your whole life for Faith?"

I Give As Good As I Get

I don't turn back. I pat down my pockets to make sure I have my wallet, phone, and hotel key. I shut the door behind me.

The events of the earlier day still play fresh in my mind. The contracts are signed, after making a few adjustments I hope the label finds agreeable. I find myself waiting for my airplane to take me back home. But the events replay in my mind over and over in their blurry remembrance. The words start forming in my head: something to write down; something to sort out my demons; something to summarize everything that is wrong with how Jacquelyn has come to view what could be our relationship. Or, at least, how I think she feels.

Vertical Fashions

(This is my love song to no one in particular)
You're choking on the words that your mouth
cannot form.
So you return to lay down, it's our rela-
tionship norm.
You preach of life's love and quick, dying passions.
Your words are flowing out in vertical fashions.

So, we stand on our morals on rock-solid ground.
But our basis for love was, and is still, lying down.
We have never moved forward or found
piece of mind.
We've only looked back on this rockstar
life of mine.

So, I scream, and you cry, and we will do it again,
Because we know you're scared to let it go
in the end.
So, I stay and I say that it might be all right,
But we know that it won't by the next eve-
ning's light.

THE FRAGILE *Finn Fairlane*

To know that we both should have just
walked away,
Because lying in bed is not where true
love is made.
So, we say our goodbyes and hope it is not the
last time,
Cause we're knowing what is stirring inside both
of our minds.

You say I can't see you, but you're lying right there,
Writhing around and twirling your hair.
You say I can't see, but you are always right there,
Flat on your back with your legs in the air.

CHAPTER 8

We Gotta Get Outta This Place

My arrival back to The City Beautiful has come: Orlando, the place where adults regress to the innocence of childhood while the real world passes them by. The home of adult tantrums and a refusal to accept the truth of reality. The problem is that reality continues. The real-world moves along, and at some point, you must pull your gaze from the castle and face your life.

While I wait for my luggage at the baggage claim, I email the new lyrical set to Logan, asking her what she thinks and if it's something she can work with. Hopefully, this will be their first single. It's a little musical distraction before the reality of my life in Orlando hits me like a ton of bricks, but the real world awaits. I grab the handle to my luggage and yank it off the carousel.

As I open the door to the outside, I am greeted by the immense humidity and heat that imprisons the land we call Florida, a stark contrast to the comfortable interior of the airport. It is only a short wait for Faith to pull up to the curb in her car. Her eyes glare at me with a newfound hatred, my real-world problems all bundled up in the most beautiful and perplexing package a man could ever hope for. There is a strained smile on her face, to where any passerby who would happen to glance into the car and see it would know that behind it, words are waiting to lash out in anger. But here I am, back, home sweet home, and the real world awaits.

"Everything is fine just so you know," Faith says sans emotion, as I throw my luggage on the back seat.

I enter the passenger side and shut the door behind me.

"I'm glad you understand," I very naively respond.

"I was talking about the doctor's appointment you missed, jackass. Remember, the ones you said you wanted to start coming to." Faith keeps looking forward while she drives.

"I know. Slipped my mind. New York and all," I defend, trying to get so much as a glance out of her.

"Yeah, and all being some whore's mouth," she snaps, still looking forward.

"Let's not label those who choose the oral route of pleasure whores," I defend again with my mixed sense of currently displaced nobility.

"Yeah, stand up for your whore," she relentlessly continues.

"I didn't know what she was doing," I start to explain.

Faith interrupts with a glance that could make a pig squeal. "You didn't know what she was doing? You know, Finn, I don't know why I expected you to want to change, to want to leave it all behind for me. I mean, right after we broke up, you established the life for yourself that you wanted. Etched your name in the annals of rock history. Why would I ever think that I could be a part of that after all these years? Why would the inkling have ever crept in my mind to think that we could work?"

"I was drugged. I was sitting at the bar, enjoying a drink by myself, when this stranger started talking to me," I say, searching Faith's eyes for some sort of acknowledgment that this wasn't my fault. "Then, Jacquelyn shows up. The next thing I remember was being woken up from some dream by a blowie."

The pain starts to creep in. I notice it—a dull throbbing in my rib. Though it's nothing I can't ignore for the moment, it is just enough to make me take notice.

"That's the thing, Finn. Normal people don't do that to themselves. They don't put themselves in situations where they can be woken up by strangers doing suckie-suckie. I know you were drugged. And I should feel bad for you, and if you were any other person, I know I would. But you have spent the last almost twenty years surrounded by drugs, and you dare say this one time it wasn't your fault! How am I supposed to believe that, Finn? How am I supposed to believe that you weren't out just plastered and high and thought, 'one last romp before I turn the page.' Huh?"

I see a tear stream down her face. I know she and I have been through rough patches before, but there's something in this one that hits her hard. A realization that her glimmer of hope has died, the pregnancy, something I haven't seen yet. But it's there, defeat in her eyes that I need to win back. I need to understand so I can explain it to her.

The thump-thump of the pain grows a little harder. I wince though she doesn't notice. She can't even look at me right now. The pounding pain slowly waxing in my chest warns me that all is not well. I don't think I need that reminder, though. Faith is reminding me enough.

"Nothing happened." My words are quiet and calm.

"You said you don't remember," Faith responds in kind.

"Jacquelyn told me they tried. She said they wanted to, but I wouldn't, even in my drug-induced state." I keep searching for signs of love's life in her eyes.

"You are so powerful you withstood the date-rapey effects of GHB?" Faith skeptically says as she turns to me.

"Years of drug use may have its benefits," I joke. "She said nothing happened and with how mad Jacquelyn got when she found out what Esther did—"

Faith interrupts, "Who's Esther? Miss sucks-a-lot?"

I nod. "And when Jacquelyn found out, she was mad too. I promise nothing happened."

"I'm moving to Chicago," Faith utters.

My heart stops. The world around me crashes against a brick wall at 103 mph. The view in my sights cracks and crumbles right before my face smashes against it, draining all life from me. I don't want her to move. I don't want her to run. What happened wasn't my fault—for once, but I can't let this happen. I mean, I can't stop it, but I don't want her to leave. I spent too long hoping for a chance. Faith was the one who said no first because she had Ronnie. Things happened. Now she's pregnant, and I don't want it to end, especially not like this.

That reminder in my chest, that heaving pain that jabs at me with ill intent, is poking harder and harder. I can still wave it away, push it aside like an annoying child. (Wow! Like an annoying child? Some father I'll be!)

"I have to get outta here. This place is no good," Faith continues.

"It's not that bad," I counter.

She raises a brow in unsurprised shock. "Really? Forget the first night where you didn't even recognize me?"

"I may not have recognized you with your curly, jet-black hair and tattoos, but you did haunt my thoughts," I protest. "I hadn't seen you since your hair was straight and blonde-ish, and your skin uninked."

"That may be, but that night aside, what has this place been for me since you arrived? Blow jobs behind bushes, a parade of girls who I actually like as humans, which somehow makes it all worse. A dead boyfriend . . . fiancé . . . whatever. My sister getting married into the life that I never wanted for her. A life that I had to read about in magazines and the internet and listen to on the radio. And you at the center of the upheaval. It's too much, Finn," she finishes, while rubbing her eyes at the thought of her words.

"What about our baby?" I throw a Hail Mary.

"I'll be fine. I have friends back there. You don't have to give up this life of debauchery and gluttonous lust you've created. It's all yours," she says as I see the tears forming.

Tears are a good thing; it means she's angry. She still feels. If she feels, then there is hope.

This momentary glimpse of possible relief from the situation sets my pain slightly at ease, giving me a little more attention to give to Faith.

"I was on a job. I'm not saying what happened didn't suck. No pun intended. But I didn't play into it, and I didn't ask for it to happen. I'm here with you. It was just business up there. Contracts for Spear Fist and planting seeds with the labels for Logan Square." I stare forward as she drives.

"That's just it, Finn. It's not your fault. It's never your fault. You were drugged this time. We weren't together the others, so I couldn't hold any expectations. But I do! If you want something, you have to fight for it, Finn! You can't just sit and let the things around you happen without regard to how they might affect the thing you're fighting for. Ever think of that?!" Faith unloads. I can feel the weight lifting off her chest as she sighs with her full body.

Perhaps it's true. Maybe I didn't take others into account as my life happened. Perchance, I just lived in the moment and damned be whoever got caught in the crossfire. Maybe my inability to see outside of my own path has left ruins in my wake, but I can't look back and see what damage has (may or may not) been caused. I can only look forward. I'm sure if I want to look back, all I have to do is look to my left and see the tears in the eyes of the woman driving me home.

I let the heat of our words settle and watch the scenery around us for a few miles. I hope the silence settles my pains.

"How serious is this Chicago thing?" I calmly ask.

"I don't know. Fifty-fifty. Seventy-five percent. I got an offer. A good one at that. I just know that after all the years between us, then seeing you again. . . it was so much, Finn. I spent so long telling myself, convincing myself, I stopped loving you. Sometimes, I thought I never did. But I did, I do." Faith pauses to steady her words. "I can't spend the rest of my life reliving the past months in different cities and variations with random women. I need some little, tiny crumb of peace of mind."

"Then stay. Don't run to Chicago." I choose my words a little poorly.

"I need to see my sister. I need something stable, and you are not it, Finn. I need to know that you won't run away from me or screw things up. So, if I push you away first, then the only person I can blame is myself." Faith sighs, as if the clawing monkey has finally jumped off her back. How I hate being that monkey.

"But you can't guarantee that I won't mess up. You can't guarantee that you won't mess up. No one can. There are no definites in this life, not when it comes to that sort of thing. Asking for that is like when we used to ask for Jeanine to stop being annoying. She was who she was." I try to calm her.

"So what? You are just going to keep messing up and telling yourself, 'that's life'?" Faith waves her hand before turning on her signal.

"No. I will try to make it up to you. I will spend the rest of my life trying to make it up to you. I can promise that." I turn to her.

"You make it sound so easy," she huffs.

"I never said it would be easy. It will be hard and frustrating at times. You will want to kick and punch and cry. There will be times that we won't like each other as much as others. But those times will thin out and become less, and the good times will be more every day and less happenstance. And I think we owe it to ourselves, if not for each other, then at least for our child," I proclaim.

"I need my sister," she says, pulling into my parking spot.

"We'll take a road trip to NOLA. It's only ten hours. We'll make a mini-vacation out of it." I smile. "Vacay!"

Faith tries to hold back a smile that creeps across her lips, a smile that wants to wallow in the moment's pity but knows that some of my words were right. A smile that hopes the words of mine that were right were the hopeful words.

"It's not that simple for me." Faith laughs. "I have a job. I have appointments that I can't just walk away from on a whim. Those appointments are what pay my bills, put food in my belly. I'm not you, Finn. I can't just travel on a moment's notice," she rationalizes.

"There's like a week and a half before that show. Can't you make arrangements? Shift some things around. We'll only be gone for like three days," I rebuttal.

She purses her lips in thought. "New Orleans does sound fun. What if I can't get the time off? I need to talk about all this with my sis. This isn't some whim of a decision."

"Then quit. I'll take care of you. I have money," I say without thinking.

"I'm not some girl to be kept. I enjoy working. I actually enjoy the color, and the cut, and the asshole people who don't know that describing highlights as caramel is different with each person who asks. I enjoy the dumbasses who say they want a completely different cut, but don't want to lose any length or add layers. I do enjoy my job and all the frustration that comes with it," she defends.

"I didn't mean. . ." My fingers shoot to my chest.

There it is, back in full force. The pain that was subsiding has been slowly creeping back in. It sends shockwaves radiating throughout my torso, tearing through me like an angry alligator in a Florida gift shop, not to mention the migraine throbbing on my left side. I open my eyes wide to try and stretch it out of my head, blinking a few times. But to no avail. Damn, this hurts. I remember I ran out as I reach for my pills. Something I shall deal with later.

"So, what do we do?" I ask, though I'm not sure what I was referencing.

"I don't know. I'll figure it out." Faith turns my direction, her hand lingers on the keys. "This doesn't fix anything. It's not like one talk can magically fix us."

"No. I know. I wouldn't expect it to. One talk is just that. One talk." I let a little optimism seep out in my words.

"Exactly. One talk. I have a lot to think about. This is about more than just us now. I have to think about the little one. I have to think about my future and how it will impact whatever this is in me. I have to think about myself. My happiness. I have to think." Her hands slip off the ignition, leaving the car running.

I don't say anything. I just let the moment linger while her swirling thoughts come to a calm. I look at my place and think about the music behind those doors. I know as well as Faith that I have work to attend to. I have my future and our future to think about. I have work to do on so many levels. But I have her right now, and that's better than nothing.

Her eyes turn toward my home. "I'm not coming in. I'm not going to sleep with you. I'm not that easy. It's going to take more than one shower in a filthy hotel room to wash the mouth slut off your dong."

I laugh through my pain. "Completely understand. I wouldn't expect any less from you. My dong will be getting a few more washes once I'm through those doors."

I exit the passenger seat and grab my luggage from the back. Before closing the back seat door, I lean my head inside, arms holding the roof. "I love you, ya know."

A sad nod is given. "I know." She forces a smile. "Now go. I have to get going."

"Well, get got." I tap the roof of her car and shut the door.

I watch her drive away while rolling my luggage to my door. There's always a little part of me that thinks every time I see her leave will be the last. There's a bigger part of me that knows I only think that because if she were any wiser, it would be.

Love makes you do many a stupid thing. My phone dings, distracting me from my thoughts of Faith. Logan. A welcome distraction she is. She likes the lyrics and is mapping out the song. How I do like musicians that can work at a fast pace.

At least something with a positive outlook is in the works.

CHAPTER 9

I Don't Like the Drugs (But the Drugs Like Me)

A t work.

Two little words, but the succinctness says it all. When relationships begin, there are love letters and poems, songs, and (back in the day) mixtapes. Of course, that stuff changes. It doesn't necessarily die down; it just changes forms. The mixtapes become buying an album she'll enjoy or letting her choose the radio station on Pandora. The songs, poems, and love letters change form, too. Those become the little notes scribbled on a scrap piece of paper under a magnet on the fridge. It's a short scribble that lets the other person know what's going on and where they are, to ensure they know that they are okay and not missing or anything that would end up on a concrete slab in a *Criminal Minds* episode.

But these two little words—there is no love. There is no letting me know that everything is okay. I figured that she would have come back later that night, but I fell asleep.

Perhaps she did come back while I slept but left. She could have found the fact that I was able to sleep a sign that I did not have any remorse for the events that occurred. Of course, I have remorse. I didn't want that girl, Esther, to do what she did. It's why I stopped it from happening. But Faith only sees the happening of the event itself. Perhaps she's frustrated that I am not angrier with the girl. The thing is, though, I can understand Esther's side. She was told I'd be DTF.

Any red-blooded, sexually awakened person would be happy if they were told they were about to meet a person of some fame who is down to fuck. She was just doing something that she thought would change my mind. Unwanted sexual advance? Sure, but unwanted advances happen. It wasn't violent. She didn't force herself upon me. She didn't hold me down. She simply made a move. Her intention, though misinformed by lousy intel, was not malicious or ill-rooted. Esther found a way to make her move that she thought I would appreciate. I think that's just part of the whole thing. Hell if I know; I could be wrong about it all. I could be the messed-up one. Faith might just be the more level-headed of us.

That would be the fine irony in it all. I wake up to some girl on my junk—a girl that I gave no permission and no sort of consent to—and Faith's mad at me, somehow rightly so. I can understand the anger on Faith's part. I can understand that without her having witnessed the events of the night before, she would think what she thinks. I'll just never comprehensively understand her inherent lack of trust in me.

Two little words: at work. Not even handwritten on a Post-It© note on the fridge. Just a text message. No love there at all. I can't help but wonder if there is something deeper bubbling below the surface. There's a part of me that wonders if Faith is in a sort of hellish torment, trapped in this life she has made for herself—knowing the feelings she had for me while still with Ronnie, and of course, how it all ended for her and him. The sadness in her eyes screams of a sort of guilt for what she has done and a desire to make things better. The last part of that I can be on board with. I think we, as human creatures, are always trying to move forward and better ourselves and our situations. We must push ever onward. However, that's what scares me, that she is pushing onward and leaving me behind—again.

But as pushing onward goes, I have work to do. If you can't be with the one you love, love the work you're with. A little more effort, and that would have been pithier, but you get the point.

I look over the lyrics that Logan has tweaked from what I sent. Minimal adjustments made can either be an excellent thing or a terrible thing. It either means that what I sent needed next to no work, or the artist is not as talented as I first thought. I'm really hoping that it's the first. I have interested labels and don't want to get them involved with a band that is less than what I make them out to be.

A rhythm ticks on in my head as I read the words she is making her own. It actually sounds nice (at least the way I hear them). I let those sit because if she is making changes, that means music is being written. I'll touch that beast when I listen to it, which means onto the next set of lyrics.

This set I actually have music for; it's an old set that's always stuck with me. The sound of the guitar was initially designed for a noisy, distorted sound. Though, if I turn down the distortion and kick in some fuzz, making it more mid than low range, it will work for Logan Square. Plus, she eats up the lyrics of heartbreak.

The Old Way

Trapped inside this thing that I can't understand.
I have no way to grab the upper hand.
I keep weighing the options, but they
only confuse.
It seems this is a battle that I'm going to lose.

Each day I look for reasons to stay inside.
Each day I find a reason to run and hide.

When I find a reason to live inside this,
confusion clears my mind, and it's then that I miss
The old way.

What I am inside is pulling me down.
Life's a circus, and I'm just a clown,
playing the one who enjoys the abuse.
If it ever stops, it's my life I will lose.
(I want to find a reason to like the abuse.)

Sometimes I look back at old sets, old songs that have been waiting for the right time to burst forth with life, and I question what the fuck was going through my mind back then. I have to ask myself what kind of person I was to stay in a situation that made me think those thoughts. I never did show those lyrics to Faith. I don't think she would have appreciated them then, and I don't think she would now. This then begs the question, "What is happening deep in my subconscious that I feel now is the time to bring life to that song?" Hell if I know. Could be the lack of communication while she bathes in her anger for me, or it could be my brain trying to tell me that this might end up the same as last time. Twenty years to repeat the same damn thing. It can't be that, though. Now we have a kid on the way, and that changes things, doesn't it?

I send the lyrics to Logan. Hopefully, she can find a good use for them. I have music if she needs it, anything to keep my mind off this pain in my chest. I'll just lay down for a nap.

The harsh light of day burns my eyes as it shines through the askew shades on my window. The sweet smell of pancakes and maple syrup hint in the background of my olfactory sense.

"Faith?" I call out, but she does not answer. "Babe, you here?" Still nothing.

I creep out of bed, my bones and joints cracking and popping in the early afternoon rising. Dressed in nothing but boxer shorts, I head to my kitchen to find a plate of pancakes topped with melted butter and syrup. The syrup has stopped running, and the butter that has since fully melted is starting to congeal again. Damn. It makes me wonder when she made these and how long I was out. The cakes are a bit cold, but nothing that thirty or so seconds in the microwave won't take care of.

As the microwave sounds out its triumphant ding of food cooked, I hear the click of Faith's heeled boots hit the floor.

"Jesus, you're just eating now?" Faith says with both shock and concern.

"Just woke up," I say, shoveling the food into my mouth.

"Well, get ready. We gotta leave in fifteen minutes." Faith's reply is curt.

"For?" I ask, oblivious to any plans.

"Doctor." She keeps it short and to the point.

The only solace I have that I might be wrong about her anger is her break from the distance she is putting up between us to make sure I am doing okay.

The pain has returned in full force, so a trip to my doctor is what I need, new prescriptions for new drugs to ease the pain.

Well, that was a crap visit. The doctor said, physically, I am fine. He couldn't determine a reason for me to still be in pain—but here I am still in pain long after it should have supposedly subsided. He said something about referred pain and psychosomatic symptoms, but it doesn't make sense to me. The pain is there, in my chest and radiating from that point of breakage. A pain that throbs. He told me it's all in my head. What the hell does he know?

Now Faith is on the psychosomatic wagon. She keeps reiterating the healing powers of positive thoughts (like I haven't tried those a thousand times before). I'd do anything to get this pain to stop, but it won't. She won't talk to me to let me explain the pain. I need something to dull it, if only for a moment, a split second of clear-mindedness. The god-damned over-the-counter pain relievers do about as much good as a non-alcoholic beer would be for keeping a buzz going—jack shit.

After my doctor visit, Faith went out with the girls from her salon, leaving me to my own devices. I pick up a guitar to try and take my mind off of the pain. The new-again music runs through my mind as I tweak it to make it Logan Square-worthy, a distraction that is quickly interrupted by the alert of my phone.

The solace I take in that dinging sound recently has become something for me, a drug in and of itself—if only a short-lived effect. At least it is something. Logan has been working with her band. Music, the all-consuming, ever-encouraging drug known as music, calls for me right now, a second round of homeopathic medicine to soothe my psychosomatically aching bones. (Damn, even I sound whiny to me right now.)

At least she likes the lyrics. Sure, she has made a few changes here and there, but the overall body of what I sent to her still reads very much the same. She just made them her own. I can dig that. She sends me an audio clip. The sound is crap, and for a band as punk-metal-whatever-label-fits-in-the-moment-here they are, she used an acoustic guitar to sample this for me. It comes across almost like a heavy march, something steady and regimented. I hear her reciting the lyrics in their timing while she is still working out the pitches. While there are no drums, bass, or any other instruments, I can hear the skank beat of the hi-hat and bass drum. I can feel where the bass line is pounding out its notes. When it all comes together, it shall be legendary. It's interesting to me that she sent me such a rough cut. I assume the excitement she feels needed to be released a little to someone who can appreciate it. I like appreciating and being appreciated.

For a split second, I feel the pain wash away. I feel good. The irony is that my momentarily alleviated pain gives me an idea.

I Don't Like The Drugs(but The Drugs Like Me)

[Finn: Hey, got any Vicodin? Dilaudid? Flexeril? Baclofen? Anything? Ribs are killing me.]

Send.

Maybe she knows someone who is holding. Possibly Logan will be my saving grace as I will be hers.

Almost no time passes before my ding sounds off.

[Logan: Slow down there, tweaker. Let me ask around. Jacquelyn's been supplying while on tour.]

I reply.

[Finn: But she's with you guys. Doesn't do me much good.]

Send.

I get a quick reply.

[Logan: She left NYC not long after you.]

I find it peculiar that Jacquelyn, who was following the bands up the East Coast, suddenly came back to Orlando shortly after I did. At first glance, that does sound awfully suspicious, but the world has more going on than my own happenings. I'm sure she had other reasons for coming back home. All I know is that right now, relief might be spelled J-A-C-Q-U-E-L-Y-N.

[Finn: Thanks. Great start to the song. Keep it up.]

Send.

I forgot to give her the new lyric set.

[Finn: Give me five, then take a look in your email. Working on something I think is right up your alley.]

All I get back is a smiling emoji, a great way to respond and end a conversation all in one little smiley face.

I switch my text message thread over to Jacquelyn. I know that if Faith were here with me, I would not be texting Jaquelyn. Faith is not here, so I can't think about the what-ifs and hypotheticals.

[Finn: Hey, Logan said you might have access to pain management.]

I hit send. Now, all I can do is hope she actually responds and isn't mad at me for what happened back in NYC. I know it wasn't my fault; it was all Esther. But sometimes people have a funny way of twisting situations to suit their needs and feelings.

[Jacquelyn: I might. Come over.]

That was quick and direct. I'm not sure if Jacquelyn knows I am actually looking to score some, or if my words were some sort of pill-popper's version of "Netflix & Chill." I'm not looking to just go over, pop some X, and do what the wild things do. Fuck it. I guess I have to go if I want the little helpers. That's the thing about my predicament; I'm not trying to put myself in bad situations or situations that can end poorly. I just need something, and she is apparently the only one who can help. For now, this is what I'll have to do until I can get the pain under control. (Isn't that what we all say?)

The drive to her house is ordinary—slightly cooler night air than during the day; some random accident with squad car lights warning oncoming drivers; the lingering smell of the day's earlier rain. But I think it is this ordinary mundaneness, the endless summer of Orlando, that has me thinking, if I never change my habits, if I am always doing the same thing over and over, I wonder how I will ever break myself of the patterns I know I need to abandon. If I can't leave those behind, I may be on the same track that leads me to be the leather-skinned, skinny man that staggers down the street midday in unwashed white shirts and torn jeans. Now I am wondering if this is the path I am on; that one day, my money will dry up, and I will be there, on the streets, with skin so tanned and leathery that when I die, some vagrant may make a perfectly good biker jacket out of me. There's a thought out of the serial killer's handbook.

I am curious as to how many of those staggering souls once started out as employees of the mouse cult. I think about how many were so underpaid, unable to cohabitate with others, that they lived out of their cars until that was no longer viable. The countless souls lost to the dark underbelly of the cult of the mouse. There's a notion in my brain that everyone in the greater Orlando area is just a casualty of the mouse in one way or another.

I shouldn't be putting myself in these situations, situations that can end the way a good majority of mine have: random sex or strangers with candy that I partake in, or sometimes both. They are the endings that give others good pause to put up fences, walls, barriers, what-have-you of some sort to keep me at bay, at least until they realize I am harmless, or meaningless, to their lives. I guess if I want to change these behaviors about myself, I need to figure out why I do them, the root cause of it all. It could be as simple as being a Mr. Self-Destruct, or it might run much, much deeper than that. It might be that the reasons I self-destruct are the same as why I got into music in the first place. Solving one of those answers may solve both. I would not want to answer the reason why I became a musician. That would bring my world tumbling down. I'm starting to think that this drive to Jacquelyn's shouldn't have happened, that this wasn't my best idea of the day.

Too late. I pull up and can see the pool lights on the far side of Jacquelyn's house are turned on. They are not lighting up the block like some obscure invention that pops out of the jacket of a small Asian boy, blinding his friends as they are making an escape from Italian mobsters. I just mean I can see the glare in the night sky peeking over the house. But if they are on, then she is in the pool.

Or was.

I put my car in park and turn off the ignition as she comes around the side of the house, wearing a bikini with a sarong wrapped around her waist in some feigned modesty. The glass of wine in each hand accompanied by the shit-eating grin on her face tells the world she is anything but.

"Come on, Finn." Jacquelyn grins. "Let's talk pain management."

With a quick pivot, she heads back to the pool, raising a glass that beckons me to follow. So, I abide. By the time I catch up to her, she is lowering herself into the heated waters of the hot tub, a glass of wine on either side of her. The mischievous look in her eye says this night is not going to be as fun for me as it will be for her.

"Come on in, Finn." She grabs a bottle of pills hiding behind her head.

As soon as I see the bottle, the pain in my ribs flares up like a dog running circles for treats.

"How much?" I ask, reaching for my wallet.

Jacquelyn shakes her head. "Silly man. Take off your clothes. Get in."

My mind is pulled back to my first time here—standing poolside, tripping over myself to be next to her perfect, naked body. Now though, the excitement is gone. All I want are the little pills.

"I'll tell you what, Finn. You take off your clothes, and I'll take off mine." She unties the top of her bikini and it slips off as the jets bubble around her. She sinks down in some 80s rock video attempt to lure me in.

The thing is a move like that would have gotten me in not too long ago for the exact reason she wants. Tonight, I must relent to her whims if I am to appease mine.

I remove my shoes, socks, pants, and shirt but leave my boxers on. I start to sink into the waters opposite from her. She hands me the untouched glass of wine.

I eye it suspiciously. "Esther's not around, is she?"

Jacquelyn lets out a hearty laugh. "You're safe. She's in New York."

I take a sip to show I trust her. Hopefully, it will move this along for me.

"So . . . now can I have the drugs?" I get straight to the point.

"Not yet. You owe me an explanation," Jacquelyn says. The flattening of eyebrows shift to a more serious tone.

I raise a brow, unsure of what explanation she needs. There could be so many.

"I'm in pain. I was in an accident, and the pain lingers." I sip my wine.

She shakes her head softly.

"We had something, Finn. We could have had more. You want the pills; I want to understand. I want to know what is not so special about me," she asks with a hint of desperation.

I try to find the answer, but I don't have one. If I did, I think I'd have been able to solve all my problems long, long ago.

Before I can answer, she puts up her hand. "No. You know what? What is so special about her that you would throw away the life you made, leave it all behind for her? Answer me that, and you can have the pills."

I look in her eyes, and we hold each other's stare. I see subtle desperation there. Not the daddy issue desperation that so many people think drives women to become strippers, exotic dancers, or whatever name you want to give them. I see a real lack of understanding in her eyes. I see a need to discern if she is so un-special, or if Faith is just that special. Either way, Jacquelyn wants to know *why*.

I wish I could tell her. I can't because some things in life have no answer. Some things have no solid foundation. They exist because of the faith you have in them. Though, in the end, if we find the answers, there is the possibility the foundation crumbles beneath us. Either that, or it will hold firm and grow stronger. This is why I think so many people are afraid to question their own faith. They are scared of what would happen to them if they were left with no foundation.

"Cause I think you're scared, Finn." She trembles a little. "I think that you don't want to be happy with me. I think that you'd rather be unhappy with her because then you can continue to write your tormented lyrics and songs. You can continue to have fans—who have no idea who you really, truly are—shower you with empty adoration."

"That's not fair." I set my wine glass down.

"No? I think you are afraid that if you stay with me, you will lose that magic touch that makes music for the ages. I think that while pushing forty, you still have these high school notions of love and life. I think you are afraid that if you choose me, those fantasies that live in your head of how life should be will shatter, and you won't know what to do. You have no idea how to be happy," she cries, a mix of anger and sad realization.

"What do you want me to say? I don't have the answer you are looking for because I don't have any answer to give." I start to rise from the hot tub.

"I want you to say that you want me." She stands up too, her naked bosom exposed. "I want you to understand that you can have it all. The music, the touring, the girl who is into girls."

She stands naked—beautiful and crying. Nothing is between us as she lays it all out in her fury and anger. But I have nothing to offer her. I have no answer that will calm her pain like those little pills would have quelled mine. Now I leave, wet and without the pills. At least the dogs trying to burst out my chest for their opioid treats have gone back to sleep for the moment.

"I'm sorry I stopped by tonight. I shouldn't have come here," I say, zipping up my jeans that stick to my wet skin.

I walk back to my car, socks and shirt in hand, and wet feet in my shoes. As I get to my car, the sound of her crying has faded. I don't know if I can't hear her because I am too far away or that she has stopped crying. I know that I can't go back and check. I shouldn't have come here. I need to leave.

CHAPTER 10

Kings & Queens of the Underground

The time between my last night at Jacquelyn's and the New Orleans show have been a slow improvement. Faith has returned to speaking to me but still no leeway on giving me any pills. The pain, of course, flares at times, coming and going in waves. But my concern has been for Faith's well-being and for what will be our future child. As the reality of our situation slowly starts to sink in, I can see the sun setting on some aspects of my life. Not all of them, mind you, but some. I think it's an okay thing to see a setting sun. It means that the day is done, and that things are starting to calm down.

I think my time in Orlando has posed more questions and ponderings than answers, but if I had all the answers, I wouldn't have needed to move. If I knew all the reasons why to everything in my life, I don't think I would have had the success I had. I don't necessarily think success comes from knowing all the answers. I think it comes from continually striving to find them all, the unrelenting push forward to better oneself. To be able to figure out the answers to the riddles of my past will give me more of an ability to guide my future on this journey we call life. So, I push ever onward.

This push forward brings us to The Big Easy, Crescent City, that place known as New Orleans and to a sweet little venue called Tipitina's. What started as a local spot in 1977 has grown into a shrine for the man who helped make New Orleans what it is today, Professor Longhair. A sad note on my part that I never got the chance to meet such a great and honored musical artisan, but life has a funny way of putting the greats ahead of my time.

After stopping off for a quick check-in at Tipitina's, just to make sure everything is set for the evening show, we head over to my favorite stop in NOLA, Cafe Beignet on St. Peter Street. Everyone flocks to the other place, the beignet place for all, or beignet for the world, depending on your translation. There's nothing wrong with that place. It's just that, to me, Cafe Beignet is a little better. But I digress.

Upon walking in, Logan rushes me and grabs me in a most unexpected bear hug.

"You gotta hear the new shit, Finn! Fuckin' rocks!" Logan says with an energy high enough to light a city.

"I shall. Let us just grab some food real quick, then we'll detour to the recording studio." I grab a spot in line.

"Did Jacquelyn ever deliver on the goods?" Logan says, with the discretion of a howler monkey looking for a mate.

"What the fuck, Finn!?" Faith glares.

"Hey Faith!" Logan tries to recover her fumble. "How's the whole growing-a-baby thing going?" Logan waves her hands at the pregnancy belly, still yet to show.

Faith laughs a little. "Good. Just doin' its thing, I guess. How's the tour going?"

Logan's eyes grow three sizes in her excitement. "Fuckin' amazeballs! Great crowds, tons of album and merch sales! Time of my life!"

"So back to the man-child next to me, what goods were Jacquelyn supposed to deliver?"

Logan looks to me for an answer, but the cat is already out of the bag. No need to call it a duck.

Logan sees me wave her permission for the truth. "He was out of pills and needed something to take the edge off."

Faith puts up a hand for Logan to stop and turns to the garden area. She heads off while Logan and I wait for the food. Hopefully, she will calm down a bit.

"I didn't know she didn't know," Logan apologizes.

"It's cool. Just another tally mark as to why she thinks we will never work out," I relent.

"She'll get over it. You're a great guy, Finn." Logan tries to cheer me up.

"Don't do the whole pep-talk thing. It's not necessary," I tell Logan.

"Thank God. I felt weird." Logan laughs.

"You sounded weird." I laugh with her.

We grab our food and head out to where Faith grabbed a seat.

"Where's my sister?" Faith says to Logan.

"Hell if I know. She meeting us here?" Logan replies, scanning the crowd in case Jeanine is already here.

"Supposedly. I have some news," Faith says, joining in the scan.

"What news?" Jeanine says, as if summoned by Faith's words. "Sorry I'm late. Got stopped by like five different people wanting me to come into their strip club."

Faith says, gesturing to a chair. "Take a seat."

"Are you pregnant? Oh, wait. Yes." Jeanine laughs at her own joke while the rest of us shake our heads.

"Seriously, Jeanine." Faith's older sister sternness kicks in.

Jeanine's face falls flat. "What's goin' on, Faith?"

"I'm moving to Chicago." Faith lays it out for her sister.

"The fuck? When was this decided?" Jeanine says, shooting me an evil eye.

"Hey, I had nothing to do with wanting this move," I defend.

"No, he didn't. But he did solidify the decision," Faith continues.

"What? How the hell did I help make that a definite? We never talked," I ask, confused.

Faith turns to me. "That's the thing, Finn. You go to New York. Things happen. Things that weren't your fault."

"That's right. They weren't! You even acknowledged that," I interject.

"Then I have to find out your most recent indiscretion." Faith gives a condescending smile.

"Nothing happened while I was there," I defend.

Jeanine shakes her head and turns away from me. Logan scoots her chair closer, trying to get a better view of the eruption about to take place.

"Then why, Finn? Why were you at a girl's house who clearly wants you for herself?" Faith pleads.

"Like I said, I needed pills. I needed something to help dull the pain. You won't give me any. The doctors won't renew my prescriptions. I needed something," I tell her with sad desperation in my voice, akin to Lt. Dan whimpering for a treat.

Faith shakes her head and turns to her sister. "So, I am moving. I want to make sure that you'll be okay down here without me."

"I'll be fine, sis. I am a big girl now. Married and everything." Jeanine smiles.

"I know. I just want to make sure being so far from family won't make you sad or whatever." Faith searches for her words.

"Of course I'll be sad. You won't be near me. You'll be half the country away, living by yourself." Jeanine shoots me the evil eye again.

"Nothing's final yet," I interject. "We haven't talked about it fully."

I try to save face here and act like my words will have an impact now or on any future decisions Faith makes. The sad matter of fact is that Faith will do what she wants for herself and our unborn without any regard for me when she is mad with me. Always the worst of times with her. When we are on good terms, it's the best of times. There's never any in-between.

Faith turns to me. "Is there something about your life that I'm missing? Something about the tours, the days at a time in the recording studio I've been privy to read about in magazines throughout the years, the decadence and lack of a real home life that I'm missing here?"

I take a deep breath. It's not as simple an answer as Faith would like it to be. The fact of the matter is that in life and love, the answer is never as simple as anyone would like it to be. There's always so much more to any given situation than is seen at surface level. But now is not the time nor the place.

"I am moving with you" is all I say.

"So, you can find some other whore to buy pills from? Some other slut to wake you up with a morning suck session?" Faith's volume is rising in direct relation to her anger.

Jeanine interjects, "Morning suck session? I'd like to think that's an old story, but the tone of your voice says otherwise."

"Nothing more to it. Just that. Though, of course, he's not to blame," Faith tells her sister in a much quieter tone.

"I'm not. It wasn't my fault. We've moved on," I try to get back on track. "So, Jeanine, Faith needs to know that you don't feel like she is abandoning you down here when we move."

Jeanine grabs her sister's hand. "You need to live your life. Whatever the reason for moving to Chicago, you need to do what's best for you."

"Plus, now you'll have another reason to visit Chicago," Faith jokes.

"Much more often." Jeanine smiles.

"Cause whatever this thing is growing inside my uterus is going to need its Aunt Jeanine." Faith smiles.

"Of course." Jeanine looks down at her sister's stomach. "I'll be there as often as I can."

"Let's hear what you've got," I tell Logan through the microphone that feeds into the recording booth. Simple words they are, but they lead to many fantastic journeys. The number of times I have said those words throughout the years is countless and, in doing so, have been on as many musical adventures in those years as well. I never know if I will hear pleasant notes, rhythms, and beats that make my heart swell, or if disappointment will set in faster than greasy-spoon, roach-motel food poisoning. But those words I have said, and the show is about to begin.

Logan sits on a stool, guitar in hand, as the drummer taps off the four-count intro to set the beat. The bassist slides down the strings into the first beat of the song. The march-style beat that played out on the phone is now in full force. The keys resonate computer noise at twice the beats per minute of the song. It fills in the empty space of the sound without being overpowering. This journey is off to a brilliant start.

The first word chokes from Logan's throat. "Ch-ch-ch-chokin' on the words your mouth cannot form."

A smile crosses my face. I know technically speaking, Logan stuttered the first word, but it works in this musical setting. There's a touch of sarcasm that carries in her words, an emotion that takes the lyrical expedition down a dark alley, and I love it. The musical collaboration and cohesiveness that travels through my headphones and tickles my ears is what will be their first hit single. I am glad I was able to nudge things along for them, do what I do—create an environment in which musicians can grow and thrive. Now, for the tweaks. It's always tweaks and adjustments. Like they say, writing is rewriting, and the same is for music.

"I love it!" I shower them with words of encouragement as they finish the song. "The sarcastic direction you took it is wonderful."

"But?" Logan says back, tapping her feet against the stool as she flicks her right middle finger against her thumb repeatedly in a nervous tick.

"Always a but," I confirm, "but nothing bad."

"Bullshit," she fires back, already on the defensive. I see the raging vein begin pulsing to life in her forehead, a violent stream of blood and anger ready to burst forth, as if I am an enemy to slaughter.

I laugh into the mic. "Relax, no need to start fires. Keys need to come up a bit. They fill in the sound nicely but get lost once the song kicks into full gear. Mainly a note for the sound guy. The keys need to create the noise that will fill in the fuzz."

Logan cocks her head with wide eyes. "And?!"

"And nothing. I think you guys have a single here. Something with radio-play potential and the ability to launch you in a big way. The rest will come in how you handle yourself with any label reps," I say with softer tones, trying to calm her down.

"So, what? That's it? You find me at a fuckin' music store, give us a tour and some lyrics, and bam! Now we will get bigger?" Logan's tone is anything but believing the words exiting her mouth.

"No, it's the work all of you have put into your sound, the hours spent practicing, the image you have created, the years spent honing your skills. Then, a little extra added in by me. That's how it works sometimes," I say.

"No way," Logan argues back.

What I love about her is her skepticism. There's no need for it. There's no wool I am trying to pull over her eyes. No tricks up my sleeve. I am not some vanity label that waves promises of fame and fortune at a cost no one can reasonably afford. I am the money man and make it back on the return. And in return, they get theirs. But Logan has been beaten down for so long by life (and whatever else) that anything good is, and always will seem, too good to be true.

THE FRAGILE *Finn Fairlane*

"That's it. You even said yourself that album and merch sales on this tour have been way up." I watch her nod. "The fans have been growing, and it is showing on the social media sites also." Again, I watch her nod. "So why not go with the flow? Enjoy this little wave as it turns into something bigger," I finish with a smile that tries to tug on the corner of her lips.

"But won't they all want something from us? Won't every label, every potential sponsor for a tour, all want something from us?" Logan tries to wrap her head around the mounting success of the tour.

"Of course. That's the nature of the business. But in that nature, you will get to create and play your music. And with me by your side, you will be able to create the music you want. Not some easily digestible and generic tune that the others would push for," I continue to assure her.

Hell, that is the whole reason I left New York in the first place and ended up in Orlando—to get away from the big labels that churned out music in laxative form, taken in one moment to be shit out and forgotten the next. It's the reason I was able to find Spear Fist and Logan Square. They are now my responsibilities to make sure they can grow on their own and can stand on their own two feet, confidently fighting their own battles without being metaphorically sucker-punched. While Spear Fist was already walking on their own two feet before me, they are finally ready to run. Logan Square is still crawling, but I will help them walk.

"So, now what?" she asks through the microphone, her voice earnest.

"Now, you guys play that song tonight at Tipitina's, one step at a time." I give them a simple answer because sometimes it is that simple.

I watch as they all look at each other with lingering disbelief in their eyes that slowly washes away as the realization of where they currently sit sets in. They are in a luxury recording studio in New Orleans, working on an album and a song that will be debuted tonight.

But this is the journey. Moments like this are why I became a musician in the first place, moments that seem so mundane without stepping back to get a view of the grand picture: the fact that she was a girl looking for a replacement, standing in a music store not too long ago, and is now touring the USA. She was angry over the fact the bandmate, someone she was supposed to rely on, count on, and trust in was more concerned about stickin' it in where it doesn't belong than the music. Now she is in New Orleans with an opportunity that may never have presented itself if it weren't for the happenstance of life. I am part of her happenstance, as she is part of mine. That is the journey or, at the very least, a small piece of it thus far.

We move ever onward into the night, which brings us to the long-anticipated Tipitina's, the big show of New Orleans. It's the last stop before Spear Fist and Logan Square head west for a short jaunt. The culmination of everything I have done for the bands has led us here. I say everything I have done as if the musicians themselves haven't been a slave to the music for years prior to my entrance into their lives. This night is the culmination of everything they have done to get themselves here. Perhaps my job is only to nudge them along when needed, nothing more. But now, at this moment, it doesn't matter. The stage is set, and Logan is on stage singing.

I am standing by the bar in a grey T-shirt, jeans, and a sports coat/blazer/suit jacket, whatever you wanna call it. My drink in my hand is keeping me company. The crowd is packed, but even in the elbow-room-only masses, I can see Jeanine and Faith talking. I am not sure this is the ideal location for Faith to have her heart-to-heart talk with her little sister, but it will have to do. Jeanine has married into the life that Faith avoided, a life that Faith had watched from the outside for years only to be dragged in now.

So, this is where they talk. I watch as the two of them exchange words while scanning the crowd (making sure I don't overhear them, no doubt). But I am a safe distance away, spying on them through parted heads and dancing bodies. What they say to each other is for their ears only. I am not interested in what they say. I can fathom a few guesses, and while none of them paint me in a good light, if any of the conversation is about me, it is for them. I am more intrigued by the mix of emotions I see on both of their faces. They both know that seeing each other every day will be a thing of the past, and that family get-togethers will be relegated to holidays and the occasional tour stop in town. But they both know that life heads in different directions at times. That, because they share a special bond, their paths may join again. They feel an emotional cupcake filled with an inner goo of hope and excitement, all on top of a bottom layer of love. But even in that weird metaphor of candied emotions, the sadness is what prevails. Like the icing on the cake, it is the first thing I see looking at them. The layers of their grief alone could make up another stupid cupcake comparison. But it is not for me to make. What I see is for me to absorb. Whether I am right or wrong about the sadness in their eyes and hidden joy creeping out of the corners of their mouths is not for me to find out. This moment is theirs, just as the moment a few feet away is Viv's.

I see Viv talking with a guy and a woman I have never seen. Judging by their wardrobe, they are the label I convinced to come down. Not a colossal name in the industry, but a start for Logan Square. Both of the reps are dressed in ripped jeans, not jeans that have ripped due to time and wear but those corporately ripped jeans. The jeans that try to say rebel, that try to say, "I march to the beat of my own drummer." They are jeans that try to stand up to the man and his conformist ways, but all they really scream is "I paid for someone else to do this to my jeans!" Even their shirts, fresh off the merch rack from some Hawt Tropics or Spenstars #metal-wannabe store, are decades behind the tour they boldly support. Damn corporate label guys.

On the other hand, it is these corporate label guys that are here because of me, the calls I make, and the ringing of my name in their ears. I just miss the smaller labels that get to wear shirts from actual tours, jeans whose holes have been worn into them from mosh pits and impromptu games of tackle football in some random field. Small label guys whose tattoos and long hair are earned, not gotten, and grown in some attempt to relate to the underground.

The woman has taken the lead over the guy, new face and new blood that seemingly takes the less aggressive approach. The female-to-female vibe could just be right. The guy may have said something that put Viv off, causing the other to step in. Maybe the woman is in charge. Hell, she could be in charge and he's just backup. Either way, I wonder about the other guy. Not my concern really, only an inquiring mind and all.

I watch as Viv's face is full of enthusiasm. I can see it in her movements. Her eyes are big as she talks about Logan Square and points to the various members on stage. While I am not sure why she would need to, I am sure she has a point. I see the label reps give courtesy nods and smiles, but I can tell they are losing interest. Luckily, so can Viv. She switches gears and stiffens her body a bit, not in a cowardly, retreating way, but in a way that exudes more authority. She has become a rock that won't let them walk away. This little gesture recaptures their attention. The female listens to Viv as she watches the stage with a hint of a smile across her face.

It's funny to me because labels rarely do this sort of thing anymore. With all the websites out there that have up-and-coming possibilities, they don't need to go to shows. They can sit back and click links, listen to submissions sent via whatever mail, and not leave their office. But for me, they come out. It's almost a way for the people in the industry to hold onto the good life, for the corporate guys to remember why they got into the business in the first place. It's a chance for them to live the life they wanted. They do it because, at the end of it all, it's the best way to see potential. Much like how movies are good on DVD in your home theater, but the experience is so much grander in a theater.

The guitars quiet down as Logan Square ends their song. This causes Viv's conversation to come to a halt while the reps listen to the group. The hushed tones, or what passes for hushed tones in a venue, break the concentration of Faith and Jeanine. Jeanine sees the reps next to Viv and sees something in both reps' eyes that cause her to whisper something to Faith.

"I hope you all're having a fuckin' great time tonight!" Logan follows with an uncontainable laugh.

The crowd cheers, which is a good sign for label interest.

"For most of you, this is all new music. But for those that know our stuff, this next song will be the first time we've played it." Logan looks out over the crowd.

The guitar kicks in. The marching beat of the bass drum follows. The rest of the band joins in, and the sound fills the venue. The crowd cheers as a small slam-style mosh pit forms near the front of the stage, only a few feet past Viv.

I watch as Jeanine watches Viv. The reps listen to the song and Viv. Jeanine starts to make her way to the three of them. I am not sure what Jeanine saw that I missed. Perhaps she heard something that signaled a need to move in. Or what Jeanine saw in their eyes was far more alarming to her than I noticed from way over here. It doesn't matter; she is there and has injected herself into the conversation with the reps. Jeanine gestures to the stage and points to Logan, as her hand gestures take on a life of their own. They are staccato in movement and sharp in their finish. She has captured the full attention of the reps. I don't think I have ever been prouder of someone who has spent so much of her life trying to annoy me.

As the song plays out, Jeanine's grandiose hand gestures are accompanied by the unconscious head bobs of the reps. They can't hide their enjoyment of the song as Jeanine looks like she is conducting an orchestra for the label.

Then I see it: a smile widens across all four of their faces. A release of tension overcomes Viv as Jeanine shakes the female's hand. I can see it in Viv; her shoulders drop and stomach arches out like she just ate a holiday dinner. Viv's smile now threatens to engulf her whole face as she shakes the rep's hand.

I make my way over to the affair. The short walk gives me a moment to pay attention to the tweaks they have made to the song from the studio earlier today. Logan and her bandmates listen well, and they adapt even better. The happenstance that was meeting Logan seems to have been more fate than anything.

All heads turn to me as I stop next to both sets of people, Jeanine and Viv on my left and the label on my right. I extend out my hand for quick handshakes.

"I see you've met Jeanine." I nod my head her way.

The female rep smiles. "Quite the firebrand you have, Mr. Fairlane."

"Finn. Mr. Fairlane is for when I die." I laugh.

The rep relaxes a bit.

"I trust that Logan Square is on the map for our next stop?" I look at both label reps.

The guy nods. "Once we get the contracts in order, we will send them over."

"Then enjoy the rest of the show," I wrap up the floor meeting. "Have a drink on me."

They both smile and part ways with us as I turn to Jeanine. "Nice recovery. What did you say that brought them back around?"

Jeanine leans in as if some big secret might otherwise be spilled. "I told them that different isn't bad. Change is different and can be what they are looking for. What they need."

I nod in agreement.

"Then," she adds, "I told them that the marketing potential for Logan Square and their talent is far higher than any pop-rock band that might be created in an office."

"Well done." I nod once more.

"Then, of course, I reminded them that you are on their team and Logan Square is on your label, which means less cost for them." She smiles.

I look her in the eyes, and while her words are about the band, her eyes scream Faith. Always the person on my mind and forever the person I default to, but I can't leave this behind. I can't put aside almost twenty years of my life for a four-year relationship I had in college. The songs I have written about Faith and the years spent yearning are the same as our relationship—in the past. Oh, but it's never that easy. Life is never that simple. Those best things worth having in life are worth fighting for. It's just a matter of figuring out which of those things are still worth having.

"Welcome aboard, Jeanine." I extend my hand.

"Don't make me regret this, Finn," she warns with a pointed smile.

I nod and take my leave. I need to find D.B. He has been absent as of late—since the tour and all. I need to hear what he thinks. I need the thoughts of someone who's on the same road as me, even if he is a little further back. I need the input of a guy—a male's perspective, a friend's honest and (almost) unbiased opinion on the matter.

I make it backstage to find D.B. talking to the label reps, except not the guys from just a few moments ago. These are the guys from NYC. Damn, I totally forgot I invited them. No matter now, though. I am here.

I overhear one of the guys say something about adding on a few tour dates. Not a bad idea if they are up for it, especially if it's on the label's dime.

"Will the tour still end on the West Coast?" I ask.

The rep shakes his head. "It'll end back on the East Coast. After they wrap up their last date in L.A., they'll stop off in Chicago again, then down to House Of Blues in Orlando."

"Sounds wonderful. Contracts all written?" I make deliberate eye contact with the rep.

He nods. "I'll just need D.B. to look them over and sign them. Tonight if he can." He pulls out a set from his brief-case and hands them to D.B.

I turn to D.B. "Got a few?"

He tosses his glances between me, the label, and the contracts. "We go on in a few. I wanna sign these." He holds up the contracts. "What's up?"

I see the look in his eyes. He's in show mode, and the contracts are the last thing he can deal with and still keep his head in the game. His look to me was a courtesy. The reaction he wants is not the reaction I want to give. I can respect his mindset because I've been there. I know how it is, so I put my concerns aside for the moment.

"It can wait." I hold out my hand. "Let me get a glance at those things before you sign."

He hands me the contracts. A quick skim has them twice in Chicago, then one in Denver and Vegas, two in L.A., one in Reno, Austin, and Chicago, then capping it off in Orlando all in under two weeks.

"Brutal but acceptable on my end. The jetlag is all on you guys. Ten shows in just under two weeks across the entire country." I raise a brow to D.B.

He nods and snickers. "Brutal for sure. It'll be great."

His smile fades and eyes get heavy. "Talk in Orlando?"

I give him a short upturn of my lips and nod. "Have a good show. See you soon."

Of course, I stay for the show and watch from the bar. But I don't just watch the band; I watch Faith and her sister. I watch the crowd. I see the world I know, the world I came from. I see how it is and possibly how the sun will set on it, the damn proverbial sunset. The funny thing in movies and books is when the old-timer passes on the torch, and the sun sets on his career, there is an unstated assumption that he is done and through. He is a horse put out to pasture, no longer useful in any way. A person who must now live out his golden years before becoming a burden to his loved ones and society. But that's the thing about setting suns. They rise soon after they go down. So, even if this is my setting sun, maybe the dawn will have something more significant.

CHAPTER II

Get The F*ck Out Of Here

M ine and Faith's return to Orlando was quiet. She slept most of the trip but was otherwise generally in a contemplative state of mind. There was a look in her eye that dared me to interrupt her thoughts, a look that silently screamed if I did challenge it, I would not end up anywhere close to well. I like that we returned home together, so I let her daring eyes rest. A battle for another day, perhaps. All I have to do is make it twelve days without blowing up my life. Twelve days till D.B. is back home and we can talk.

Day one.

Though we made it back to my place without any fights, casualties, or adverse happenings, I feel like we are in two different worlds. After an almost silent trip, she heads to my bedroom and lays down. No "goodnight" or words to have me join her. No pithy thoughts on her mood to break the tension that is slowly suffocating us. She just sleeps.

I still do not know what was said between her and her sister at the show. I try not to think about it, but my mind has to. Obsessing over the things in life that should be insignificant is what I do because, to me, nothing is ever that insignificant. Whatever was said has caused a sort of radio silence. I am done fighting with Faith. I do not want to cause any more stress, rile her up, or hear her yell. I want us to be okay, whatever that word means now. In a sense, I should enjoy the silence, relish in the fact she hasn't completely shunned me. Enjoy whatever time she has decided to give me before I blow it all up again, before she finally leaves me permanently.

But, in our silent thoughts, the truth wanders like a lost madman in a darkened alley. In my unwanted silence, my thoughts betray me and turn to Jacquelyn.

Our romance was short compared to most, but to others, it may have been a lifetime. But it was uncomplicated. It was new. Even in the end, there were still surprises; perhaps because even then, it was still fresh in many regards. Maybe I was drawn to Jacquelyn by her mysteriousness, a mysteriousness that hid who she was. A cloak of secrecy to hide her profession out of some intertwined sense of pride and shame. But she accepted me. She wanted me for who I was, not who she thought I could be or perhaps who I once was. With Faith, it is always so much more complicated. Complicated things attract us; it's the intrinsic human curiosity that drives our species to better ourselves and understand the world around us. The interest of the complication and the intrigue behind my eyes keeps pulling me to Faith, the eternal struggle between the Id and the Superego. Jacquelyn, on one side, is the comfortable side of things known and the peace of mind that comes with that. Faith, on the other side, is the one that knows it is where I belong if only I can figure out a way to get there without killing myself—metaphorically or literally.

All I know is that the longer she is silent, the more the pain slowly creeps back in. But as long as I am near her, even in her silence and sleep, the pain stays at bay. I must think. I must find a place to think and figure out my pain, my purpose in her life, and everything in between.

Letting you sleep. At George's Music. Love you.

The store is peaceful today, quiet and slow with only the employees wandering about. Well, the employees, me, and like one other guy. I let the thoughts wander through my mind while my guitar gently weeps. There is no budding musician that catches my eye. No talent that cries out my name. I just sit and strum, marinating in all the potential outcomes of any possible actions. But being away from it all seems to help calm my nerves. It instills me with a sense of serenity.

Looking outside, I see the sky is starting to darken. Either I've been in here much longer than I realize, or a scary storm is brewing. Any way it goes, I need to get back to my Faith.

I park my car and head inside as a flash of light illuminates the dim sky, followed by a roaring thunderclap overhead. It's only a matter of time until the storm hits. It's nature's way of telling me this is where I am meant to be at this moment. There's no leaving now.

The ominous weather outdoors is a stark contrast to what I walked into indoors. I smell cooking. If my nose is correct, I detect mushrooms and onions being sauteed and burgers whose aromas indicate my timing is perfect.

As I enter the kitchen, she greets me with a smile. "Dinner's just about ready." She flips the patties onto their buns and tops them each with the onion and mushroom mix. She carries the plates to the table.

I walk to the refrigerator. "Anything to drink?"

She nods her head. "A Coke, please."

I grab a can for each of us and join her.

"I wasn't sure when you'd be home, but I got hungry and thought you might like a burger as well," she says, taking a bite.

"I'll thank the storm for sending me back home." I smile. "Thank you for cooking."

"All the way back home, you never asked about Jeanine," Faith says in an unusually calm tone.

"I figured whatever you two talked about wasn't my business," I reply, swallowing a bite.

She sips her Coke, squinting her eyes at me. "She really has become a sister to be proud of."

I nod my head. "Quite the turnaround from back in the day."

"There's a tribe of monkeys, or apes, or some sort of primate somewhere," Faith starts on a seemingly off-topic tangent.

I raise a brow but stay silent.

"I read about it somewhere. An article. . . Facebook. . . some magazine. I can't remember. But I read about this troop, or congress, or whatever they're called, and how there was this male that joined their tribe after being ostra-cized from another," she continues.

"Okay?" I say, not really sure where this is going.

"At first, the male was aggressive and domineering. But the original males in the tribe wouldn't have any of it. They would defend against it, but not give in to the demands. Eventually, the new male calmed his aggressions and joined in the peaceful ways," Faith says, taking a quarter of her burger in one bite. She smiles as she chews. "These are really good."

"Yes, they are," I confirm.

"Then Jeanine asked if I knew the fable of the scorpion and the frog," she continues with a leading tone.

"Of course," I respond. "Scorpion needs a lift across a river. The frog agrees, and halfway across the scorpion stings the frog. Knowing they'll both die, the frog asks why."

"'It's in my nature' the scorpion responds," Faith finishes.

"So, you and Jeanine talked about Aesop?" I say, chug-ging down some Coke.

"She told me I can't be mad at who you were or who you are. Our past is our past, no matter how far back or recent. You didn't kill Ronnie. You didn't manipulate any-thing to be vicious or vindictive. The situations you inevi-tably find yourself in are not sought out by you, but rather, they seem to seek you out," she explains.

"Yes! Yes, they do," I start to defend.

She quickly throws up a hand and tightens her lips, a clear signal for me to shut the fuck up. So, I do.

"But, like the frog cannot be mad that the scorpion stung him, the frog could hope that the scorpion could learn from the monkeys," Faith wraps it up.

"Now I'm just confused," I admit. "The whole thing got a little convoluted."

She huffs in frustration. "I'm saying, hopefully, you can learn to see farther down the road to where your daily actions and the day's events might lead you back home and not to some rando girl's mouth around some random body part."

I smile and nod. "So, she stood up for me?"

"Hey, first time for everything, Finn." She takes down the last bite of her burger.

But this moment with Faith—the calm and quiet, the peaceful tranquility—it feels different. It feels almost calmly unsettling, the way the world quiets down right before a storm. It's like looking outside and seeing there's no wind yet. The sky might be darkening a bit, but it's calm. No signs of the approaching chaos until the wind kicks up without any lube to easy it in. Just full force, flinging loose furniture and ripping branches off trees. Now, all signs that things might be fine have disappeared—vanished from the surrounding landscape, replaced by the start of the show. The cosmic ballet played out by the wind, the rain, the lightning, and thunder leave no doubt that you thought calm was good.

Day two is rather mundane, just busy work for the bands, contracts, and all the boring stuff that comes along with the music industry. Faith is at the salon for the day, then heading out with her co-workers. This day is a day to ourselves.

Day three.

I decide to head back to Coffee Shop of Horrors. I haven't had their coffee in a while, and my body is jonesin' for it. There's a shortage of perfect coffee in the world, it'd be a pity to drink anything else. But my drive to the shop stops about a block short. They seem to have relocated since my first visit. This is a larger location, now full of baked goods and coffee-infused ice cream with nitro coffee on tap. They have really stepped up their game since I popped my cherry. Hell, they have a wall of board games for customers to play as well as hot sauce, art, books, pillows, bags, and other stuff for sale, all with the perfect horror/fantasy theme. Not to mention the giant television playing out some horror show. Time has definitely been kind to them.

I peruse the coffee selections for a moment when the owner steps out from the back.

"Been a while," the owner says.

"Sorry?" I didn't quite hear her.

"Haven't seen you since the hurricane," she rephrases.

"Good memory," I say.

"You're not easily forgotten," she quips. "You need help, let me know." And with that, she sits down in front of her computer. The location may have changed, but habits have not.

I grab a bag or two of almost every flavor because I am not sure when I'll be back in the area. Even so, it's not like it'll go bad. As I said, perfect coffee is hard to come by.

The owner laughs at me as I carry handful after handful of close to thirty bags of coffee in total to the counter, including four bags of a peanut butter roast.

"Can't decide or are you going somewhere?" she asks with a dry sense of humor in her tone.

Though it was meant as a joke, it hits me. I don't know. Neither. Both. All of the above. Some weird, unseen fourth option.

"A gift for that girl I was with. Plus, some for myself," I say.

"Still together, I take it," she keeps it short.

"Not sure we were ever apart," I ponder out loud.

Luckily, her life experience has taught her not to delve too deep with customers. She simply smiles and continues ringing me up. But her casual conversation has struck a nerve somewhere inside me. In all the years we were apart, she must have been thinking of me as much as I of her. Otherwise, that first night back outside that greasy burger joint in Old Town, she wouldn't have said anything. She would have just passed me by without so much as a peep or a whisper.

"If I don't make it back in, thank you for letting us stay as late as you did that night. Your kindness means a lot." I grab my many bags off the counter and slide them up my arm.

"No worries" is all she says. "You can always buy online. We ship."

I stop and look down at my armloads of hundreds of dollars in coffee. I just laugh in spite of myself. Something I could have figured out if I opened up a search engine before driving here. Well, ya live and ya learn.

"It's more fun this way," I joke at my own expense.

Day four is spent on the phone with the label from New Orleans. Sometimes, no matter what concessions I am willing to make to gain ground in the long run, things just don't pan out. I don't know if it was something said between Viv, Jeanine, and the label before I approached or if I said something. More than likely, it was nothing that was said. It was the simple inevitability of time. The label thought on their preliminary decision and decided against it. There was nothing I could say on the phone that would change if we were in person. In the end, the label felt that Logan Square wouldn't be a good fit.

Now, when I tell Logan, she will be crushed. It will feel like all her hopes, dreams, years of hard work, and sacrifice to the craft will have amounted to nothing, to being told her music isn't good enough. It will be my job to convince her otherwise. It will not be easy, and she will put up some sort of teenage resistance in the matter, as if I am fighting against her. I will be okay with that because getting her calm is my job. I will tell her there will be others. That I will find her the right fit and she will make something of herself and her band.

Day five arrives, and Faith again is working. I spend the day in my studio working on ideas for songs. It is a day of self-reflection and inner steadiness: a day to write and revise lyrics and music, and a day to think about whatever Finn needs to think about. (It's nice to know I still refer to myself in the third person.)

Dinner is just as pleasant. I decided to make a dish that is sure to please—grilled cheese and ham with oven-baked French fries covered in cheese, sauteed onions, and Thousand Island dressing, otherwise known as Animal Style for all you Hollywood burger joint peeps.

Day six.

The halfway mark and the point of no return (if this were a mission of miles) so to speak. I make a stop off at Park Ave CDs. I need to distract myself from the talk I desperately need and am being forced to wait for. The conversation with D.B. will give me much-needed insight into what I should do. The idea of my own label sounds fantastic. It really does. But this supposed move forward could be the proverbial sun setting on my touring days. It definitely looks like the sky is a few shades darker. Here's the problem with the sun setting metaphor: there's no clock. There's only the presumption the day is ending. No actual way to tell if the darkening sky is from the sun going down or storm clouds approaching.

I make my way to the store and finger through old vinyl records from when rock 'n roll ruled the world. Yeah, it still does in a sense, but it's changed so much. It is no longer the monster we once knew and loved. It has morphed and grown into something so different from what it once was. To look at the old and the current side by side, without what came between, the two would be unrecognizable. I look through old Rush albums, Talking Heads, Iron Maiden, The Animals, and so many more. I look at the inner sleeves (much to the chagrin of the employees) and stare at the pictures; the days of sitting in a studio—a my-hand-to-God, good, old fashioned analog studio. The mixing boards, reel to reels, microphones that by today's standards either sound like complete crap or have made a retro comeback. I stare at the look on each of their faces, the photos of them on stage or walking the back halls to the stage. The look in their eyes bares an excitement, an in-the-moment high and energy that never fades. Not just because it was captured in that one instance onto a photograph, but it never diminishes because the fire that burns inside of us never dies. Sure, it dwindles from time to time. The heat lessens like a bonfire in need of more wood, but unlike that bonfire, it never truly dies.

Maybe it's all just some nostalgic yearning for the early days. If I keep going this road, I may end up the guy who's holding onto his better years like the forty-five-year-old still reliving his glory days as a high school quarterback. Sure, my time was sweet. But perhaps my desire to create new music and new sweetness are blinding me to the best-of-times that are passing me by right now.

Whatever the reason for my thoughts, I am distracted by the sounding alert of a text message.

[Jacquelyn: Can we talk?]

Three little words. Three little words that will lead to so many more. I stand, pondering how to respond for far longer than I should. Anyone who stares at a phone this long without moving is clearly not in a proper state of mind. But here I stand, staring down onto the 3x5 screen, or how-ever big a cellphone is, pondering those words. Frozen in the unknown of how I should answer, not because my words have escaped me but because I want to say yes and know I shouldn't.

Jacquelyn is my savior to stay in the life that I love. She doesn't judge me by my past and still wants to be a part of my future, a girl who never did get a fair chance to state her case while being told a verdict she didn't agree with, and rightly so. Life options aside, I enjoyed my time with her. She made me feel like the man I always wanted to be. She made me feel special. How fuckin' cheesy. A grown-ass man, with money in the bank, fame (fading or otherwise), and a history all his own wanting to feel like he's special to someone.

[Finn: Meet me at Old Town.]

After checking out with my handful of Talking Heads and Rush vinyl and some CDs, I head on over. The traffic is surprisingly light for this time of day, and I arrive at Old Town in what could be record time.

Jacquelyn isn't here yet, so I wait in line to order a burger from that same greasy burger stand that started this whole Orlando experience and the reunion of Faith and me.

It's funny, time passes differently in Florida than it does up north. There's no snow or real changes of season to let you know that the world is spinning, that time keeps ever marching onward. There's only the daylight and the darkness. It is the darkness that is setting in, a cool breeze that blows, and the multi-lingual noise that drowns out all distractions around me. I know I've said it before, but there really is magic in the night air. It's something you miss if you don't stop and look around.

Everybody needs to take a few moments to look farther ahead than ten or twenty feet. To look outward in the further down close distance—to where the sound doesn't carry into your ears, where your ears stop listening to the sounds around you—where you can really see the beauty in what has become so familiar to you. Like visiting Vegas for the first time, you stop and take it all in. The lights of the strip and the casinos whispering your name are all so much that when you first arrive, you stop and try to comprehend the vastness that is Vegas. That is what everyone needs to do with their surroundings now and again. It is what I am doing while I wait. If only because you never know what might inspire you, what might be found lurking in the ethereal surroundings that gets missed by those glued to their phones or focused on the immediate.

As I continue to take it all in, eating my burger and fries under the fiberglass umbrella, I feel a pair of arms wrap around me. I know these arms. They have a distinctive embrace that a part of me misses.

"Hey you," Jacquelyn says, slipping her arms from around me and taking a seat.

I pull a relatively fresh burger from the bag sitting in front of me. "Thought you might be hungry."

"Thanks." She unwraps the burger.

"It was funny you texted when you did," I say.

"Why's that?" She chomps down on her burger.

"I was at the store where we first met," I say with a bit of reminiscence.

"Look, Finn," she tries to interrupt.

"It's funny." I don't let her speak yet. "This little hub of the peninsula. The Orlando area. Things happen here that I don't think can happen anywhere else. The rain we get. The weather. It messes with our heads. With how we think. Personally, I think it's why this state has such a big drug problem. But hell, I'm just a rocker. What do I know?"

"Finn!" She gets a little louder. She will demand the time to say what she wants. "Listen, I need you. There's something about what you do, who you are, that pulls me to you. A gravitational pull I can't escape. I can't stop thinking about the shows, the night in New York, the days spent at my place. I need you, Finn. And I think you need me, too."

Jacquelyn pulls out a bottle of pills from her pocket and places it on the table. Not exactly a subtle thing to do in a crowded area teaming with cops, but as I said, this place makes people act differently.

The pain that always lingers just beneath the surface starts to rise up. Like a starving dog that sees food, it hungers for it. It crawls toward it but still has to inspect it first to make sure that this won't be his last bite.

"Jacquelyn, you never got a fair chance," I begin.

"We've already talked about that. Discussed the you and the me. You still owe me an answer," Jacquelyn says, wrapping her hand around the pill bottle.

"I'm not sure I can properly give you an answer," I say. I try to look Jacquelyn in the eye but keep wandering to the bottle.

"Why not?! Did we not have fun? Were you not falling for me? It's easy, ya know, being on stage or at the club. The guys, they crawl all over me, fall at my feet, trying to get a piece. They throw money at me. Some even shower me with gifts to feed their illusion that we are in some sort of relationship or that we will be if they spend enough. Tell me that's not all I was to you?" she pleads. The tone in her voice is filled with quiet desperation calling out from behind her false bravado. "Tell me I was more than an illusioned girl vying for the attention of someone who was never going to make themselves available. Tell me that I mean something to you."

"I have never been with someone who didn't mean something, even if only for the moment. You mean so much more than just that. The ineffableness of the whole situation. Faith's pregnant," I start to say, but I stop. I know those aren't the words I am looking for even though they were spoken.

"Her having your kid doesn't tie you to her. It ties you to the kid. You don't have to make something that represents a relationship work because of a kid. We had something. We felt something. I still feel it, and I know you do too," she continues pleading.

"You're right. Having a child with her doesn't mean I need to make some vague semblance of a relationship happen. What I feel for you is . . . not relevant anymore." Not my most choice words for a delicate situation.

She pulls the bottle away and stands up. "Of course your feelings are relevant, you ass. People think it's easy, doing what I do. It is, in a sense, if you are physically fit. Spinning, dancing. Those are easy if you can already dance. The tableside service, the private sessions you have to fend off the drunkards who think that, just because they took you private, they can assault you. That's the hard part, but you get thick skin in my line. It comes with time. But this..." She waves her hand between the two of them. "...this right here...it hurts no matter how thick my skin. I'm trying to offer you a way to the life you never wanted to leave and the life that I'm made for."

She turns to walk away, leaving me with the remnants of the food. She takes a step and stops, turning back toward me. "When you finally figure out yourself, you'll look back and only see everything you missed. Everything that could have been will have moved on. You'll look back and realize everything you once loved has relegated you to a footnote."

"You don't mean that." My words creep out.

"I'm pissed, Finn. You are doing a big thing poorly." Her tone is quiet, sullen. The weight of her words sits heavy on her shoulders. Her head hangs a little.

"Can I get a couple of pills?" I throw out a Hail Mary.

She laughs, even though her mood is still grey. She shakes her head. "The audacity of your words earns you nothing. You still haven't answered."

She walks off and disappears into the evening crowds. I finish my food and head back home to Faith.

Six more days.

Days seven through eleven were surprisingly calm. Faith and I decided to visit old Downtown Disney on the eleventh day, a relaxing stroll through the shops and restaurants.

"I leave in a week," Faith says, with a hint that she still wants me to go with her. It's an answer I still have to give.

"I know. Your boxes are packed and stacked," I say, watching a couple of kids turn the wheel on a mock cannon. They pretend to shoot at some unseen enemy.

"I'm not going to let that answer ruin our day." Her passive anger creeps out.

She drops the subject and turns her attention to a hat store. Nothing but hats. We stop inside and window shop for a while. She does her best job modeling the various styles, most of which look great on her.

She doesn't want any, though. Nothing extra to pack up. No excess baggage. She says this to me, as if it was a metaphor veiled in wide-knit lace made from thread-weight yarn. It drives the point home.

I just need to sort out my head.

Day twelve.

Twelve days was the time between D.B. telling me we'll talk once he's back in Orlando and him returning home. Twelve days can go by in a flash. Other times, twelve days can seem like forever. I never thought he would make it back home. Not that anything adverse happened to him while he was on tour. No, that all went swimmingly. But twelve days of watching Faith slowly pack up her life down here, twelve days of helping Faith pack up her life down here puts things into perspective. It says that the end is coming. By helping her pack, I am pushing the inevitable end closer to the present than it was moments ago.

I guess now I have to choose the ending. Always the dilemma. The sun will set on some aspect of my life. In some way, a part of my life will forever change. I have to figure out which part and the why behind it. That's why I am sitting with D.B., double-decker cheesy tacos in hand, as we once again surround ourselves with the hot sauce bar and local art.

Here's the irony in my mind on this whole conversation we are about to partake—I am in no pain. Perhaps it is my body's way of telling me that everything is gonna be all right. Maybe the pain that has been dwelling inside me now has a place to go, that sitting here is someone opening the floodgates and giving my suffering a place to escape. Whatever the reason, I am glad it is subsiding.

"Here's a strange turn of events: Jacquelyn and I have been talking a lot lately," D.B. says, picking up his taco.

My hands stop lifting the chip to my mouth as my eyes lock on his face, searching for the words he just spoke to repeat themselves with clarification.

"Yeah," he says, as if I had responded with words. Maybe I did, and I didn't realize it. Perhaps he knows what I am thinking and thus his response. "She's been at a ton of the shows on this tour." He looks down at his food to take a large bite.

While he chews on his food, I chew on his words. There's a hesitation in his words—a world of silence he is not saying—he covers like he has been practicing this moment.

"She must be a big fan," I say.

"It started at the bachelor party." He swallows his food. "After you were . . . under, she was cut off. Didn't know what to do or if she should do anything. Not that there really was anything to do."

He stops talking and looks to me for permission to continue, as if I can stop him. But I know that his look isn't seeking permission to go on talking, but that he has a more profound confession. I know all too well this tale he has yet to tell.

"So, you and Jacquelyn talked while I was under. Became friends," I say as he nods in relief and confirmation.

I leave it at that. There's more to D.B.'s story, more he wants to get off his chest. But it doesn't matter. The things he wants to tell me are all just part of the life we live. This moving sea of twirling space dust that envelops us tells our story, whether we want it to or not. I know what he wants to say, so he doesn't need to say it.

"She's not your average woman, Finn," he says with a hint of a smile in the corner of his lips. "Don't be afraid that your guys' sex will become stale or moldy. Not all relationships burn out in the bedroom. Don't think that every day will be a honey-to-do list of chores. Or that you'll walk in on her riding the cabana boy's pool noodle."

D.B. says these words, but he doesn't speak to which woman he is talking about. Maybe that's his point. Perhaps D.B. is much more a Rhodes Scholar than I ever gave him credit for.

"Jacquelyn told me about your growing obsession with those round, little pills. She also told me the question that prevents her from giving any to you. Jacquelyn's a good girl. Stripper with a heart of gold, if there ever was such a thing," D.B. says with bright eyes. "I love you, man, and don't want to see you end up just another rock 'n roll statistic, found dead on a floor in some hotel room. Make a choice. At least you have one."

His last five words were hard for him to say. They came out through gritted teeth. Teeth clenched by my position to have either woman—both of whom want what they think is best for me. One of whom no longer has a significant other, as tragic as those circumstances were. And another woman who wants it all.

Maybe I'm missing the point. Maybe the choice isn't between the women, but that I can choose to not end up a statistic.

Either way, as he said, at least I have one.

CHAPTER 12

Once In A Lifetime

"Fuck them!" Viv says, downing her Jack and Coke (mostly Jack). Though I guess to get to this moment, I need to explain the surroundings.

The final stop on the Spear Fist/Logan Square expanded North American Tour—House of Blues Orlando, a night to cap off what has been a majorly successful tour, not only for Spear Fist but for Logan Square as well. Hell, up to this point, it has been a helluva ride for Viv and Jeanine too. Jeanine's marriage seems to not only have survived the tour but strengthened their relationship without destroying the band, which was a point of significant concern for D.B., Vincent, and Neil at one time. Viv, also, seems to be thriving on her childhood dreams of a rock 'n roll life. She and Logan are still happy, though, at this given moment, frustration has her grounded in the reality of the lifestyle.

At the bar, located to the left side of the stage, Viv and Jeanine chug drinks, telling me their thoughts on the label from New Orleans, the label that was supposed to pick up Logan Square. The label that has decided they weren't quite the perfect fit I thought they were. I know all these things they are telling me, having heard them time and again from the current label and others in slight variations. To Jeanine and Viv, this is the first time in the history of music a label has backed out of a deal before signing the contracts. To Viv and Jeanine, this is the worst thing that could happen. To me, it's just another in a long list of bumps in the road, hurdles on the track, whatever. To them, it's a first. So, I must treat it like it is a first.

"Fuck those guys!" Viv turns to the bartender. "One more round!" She then turns back to me. "We were so close."

"Viv, there's a lot to this business that you are learning. But nothing ever comes easy. After they passed, what did you do to convince them they were wrong?" I ask, sipping my vodka and lime.

"What do you mean what did I do? Nothing. They passed." Viv tightens her stance and scrunches her face as she defends her words.

"Okay, a little bit of knowledge is about to drop. First, you're fine. Don't close off now. Don't drop out of the race because they did first." I pause to make sure she is still focused on my words. I watch as Viv and Jeanine soak in each and every word I say while sipping their drinks. "It's been twelve days. Send them an email or give them a call explaining why they are wrong. Why I, Finn Fairlane, said they are wrong."

"But wouldn't they want to hear these things from you?" Viv asks.

"You work for me; your words are from me. State your reasons with confidence. Tell them whatever you think will get them to take the hook." I watch Viv's facial expressions to make sure she is understanding.

Her lips slightly show a small smile as she nods. She understands.

"Now call them," I urge her.

I watch through the growing crowd of people, to the opposite end of the venue, as more concert-goers flow through the entrance. I see the familiar face of Jacquelyn stroll through the door, only for a brief second. Then she is lost to the swelling sea of people. Maybe I was wrong. Perchance it was not her. Just my imagination. I continue scanning the crowd for her, but she is lost.

"It's ringing," Viv says.

As she says her words, the sound of a nearby ringing phone screams beneath the music.

A finger taps Viv on the shoulder. It is one of the reps from New Orleans, though he is no longer dressed in the factory-torn jeans and reprint tour shirts. He is not on official business but dressed in jeans torn from the stress of time. He dons a shirt that has been to more concerts than most people in this building.

Viv's normal flesh tone is taking on a deep red hue as the anger and frustration grow in her face. Her breathing is more shallow and forced.

As I walk by her, sipping my drink, I whisper, "Just relax. You got this."

"I believe you are trying to call me?" the rep says.

"I didn't expect to see you here," Viv starts off with a steadier tone and pacing to her words.

"After the New Orleans show, I had one of their songs stuck in my head. I ended up picking up a CD to mull it over," the rep starts off. "There was something about your words." He turns to Jeanine. "And yours, that made me think my colleague and I had it wrong."

Viv takes a chest-swelling deep breath and holds it while she chews her words. "You need Logan Square. They may have been the opening act on this tour, but their performance on stage and merch sales have been anything but opening act."

The rep nods his head in agreement.

I continue watching as Viv settles into a comfort level that allows her the confidence to reel this guy in. He continues to nod with each of her words. I smile as I see my legacy grow. Never a bad thing, though my whimsy thoughts of a rock empire are interrupted by a buzzing on my phone. An email from Spear Fist's other label. I open it and read the body of the email but not the attached contracts.

I walk to Viv and whisper in her ear. She stops talking, and a smile crosses her face as she turns to me. "Are you serious?"

I nod and step away.

Her forced confidence from earlier has left, and genuine conviction, backed by a label that is willing to sign Logan Square, has given her all the backbone she needs to talk with this guy.

Jeanine steps in and joins the conversation. The rep tosses glances between the two women as they all have a friendly chat. After a while of talking and drinking, the rep extends a hand and shakes theirs.

I walk away as the three of them lean against the bar and order another round. Sometimes, the things in life that seem like a sure thing are a sure thing. But it doesn't mean it will come without effort, patience, or some frustration. Both those ladies fought passionately to keep that rep on their side. Sure, the music being stuck in his head helps; it is always about the music. Though, no matter how good the music might be on its own, it is still good to have someone fighting on your side to make sure the world sees how wonderful you are.

As I watch them all laugh and talk it up, I can't help but feel a little melancholy, a little weight sitting on my shoulders, slowing me down, a trudge in my step. I don't want this night to end. I don't want the butterflies in my stomach churning my insides and making my chest feel the my-heart-is-about-to-burst-out excitement to end. Not that I've never finished a tour before. It's not about that. Tours end; it's what they do. But this moment, this uniquely stellar moment where everything aligns is what I want to last forever. The end of a one-man machine known as Finn Fairlane and the start of Fairlane Records (or whatever off-the-cuff name I came up with in that meeting) is being solidified right now. Viv and Jeanine cementing the deal all because I showed Viv an email that Spear Fist's other label wanted Logan Square as well. Viv saw the opportunity and seized it. This moment is what it is all about, a stellar moment in time where everything is perfect. Perfection is not a state of being by any means. Nothing is perfect. But if we look hard enough at the hours, days, months, and years spent honing our craft, we can see perfect moments. Moments where all the stars align, and the universe has blessed us with a perfect moment. This is it.

On stage, Logan Square is finishing up their set and will walk back to the green room to be greeted by someone they have only met in quick handshake meetings. Now, they will be talking about contracts, tours, and much more.

There is an irony in this night that is not lost on me. The place that ends the tour, the building that finalizes my need to work for myself and on better things than corporate-produced pop hits, this town that I loved to loathe for that magical, talking rodent, has me standing in the belly of it all—House of Blues Orlando. This place has taken me back to my earlier years, a time when everything was so much simpler yet so much more complicated. It transports me back to a time when I knew everything, and nothing was going to stand in my way. This place, right here, takes away the jaded eyes of adulthood and transports me back with rose-colored glasses. Clichéd, perhaps, but it's why it was built. I know it's just a moment in time, but it feels so perfect. Nothing going wrong. Nothing being screwed up by good intentions with no forethought. No pain. No regrets. Just this moment. All in this place of childhood innocence that is washing away the misanthropy that adulthood inevitably brings.

So, the irony is that perhaps I am wrong. Maybe, just maybe that magical kingdom I have held such contempt for isn't the horrid, gilded place I preach that it is. Perhaps, that empire is doing what it is meant to do—take you away from the pressures around you so you can see clearly. So you can look at your world with fresh eyes and see exactly what it is you are looking at—the forest and the trees, if only for a moment.

This stellar moment of perfection will end, and I shall be okay with that. There is a truck in the lot loaded up with all of Faith's belongings, packed and ready to make the trek 1100 miles to the place where she and I first began— Chicago. Chicago is where she is meant to be. It is where a salon awaits.

A tap on my shoulder brings me out of my daydream and crashing back down to reality. Faith needs to head out. She has to be settled into her new place and start the grand opening of the salon in two days. I told her she should have left yesterday, but she insisted on staying for the final show. I am not sure if it is some lingering suspicion or distrust that she still holds for me, or a need to be near her sister as long as possible to make sure that Jeanine will be all right once Faith leaves. But Faith stayed, and now she will be arriving in Chicago within a half-day of opening her salon. If Faith stayed the night, she wouldn't even make it on time. Now is the time she must leave, a forced end to all things.

We elbow our way through the crowd of people, gently pushing those aside too enthralled in the show to see us trying to pass. I hear my name being called out, my name drowning under the waters of the music. I look around for the source of my name, but I see no one. We continue walking toward the exit when I hear my name called again. As Faith passes through the no re-entry part of security, I see who is calling me—Jacquelyn. Her voice is distorted by the blaring music and the night of shouting at the stage. I stand outside with Faith as Jacquelyn approaches. The whole no re-entry thing doesn't apply to my friends or me, but the metaphor is not lost.

Faith stops to let her have this moment.

"You can't just leave, Finn," Jacquelyn says with a plea in her voice.

I can already feel the pain start to creep back in. The restlessness in my lower extremities starts to shift from one leg to the other. I see what is happening here. The two women I am torn between, representing the duality of my life, are standing on each side of me.

"She needs to head out," I say, gesturing to Faith.

Of course, my words were not perfect. They rarely are when I speak. But the words were spoken, and Faith heard them. I did not say "we need to head out." I didn't say "I am heading out." No. I stated that Faith needs to head out. And that is what Faith heard, a choice unconsciously made in my words. It will not be an "us" heading out, not a "together" event. Just her, heading out on the road to her new life back in Chicago and leaving me to the life I have made for myself.

Jacquelyn steps out past the security of the no re-entry. We step away from the crowds of people to a quieter location. As Jacquelyn finds a place to stand, I can't help but notice her head is framed by giant mouse ears whose silhouette is a neon-light on some distant storefront or billboard.

Jacquelyn's framing in those ears is everything the corporation wants, for adults to hold onto their innocence against the rising tide of all that tries to tear it away. But my naiveté is lost. It has been for decades, and no amount of time spent wearing mouse ears or frolicking in the magical kingdom will bring it back.

"So, you're not leaving, Finn?" Jacquelyn attempts to clarify.

I look back to Faith, who is framed by nothing. No mouse to make her look like an overgrown child. No magic lights surrounding her. Just a brick wall behind her and a stark realism that is her showing her baby belly. Her long, curly hair that disappears into the black of the night sky and the heaviness in her eyes that look to what the future might hold. It scares her, and you don't need to be a mind reader to see how she tries to hide the consuming fear behind timid smiles and squinting eyes.

"What do you want, Jacquelyn?" I ask. I figure a straightforward question is what's needed.

The lights that line the silhouette of her distant mouse ears flicker and brighten for a moment. "A reason, after everything we've been through. After everything. . . I deserve a reason."

"What is she talking about?" Faith interjects from the stark darkness of where she stands. The clouds clear their cover of the moon, and its light shines down on her.

I smile at Faith. Her anger toward me only exists because perhaps I do not communicate those things I feel do not need communicating. And it is those things that I keep to myself, those things I think don't need be said, that maybe should have been told. It is within those quiet thoughts we keep to ourselves that reveal the truth about who we are more than the things we say ever could.

"Jacquelyn asked what it was about you that was so special. She wants to know what it is about you that keeps me from being with her," I say, turning back to Jacquelyn.

"We could have something great, Finn," Jacquelyn starts before I can tell her. "We could have this life together. Something for the ages. Something that will be written about in songs for the whole world to sing. This life. . ." she looks to the House of Blues, ". . .this is what you made for yourself. This is the life you carved out for yourself in this world. Your own little slice of heaven. I want to be a part of that with you."

Jacquelyn says those words, but they are not what I hear. I hear the truth behind them. I listen to the words that Faith never spoke because she didn't feel the need to express them.

"You want to know why Faith will always be where my heart lies?" I ask Jacquelyn.

"Yes!" she says, sighing out all the air in her lungs.

"You want the life. You want what I have. The elements that make up the lifestyle of the moments I have lived. You don't need me to have those things. You need to find someone who has those things. The person that you could still be with even if they lost all those things. Faith has never cared about any of that. From before our first big break-up at that graduation party, she never cared about the lifestyle. She never cared about being famous or the consequences that came with it. She just wanted me, and I was too stupid to see that.

"But Jacquelyn, you, you have someone you've been talking with. Someone who met you at your most vulnerable and still had a look in his eye when he said your name while we ate hot sauce-covered tacos. A look that said you mean more to him than you could for me. But I guess, more than anything, Faith gave me the inspiration to be great. She gave me the passion to write the words I have left behind in song. She planted in me the ideas that drove me to end up where I did. If I stay with you, it wouldn't be fair to any of us. You would always have someone else on your mind, gnawing away at the could've and should've. I will always be thinking of Faith.

"Faith is the reason I am who I am. I am not leaving rock 'n roll behind. I am stepping further from the limelight and into a much more comfortable seat. There is no other woman I would rather watch a new sunrise with than her. I never needed a girl who would strive to give me everything. I need someone who pushes me to be a better version of myself."

"But we could have had something so beautiful," Jacquelyn cries in one last attempt.

"No. We couldn't have. But you can. You can have the life you want with someone much more suited to provide it to you," I gently finish. "I say sunrise because I am not done. I am not leaving behind a legacy. I am still making one. There is no end to my career and no end to what I do. Now, I shall do those things differently. A way in which I can be with the one I love."

I turn to Faith, who holds back tears. At this moment, I can't tell if they are tears of joy or anger, frustration, or fear. But she is smiling uncontrollably, and there isn't a sight in the world more beautiful than what I see standing before me now.

I turn back to Jacquelyn as she tosses me a bottle of pills. "Something to tide you over for the ride up to Chicago."

I look at the bottle and back to Jacquelyn.

"I told you, Finn," Jacquelyn continues. "When you tell me why, you get your pills."

I look to Faith. Her raised eyebrows, tight smile, and shaking head tells me that she understands she was wrong about me this time.

I look back at Jacquelyn and toss her the pills. "Thanks, but I'm good."

I toss Jacquelyn my all-access pass so she can get back into the show and see the man she has secretly been falling for.

Jacquelyn looks down at the pass. "So, you're just walking away from it all? From everything you've built down here?"

"I'm not walking away from it all. Just moving it to a new location. That's the joy of music. It's everywhere."

Faith and I make our way to the truck and start the engine. As I pull away from Disney Springs and onto the roads leading away from Orlando, my thoughts begin to wander. I start to think about what my life would have been like with Jacquelyn. More nights of debauchery and hedonism that I lived out the past couple of decades. More of the same that is the game of rock 'n roll. It would be a comfortable life, a life where the challenges are familiar and comfortable. A world where I stay exactly where I was when I moved down here. But Jacquelyn, much like everyone else, deserves happiness. She deserves to be with that someone who doesn't resent her or think less of her because of the things he never was able to do. I would. I would resent her for staying. D.B. holds no resentment.

Now, as I start our journey to where we began, I think back on the life I lead. I imagine the moments in between what Faith told me. The quiet moments that Faith keeps to herself for all those years between.

I think back to a moment we shared on her parent's patio back in college. We sat under the stars on a chilly fall night, just her and me. We spent the night looking up to the stars, imagining the possibilities of what life had in store. We shared our guesses and had a good laugh before making love under all the possibilities. There was an innocence in that night, a naivety that the mouse strives for us to hold onto for just a little longer. I think it's okay to do so. The world is a relentless place, so stay young as long as you can.

The possibilities—that is what life is all about. Of all the different scenarios we played out that night under the stars, not one of them was what actually transpired. Our young minds couldn't even conceive of what would actually manifest. Not one of those ended with us having a child, moving back to Chicago, and starting over. Sometimes life is like that.

That was years ago, when we were young and embraced the world with open arms. When we let things come what may and smile while being battered by life. A time before we closed our grip and held our fists ready to strike, to defend ourselves from those which we once embraced.

Whatever tomorrow holds for us, I do not know. I can only hope to again embrace the ideals we once held onto so dearly, ideals that made the world a better place, if only for a while.

THE FAIRLANE INCIDENTS
BOOK CLUB QUESTIONS

1. Which characters in the book did you like best?

2. Which characters did you like least?

3. If you were making a movie of this book, who would you cast as Finn and Faith?

4. With all the music references throughout this book, do you think you'll look up any you aren't familiar with? If so, any in particular?

5. What do you think of the book's cover? How well does it convey what the book is about? If you have seen the previous covers, which one do you like best?

6. Did you find the ending of the book satisfying?

7. How does the setting contribute to the story?

8. Did you guess the ending of the book, and if so, how?

9. What do you think happens to the characters after the book ends?

10. Which parts of the book stood out to you?

THE FORTUNATE FINN FAIRLANE
BOOK CLUB QUESTION

1. How did the book make you feel? Did you find it an easy, light read or a more emotionally driven?

2. What did you think about the ending? How do you think that will drive book 3?

3. Based on this book, what do you think about Nick Savage's writing style for the story? If it were different, would his story-telling ability change the way the story developed?

4. How does this book compare to others you've read?

5. Which character was most like someone you already know? How did that affect your perception of the character?

6. Are there any events in the book similar to something you've personally experienced?

7. What scene would you point out as the pivotal moment in the narrative? How did it make you feel?

8. What surprised you most about the book?

9. What was your favorite chapter and why?

10. What (if any) questions do you still have about the plot?

THE FRAGILE FINN FAIRLANE BOOK CLUB QUESTIONS

1. What is the significance of the title? In what ways is Finn fragile?

2. This books deals with several themes: fame, addiction, the rock 'n roll lifestyle, inspiration, dreams. Which ideas stood out to you? How were those themes brought to life?

3. Finn Fairlane has definite opinions about the effects of the mouse on Orlando. What do you think of his assessments?

4. Jeanine and Gregg seem to have a healthy relationship despite the pressures of the industry. What does this say about the possibility of this life for Faith and Finn?

5. Finn's choices seem to boil down to two women who each represent a different future. What do Faith and Jacquelyn seem to promise? What are some alternatives to the futures they represent?

6. In the end, Finn chooses to go with Faith to Chicago. What do you think of his decision?

7. What do you think will happen to Finn and Faith in Chicago? Will they ride off happily into the sunset

to raise their baby or will the same problems follow them to a new city?

8. Should Finn be willing to give up his life in the music industry to become the man Faith wants him to be? Why or why not?

9. This series showcases several strong women. What do you think of Viv, Logan, Jeanine, and the other supporting characters?

10. Finn Fairlane has starred in three books now. How has he changed from the Finn you met in book one (the one standing naked in a rainstorm) to the one who gets in the truck with Faith?

ABOUT THE AUTHOR

Nick Savage is an award-winning and Amazon best-selling author. He lives in the greater Orlando, Florida, area with his wife and two cats. He is an avid video game nerd, artist, and musician.

Series by Nick Savage:

The Fairlane Series:
The Fairlane Incidents
The Fortunate Finn Fairlane
The Fragile Finn Fairlane

The West Haven Undead:
Us of Legendary Gods
So We Stay Hidden
The West Haven Undead

Other Works by Nick Savage:
World Whore, D

MORE BOOKS FROM
4 HORSEMEN PUBLICATIONS

ROMANCE

ANN SHEPPHIRD
The War Council

EMILY BUNNEY
All or Nothing
All the Way
All Night Long: Novella
All She Needs
Having it All
All at Once
All Together
All for Her

KT BOND
Back to Life
Back to Love
Back at Last

LYNN CHANTALE
The Baker's Touch
Blind Secrets
Broken Lens
Blind Fury
Time Bomb

VIP's Revenge
Chef's Taste

MANDY FATE
Love Me, Goaltender
Captain of My Heart

MIMI FRANCIS
Private Lives
Private Protection
Private Party
Run Away Home
The Professor
Our Two-Week, One-
Night Stand

SHAE COON
Bound in Love
Controlling Assets
For His Own Protection
Her Broken Pieces
The Roma's Claim
The Roma's Promise

DISCOVER MORE AT
4HORSEMENPUBLICATIONS.COM